DRAGONFLY GIRL

MARTI LEIMBACH

DRAGONFLY GiRL

 KATHERINE TEGEN BOOKS
An Imprint of HarperCollinsPublishers

FOR TOM

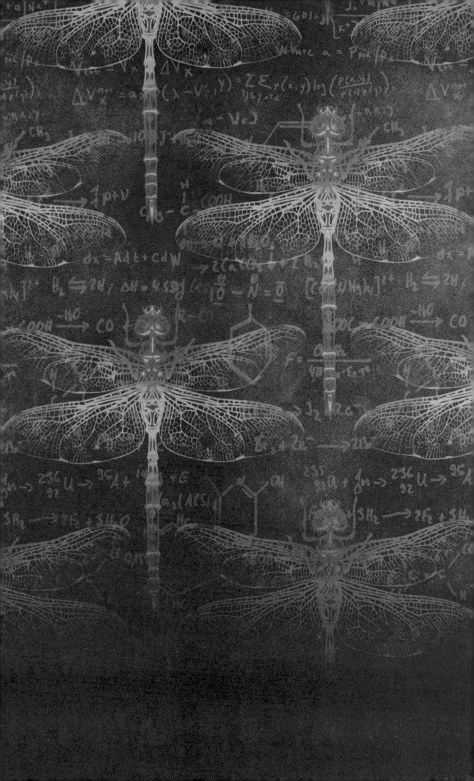

PART ONE

PRIZEWINNER

If you know you are on the right track, if you have
this inner knowledge, then nobody can turn you off . . .
no matter what they say.
—BARBARA McCLINTOCK, cytogeneticist and
1983 Nobel Prize Winner for Physiology or Medicine

1

MY BRAIN ISN'T normal. I forget all the dates on history tests. I can't memorize verb tenses in Spanish. Important facts escape me: the order of presidents, the start of World War II. Please don't ask. I know this isn't what you'd expect of a supposedly "high IQ individual," but it's just how I'm wired.

There are other embarrassments: my stubby bitten fingernails, my pencils with chewed-off erasers. The art teacher who said that I should stop taking the class if I couldn't actually make anything.

Science is different. When I'm studying science or math, my concentration is smooth, complete. I don't fidget. I don't chew my hands. Instead I glide through equations, seeing numbers and symbols as though they are there in front of me. It's not as freaky as it sounds.

But I get teased a lot. In school, they call me a cyborg. They say I should donate my brain to science—like, immediately. Or a girl might say, "My hair is doing a Kira," meaning her hair looks bad. Or she'll say, "I've got a Kira face," because she thinks she looks bad. Most people just ignore me. Ignoring me might be worse. I'm invisible until I do something stupid. Then I'm laughable.

And because I can *only* do math and science, it's not exactly like I'm getting much love from the teachers either.

Not that smart after all, I heard one say. I was behind her on the staircase between periods. She didn't know I was there. *Very inconsistent,* the other agreed. Her little friend.

Are you angry at your teachers? the guidance counselor asks me. It's the same question at the end of every year.

No. It's me that's the problem.

Everything all right at home?

She knows it isn't. My mother is sick. But that's not why.

Will you please try harder next year?

Yes, I always promise.

As though I'm not already trying my guts out.

Senior year, fall semester, the school's principal, Dr. Jackson Greevy, walks back to his office sloshing the coffee in his mug to find me waiting for him on the bench with a note in my hand. I've been sent by Mrs. Callahan, my English teacher.

"Let me guess why you're here," he says. "You got too rowdy at the pep rally."

It's supposed to be a joke. Greevy knows I am incapable of getting "rowdy" at anything. And I can't stand pep rallies. All that stomping of feet, all that whistling.

"Maybe you got caught smoking in the bathroom?" He grunts out a laugh. I think the "joke" is supposed to be funny because last year I developed an idea for measuring the toxicity of chemicals that linger on clothes after a cigarette is put out. I won a hundred bucks for it. It's what I do: enter student science contests to win money. We have a lot of bills, but, as my mother says, at least there are a lot of contests.

I follow Greevy into his office, the only room in the building with carpet. I stand grimly in front of his desk, fiddling with my hair, a mop of loose curls that always escapes its elastic. On the desk is a photograph of the Greevy family: two girls in summer dresses and a baby in the arms of a pretty woman with ebony skin, smiling into the camera.

I'm in so much trouble.

"Don't sit down," he says, lowering himself into his big office chair. "I don't want you here that long."

He puts out his hand for the note from Mrs. Callahan, tips back in his seat, and takes a long breath as he reads. Then, I see his expression change. He sits up straight, staring hard at me.

"You walked out of English class without permission? You then went to your locker to conduct a *chemistry experiment?*" he says, his voice rising. "A chemistry experiment in your *locker?*"

"I was just . . . uh . . . storing the experiment to bring home later. But I thought I smelled leaking gas—"

"Did you say *leaking gas?*" Suddenly, his hand is on the phone, his eye on the clock.

"But it wasn't!" I add quickly. "It was only residual fumes. So I came back to class and—"

I see him relax about the experiment. That is, the worry is gone, but here comes the anger.

"So, you're storing chemistry experiments in your locker—that stops *now*, by the way—and you walked out of an in-class essay for which you now have a mark of zero. Are you *trying* to sabotage yourself?" He shakes his head as though ridding himself of a bad thought. "Everyone *knows* you can write an essay! Didn't I read that you won a big prize for a science essay?"

The newspaper announced it last week. A big cash prize, money my mother and I desperately need. But the "essay" Greevy is talking about, the one that got me the prize, might be the worst mistake I've ever made. If we didn't need the money so badly, I'd rip that prizewinning paper into little pieces.

Greevy says, "You want to tell me what's really going on?"

I keep my mouth shut. I'm hardly going to tell him I fudged my entry for an international science prize. Or worse, that my mother keeps borrowing money from a loan shark (his name is Biba) who is now *threatening* me for repayment. I found him leaning against my car this morning, looking like the gangster that he is. He pulled out a square of newspaper from his back pocket, a clipping of the article that mentioned my prize. *You won some cash!* he said. An accusation. *So why haven't you paid me?*

I chewed on my thumb, unsure what to say. It's hard enough for me to speak up for myself, let alone when someone like Biba is glaring at me. I mumbled something about not having the money yet and having to go to Sweden to collect it.

Sweden? You're lying! He knows someone like me never goes anywhere, at least not out of the country. But I wasn't lying. Not about that, anyway.

I wish this piece of junk was worth the money you owe me, he said, gesturing at my car, then kicking at a tire with his boot. *You don't make me wait for my money too long, understand?*

This took place only a few hours ago as I was setting off for school. Now, in Greevy's office, I try to hold it together as he rants about my grades. Then he says, "How am I supposed to sign you off for a long absence just before Christmas break so you can fly off to Switzerland when you aren't keeping up with your work *here*?"

Sweden, not Switzerland. They hold the Science for Our Future conference in Stockholm. But I don't think it's wise to correct Dr. Greevy.

"I asked you a question!" he says.

A question . . . oh God. What was it? Oh, yeah, about signing me off for an absence. "Um . . ." I say, not knowing how to answer.

"We are talking about an *entire* school week!" he says, shaking his head as though it's an outrageous idea.

"It's very important to my family," I squeak. We owe thousands to Biba. The money from the science prize is my only way of paying it. But I've got to participate in the conference in Stockholm first.

Greevy returns to his files. After a long pause, he says, "I will *reluctantly* grant you the time. But you need a high school diploma, you understand? Please keep that in mind on your way to Switzerland."

Greevy was never going to stop me going; he was just trying to scare me. Even so, my eyes sting. There's a painful knot in my throat. I'm shuffling toward the door, ready to leave, when I find myself unable to contain a little burst of defiance that sometimes visits me.

"Sweden," I mumble, my hand on the doorknob.

Greevy looks up from his papers. "Excuse me?" he says.

I turn around to face him. I know I should keep my mouth shut, but I can't help it. "Prizewinners go to the Grand Hôtel in Stockholm," I say.

There's a silence between us. His face is a hard stone. I think he's going to tell me he's changed his mind and I can't go, but instead his expression softens. "Okay, Sweden," he says.

I exit Greevy's office, my mind filled with thoughts of the award ceremony that takes place in a ballroom in the Grand Hôtel. The room is called the Hall of Mirrors and is the same hall where the very first Nobel Prize was awarded in 1901. For a moment, I forget about being hauled into the principal's office, about failing English, about the endless struggle with money. Instead, I think about that magnificent ballroom, a room made of gold—gold everywhere, even on the ceiling—and the full scale of what I'm doing hits me. I'm going to Sweden to collect a prize I'm not really entitled to have won.

If I were smart, I'd turn around and tell Greevy he's right. That I shouldn't miss that week of school. Forget Stockholm. Forget the Hall of Mirrors.

But I'm not smart. See what I mean? So I keep walking.

2

MY BEAUTIFUL FRIEND, Lauren, also has a beautiful a car. You can't miss it: a Mercedes C-Class Cabriolet that her father bought as a gift for his secretary. Big mistake. The dealership called to find out how they were enjoying the new car, and Lauren's mother was like, *What new car?* She scored the Mercedes in the divorce that followed, but because the car reminded her of the secretary she wouldn't drive it. So Lauren passed her driving test, bought fingernail polish to match the car's color (hyacinth red), dug out the keys from a kitchen drawer, and declared the Mercedes her own.

I watch through my bedroom window as she pulls up, parking along the rusting chain-link fence that borders our tiny front lawn. I'm worried Biba is going to see the car on one of his lurking missions (he occasionally drives past our house slowly in order to be intimidating, and believe me, it has the desired effect). I don't trust him near Lauren's car.

But so far, no Biba. Lauren cuts the engine and twists around to gather some bags from the back, hoisting them onto her shoulder. I go to the front door, tiptoe in my bare feet across the dirt path, and help her with the bags. There's a lot. She's even trailing a suitcase.

"How do you feel about big, chunky earrings?" she asks. She's sporting some hefty ones herself, long dangles of gold moons and stars broken up by pearls.

"Like I don't have pierced ears."

"Oh yeah. I always forget that. Why the hell not?"

In lots of ways, Lauren is my opposite. She lives in an enormous house, goes to a private school, loves jewelry and short dresses and shoes with big heels. But there are things we have in common. She might look like a supermodel, but the truth is she's a science geek. Her great loves are zoology and botany. And she treats her fancy car like a truck, clocking miles along the coastline or across mountain ranges in pursuit of birds and other wildlife. Outdoors in a field coat with pouch pockets for her camera lenses, her blond hair bundled into a cap, she'll sit for hours in the dawn light waiting for the right shot of a rare bird.

"Here," she says, and throws me a bag of makeup. My expression must give me away, because she says, "*Pleeease*, just play around with it."

We drag the bags of clothes down the narrow hall. Lauren says, "Where's your mom?"

"Resting," I tell her. My mother is always resting. Once in a while there's a crisis and I brace myself. Everybody knows you can't live forever with her kind of cancer. But my mother isn't everybody, and sometimes I think she may just pull it off.

"I'll keep my voice down," Lauren whispers.

Lauren loves my mom almost as much as I do. And my mother calls us both "her girls."

"Do I hear my girls?" my mother calls from her bedroom.

We pause by the door. She's in bed, propped up. I can hear the live lottery drawing on the television. I know without looking that there's a fan of lottery tickets in her hand that she's checking carefully as the winning numbers float across the screen.

Lauren steps into the room and waves. "Hi, Diane!" she says. "You win anything?"

"Not yet. But last week I got ten dollars."

"Fingers crossed!" Lauren says.

"Please don't encourage her," I whisper.

"It's harmless," Lauren whispers back.

But it's not harmless. The odds are one in forty-five million. We go into my bedroom and I tell Lauren, "She might've won ten dollars, but she just spent thirty on new tickets."

I don't mention Biba. Or the monthly bills we can't pay. I've never told anyone about our problems with money, not even Lauren.

"Fine, whatever," she says, standing at the foot of my bed, unsheathing dress after dress from veils of dry-cleaning plastic, then tossing them onto the mattress. "Some of these might be a tad short for you," she says. We're interrupted by the booming sound of loud music from a car outside driving slowly past, windows down, stereo blaring. The sound vibrates through the air, practically shaking the walls. Finally, the car passes. "I guess the children are out tonight," she says.

"The children" is what Lauren calls the gangs of kids that

used to be in abundance in this neighborhood. It's better now, but vandalism and burglaries are still a problem, and frankly, the kids aren't kids anymore.

"I feel bad about borrowing your clothes," I tell her.

"And now I feel bad that you feel bad. Let's all feel *bad*, okay?" she says, and we both laugh.

She lays out dresses and suits and shoes. It reminds me of the day we met in science camp back when we were ten years old. My mother had applied for me to get a scholarship to the camp, which was an expensive residential thing that would have been impossible for us to afford. I was always entering contests, even then. But guess what? I won the scholarship, and Lauren and I got bunks next to each other. She brought so many different outfits, she needed all her trunk space and most of mine. Since then, we've been best friends.

"Anything useful in here?" she says, flinging open the thin doors of my closet. She quickly scans the few clothes on hangers and says, "Why is everything you own black?"

"Because they haven't come up with a darker color?" I say, staring at Lauren's designer dresses and boxed shoes now covering my mattress. The colors here are deep and regal: gold, crimson, emerald, ivory. All delicate, perfectly made, and from what I can tell, hardly worn. It would be easy to wreck something. I could snag a hem or stain a cuff or break a heel. "I'm worried your stuff could be, like, injured," I say. "And what if the airline loses my suitcase?"

"They won't. *This* is your suitcase." Lauren points to the suitcase she's brought, a candy pink Rimowa on four wheels.

"I can't take that," I say. I'm thinking of the price tag, not the garish color.

"It's just sitting in my closet, which isn't really the life a suitcase wants to lead, is it?" Then she looks at me more carefully and says, "What's wrong? You're going to freaking Switzerland! You should be psyched!"

"Sweden," I say, breathing out a sigh. I'm not only un-psyched, I'm seriously nervous. How do I explain this? "It's just that the event . . . well . . . it isn't a high school thing. I mean, I can't look like a teenager."

She holds up a cashmere tunic. "Nobody will think you're a teenager wearing this!" she says, then, "Wait . . ." She peers at me closely, no doubt noticing the strain on my face. "You don't *want* to go, do you?" she says finally.

"I *have* to go." I glance at the table by the bed where my brand-new, immaculate American passport waits. "I'm just not sure I should go."

"Why not? I mean, look at this *dress*!" She twirls a gauzy gown into the air. A sparkle of beads float throughout the fabric, which seems to go on forever, the hem grazing Lauren's shoe. "This dress guarantees you'll have a great time!"

She thinks it's nerves holding me back.

I look at the dress. I swear I've never seen anything so elegant. The lines of beads woven through the cloth are actually sparkling dragonflies. Coincidentally, the paper I wrote—the one that won a prize—discusses the hunting skills of dragonflies.

"You worked yourself blind on that stupid essay," Lauren says.

I can feel her mind racing, ticking through any reason I might suddenly not want to go to the prize ceremony, the banquets, the whole week of activities that are focused on the subject I love.

Lauren is the only person I can tell. And she deserves to know, so I say, "I don't want to go because I'm not qualified to win. My entry isn't . . . um . . . well, it didn't follow the rules."

"What do you mean?" she says, genuinely concerned.

"I had to . . . fake it . . . a little," I say, forcing out the words. "I lied," I add miserably, "and I'm terrified they're going to find out."

She drops down onto the bed, the dragonfly dress spreading out across her knees. "You *lied*?" she says, looking mortified. Lauren, who usually has an answer for everything, is stumped. After a long pause she says, "Please tell me you haven't taken the money yet."

I haven't. But they've already sent me the airline ticket.

"Don't freak!" I say. "I'm going to fix it . . . I'm figuring it out."

Lauren looks around the room as though searching for an escape. "How do you 'fix' plagiarizing a scientific essay that wins an international prize? Kira, I think you're brilliant. But there are some things that even *you* can't figure out."

Now it's my turn to be shocked. "You think I *plagiarized* the paper?"

"Or made up the findings, right? I mean, maybe not for the entire paper, but—"

"No! Why would I do that?"

"I don't know, people do!"

"Not *me*!"

"Then what's the lie? Tell me before I dig out the shoes for this freaking dress that I don't even know if you'll get to wear now!"

I reach under my bed and draw out a group of stapled papers. It's a photocopy of the Science for Our Future application, an application I've read dozens—no, hundreds—of times now. I hand it to Lauren, saying, "Read the part about qualifications of entry. It says you have to have received your doctorate. You know, a PhD."

Lauren's eyes grow wide. "Your *PhD*?"

"It says you can't have received a PhD more than a year ago," I say, quoting from the rules. "But I entered anyway because . . . well . . . the big money in science contests *always* goes to graduate students and postdocs." And right now we could use some big money.

She begins reading through the application, her brow furrowed, her finger tracing the words in their tiny script across the printed page. "Did you actually *tell* them you have a PhD?" she asks.

"No, but I didn't tell them I'm in high school either. I just left that part blank. It must have slipped past them."

A smile creeps across her face. "Then what are you worried about? They may not even notice!"

I shake my head. "But what if they do? I've broken the rules—"

"Don't say anything and it will be fine! You want this prize, don't you?"

I'm desperate for the prize. We need the money so badly. And of course I'd love to visit a foreign city, to participate in the conference, to feel good about something I've done for once in my life.

Lauren is saying, "If you get cornered, say you wrote the essay without the benefit of a PhD and that you'd like your prize, thank you very much. . . ."

"I can't—" I begin.

"But Kira, you left the PhD part blank. *You've* done nothing wrong! It's their problem if they didn't notice."

"Really?"

"Really." She stands, pushes the dragonfly dress toward me, and says, "I want to see if this thing is long enough."

"It still feels like cheating," I say.

"Not cheating. Put on the damned dress. Wait, let me get the zip."

I slip out of my jeans and hoodie, then into the dragonfly dress. It's a bit loose in the bust and the sleeves are an inch too short, but it is a dazzling dress in a sheer fabric, like something a movie star might wear. I love how the material moves, the beaded dragonflies, the floating hem.

"I feel like Cinderella," I say. For a moment, I imagine being in the Grand Hôtel in Stockholm, standing among a group of people in an airy lobby in this dress.

Lauren flashes a smile. "Good! And remember, Cinderella got a prince! By which I mean, not just a handsome royal, but substantial real estate in the form of a castle, footmen, gowns, plus a fabulous scepter."

"I just don't know if I can pull this off," I say.

"But you've *already* pulled it off. Nobody is going to ask about the PhD. We'll figure out a plan if they do, but for right now I want you to see this!"

She reaches above the chest of drawers and unfastens the mirror that hangs on the wall there, angling it in front of me.

"Look at you," she says, and whistles softly.

I glimpse the mirror and see, indeed, that the dress is stunning. The romantic neckline softens my angular shoulders, and the bodice is cut so I look more shapely. The color is good with my dark hair; its shades of blue tone down the patches of acne that sometimes flare around my chin.

"I look . . . not bad," I say.

"Not bad?" Lauren sighs. "You look *amazing*."

3

I'VE NEVER FLOWN on a plane, visited a foreign country, or even stayed in a hotel. When I finally arrive in Stockholm—groggy, wrinkled, ecstatic—I feel like a visitor to my own life. I'm fascinated by the sounds of foreign voices, the signs I can't read, the brand names I don't recognize. Stockholm is an archipelago, a city of islands; lamplight glows on the famous bridges. Christmas lights outline storefronts and windows, the branches of trees, and the sides of red market stalls, above which hang garlands of pine.

I take a wrong turn and end up in the old town, Gamla Stan. All around are people dressed in parkas and scarves, carrying umbrellas in case the snow grows heavier. But the snow is as soft as confetti, gathering gently along the edges of the cobbled streets. The smell of hot food drifts through the air, the scent of caramelized sugar floats from pastry shops in clouds I feel I could stick out my tongue and lick. Entering a patch of green that makes up a city park, I wander unnoticed in a wooden corral among statues of Santa's reindeer, lit with thousands of tiny bulbs.

I may be the happiest I've ever been.

And, of course, the minute I have this thought, I wish my mother could be here with me, that I hadn't had to leave her behind. Lauren is going to check in on her so she won't be entirely alone. Even so, I want tell her everything I see. But it's dawn in California and she won't be awake. However, I know someone who will be.

In the early hours, you can often find Lauren at Don Edwards Wildlife Refuge. I've been with her many times, huddling in the brush, waiting to see something interesting, the endangered Ridgway's Rail, for example, a bird that has proven more difficult to photograph than it ought to, given it's the size of a chicken and can't really fly.

I get out my phone, pull off my glove, then type:

Myth: people who live in warm climates have thinner blood.

A minute later I see two blue tick marks that mean the text has been delivered. A message back from Lauren reads:

Fact: everyone wishes they lived in California.

I'm not so sure. Crossing a bridge that my map tells me connects the old town to Blasieholmen, my destination, I peer out over inky water reflecting the sky and a small sea of ships strung with lights like hundreds of floating Christmas trees. I can't imagine anywhere more beautiful.

A few seconds later my phone rings. I hear Lauren's voice a continent away.

"Is it amazing?" she says.

"Incredible. But also negative four degrees. Sorry, I mean 24.8 Fahrenheit."

"Did you just convert that in your head? Never mind. How fabulous do you look in my mother's Moncler parka?"

"Pretty good if I keep the hood up."

I hear Lauren's groan. "I bet you look great. Have you been to the banquet yet?"

"I'm still looking for my hotel."

"You haven't even found the *hotel*? But you left here *yesterday afternoon*!"

"The flight takes fifteen hours, and anyway, it was delayed. It gets dark here at, like, two o'clock. Seriously, I can see the moon."

"Well, buy some chocolate. They make the *best* chocolate."

"You're thinking of the Swiss again."

"Well, what do the Swedes make?"

"Clogs, I think?"

"Aren't clogs Dutch?"

"Oh. Then maybe nothing."

I turn a corner, still chatting. Then I stop. There, facing the water over which I've just come, is the Grand Hôtel. It's huge, with a majesty difficult to achieve outside the nineteenth century, when it was built—the same century in which the Houses of Parliament, the Eiffel Tower, and the Paris Opera were imagined. Suddenly, I don't want to take another step. I want to turn around, seek out a small room above one of the cozy restaurants in the old town, or go back to the little park of reindeer. The hotel is too imposing, too splendid; I can't imagine visiting it, let alone staying here for days, eating and drinking and talking with scientists from all over the world.

"Lauren, I found my hotel," I say in a whisper.

"And?"

"And it's . . . I better go."

I hang up and stand there in the cold, feeling the winter's chill even through my fleece cap. Somehow, I have to enter this hotel and convince everyone inside that I'm a person I'm not. A scholar, a PhD. What felt possible back in California feels foolish and naive now that I'm here.

But I have no choice.

I walk with trepidation toward the giant, lit facade, feeling all the while like a beggar approaching the palace gates. Through the glass windows I can see people in fancy clothes, a lady in a plumed hat, a man sneezing into a pocket handkerchief. Two children race around their father's legs as he swats at them like flies. It is like peeking into a different world. I'm an intruder who should never gain entry. I'm Cinderella, arriving at the ball with the damning voices of her stepsisters in her ear. At any moment the powers that be will identify me as an impostor and turn me away. I'm sure of it. I'm waiting for that moment of humiliation, and yet nothing happens. Or nothing bad anyway. The doormen, wearing overcoats and top hats, hold open the enormous doors. One of them, in practiced English, offers to carry my bag.

I'm given room keys, a welcome pack, and a chance to "freshen up" before tonight's dinner. None of this feels real but within a few short hours I'm sitting in a dining room with chandeliers that sparkle against a painted ceiling, surrounded by scientists and scholars from all over the world. The four winners have our own table as well as our names listed on the evening's program. *Dr. Kira Adams.* It looks strange with the others, and not just because I don't have a PhD.

Lauren's "little black dress" is just right, but Lauren isn't here to explain the formality of the dinner table. I'm baffled by all these glasses and side plates. I get out my phone and sneak a photograph, sending it to Lauren with the message, Heeelp, plz! Meanwhile, I copy what people around me do, bumbling my way through.

I'm relieved when Carlos Ruiz, a prizewinner from Texas who is seated to my left, reveals he's overwhelmed by the place settings too.

"This is a lot of forks!" he says with good humor. I'm not even sure which plates and glasses are mine, let alone what to do with the forks. There's a large spoon at the top of my plate that's also a mystery. At last, Lauren messages back the photo of the place setting. She's marked it up in lime green writing, identifying every item on the table, including which glasses I should drink from.

Phew.

Carlos tells everyone he's glad his PhD research won a prize, because his master's research nearly killed him. "It was like murder by microbes," he says. He laughs, his dark curls shaking on his head.

Apparently, a handful of bacteria from a dangerous gastrointestinal illness mysteriously wafted into the laboratory's ventilation system. Several people, including him, had ended up flat on their backs under the care of a tropical disease specialist.

He explains that it turned out to be a good thing. The illness persuaded him to move from disease ecology to his current field, which deals with dead tissue but not with disease. "If I hadn't changed fields, I'd never have stumbled onto my current research or won this prize," he says. "So I'm grateful for faulty lab procedures and escaped bacteria. Hey, what's this whipped-up stuff in here?"

"Butter," says the tiny woman next to him. Her square-framed eyeglasses remind me of my biology teacher. She wears an olive dress and her name tag, bearing the name Helmi Korhonen, pulls at its delicate fabric. "I know all about faulty lab procedures," she continues. "People throwing risk group two cells straight into the trash along with sweet wrappers."

"If the biohazards don't get you, the lack of sleep does," says Will Drummond, the final member of our group. Will is from England. Cambridge University, in fact. And he isn't merely a category winner like the rest of us. He won his own category, of course, but he's also the winner of the grand prize, along with its hefty cash award. He's the sort of person who is perfectly at ease in the timeless elegance of a hotel like this and has no trouble with the place settings. "It's amazing how many mistakes one can make in the middle of the night," he says.

"Are we still talking about lab science here?" Carlos laughs.

I want to join in but can't think of anything to say. Also, I'm wary of Will. He singled me out earlier, cornering me at the hotel bar where we all convened for a cocktail before dinner. "Ah, it's the dragonfly girl," he said, referring to my paper. I was standing there, teetering on Lauren's high heels and trying to fit in. He asked what I wanted to drink. "A glass of something?" he offered.

The problem is I'm not eighteen yet, which is the legal drinking age in Sweden, but of course I'm supposed to be carrying off the illusion that I'm a real adult. I tried spluttering out an excuse, but Will reached for one of the fluted glasses set out on a table and placed it in my hand. I'd never had champagne before and I didn't know how to drink it. I sipped too deeply and the champagne filled my nose.

"Careful," he said, raising an eyebrow. "The carbon dioxide in the bubbles speeds the flow of alcohol into the intestines." When I appeared confused he looked at me more closely. Then he leaned in and whispered, "You'll get drunk fast if you drink it like orange juice."

And it was like he knew—I swear he knew—that I was underage.

He addresses the dinner table now, saying, "One time I was so exhausted I spilled cancer all over myself." He positions his hand as though holding a petri dish, then pretends to knock into something and tip it, his face aghast as he stares down at his dress shirt. Everyone laughs at his skillful mime. "I had to ring my girlfriend in the middle of the night to bring me new clothes. She wasn't entirely pleased."

"I once set my sleeve on fire with lit ethanol," says Helmi. "I didn't even notice until my arm started to burn."

I follow along, saying nothing. It would be all too easy for me to open my mouth and reveal that I have zero practical laboratory experience. Our school doesn't have money for any kind of laboratory, let alone a professional one. I hope my silence on the topic goes unnoticed, but of course they all eventually look at me, expecting me to come up with a war story of my own.

"What has been your experience?" Helmi says. She's from Helsinki, her English charmingly accented.

"My experience in labs?" Oh God. "Um . . . I find some things, like, really annoying," I say. I roll my eyes as though it's been a trial, these labs. "And what about paywalls?" I say, a genuine concern. My biggest problem is not being able to buy the research papers I want to read. Most of the time, when I click on a citation I hit a paywall. It takes time to find a way around it.

"Doesn't your university offer you access?" says Helmi, confused.

"Oh yes, of course!" I say, feeling a tickle of panic. "I mean when I forget to log into our . . . um . . . thing."

"You're quite young, aren't you?" says Will, as though he's just completed an assessment. He's handsome and horrible at the same time. His blond hair shines softly in the candlelight but his eyes are fixed hard upon me. "I always worry about young people with great intellectual promise. They tend to get pushed too fast for their own good."

I stare at him, frozen. It's as if he's figured the whole thing out, and he knows I'm still in high school, that I don't have a PhD or any diploma. Luckily, dessert arrives, interrupting our conversation. White mousse in a chocolate cup. But I'm too nervous to even enjoy chocolate.

Carlos says, "Every kid starts out as a natural-born scientist. That's a quote from Sagan."

Will begins a story, telling everyone at the table how as a boy he'd spent summers conducting experiments at his family's farmhouse in Devon. He exploded goose eggs using hydrogen gas and kitchen matches, much to the annoyance of his father, a geologist.

I don't think I've ever seen an actual goose egg. And I can't imagine Will as a child. He gives the impression of a man whose youth had been an unnecessary impediment he'd stepped over on his way to adulthood.

"Were you aware that my brother was in line for the prize you won?" he says, turning to me again.

I don't know how to respond to that. "Your *brother*?" I say.

"Aiden Drummond," he says, as though I ought to know the name. "He's the runner-up. Had he won the prize, the university would have given him matching grant money for his work. The fact you referenced some of his research in your own paper was a double blow."

"Oh," I say, feeling my face redden.

"He's interested in unihemispheric sleep," says Will.

Unihemispheric sleep is when half the brain rests while the other half is awake. Flocks of birds migrating for the winter are often half asleep, so to speak, as they travel. But it's hardly a new or specialized subject. Lots of people study it.

"In any case, Aiden is arriving tomorrow to sit in on the conference," continues Will. "I'll introduce you." Without taking his eyes off me he reaches for a carafe of water and fills my glass. "I just thought it was interesting that you quoted from his earlier research. And that for some reason, he didn't win the prize."

I hear a note of bitterness in Will's tone, as though I have no right to win if I'm referencing any of his brother's data to make my own argument. It's understandable that he feels that way, and I wish I could think of a response. But I'm distracted by Helmi, who announces excitedly, "Did you hear that last year one of the winners was disqualified? His data was incorrect. They had to give it to another."

She makes her eyes large and round, as though this is a delicious scandal.

"I heard that, too," says Carlos.

"Oh," I say, even more nervous now. "Does that happen often? That they remove someone's prize, I mean?"

"It has been known," Will says, "though I'm sure your data is perfect. Your math is certainly impressive. Where did you do your PhD?"

So there it is, the perfectly reasonable question I prayed nobody would ask. I'm not sure if I hear suspicion in Will's voice or if I'm just paranoid.

Luckily, Lauren helped me prepare for this moment. According to her, I don't answer the question that's been asked. Instead, I answer a different question, as though he asked me *what*, not *where*, I studied.

"Biochemistry," I say, with as much confidence as I can muster.

But Will's not letting me off that easily.

"I meant," he says slowly, "at what university?"

So, the strategy hasn't worked. Or at least not yet. Lauren said that if I didn't succeed in distracting him through conversational evasion to try staging a minor accident, like dropping my purse. But just as I have this thought, Will does what I hope he'll do—in fact, exactly what Lauren had promised he would do if I avoided answering—and asks a second question, allowing me to dodge the first.

"I mean, you're American, right?" he says. "Or are you Canadian?"

"I'm from California." Experience tells me that he will now ask me about California. The image, popular among tourists, is that the whole of the coast, from San Diego to Crescent City, is one long beach vacation spot filled with movie stars.

Will bites the bait. "Where in California?" he says.

"Near San Francisco." I'm about to launch into a description of the state parks, the wildlife, the beaches, as well as Los Angeles and the occasional movie star sighting, but Will isn't interested. He turns fully toward me so that I feel pinned between the oak slats of my seat back and his serious, heavy face.

"Palo Alto? Don't tell me you were a student of Dr. Munn. That wouldn't have made for a fair contest, would it?"

By Palo Alto, he means Stanford and, of course, the Mellin Institute, where Dr. Munn has his laboratory. Munn is on the board of the Science for Our Future prize and, no doubt, holds great influence with the committee that chooses the prizewinners. He's also tonight's speaker. What Will is saying is that a student of Munn's might have an unfair advantage. Maybe he thinks this is why my paper was chosen over his brother's. I shake my head quickly.

"I've never even met Dr. Munn!" I say, sounding mildly hysterical even to myself.

"Then where exactly—" Will begins again.

"Rimowa University," I blurt out. *Rimowa?* That's the brand name of Lauren's *suitcase*. What the heck made me say that?

Will looks as shocked as I am. "I've never heard of—"

I can't let him continue. I feel the sudden jab of a headache, as though Will's attack is physical, not verbal. I need a distraction like Lauren spoke of—an accident, that's it! I feel myself shaking as I reach for my water glass, the one that Will just filled. It's a shame to tip it onto the white linen, but I do so easily enough. In fact, I knock it too hard, sending the glass tumbling, colliding with a dessert fork so that there's a sudden *twang*, then water all over the table. I gasp and push myself away from the table as icy water fills my lap. I manage to give an impression of utter surprise, as though it truly had been an accident, and am joined by Helmi, who squeaks an "Oh dear!"

A couple of waiters step forward. Will and I have to stand aside, out of the way, as they dry the floor. Suddenly there is someone else in front of me. He isn't Will and he isn't a waiter either.

"You okay?" he says, smiling. He's holding a small box of recording equipment he'd been taking up to the stage, passing our table just at the moment the glass fell. He puts aside the box now and takes my hand. "I'm Rik Okada. I work for Munn."

His accent is distinctly American. In a dinner jacket and bow tie, his blue-black hair casually tousled, he might also be the best-looking guy I've ever seen, with large dark eyes and a pronounced angle to his cheekbones. Young, too. He couldn't be much older than I am. I'm suddenly aware of how awkward I look, standing in a puddle in Lauren's dress, which has a giant wet spot down the front that I now try to shield with a dinner napkin.

I say, "I'm fine, I think. I didn't get any water on you, did I?"

"Not at all," he says. He seems to find it amusing that I would worry about spilling on him. Like he wouldn't have cared if I had.

Meanwhile, Will is staring at me again. I get the sense he's figured out that I staged the accident. This may make him more determined than ever to find out the truth.

"I'll let you get back to your dinner," Rik says, and I think, *No! Don't do that!* He's about to dissolve back into the other guests, leaving me with Will, when I say desperately, "Are you a scientist?" which is perhaps the dumbest thing to say in a place like this.

But if he thinks it's a lame question he doesn't show it. "I work around scientists, does that count? I've only just finished at Berkeley."

Will interjects, saying, "Tell me, have you ever heard of a *Rimowa Univ*—"

"Berkeley!" I interrupt. "That's so nice!" I say, sounding frantic and strange.

Rik smiles, then collects his box of equipment and looks toward Munn, seated at the other end of the room. "It seems so long ago now," he says, then excuses himself, telling me he hopes I enjoy the conference and to come to him with any problems. "I keep things running," he adds.

"Can you keep her from tipping things over?" says Will, clearly annoyed. He's about to say something more when, as though by divine intervention, a spoon taps a glass and we are called upon to hear tonight's talk.

Dr. Gregory Munn is a tall, spare man with white hair that flows over the collar of his jacket and an academic shabbiness that feels exotic to me. But then, I've never met a real-life professor.

He stands at the front of the room looking through papers, readying himself for his after-dinner talk. He then steps forward, welcoming the prizewinners, the judges, and all the distinguished guests, addressing them with the sort of ease that comes from years of public speaking and the confidence of someone who is never lost for words. Behind him, the screen fills with the academy's logo. To one side is Rik, recording the event. I can see his dark hair, his handsome profile.

I really shouldn't stare.

The room smells of coffee and chocolate, stringent whiskey and the ash from a fire that crackles and burns in the fireplace. Amid the tinkling of glasses and rustling of fabric, Munn rubs the lenses of his reading glasses, then settles into his talk. Across the screen arrive words written large against a background of space, studded with stars:

WE KNEW THE WORLD WOULD NOT BE THE SAME. A FEW PEOPLE LAUGHED, A FEW PEOPLE CRIED, MOST PEOPLE WERE SILENT.

Munn says, "Of course, we all recognize this quote. It's Robert Oppenheimer reflecting on the awful spectacle of the atomic bomb exploding upon the unready city of Hiroshima, Japan. I read it every so often to remind myself that while advancements in science miraculously improve and extend our lives, they can also end them. With each passing decade, I become more concerned about the increased involvement of the military in all areas of scientific endeavor."

A picture from Mellin flashes across the screen. It shows Munn in a lab coat standing among a group of people working at bench seats along a white table. All of them are pristinely attired, some with goggles hoisted upon their brows.

"As many of you may know," Munn continues, "I began my career in regenerative medicine many decades ago in Cambridge, England. But these days, when I'm not working on my California suntan—" He waits now as a few chuckles drift through the room. If Munn has ever visited the beaches along the California coast, there's no evidence of it on his pale skin. "—I'm inside the laboratories at the Mellin Institute working alongside very talented men and women. We are under tremendous pressure to respond to advances in the area of bioterrorism and other forms of weaponry. The threat is very real."

Mellin isn't a place I associate with anything of this kind. It's famous for stem cell research. You want to grow a heart? Ask Munn about it. You want to see a "mini-brain" in a petri dish? That's also at Mellin. It's most famous for the invention of a revolutionary kidney machine. These machines, used all over the world, save thousands of lives by making it possible to repair even very damaged donor kidneys so that the organs are serviceable as healthy transplants. I've never heard of Mellin's involvement in countering biothreats. The lab certainly doesn't tweet about it.

Perhaps that's why the room is still, not a movement nor a sound. Everyone is captivated as Munn continues, describing the dilemmas scientists face in today's world. "Funding comes with strings attached. And those with the money and power push us to apply our findings too early. We must be cautious with what we do, who we work for, and how we apply our talent and skills. Science for profit is a growing worry, and not every business or government is as scrupulous about ethical issues as we would have them be."

It's a sobering message. When at last he draws to a close, a silence falls, then a thunder of applause fills the air. Munn promises to answer questions, and a microphone is passed around in an orderly fashion. Ten minutes later people are on their feet again, this time making their way to the after-dinner celebration. Guests, judges, speakers, and committee members will stay up late into the night, lounging in empire chairs and on velvet chesterfields, sipping schnapps and talking.

I don't join in. Instead, I slip away as soon as possible toward the back of the room, then out to the hotel's wide corridor and into the ladies' room, where I hide inside a stall. It's the one place where Will can't reach me. He seems determined to uncover the truth about my education, or lack thereof. He wants me disqualified. After all, his brother is the runner-up.

It shouldn't be difficult to avoid him, at least tonight. But as I come out of the ladies' room, he is standing right there as though he's been waiting.

He smiles like a host receiving a guest. "I believe we were having a chat about your degree work," he says. He holds up his phone.

"Google has no record of a Rimowa University in California."

"Who said it was in California?" I'm panicking now. It's not the award that concerns me. It's the money. If I'm disqualified, I can't pay Biba. And the luxurious room with its magnificent view of the Royal Palace—a room that I can no more afford than I can swim the Baltic Sea—will also become my debt. The plane fare, too, I imagine.

"Kira," he says, and makes a little gesture as though calling me toward him. There really isn't much choice unless I want to push back through the bathroom door and spend the rest of the evening sitting on a toilet seat. But just then, something remarkable happens.

It's Helmi. She's been drawn to the ladies' room for reasons other than escape, and she brings with her a journalist from the Swedish newspaper *Dagens Nyheter*. The journalist wants to interview the prizewinners. Most important, the grand prize winner. And that is Will.

"Hello!" the journalist says, extending her hand to him. "I am Elsa!" She has gleaming pale hair and a stylish faux-fur hat. In her long dark coat and leather boots that rise above her knees, she is urban and chic, and altogether more glamorous than the science crowd.

I watch with amusement as Will transforms like a flower. The menacing glare he'd fixed upon me evaporates. In its place, he affects an expression of humility and charm, almost managing a blush as he takes Elsa's hand.

"So, you are the shining star of the competition, no?" Elsa says, thrusting the microphone in Will's direction.

Time to escape. I move quietly away from Will, now powerless to follow me. He watches with dark disapproval before redirecting his attention to the beautiful Swedish journalist, who seems thrilled with him, as though he were royalty from another world, an alien prince.

4

I MAKE THE mistake of checking out the person who was disqualified last year. It turns out the researcher got some data wrong, that's all. It was an *error*. But the committee ruled against him anyway as his conclusion was not considered to be "genuine."

Apparently the committee is very strict.

And now I can't sleep. I toss and turn all night in my giant bed. Nagging at my conscience is the fact that somewhere in the hotel is Will, waiting for morning so that he can hound me again. It feels like the night's hours are carrying me toward a terrible end. I am sure I'll be disqualified. It's only a matter of time.

By dawn I give up and pull on some clothes, then wander through the wide, lit halls of the hotel until I arrive at the restaurant. It's called the Veranda because in summer the glass walls fold back so that guests can dine in the open air. Through this glass I watch the winter snow glow with the sunrise.

It's so beautiful I think it might be worth the insomnia.

Around me, waiters in waistcoats come and go, ignoring the

drowsy girl folded in a chair. The buffet is filled first with a continental selection, baskets of bread smelling of pumpernickel, sourdough, and rye, pastries dusted with sugar on tiered plates. There are croissants and iced braids and fruited buns with colorful centers of cherry, apple, and peach.

But anxiety about Will has sapped my appetite and I sit miserably with a *kaffe latte*, wondering when he plans to launch his next assault. As always when nervous, I'm biting my nails, which seems even weirder than usual because I'm wearing Lauren's clothes. I don't think elegantly dressed people are supposed to be nail-biters.

Finally, I wander over to the buffet, selecting one of the cinnamon *kanelbullar* that arrive warm from the oven. It turns out that this palm-size delicacy is the most delicious cinnamon bun in the world. I eat eagerly, feeling the warm butter like a balm. The taste of sugar and cinnamon have a calming effect, reminding me of Sunday mornings when I used to wake to the scent of my mother's special pancakes. Back then, when she was well, there were no loans. Thinking about those days, which are many years ago now, I'm at peace. As the waiters place bowls of fresh berries on a shallow shelf of ice behind where I am seated, I fall asleep.

I wake to the sound of cutlery, of china touching china, of eggs crackling in butter and the rustling of voices. The air is steamy with coffee. Hot breakfast warms in silver dishes with decorated lids. The tables nearby, once flawlessly laid with shining goblets and napkins folded into swans, are now filled with people. I think I hear Carlos among them. There's no mistaking his Texan accent. When I open my eyes I realize he is sitting beside me, speaking to Helmi across the table.

"This is . . . what, exactly? This is *fish*?" he's saying. His plate is full of the buffet's many delicacies, including wedges of quiche, slices of cured ham, and Sweden's famous creamed cod roe, which he stares at as though it might hatch.

"Yes, fish," Helmi says matter-of-factly. She is dressed in a long woolen skirt and ankle boots, and a silk blouse buttoned high, above which she has tied a neck bow. The heavy frames of her glasses hide large, hazel eyes. With the dark clothes and her hair braided into a bun, she looks less like a biology teacher and more like a friendly pilgrim. She says to Carlos, "In Finland, we have fish. Fish is normal."

"But fish isn't a breakfast food."

"What is breakfast food in America?"

"Something that says the word *breakfast* on the box or is an egg," Carlos says. He notices I've woken now and looks down at me, curled like a pretzel inside the curved arms of the chair. "Oh, look, it's sleepyhead," he says, smiling.

With effort I sit up. Even the weak light makes me squint. "What time is it?"

"Don't tell me you stayed here all night?" says Helmi. "Did you think you'd miss breakfast?"

"I couldn't sleep."

"I have evidence to the contrary," says Carlos. He picks up my phone and hands it to me. There, splashed across the screen, is a photograph of me asleep. He'd draped a napkin over my shoulders like a tiny blanket so that I look like a giant slumbering doll. "We thought you'd want it for a souvenir," he says.

"How did you know my password?"

"Because it was pi," says Helmi. "Which was obvious."

Carlos rolls his eyes. "It was *not* obvious."

"I got it first try!" Helmi says, looking slightly affronted.

They argue gently back and forth about who knows how many digits of pi, about cybersecurity and how these days any eight-year-old can hack a phone, so why have passwords anyway.

It occurs to me this must be what it feels like to have two parents.

Carlos pours a cup of coffee from a cafetière, hands it to me, and says, "Here, drink this before you fall asleep again."

I'm grateful for the caffeine. With a more alert brain I realize, however, that here at the breakfast buffet I am a sitting duck for Will, who will undoubtedly be joining us at any moment.

"I've got to go," I say, feeling suddenly panicked.

"Go where?" asks Helmi. "You haven't eaten."

The smell of hot food is difficult to resist, and I long for another of the cinnamon rolls I had earlier. If I can get out before Will arrives and pilfer a *kanelbulle* along the way, I'll consider breakfast a success, even if I looked pretty foolish dozing in a chair like that.

"I need to prepare for my talk," I say.

This isn't the reason. I just want to avoid Will. But it is true that each of the winners must present his or her paper, followed by a Q&A session. I've worked out my speech, but only in my head. And given I'm the girl who can't string two sentences together in a class of high school students, I'd better practice.

"You're not until tomorrow. It's Helmi, then me this morning," says Carlos.

"Even so," I say. *God, I need to get out of here.*

But it's too late. Suddenly, I hear Will's voice behind me. "Don't go just yet, Kira. You'll miss those nice glazed fruits and all those sticky buns," he says, sounding as though he's talking to a child.

I try to get away, but he puts a hand on my shoulder and eases me back into my chair. "Let's have breakfast together," he says. "I have a proposition for you all."

"I'm already on my second breakfast," Carlos says, patting the folds of his stomach. "Are you suggesting I have a third?"

"If you wish!" says Will, laughing.

Something has changed about him. Rather than launching into an attack on me, which is what I expect, he seems jovial and friendly with all of us. He tells Helmi he came across a reference to her work in a journal he was reading before breakfast. He compliments Carlos on the quality of his thinking in the paper that won Carlos his prize. He's happier, moving with more ease in his jacket, laughing loudly and almost genuinely at Carlos's jokes. He even manages not to sneer at me.

"Enough of Mr. Nice, what is this proposition?" Helmi asks.

Will chuckles. "Hang on, I'm trying to charm you," he says.

Helmi rolls her eyes, but I can see that Will has, indeed, charmed her. It's only that Helmi will not allow herself to stray far from the point, and Will had, after all, begun the conversation by stating outright that he had a proposition.

"I'd like to rearrange the order of delivery of our papers," he says, pausing to take in the astonished faces around the table. "That is, unless any of you object."

He explains that it isn't such an exciting proposition. It's really just a favor. Traditionally, the competition's grand prize winner delivers the final paper in the Hall of Mirrors. He wants to trade places and let me give the final talk.

"*Me?*" I say, poking myself in the chest. "Are you *kidding*?"

"And I'll take your spot tomorrow morning," he says, bowing his head as though to thank me.

Carlos makes a *hmmm* sound, then says to Will, "Why would you want to do that?"

"Yes, exactly! The grand prize winner doesn't just give away his place at the final celebration!" says Helmi.

"I have my reasons," Will says, leaning back in his chair. "Good reasons."

"You must, buddy, because nobody would give away the chance to deliver their paper on a candlelit evening in the Hall of Mirrors unless he was half crazy or avoiding sniper attack," Carlos says, then turns to me. "Go for it, Kira, before he comes to his senses."

My brain is working like a slot machine, rifling through one combination of reasons and then another, trying to figure out what Will is up to. The evening presentation is followed by a banquet. Why *wouldn't* he want to lead the show?

"Why?" I ask flatly.

Will gazes at me, unperturbed. "Why not? You're the youngest among us. Surely this means you deserve all the attention."

"How old are you, anyway?" asks Carlos.

I feel myself panicking but am saved, once again, by Helmi. She shoots Carlos a disapproving look and says, "Don't ask a woman her age!"

"But you won the grand prize," I say, addressing Will. I'm sure he has a reason he wants me to give the final talk, and it can't be to put me in a good light.

Will waves away my remark with the back of his hand. "I've won many prizes. And I wonder, Kira, have you won many other prizes?"

He knows that I haven't, at least none that I am able to name. All my prizes have the word "junior" or "high school" attached to them. The conversation is taking a dangerous turn. Soon it will focus on degrees. "Not any of significance," I admit quietly.

"Then it's settled! You'll have the spotlight," Will says. "You deserve it."

"I really don't want it," I say.

"Is this a British chivalry thing?" asks Carlos.

"I suspect it has something to do with a certain young Swedish reporter," says Helmi, narrowing her eyes, "and nothing to do with Kira."

Perhaps it's that simple. I recall how enamored the stunning reporter from *Dagens Nyheter* had been with Will. Also, how her black leather boots rose high on her legs, almost reaching her thighs. It's easy to imagine that Will would go to great lengths to kindle the reporter's interest.

"You got me," Will admits, then winks. "Elsa really wants to be there when I give my talk. But as it happens, she is on assignment that evening, attending a gala being thrown at the Royal Palace, to which she has invited me. If I give my talk in the morning and Kira takes my place in the evening, Elsa can attend my presentation and I can visit the palace as her guest later. It seems a no-brainer."

"I get it now," says Carlos, nodding. "Elsa. That's a nice name."

"So there will be a second and very positive news story in *Dagens Nyheter*, this one about Dr. Will's award-winning paper, followed by a magnificent party with the woman of his dreams," concludes Helmi.

"I really can't get anything by you, can I?" laughs Will. "And yes, she does work for Sweden's biggest newspaper and my talk will feature largely."

"But it really isn't up to us, is it?" says Helmi. "We can't decide the proceedings."

"I'll explain to the committee that I'm coming down with a spot of laryngitis," Will says, and coughs as though to give the idea some shape. "And that's the reason for scheduling my talk ahead of time."

"You would lie?" says Helmi.

"Oh, not a real lie." Will looks directly at me now. "Not a *big* lie, anyway. I'll hardly get disqualified for giving an earlier presentation. And I really do have a little tickle in my throat."

"I'm cool with it," says Carlos.

Helmi takes a long breath. "I don't care anyway," she says, spearing a square of hard cheese on her plate. "I'm still going first." She rolls her eyes as though lamenting this fact.

"So, how about it?" Will says to me. "Surely you understand? After all, not every secret needs to be disclosed."

There it is, the real proposition: *Trade places with me and I will keep it secret that you are not qualified to have entered this contest to begin with.*

Maybe it is as simple as it sounds. Maybe in the glow of Elsa's attention, he's decided to discontinue his mission to have me stripped of my prize. But I don't trust him, and it makes me uncomfortable to take his place. Terrified, in fact. The Hall of Mirrors is too grand, the last talk of the conference too weighty. But I have no choice, it seems, and mumble "Okay" into my coffee cup.

"Good girl." Will beams, and holds up his juice glass for a toast.

5

WITHOUT THE THREAT of Will looming over me, the day brightens. The hotel feels more inviting, its stately rooms like stages for great things to come, its windows revealing a city I want to explore. Even the air tastes fresher. It's time for me to stop obsessing about Will and have some fun. I march up to my room, pull a swimsuit from my suitcase, grab the terry cloth robe provided for my use, and make my way down the corridor, determined to enjoy my morning. I take the elevator to the very bottom of the hotel to experience firsthand the famous Nordic spa.

The idea is that you go from a steaming sauna to a cold plunge pool. It sounds totally uncomfortable, but apparently it boosts your immune system. There's no way I'm returning to California without having tried it. So, in my bikini, with my towel tied around my waist like a long skirt, I step through the glass doors of the changing room and quietly enter the spa.

Strangely, it is empty. I pass under a stone arch to the summer pool with its temperature fixed precisely at 98.6 degrees Fahrenheit, in line with that of the human body. The long rectangle of warm water gives way to another arch, through which I enter the area that houses the cold pool, a smaller oval with a pattern of decorated stones across its floor.

Beeswax candles bounce light against the walls. My lungs fill with their honey scent. Finally, I reach the sauna. Pushing through its heavy door, I step into the warm wooden interior as though into a cave of fire.

At once, a hot mist condenses over my skin. I fold my towel over the sauna's wooden ledge and stretch out upon it. The room is thick with steam and the dark pine scent of the timber that lines its surfaces. Droplets of water settle over my skin. I feel my hair go wet. The brick fire steams in the center of the small room as I drift into the spell of its warmth. My body becomes heavy, my mind light.

I might have fallen asleep, which is not a good idea in a sauna, except that beyond the steamy clouds a body stirs, bringing me to attention. Squinting through the dark light, I see the sauna's other visitor is Munn's assistant, Rik. He wears a pair of trunks low upon his waist. He passes the corner ledge where I sit, then opens the door. A shelf of cool air wafts inside as the door shuts, leaving me to peer through its glass at Rik's back as he makes his way out to the stone pool of chilly water.

There's no reason for him to have recognized me. In the sauna's dim light, I could be anyone. I sit quietly upon the warm surface of spruce, listening to the spit and sizzle of the brick hearth and wondering what to do. It feels altogether strange to be half naked near this guy, but he might think I'm avoiding him if I race off back to my room. The sauna is so hot, I'm going to faint if I don't move, however. At last, I rise, open the door, and feel the relief of cool air as I step out toward the small stone staircase that descends into the cold pool.

Maybe if I'm lucky, Rik will be gone.

But when I come out of the sauna, there he is. One look from him and I know that he's recognized me, both in the sauna and now as I stand at the top of the stone steps, my towel around my waist. He's already deep in the water, his skin pricked with cold, his hair sleek and dark as a seal's. He's handsome and inviting, and every atom of my body wants to run away.

But also to stay right here.

I'm about to say something to him, but he presses his finger to his lips to signal that I shouldn't speak.

I'm so nervous, I can barely stand. Somehow I step into the pool, feeling the chilly water grab at my ankles. Leaving my towel behind, I take another step down, the cold climbing my legs, my heart beating in my chest. At last my feet meet with the stone bottom.

Rik stays where he is as I lean my back against the pool's edge, a crown of lit candles flickering near my skin. I've never before been in a spa, or a sauna, or a plunge pool. I've never locked eyes with a guy. It feels mildly intoxicating, allowing him to watch me as I sink into water so cold, the surface of my skin prickles with it. Rik's flagrant staring might seem rude, but not to me. He doesn't ogle me. He simply holds my gaze.

It's like a game, one I've never heard of, but one that I wish to play. It requires me to watch him, to move in sync with him, to refrain from puncturing the noiseless air with speech. I understand that he will abandon the game if that is what I want. His invitation is simply to share the experience of the otherwise empty spa, the wet heat of the sauna, the unforgiving cold of the plunge pool. He doesn't insist upon it, but when he steps across the water and up the stairs beside me, rising into the warm honey scent of the candles, I follow. I focus on the long muscles of his back, his broad calves, the dark bowl of his hair. We move from the cold into the sauna once more, not speaking, then take our places along the welcoming wood. It's as though the sauna and plunge pool provide a gentle sedation. I watch his lean body grow rosy in the hazy light. I feel my own fold loosely around me.

We stay like that, together and silent, while the rocks in the fire hiss. So close, I can feel the small exchange of heat between us. We enter the plunge pool once more, this time with me leading, then farther, into the warm pool, before eventually parting wordlessly into our separate changing rooms. When finally I emerge from the spa room and into a corridor with glass walls through which I can see snow, a group of trees, and the weak Nordic sun with its fairy-tale light, he is gone.

It's bad timing to have a crush. I try to shake Rik from my mind and concentrate on why I'm here. I need to stay alert, avoid Will, and collect the prize. Biba will be waiting for me back home. There is no Plan B.

I get dressed and rush to Helmi's talk. It's in a conference room with decorative paneling and big oak doors. Rows of chairs fill the space, arranged theater-style. Those for the prizewinners are positioned centrally in the first row and decorated differently from the

rest, with carved arms painted in gold leaf and seat cushions uphol-
stered in brushed velvet. Prizewinners are expected to sit together
during the presentations, and I have no choice but to squeeze in
next to Will. Carlos is on his other side. Helmi's chair is empty
except for her tablet and bag. She's already onstage.

A technician clips a microphone to the lapel of Helmi's jacket.
A sound check ensures the audio is working properly. Across the
big screen is Helmi's first slide, a giant picture of colorfully stained
neurons.

The room is filled with leaders in every avenue of scientific
endeavor, but if Helmi is nervous she hides it well.

At last, the lights across the audience dim and a tall man with
a graying goatee steps onto the stage. This is Dr. Biruk, a geneticist
from Ethiopia who is also the chair of the committee. He takes
his place at the podium, checks the microphone, and says a few
words. His accent is beautiful, his English perfect. He introduces
Helmi, leading a round of applause, and she jumps up as though on
a spring and begins her presentation.

She addresses the audience confidently, explaining how she
manipulated stem cells to form three-dimensional structures that
contain the neural contents of a developing human forebrain. "We
can see here how the cells have differentiated," she says, flipping
through her slides.

The reason the research is important is that it helps us understand how genetic mutations take place and may inform ways of
tackling unwanted mutations. "We may be able to use this research
in adult brains as well," she says, then lists all the ways in which this
could be helpful, especially for those suffering dementia.

I'm amazed by her; the audience is amazed by her. She finishes her talk with great style, bowing like a stage actor as applause erupts loudly across the room.

"She's brilliant," Carlos whispers.

"I agree," I say, watching Helmi stack her notes neatly and prepare for the Q&A that follows. The first question is from a University of Sweden microbiologist. Helmi stands high on her heeled shoes, craning her neck to address his question about radial glial cells.

I whisper, "You know, I hadn't realized how short she is."

Carlos and Will look at me strangely. "*What?*" Carlos says, as though I've just said something crazy.

"I mean, she's just not very tall. Not that it matters," I say nervously.

"And you just noticed this?" says Carlos.

"I believe what Carlos means," says Will, sounding uncomfortable, "is that Dr. Korhonen has hypochondroplasia."

I haven't heard the word before and have to figure this out. *Hypo* comes from the Greek word *hupo*, meaning "under." In biological terms, the expression *chondro* normally has something to do with cartilage, while *plasia* refers to growth or formation.

Suddenly, I get it. While most of her is a normal size, Helmi's legs are shorter, her hips wider, her arms truncated. She has underdeveloped cartilage. How could I not have noticed? But I suppose there's so much else about Helmi—she's so smart and astute, missing nothing—that it draws attention away from her being physically small. Anyway, I'm used to being taller than everyone. In Lauren's winter boots with their fashionable heels, I'm up around six feet. Almost everyone looks short to me. "How do you guys know for sure?" I ask.

"She told me," Carlos mutters, distracted. He's totally focused on Helmi's talk. "God, she's awesome," he says.

After lunch, Dr. Munn takes the floor and speaks briefly about his laboratory's work with zebrafish, which first made scientists aware that genes can remain alive after death.

"We were able to prove that many genes remain active for hours, even days, after death. The young man to whom I now introduce you has applied these findings in a very interesting way." He nods at Carlos, who is onstage exactly where Helmi had been seated. Unlike Helmi, he is nervously gripping the arms of the chair and running his tongue over his dry lips. "May I introduce Dr. Carlos Ruiz, who will explain how his work determining the exact time of death in cadavers has been of vital importance in helping police in murder investigations."

He might be nervous, but Carlos is well prepared. He gets a big laugh by confessing that for the past few years he's often thought of himself less as a scientist and more of a recycler of dead mice.

"So many mice," he says, shaking his head in mock disbelief. "Eventually, my grant ran out and I couldn't afford more lab mice, but luckily, there are sixty-four native rodents in Texas, so really I was well resourced. I needed only to take on a lab partner. My mother's cat, Luna."

I smile as a black-and-white cat fills the screen, its green eyes narrowed as though scrutinizing the audience with some distaste.

"It turns out that Luna kills between the hours of four a.m.

and six a.m., which is reflected in my data," continues Carlos. "The most dangerous time for mice in my neighborhood is 5:43 a.m."

He then refers to Munn's discovery of genes that stay active for up to four days after death in zebrafish, explaining how he built upon the discovery, developing a way to tell exactly when a person died. Not just which day, but the precise hour and minute. "That kind of precision makes it easier to narrow down a suspect in a murder case," he says, "which is why I'm wanted by law enforcement across the country."

Again, the audience laughs.

It is impossible not to love Carlos, who seems always to be smiling. With his floppy curls and soft cheeks, he is like an overgrown child who has been dressed up for an occasion, and his laugh is infectious.

"Okay," he announces, "just to show you how this all works, we are going to play a game I call 'When Exactly Did They Die?'"

The idea of a game causes a stir of excitement in the audience, who are not used to games during the presentation of serious scientific papers. Carlos quickly hands out cards on which he has written some data. On each card is a person's photograph as well. "Everybody has to play," he says.

Our row's card shows a sepia photograph of a man with neatly oiled hair and a bushy beard. I know who he is even without his name written beneath the photo. However, the data given is a total mystery. Tons of numbers, symbols, and chemical equations.

Carlos takes the stage once again and says, "You may notice that each of your subjects was, in fact, a famous scientist."

"Alexander Bogdanov," Will reads. "Soviet-Russian physician."

"What did he do?" whispers Helmi.

"Wasn't he a hematologist?" asks Will.

Helmi shrugs.

I don't want to sound like a know-it-all, but I say, "He thought the secret to long life was having young blood in your body. So he transfused himself with blood from students in his pursuit of endless life. But he didn't screen the blood and caught malaria. He also used to evade the tsar's police by using fake names. Riadavoy, Werner, Maximov. Bogdanov wasn't his real name."

Will turns to me, his mouth open in surprise. "And you know this *how*?"

"Because his real name was Malinovsky."

He scowls. "That's rubbish! He was Bogdanov."

Will's pronouncement that my information is rubbish seems to make it so. I keep quiet and am relieved when Carlos's voice finally booms across the room again.

"I'm going to give you some instructions and you're going to use the data on the cards to figure out when the person on your card died. Of course, I've invented the information that gives the exact time of death, but the day and year are historically accurate, and I think we can all agree it is more fun when we are dealing with historic scientists rather than the mouse victims of my mother's cat."

He gives us the instructions and tells us we have ten minutes to work it out using the data on each of the individual cards. The silence in the auditorium gives way to a cacophony of voices as groups begin discussing how to answer Carlos's questions. Finally,

Carlos holds his phone next to his lapel microphone and a ringtone from a horror movie chase scene signals that time is up. Now he asks each group for the time of death. A member of each row is chosen to give the answer, standing briefly to announce the name, date, and time of death for the subject on the card.

"Michael Faraday, twenty-fifth of August, 1867, at 9:52 p.m.," says one of the judges in a back row, then gives a little laugh. "Oh, sorry," she says. "It isn't really funny, is it? Didn't he die of chronic chemical poisoning?"

"Yes, he did," says Carlos with gusto. "But not before making important discoveries in the field of electromagnetics."

Then Rik stands up, speaking for his row. Since our meeting at the spa, I've been aware of where he is in every room of this hotel. I keep thinking about how he passed by me in his swimming trunks, how he put his finger to his lips.

"Elizabeth Fleischman," he announces loudly. "August 3, 1905, at 3:01 a.m."

"That's right! And very sad, too," says Carlos. "She was a pioneer in radiography. We didn't know what endless exposure to X-rays did to a person back then, and Elizabeth died of radiation poisoning."

When finally Carlos arrives at our row, Will takes the lead. He stands straight, his shoulders back, and pushes the hair off his forehead. "Alexander Bogdanov, April 7, 1928, at 5:02 a.m.," he announces.

"*Correct!*" says Carlos. "By now, you've all gleaned that the scientists on your cards died as a result of their own experiments. So, Will, do you know anything about Bogdanov?"

"Hematologist," begins Will. He scratches his head as if to recall a fact. "I think he was pursuing his dream of eternal youth, receiving blood transfusions from young men in hopes that they would keep him alive forever?"

"Absolutely right," says Carlos, intrigued.

"He didn't actually screen the blood, however, did he?"

"No, he didn't," says Carlos, and clucks his tongue. "And that was his downfall. He died from the infected blood of one of his students."

"Yes, I seem to recall as much," says Will, still standing. He glances at me now. He's wicked and playful, and utterly unstoppable. "Didn't he evade the tsar's men for years?" he says.

"He did, indeed," says Carlos. It's clear he's impressed by Will's knowledge. In fact, the whole room is impressed. I wait for Will to mention that it had been me who had told him these facts about Bogdanov, but he only clears his throat, rests his chin in his hand as though trying to call to mind some great thought, and says, "I believe I am correct that he used a number of pseudonyms to avoid capture. His real name, of course, was Malinovsky."

Like he knew.

The audience applauds him, and Will gives a little bow as though reluctantly acknowledging their appreciation. Then, as casual as ever, he takes his seat.

"Your information appears to be accurate," he says, in a voice so low that only I can hear. "If you have a doctorate at all, I assume it is in the history of medicine."

6

I'M STANDING IN my underwear staring at the gown with the beaded dragonflies sewn into the fabric, one of many beautiful things Lauren packed carefully into the pink suitcase. I want to slip between the folds of silk and zip myself into the dress, pin my hair up away from my face, and parade down the softly lit corridors to join the others gathering downstairs in preparation for tonight's cruise.

But Will is downstairs.

It would only take a change in his mood for him to get me disqualified. Anyway, I feel a creeping anxiety, as though I'm straying further and further into a trap that I'll never be free of. It's not only the lack of credentials that unnerves me. It's that ever since arriving at the Science for Our Future awards I've been playacting, pretending to be older than I am, educated, accomplished. I wear Lauren's clothes, designer numbers that make me appear rich and sophisticated, with an eye for fashion. Meanwhile, my real self is folded into the suitcase along with my jeans and red sneakers.

The ball gown is a step too far. Who will believe that I could own such a dress? The trouble is that everyone will believe it. Just as they believe so many things about me that I've planted in their minds or allowed them to assume. I've met many new and wonderful people over the past couple of days, but they haven't met me, the real me.

I reach out, touching the dress. I think of Rik, who is already downstairs. I want him to see me in this dress, but what would he think if he knew it was all pretend? I bet he wouldn't like me so much if he knew my regular outfit is jeans and sneakers, with a school bag over my shoulder.

I know exactly what Lauren would say if she were here. She'd say, *Shut up and put on the damned dress.*

So I do.

I arrive downstairs, stepping carefully in Lauren's high heels. My dress attracts the attention of a man with red hair who hands me a glass of champagne and tries to engage me in conversation. But I melt away into the crowd of people in dinner jackets and evening gowns. A bell rings and we gather around a guide in a bright uniform carrying a lantern the size of a hatbox. We follow him through the doors of the hotel and out into the night, the snow around us like feathers. I'm freezing even under the velvet cape that Lauren chose for the dress, but I'm also enchanted by everything around me as we make our way out to the jetty that stretches into the inky water, not quite a lake, much less a sea, that filters through all of Stockholm. Some draw out umbrellas as shields against the snow. Others laugh and flick wet flakes from their hair. I look over the lapping darkness of the water, marveling at our ship lit with hundreds of white bulbs.

And then the red-haired man appears again. He finds me by the waterfront and makes a beeline for me. Close up, I see that his cheeks are pockmarked and that he has a withered quality to him so that he seems too small in his overcoat. He buries his hands in his pockets and leans toward me, his hair studded with snow.

"Where do you teach?" he asks, his accent thick and familiar. Maybe it's the intoxication of a wintry night or maybe it's the champagne, but I say something true about myself for the first time since arriving in Sweden. "I don't teach," I say, then stick out my tongue to catch a snowflake on its tip.

"Because you are only in secondary school," he says. A flat statement spoken so heavily I can almost hear a thud. "Don't be concerned," he continues. "I have no interest in harming you. In fact, quite the opposite. I'd like to offer you a position."

"A position?" I say.

"You have unusual talents. I can introduce you to people elsewhere, people who will recognize your abilities and compensate you well for them."

I'm a little freaked out. Perhaps he realizes this, because he offers a reassuring smile, then shrinks away into the crowd while I recover. How does he know anything about me? What kind of "position" is he talking about? Questions spin through my mind as I climb aboard the ship, entering a large, glass-walled room that smells of mulled wine and spices. There's a jazz band playing. One of the musicians checks his trumpet before returning the mouthpiece to his lips. I'm glad for the distraction, the noise, anything to fill my head and push out the fear that has lodged itself there.

Suddenly, a succession of pops explode into the air and now there's more champagne. The glasses are stacked beside an ice sculpture in the shape of an angel. I don't even need to put out my hand before one is offered. In the regal dress, in heels that make me as tall as the men, I have discovered what it feels like to be beautiful. People make way for you as you walk. You don't have to ask for anything.

The second glass makes me feel less troubled, but now my head is swimming. I think I should find Helmi and Carlos when I feel a touch on my shoulder. I imagine with dread that it is the redheaded man, but when I turn, I see Rik, holding a camera. A flash erupts in my vision and he apologizes for startling me.

"You dazzled me!" I say, blinking.

"That was my intention." He steps forward, shows me the photograph on his camera's screen, and says, "I'm supposed to be filling up the Instagram and Twitter feeds for SFOF. Can I add this to the pile?"

The photo is flattering, but the last thing I want is my face connected to this prize on social media.

Rik must sense my hesitation. "I don't have to," he says. "I'll do what you want."

Out of the corner of my vision I see the redheaded man again, watching me as I speak to Rik. He'd said he had no interest in harming me, but making such a statement is, in itself, threatening. If he walks over to us now and announces I'm a high school student, everything will change in an instant.

"Dance with me," I say to Rik. I'd never normally have the courage, but I'm more scared of the red-haired man than I am of embarrassing myself with Rik. Anyway, Rik seems pleased. He smiles, then plucks my champagne glass from my hand and leads me to the dance floor. He looks at me with the same warmth as he did in the spa, and a feeling erupts inside me that is both peculiar and thrilling.

"I shouldn't have asked you to dance, really," I say.

"Why not?" says Rik.

"'Cause I don't know how to dance," I admit, which is hilarious and tragic at the same time.

But Rik only smiles and pulls me closer. "Sure you do," he says.

At first, he kind of drags me around, but eventually I can manage without literally falling over. At some point I realize nothing awful is going to happen. I'm not going to fall down or step on Rik's toes. We sway to the music amid other couples, dancing in silence. The red-haired man has disappeared, and now I begin to relax, even to enjoy myself. I look into Rik's eyes and feel again that connection we had in the spa. I wonder if he will say anything about the spa, the sauna with its furnace of fiery bricks, the dark chill of the stone pool. I can think of no natural way to bring up what happened there. It's as though it's so private that it cannot be discussed at all, even between us.

"I'm looking forward to hearing your talk tomorrow," he says.

"Hmm, I don't want to think about that," I say. I want to focus on where I am right now, dancing in a room full of ice sculptures and frosty wreaths and winter flowers, feeling Rik's hand in my hand, the cloth of his jacket against my skin. I've seen posters for dances at school. I've certainly witnessed the spectacle of the "promposals" that occur in spring, when senior guys make a great display of inviting the girls they like to the prom. But I've never actually been to a school dance. I wonder if they are as good as what I'm experiencing now.

He says, "Munn and I have breakfast together in the hotel library in the mornings to go over the day's schedule. You should join us sometime. You two have a lot in common," he says.

"Like what?" I murmur.

"Zebrafish, for example. You mention them in your paper."

That makes me smile. "Hmmm," I say, "they can repair their own hearts."

"I think Munn would like you."

"That man with the red hair and the accent likes me. But I don't like him."

"Which man? Everyone has an accent."

I realize suddenly that nothing I'm saying makes any sense to Rik. Also, that I'm feeling a little light-headed.

"You sound like you've had some champagne," he says.

"Maybe, yes." I've had two glasses of champagne in a row, which is more alcohol than I've had in my entire life.

"I like your dress," Rik says.

"All her dresses are amazing," I say, then realize that I've said "*her* dresses," meaning Lauren's. I quickly correct myself. "I mean the designer. All of this designer's dresses are amazing."

"Ah," says Rik.

Maybe it would have gone like this all evening. Maybe we'd have danced and talked and stood together with cocktail plates and canapés. I like to think so. But as the music ends Helmi arrives at my side, explaining that I am needed upstairs for a group photo, all the prizewinners together.

"Sorry," she says, glancing at Rik.

He makes a little sad face, then says, "Does this mean I have to get back to work, too?"

I follow Helmi reluctantly, the thrill of dancing now replaced by anxiety, knowing that Will is upstairs. I try to remember that the award isn't about what Will thinks of me but about my paper, the one I'll deliver tomorrow. The paper is about how dragonflies track their prey, calculating distance, direction, and speed, a talent usually reserved for creatures with complex nervous systems.

I say, "Did you know, Helmi, that dragonflies track prey so efficiently that they catch ninety-five percent of what they hunt?"

"No," says Helmi, calling back over her shoulder. "Nobody knows that."

"They have one of the highest predation efficiencies in nature."

"Have you had a glass too many, or do you always talk like this?"

"I think I always talk like this."

I hear Helmi's laugh as she pushes her way through the crowd, calling "excuse me" and "pardon me" and "hello, can you please move?" It's a little embarrassing, but I'm in my own world right now, floating on champagne as the ship inches its way through the icy water, thinking about how I just danced with a guy.

But at the top of the steps it all evaporates. I see Will poised like a movie star between huge lights on black stands, electrical cables coiled at his feet. In the glow of the spotlights, he looks more commanding, his hair more golden. He speaks to a television crew, then turns to his date, the lovely Swedish journalist Elsa. Toward Elsa he seems a wholly different man, someone capable of smiling sweetly and pushing a strand of beautiful white-blond hair away from her cheek.

He switches back to the usual Will when he sees Helmi and me, his face tightening into a frown. He marches toward us as though we are a couple of schoolgirls late for assembly. "There you are," he says impatiently.

He motions for us to move forward into the light for the photographer. Suddenly, Carlos emerges, finishing a last bite of gravlax and licking his fingers before positioning himself next to Helmi. I'd like to tuck myself between him and Helmi, but the photographer gestures for me to stand next to Will, who gives a jerk of his head, as if to say that I need to move a little faster.

I feel so awkward beside him, like a lamb sidling up to a lion. He's certainly not thrilled with me, either. He looks down at my dress, as though at a specimen jar. "Don't you look grown up," he says, smiling. I look daggers at him as he says, "Very put together."

I want to tell him I don't care what he thinks of my appearance. That I know what he's up to. But even if I could get up the nerve, I don't dare speak. Will instructs everyone to stand close, but then, just as the photo is being taken, he moves toward the camera so that he is front and forward of the rest of us. It's as though Carlos, Helmi, and I are there only to reflect his glory. I wouldn't mind if he were pleasant. But as the flashes pop, I feel Will's dark mood all around me. Not even the champagne helps. The gloom of the past forty-eight hours descends at once.

If anything, the alcohol makes it worse.

"Have you met my brother, Aiden?" he asks pointedly. In front of me suddenly is a man very much like Will in appearance, but thinner and taller, as though someone has taken Will and stretched him. "You already know his work. After all, you make reference to some of his research in your own paper."

Will's bitter tone rings out, noticed not only by me but also by his brother, who I realize now is older than Will, something I hadn't expected. Aiden gives me an embarrassed smile. "I'm honored to be a runner-up to your excellent work," he says.

"You weren't *a* runner-up, you were *the* runner-up," Will corrects. "It's just a shame you won't be getting the matching grant money for your research. But we have to abide by the judges' decision." He sighs.

Aiden looks even more embarrassed. Unlike his brother, it's clear that he prefers not to be in the spotlight or have his achievements unduly noted. "I am certain I was *very* much behind you," he says graciously. He's about to say something more but is interrupted by Will, who pushes him forward, toward the camera, asking the photographer for a few snaps of him with his brother. The last thing I see as I move away from the hub of media people and back into the party is Will urging Helmi and Carlos to stand along with him and Aiden. As though these four are the rightful winners of the prizes.

7

I WAKE WITH a pounding head, my mouth so dry it's as though I've been sucking cotton all night. The darkness of Swedish winters means there's no sun filtering through the curtains. I use my phone to navigate to the bathroom so I don't have to switch on a lamp. Bending over the sink, I swallow tap water. This is my first hangover.

But my headache doesn't stop me thinking about Rik's hand on my shoulder, on my waist. I'd put up with a week of hangovers just to feel again his broad palm as he led me to the dance floor and the solidness of his body next to mine.

A shower would be too noisy, plus I don't think I could stand water pounding on my head. It's going to have to be a bath. I fill the tub, then lower myself into the warm water, thinking this time tomorrow the awards will be over. I'll be packing up, readying to vacate the pretty room, the luxurious hotel, the cold wonder of Stockholm. But meanwhile, I have two important things to do. First, prepare for my presentation. Second, avoid Will.

For my presentation, Lauren packed a black wool turtleneck and dressy trousers with French pockets. A note in her handwriting reads "Good luck!" She's also included a silky camisole for under the top and a chunky necklace made of gold shells to break up all the black.

The outfit is just right. In the mirror, I look serious, professional, stylish. Only my eyes, puffy and small in my head, give away the hangover. I can almost hear Lauren's voice coaching me on that one, too. *Open the makeup bag I gave you! You'll need a cold pack, then lots of concealer and even more mascara.*

I get some ice from down the hall and lie with a wet washcloth over my face. I know I can't give a talk even half as interesting as Helmi, who had been so masterful and quick-witted, explaining complex procedures with lucidity and style. Or Carlos, who acted the part of a charming MC as he conducted his game with the cards. And I can only imagine Will's talk. He is so full of himself, plus he can say the word *humdrum* and make it sound important.

I tell myself, *Stop thinking and dry your hair.* But the sound of the blow-dryer is like an airplane engine. I need coffee, but my legs are shaky. I carry the ankle boots Lauren supplied for this outfit, because even short heels seem too much. At least the elevator is empty.

The lobby is full of soft morning light and the pine scent of its enormous Christmas tree. I slip on my boots and make my way toward the Veranda. The smell of butter and toast and cinnamon, all of which I normally love, makes me queasy. Passing a table of people feasting on various cold meats and boiled eggs, I feel my stomach lurch.

I find a tray of orange juice by the waiters' station and drink two glasses in a row. Under normal circumstances, I'd devour another *kanelbulle* or two. But all I can cope with is a plain white roll from a basket of bread, which I nibble like a mouse.

"How are we this morning?" Will's voice, unmistakable, loud, blasting into my left ear.

"Fine," I say. I search for a means of getting around him without actually pushing. I try going left, but he holds out an arm as though to steady me, effectively blocking my way.

"You don't look fine," he says. "Didn't you enjoy our sail through Stockholm by moonlight?"

He seems to be speaking exceptionally loudly. "Yes," I say. I really hope he'll get out of my way.

"Why don't you join us?" he suggests, gesturing toward a table by the glass wall. I look across the room. Beside Will's empty seat are several committee members in conversation with Will's brother, Aiden, who smiles a lot. It's like he's campaigning for my position of prizewinner once I'm deposed.

And yes, I'm sure Will means for me to notice this.

"Perhaps you'd enjoy a chance to chat with the committee?" he says.

It feels inevitable that I will be disqualified. But if Will expects me to march over and sit with the committee as he unveils the truth about me, he's wrong.

"I'm having breakfast with Dr. Munn," I say, a lie that blooms out of nowhere. It throws Will for a moment. I watch the shock in his eyes before his face darkens with disbelief.

"How nice for you," he says. He scans the room, then adds, "I don't see Munn about. Where exactly are you having this breakfast?"

According to Rik, Munn has breakfast in the library. If I had a meeting with him, it would be there. But I say nothing as Will stands impatiently before me, waiting for an answer.

"You're making it up, aren't you?" he says, then folds his arms over his chest. "You're good at making things up."

I swallow hard. I feel my stomach tighten as I continue. "Follow me to the library if you're so sure," I say.

Will flinches as though I've poked him. He opens his mouth, then closes it again. "I'd like to know why he wishes to see you."

As if he is entitled to know why. Just as he imagines he is entitled to know my educational standing, my background, everything about me. Perhaps he thinks that winning the grand prize in the Science for Our Future awards makes him king.

"Me too. I'd like to know why he wants to see me," I say, turning on my heel. "I guess I'll find out."

I think that's the end of it, but it's not. I hear his voice again and realize that he's following me. I feel the cool sweat of fear as I move through the corridors toward the library. I hear Will's footsteps behind me, a kind of drumbeat that echoes in my head as I move out of the restaurant, through the elevator lobby, and then along the corridor.

A shiny brass sign tells me to turn right to the library and I do so abruptly, pressing my fingers to my throbbing temples. Will's footsteps quicken. He's beside me now. He is certain that there is no breakfast, no meeting. It infuriates me that he's right, that I'm bluffing.

"My brother has been very gracious about this matter of the prize," he says. "I'm not so sure he ought to be."

And there it is again: the threat. Like a spot of fresh blood from a wound that won't heal. Maybe I should confess to the committee myself. Or slink away before tonight's banquet and leave the prize to Aiden. But doing so would have consequences. I think of my mother. I can't let her down. I think of her health, of our little house back home, of all those bills.

I see the brass placard with the word *Bibliotek* ahead and I regret being so bold, so foolish. I've walked into a trap. It's all I can do to continue. Finally, I come to a halt outside the library's double doors, one of which is open.

I'm not sure if I should knock as though I were going into Munn's office or enter as though I'm a legitimate hotel guest. I compromise, knocking just once before stepping gently through the doors.

Suddenly, all the chaos of rushing through the hotel ends. Everything is still. The library, filled with soft light, its walls brimming with leathery books, holds an array of cherry tables and inviting plush chairs. There's Munn, sitting beside Rik in an armchair, a cup and saucer in his hand. Resting between them on a low table is a pot of tea and the last remnants of toast. Rik must think I've gone nuts. Last night, he told me that Munn took breakfast in the library. But he hadn't said arrive in the morning and barge in as though escaping enemy fire.

Munn regards me with a curious expression. I can barely bring myself to look at him. I've followed his research for years, read his acceptance speech for the Nobel Prize, and listened to podcasts in which he discusses his work. His mind is progressive, extraordinary. In England, he holds a knighthood.

"Kira Adams," he says in his clipped English accent. My name comes out sounding like *Kira Eddems.*

He has good manners. He'd never show that he feels intruded upon. Instead, he acts as though he's been expecting me. He puts down his teacup. "Please join us," he says.

I glance at Rik, whose face registers mild surprise, then over my shoulder to where I expect Will is glaring at me. But the entrance to the library is empty. Will is gone.

"I was actually hoping to speak with you," says Munn.

I can't imagine this is the case, but I try to smile.

"Here," Rik says, pulling out a chair.

I'm given a cup of tea, a lump of sugar, a slice of almond cake. I try to say thank you, but it comes out as a squeak.

"Am I correct in saying that you're from Palo Alto?" asks Munn. "You must visit us at the Mellin Institute. We're not far from you."

Not far in distance, but light-years away. Palo Alto is the home of Stanford University and the Cantor Arts Center, as well as some of the richest neighborhoods in America. Lauren lives there, surrounded by newly minted tech entrepreneurs. It couldn't be more different from my neighborhood, crammed with tiny single-story houses and manufactured homes on unkempt plots.

"Tell me about your family. Any brothers or sisters?" Munn asks.

I shake my head. "It's just my mom and me."

"Any special schooling?"

"Um . . . no."

"Your mother . . . is she an academic?"

I might have said that she never even went to college, but that would feel as though I'm admitting to some great failure in her life. Or that she didn't try hard enough. Neither is true.

I shake my head.

"Are you going to ask me why I hoped we'd have a chance to chat?" he says teasingly.

I feel myself blush. The truth is I'm almost afraid to speak.

"Because I knew your father. Your father," he says, as though reminding me I had one, "Cyril Adams."

My father's name is so unexpected, and for a moment it's as though his ghost has entered the room.

"He was an extraordinary young man. When I was reading your paper it was like déjà vu. It could have been his work."

I never knew my father. He had a drinking problem and made stupid decisions when drunk. One was to try to interrupt an armed robbery not far from our house. I was only a baby when he died.

"You are very like him," Munn says.

I can't just sit here mute. He'll think I'm even more ridiculous than I am. "How did you . . . how did you know him?" I say.

Munn clears his throat and smiles. "I was a fan, really. I take an interest in people who are, one might say, preternaturally gifted. He didn't have the benefit of higher education, yet there he was. Something bordering on the miraculous. I used to visit him in that garage where he worked."

I nod. The garage was an outbuilding on a poultry farm. More like a shed. And the reason he was there instead of at a proper engineering lab was, again, because of the alcohol.

"It was as though he could pluck things from the future and

bring them back to the present day," Munn continues. "I'd find him in his workspace in grubby coveralls with heavy tongs, forging a tool he'd had to invent himself because whatever he'd dreamed up couldn't be built without it. Do you understand what I'm telling you? He was so far ahead of us that the tools needed to make his inventions had not yet themselves been invented." He leans back in his seat and smiles. "He must have found us all a very dull lot."

There's a pause, and I don't know what to say. My father was very smart. I know that. He was also very troubled.

"My mother told me stories," I say.

Munn nods, as though he can imagine stories, many stories. In fact, there have been few. My mother doesn't talk about my father, or anything about the past, really. It's as if her whole life began the day I was born.

"He was a true genius, Kira," Munn says quietly. "An impossible maverick, and yes, he had his problems. But he was remarkable. And so are you."

I don't know what to say to that. I stare down at my knees. Rik senses that I'm overwhelmed and fills the silence, discussing a detail of my dragonfly paper. I try to nod along and act, you know, *normal.*

At last, it's time for Dr. Munn to go. Rik holds out Dr. Munn's coat and valise for him. "I've enjoyed our chat," Munn says, and extends his hand. "Keep your work as pure and honest as you can while still keeping the wolf from the door."

This last remark rings through my mind. It sounds almost as though Munn has figured out that I'm here to do exactly that, keep the wolf from the door. And that in order to do so, I can't be completely honest.

By the time we gather for Will's presentation, my hangover has mostly resolved, but I'm still a bundle of nerves, sitting in the front row on the gold-leaf chair and waiting for him to begin. I feel my heart vibrating in my chest, my skin growing hot, then cold.

"What's happened to you?" asks Helmi. "You have the fidgets."

"Are fidgeting," says Carlos, correcting her English.

Helmi rolls her eyes.

It's true, my legs seem to vibrate with their own power as I try in vain to keep still. I pretend to Helmi and Carlos that I'm nervous because I ran into Munn at breakfast, but that's not the real reason. The reason is the man in front of me, preparing for his talk. Every so often, Will glances my way, and it makes me shudder.

"What did Munn say to you?" Carlos says.

"That she never stops moving," says Helmi, then smiles at her own joke.

The room's lights dim. Will begins.

First, he thanks the committee. Then he thanks the judging panel. He goes on to thank the organizers of Scientists for Our Future, its sponsors and contributors. Finally, he starts thanking individuals by name. Anyone would have imagined this was the last talk to be given at the event; it certainly feels like it is.

I have fresh regret at agreeing to speak after him. But, of course, I'd had no choice but to agree. Even now, I can see Aiden off to the side, one row behind. Next to him is Elsa, who sits elegantly with her long legs crossed, recording the talk on her phone.

Will begins by describing how the brain doesn't age as we once imagined. Each of us has genes that express what we understand as "aging" according to a schedule within our own individual genome. That schedule is difficult to influence. "Yes, we can delay certain problems like heart attack or cancer through lifestyle choices," says Will, "but our cells possess their own time clock, so moving the dial on our overall life-span is unlikely no matter what the health gurus say."

He flips through a series of slides. The screen fills with different kinds of cells. Neural cells grown from stem cells, glowing purple and red, burst with color rising from their surfaces, looking like the solar flares on tiny suns. Skin cells make patterns like a kaleidoscope. "Stem cells often don't perform in the human body the way they do in a lab. The question I am asking is, why not? My hypothesis is that they lack the time clock I've just spoken of."

Will's presentation is exciting, even profound. The whole room is enchanted by him. He times his talk beautifully, filling the screen with graphs and slides. He makes jokes, gets serious, draws unlikely parallels, and convinces everyone.

Helmi scribbles notes hurriedly onto a pad. Carlos scratches pencil marks onto the margins of a printout of Will's original paper. But all I can focus on is whatever trap he's set up for later tonight.

Finally, the talk ends. The audience erupts into applause. Will is nothing if not impressive: a handsome, brilliant scientist whose qualities make it all the more withering that he has taken a dislike to me. I watch him nod to the audience, first to those on the right, then those on the left, then finally us in the center. He levels his gaze straight at me and purses his lips disapprovingly. *Follow that,* he seems to say.

Lunch is short. That is, I can't eat. The conference continues through the afternoon with talks given by different groups. A class of schoolchildren arrive for a hands-on experiment conducted in the small courtyard. A petition or two floats about. Private meetings take place in the far reaches of the hotel, some of them quite secret.

"Do you want to know why they have locked that door there?" Helmi says, pointing toward a heavy closed door, as solid as a wall. "Because Dr. Munn and his group are discussing work for the military."

"What kind of work for the military?" I say.

Helmi raises an eyebrow and shrugs. "Unlock the door and I will tell you."

I wade through the afternoon, mostly hiding in my room. Everyone is excited about the final presentation in the Hall of Mirrors—my presentation—and the award ceremony afterward. Everyone except me.

I don't know how this great gift of coming to Stockholm has been transformed into such a grim task. Well, I do know. It's been ruined by Will. Or maybe it was doomed from the moment I sent in the award application with a blank where the degree and date should have been written. At least Will is gone now, off with his lovely journalist. Elsa is taking him to the party at the Royal Palace. I hope she keeps him late.

Evening arrives and I wish more than anything that the schedule hadn't changed. The idea of taking the stage in the Hall of

Mirrors terrifies me. So much buildup, so much expectation for this last presentation. I'm not even sure I can talk in front of an audience. I've never done it before. And my paper, once orderly in my mind, now seems a disarray of facts and numbers. I force myself to review my notes, then stand in front of a mirror and practice. At least Lauren's clothes are right for the occasion, but my wild hair is especially uncooperative and my skin sports a new constellation of acne brought on from lack of sleep.

I arrive downstairs at the expected time feeling wobbly and breathless, as though I've just run miles. But I suppose I'm as ready as I'm ever going to be. I make my way through the hotel, head down, avoiding eye contact with anyone, and step into the Spegel-salen, the Hall of Mirrors. The room, locked except during events such as this, is so richly beautiful, it feels like walking into a fairy tale. Fashioned after the famous Hall of Mirrors in Versailles, its vaulted ceiling is painted richly above a giant chandelier reflected in walls of gilded mirrors. I can't bear the thought of being the center of attention in such a room. It doesn't seem right.

But there is no backing out.

People are taking their seats already. A buzz runs through the air. I walk up the center aisle amid candles that flicker and reflect all around. I am more than overwhelmed; I am *mortified*. My lungs feel as though they've shrunk inside my chest. I can't get enough air. And I have to think carefully about each footstep so that I don't trip. It's a relief to find Helmi and Carlos in their seats. They smile encouragingly and I give a little flicker of a wave. But then I see something that brings me to a sudden halt.

There, in front of me, is Will. He stands regally as though the

Hall of Mirrors is his very own ballroom and we are all his guests. He isn't supposed to even *be* here. The whole point of me giving my talk now was so that he could be out with Elsa. I search wildly for Elsa, hoping she's nearby and will soon whisk him off to the gala. But Elsa is nowhere to be seen.

So.

It's obvious he has no plans to be at the Royal Palace tonight. The story about Elsa and the gala at the palace was a ruse. I'm not sure exactly what Will is up to, but I'm certain the reason he is standing so prominently in front of me now is so that I will notice him.

I notice him, all right. And I see his brother in the row just behind Helmi and Carlos. Will is so sure Aiden deserves the prize instead of me. Maybe he does—I don't know.

I push myself forward. I tell myself I've done many difficult things in the past and this is just one more. But oh, how I pray Will won't speak to me, at least until after the talk. I continue, walking deliberately. I get almost to the front of the room before I hear his voice. It stops me like a wall.

"You look as though you've been caught in a storm," he says.

Drop dead, I want to say. Instead, I smooth my hair, making sure the bubbles of curls are held back, away from my face in a clip. I check my clothes for lint.

"Have you been caught, Kira?" he says.

"Pay no attention to him!" Helmi says, and smiles encouragingly.

"That's right, pay no attention to me," Will agrees.

The talk would have been difficult enough without Will here.

Now it seems impossible. I can almost hear my mother's advice whenever I'd been bullied in school. *Walk on by*, she'd tell me.

I walk purposely past him and up a short tower of steps to the stage. I take my place in a chair to the side of the lectern, waiting to be introduced. It's awkward to sit onstage. I'm suddenly aware of the racks of lights above me, the screen to my right, the entire room spread out in front of me. But at least Will can't bother me here.

The lights grow dim in the back and the stage lights beam brighter, shining hard onto the top of Dr. Biruk's head as he approaches the podium. He seems uneasy as he introduces me. Unlike all the previous winners, who have worked in illustrious laboratories and published numerous papers, there is little to say about me. In fact, nothing at all. He squints at his notes as though he's missing something before finally giving up and calling my name.

I'm no good at public speaking. It's always the same. The teacher calls on me for an answer, one that I know, and I suddenly feel as though my mind has been scrambled. It's even worse now, standing in front of the audience, hearing their polite applause. Plus, Will is glaring at me, making me feel fraudulent and wrong. But I *am* going to give this talk. There's no question about that. It's part of the requirements for prizewinners.

So I begin the only way I know: by reeling off a list of facts.

I say, "Dolphins have a corpus callosum just like we do, so both sides of their brains are connected. But they sleep with one half of their brains at a time, while the other continues as normal."

On the screen, I click into place a slide of a coastal bottle-nose, the type of dolphin you can see from the beach. "Maybe you already know unihemispheric sleeping isn't unusual in dolphins or in migrating birds?" There is an awkward pause, and I realize all at once that you can't ask a question to an audience of over a hundred and expect an answer. "Sorry," I say, and quickly switch to another image. Where there had been the dolphin is now a close-up of a duck with a glossy green head. "This is a duck," I say, but I can't for the life of me remember what else I am meant to say about the duck. That it's a mallard? I hear an awkward laugh from the back of the room, then stony silence. I move on quickly.

The next image is of a subarctic darner, a type of dragonfly with a colorful, patterned abdomen and a broad net of wings.

"Dragonflies hunt prey like mammals do, even though they have no central nervous system. In other words, they can't actually think. They measure rotation while tracking their prey's angular displacement, using that information to determine not where their prey is, but where it's going."

There, that sounded almost like a scientist. But I squint out at the audience and see that I haven't had the effect I'd hoped for. The judges and committee are watching dutifully while others have sunk into their seats or are stealing glimpses at their phones. I'm not telling them anything new or even interesting. It's the same problem I have in school—call it awkwardness or stage fright or whatever. It always ends in shambles.

I press the button on my remote several times until at last I come to an image of numbers and equations.

"I made this mathematical model to explain the steering maneuvers of dragonflies in response to visual cues of their prey. On the left are the numbers that would be required if experts in the field were correct in their current theory about how dragon-flies track prey. On the right is what actually happens. At least, I think so. On the face of it, this looks like a whole lot of numbers, but let me take you through it and show you how, if we follow the column on the right, we understand how dragonflies hunt so successfully—"

I swallow hard, hoping that doesn't sound too arrogant. After all, I've just said that the experts are wrong. I begin explaining the math. And with this comes a kind of calm. I love math; it's the language of science and the only language I feel truly comfortable in. For a moment I even forget where I am, forget the stage and lights and the audience in their seats. It's just me and the numbers. I feel happy, floating.

"My theory is that the reason dragonflies can predict the movement of their prey is that they use motor neurons from their wing systems as predictive sensory apparatus. I show my calculations for those predictions here," I say, flipping to another slide. "They switch from visual neurons to motor neurons in rapid rotation, shutting one off, then the other, much like the way a toggle switch works."

I give the audience a moment to take this in. I can see people studying the slide, others writing notes. One gets out a phone and snaps a picture of the screen.

I sum up with something not in the paper, but that I've been working on. "This ability to shut off part of the brain is also why some animals can sleep with half of their brain. It's a toggle system that, if properly understood, might be useful in staving off death," I say.

I explain that in theory, we could limit the scale of cell death in the brain and encourage neurons to repair themselves even as we are dying. The first step is to stop signals that tell the brain *not* to repair itself and *not* to generate new cells. "We need to switch on those repair signals while simultaneously turning off the 'executioner cells' that invade our neurons and carve up DNA. I'll just show you how that works. . . ."

When I check again I see the audience looking expectantly up at the screen. Almost everyone is taking notes. I get through a lot of slides of different chemical processes and a lot of explanation, but I hold the audience's attention right to the end of my talk.

And then I'm done.

"That's all I have," I say. To my astonishment, the audience applauds loudly. I even hear a whistle from the back. For a moment, I think to myself that I've completed the mission that was set before me: arriving in Stockholm, sitting among the great and good of scientific experts, delivering a paper—my very first paper—here in this room. Despite all my worries, I'm going to collect the prize money we need.

I am joined onstage by Dr. Biruk. He leads a second round of applause, this time congratulating all four of the prizewinners. I watch as Helmi, Carlos, and Will rise from their seats, turning to the audience and bowing their heads as they acknowledge the praise being heaped upon them from every corner of the room. Then, in groups of two or three, members of the audience stand, cheering. Helmi glances back at me, her face registering delight, and gives me a quick thumbs-up.

"Ladies and gentlemen, this year's Science for Our Future

award winners!" calls Dr. Biruk in his deep, resonating voice.

It's almost more than I can take in. The atmosphere is electric, everyone cheering. I catch a glimpse of Rik, who is applauding the most, I think. Beside him is Munn, clapping in a slow, methodical rhythm and looking at all four of us as though trying to decide something.

The audience settles down into their seats. Rik steps forward, a microphone in hand to record the Q&A. As he readies it to take questions from the audience, I notice people eager to participate. Some are perched upright in their chairs, waiting. Others lean forward, looking for Rik. I'd been worried that nobody would show any interest at all in my presentation and that there would be no questions. But instead, the whole room seems eager to hear more.

But something is wrong. While the rest of the audience has settled back down into their chairs, Will remains standing. I look at Will as though to ask what he's doing, and he gives me a smug smile before signaling Rik to bring him the microphone. I feel a cascade of nerves float through my body so that I'm buzzing with them. I look to Dr. Biruk to do something, but he stands motionless, as confused as I am. Meanwhile, Will gestures again to Rik.

Too late, I realize what's happening. Will has chosen this moment as his chance to finally speak publicly about me, not just to the committee, but to the whole of the scientific community in attendance. As Rik crosses the room toward Will, I shrink back, feeling a sudden pressure in my solar plexus as though I've been hit by a brick. I pray that Rik will stop, that he won't let Will ruin everything. But he doesn't know there is any reason to stop. He gives the microphone to Will, who grasps it with both hands. Will now turns, staring at me like prey he's been hunting for days and has finally cornered.

"Dr. William Drummond, University of Cambridge," he says, identifying himself for the record. Then he states flatly, "Kira, early this week you informed me that you received your doctorate from Rimowa University. I have found no record of this university, and my question is, where did you receive your doctoral degree?"

A murmur runs through the audience. Some are confused, others are impatient with questions of their own that pertain to the talk. I am too shocked to say anything. But when I don't answer, Will asks the question more forcefully. "The rules of the Science for Our Future prize give a time frame for when the entrant has received a doctorate. So, where and when, exactly, did you receive *your* doctorate? Because it certainly was not at the nonexistent Rimowa University," he says.

The room becomes unsettled. People are embarrassed, whether for me or for Will, I can't tell. Meanwhile, I say nothing. My only hope is to stall long enough that Will is forced to yield the microphone to one of the others who wait with their own questions.

"Are you refusing to answer?" he demands finally.

I can see Carlos sitting in the chair beside Will, his face filled with confusion. And there is Helmi, looking shocked that Will is making everyone so uncomfortable. I don't dare look at Rik.

All my life I've been worried about not being good enough, and that one day not just the kids at school but the whole world would reflect back to me an image of myself as a loser, a freak, a fake.

And now it has.

I force out some words. "Do you want to ask something about the research?" I say.

"I want to know whether or not you have a PhD. Do you have a doctorate?"

"I'd be happy to answer any questions about my presentation," I say. I hear a murmur rise in the room, then Will's voice again.

"I repeat: under the rules of this prize your presentation ought to have been associated with your doctoral work, the same as every other candidate. So please, do tell me, Dr. Adams, where did you receive your doctorate?"

I have no answer. I stand dumbly before the audience. I sense that everyone is taking in what is happening. They've figured out that I've cheated. I'm humiliated. In the awful quiet of this great room, I am ground to dust. All because Will has an older brother who he wants to receive the prize. And because, of course, he's right. I have no PhD.

I look out at the many faces staring back at me. Are they shocked? Angry, even?

I can't blame them.

"I made up Rimowa University in conversation with you," I say, directing my attention to Will. "But I never stated on my entry form or to the committee that I had a PhD."

I look out at the audience again. "I'm very sorry," I say.

I unclasp the tiny microphone clipped to my collar, then the transmitter tucked into my back pocket. But my hands are shaking, so I drop the microphone and it hits the stage, making a noise like a firecracker.

I begin to walk, feeling the room lurch one direction, then another, adrenaline coursing through my veins. It's as though I've taken a drug. My vision tunnels, then expands. My heart is pounding. The muscles in my legs don't hold me upright. But I fix my sight on the big doors at the end of the room and go for it.

I have to get away.

Dr. Biruk is addressing the audience through his microphone. "Please stay seated!" he insists, but he can't calm the crowd. Meanwhile, I reach the doors, ahead of everyone else, and push through them into the plush lobby.

I hadn't expected to see the hotel staff waiting in lines. But they are all assembled just outside the entrance to the Hall of Mirrors, standing like soldiers with trays of cocktails. They were expecting the guests to arrive shortly, and here we are, just a bit ahead of time. Several offer me champagne as I race forward, head down, with an urgency that won't go unnoticed.

The grand staircase is too long and too visible, so I aim for the elevator lobby at the end of the corridor, behind which is an emergency staircase. I push through a set of doors, then climb, racing up the stairs, one flight, another. I understand now that Will rearranged the speeches so that Elsa would write an article about his talk and take it to press before the final talk (mine). If I'd given my talk ahead of his and Will had pulled the stunt he did tonight, the main story about the Science for Our Future award would feature me, not him. He'd wanted to have his glory before launching his attack. By rearranging the order of speeches, he'd managed both.

At last I reach my own floor. I fly through the door, then down the hall to my room with its brass-plated number. Flinging open the door, I see the bedsheets have been carefully folded down, the room made tidy. There's chocolate on the pillow, two mints in green foil. It's all beautiful and perfect, and, for some reason, it makes me even more upset. I throw off the bedsheets, launching the chocolates across the room. I bang open the pretty wardrobe with its delicate key and pull out my suitcase. I can't stand to imagine what will be in print now: how the girl from California was sent home in disgrace, how the prize was awarded to another.

I wish more than anything that I'd never entered this stupid contest. It was ridiculous to imagine that I could get away with it, that I could dress up like someone better, someone stylish and urbane, grown-up, valid. I'm a fraud. I'm stupid. I'm also deeper in debt than ever and with no one to blame but myself.

8

AT FIRST, I'M too upset even to admit to myself what just happened, but as the hours pass, I eventually text Lauren, revealing every excruciating detail of the night.

Lauren is nothing if not consistent. She texts back that if all hope of getting the prize is lost, then I should put on the fabulous wool tunic and tall boots she packed and leave loudly and with passion: Act like none of this matters! Let all those cranky scientists think you've been thrown out of much better conferences!

That's just what Lauren would do. I know she would.

At dawn, before anyone else is awake, I drag the pink suitcase down to the lobby wearing my own clothes: jeans and sneakers, a gray hoodie, my hair in a ponytail. Outside in the freezing morning, I text as I walk, telling Lauren that I don't really care what anyone thinks. The first lie. Also, that I am exiting the scene with great style in the wool tunic and tall boots. Another.

I can no longer wear Lauren's chic clothes and pretend. It's not honest and it's not me. I'm tired of faking everything.

Nothing is open this early in the morning, so I sit on one of the long black benches in Stortorget square. The city is frozen in snow and ice, a dusting of white filling all the spaces between cobbles. Above me is a sliver of moon. The morning light illuminates the square's colorful houses, centuries old, painted burnt orange, olive green, mustard, red. It's like sitting inside a postcard.

I tell myself I've got my suitcase. I've got my passport. I've got everything I need to go home.

Except the prize. If I show up without the prize money, what do I say to Biba? I shake my head. It won't matter what I say. Only money talks.

I search out a café and sit in the warmth beside a window, watching the sun emerge. Ice melts in pieces and slides downward against the glass as cathedral bells ring out the hour. The air smells of sea and snow and the smoky flames from the fire lit in a tiny hearth set into the café wall. My coffee is thick with cream.

It seems wrong to feel so gloomy when all around me is beauty.

I didn't go to the awards ceremony last night, but I assume my award was given to Aiden after all, just as Will wanted. At least I had my moment before Will ruined it. Amid the arched mirrors and magnificent chandeliers of the Spegelsalen, I'd felt the approval of people I respected, PhD or not. And while I hate what happened next—the profound humiliation—there had been a parcel of time when everything was perfect.

I feel someone watching me. When I look up, I see a man standing above me, snow dusting his shoulders. It's the red-haired man from the ship, the one who told me he knew I was a high school student.

"We have a mutual acquaintance," he says now, unwinding a scarf from his neck. He glances around the café before sitting across from me at the table. "Where are your friends?" he says.

He must mean Helmi and Carlos. I wonder if they will still be my friends now that they've found out I lied.

"I'm not going to be awarded my prize," I say.

"No?" he says, as though this is news to him. He leans back in his chair. "Does this mean you will not provide Biba with his money? He won't like that."

Biba. That's our mutual acquaintance? I think of him in his oil-stained jeans, his sun-bleached leather jacket that gives off the smell of exhaust fumes. He's nothing like the well-dressed man before me with his delicate features and tidy beard. That they should know each other at all is incredible and frankly scary.

As though reading my mind, he says, "Biba has a cousin who works as a science scout for us. We are always looking for young people with great talent. He found out about you and brought you to our attention. We don't mind if you are still in your American high school. We don't have rules like this silly committee with its small prize."

"It's not a small prize," I say. "Not to me."

"You needn't concern yourself about the prize. Let them keep it. Come along with me, and the debt will be taken care of." He makes a gesture as though he's flicking the debt away.

"You'd pay the loan?" I say.

He looks at me disapprovingly. "Do not act so grateful. It's unbecoming." Then he adds, "The loan will be repaid once you've met with the gentleman I work for. An introduction, nothing more."

"But . . . why?" It astonishes me that there are people in this world who can treat thousands of dollars like the price of a cup of coffee.

"You have unusual abilities. The man I work for creates scientific think tanks with people such as you. We will pay a small finder's fee to Biba and he will disappear. No more a problem."

He gives me a look as though he's assessing my reaction. Then he says, "The world has changed. People who are good at science have no need to rely on the qualifications they make such a fuss of in your country. All this credentialing!" He nearly spits the word. "PhD *this*, master's *that*. *We* will educate you. We have a facility for young people like yourself."

A *facility*?

When I say nothing he looks at me sharply. "I give you a choice. You go home and wait for trouble with Biba. Or you allow me to introduce you to the gentleman I work for. He is in Moscow, a short plane ride away."

A *plane* ride? He terrifies me, but I don't want to show that.

"Who is he?" I say finally. "The man you work for?"

"Someone interested in the sciences."

I think, *Everyone I've met this week is in "the sciences," as he puts it*. But I don't say anything.

A waitress approaches. He quizzes her about the menu while I think fast about what to do. If I return home without the prize money, it's impossible to pay Biba. If I agree to meet this guy's boss, whoever he is, the debt is paid. It should be easy to decide, but something about the red-haired man tells me that there would be no question about my being required to join their "facility." They won't easily let go of a girl they've paid thousands for. I feel like a bag of groceries that can be bought and sold, like I could disappear altogether into whatever terrifying world this man comes from. My heart is racing. I feel a bead of sweat running down the inside of my shirt.

"Would you care for another coffee while you think it over?" the man asks. He's utterly relaxed while I secretly fall apart. "Though it's an obvious choice, is it not?"

I think about what Munn said in his after-dinner talk. He'd said to be cautious about what kind of science we do and who we work for. This man before me, this person who knows Biba, hardly seems like someone I can trust. "Hot chocolate," I say, the words barely audible.

"As you wish." He shrugs. The waitress disappears to the kitchen with our order.

"The man you will meet is very important. Very wealthy. My advice? No matter how easy he makes the conversation, never forget you are speaking with a man of great power—"

A man of great power. I wonder how he uses this power.

"Sorry to interrupt," I say, trying to sound casual, relaxed. I want him to believe that he's made a friend of me. "I just have to use the ladies' room."

A flash of annoyance crosses his face as I excuse myself. I don't want to stay in the coffee house with this man, but I'm not sure how to get away either. I go to the bathroom, shut the door, then open it a crack and watch.

I can see him there at the table, looking at nothing in particular. I'm hoping for a distraction. I wait, spying through the crack in the door until at last something interests him on his phone. As he begins typing a message I silently count to three. Then, I slip out of the bathroom and move quietly, swiftly, through the door leading to the street.

Without my pink suitcase with all of Lauren's precious clothes. Without my coat or hat.

I keep moving—I don't even know where—until I see a sign for the Nobel Museum. Inside the museum, I catch my breath and tell myself to calm down. The man with the red hair doesn't seem to have followed me. I shouldn't be so scared. He was just recruiting. Plenty of people show up at SFOF to do that. It's only weird because he knows Biba. Even so, I'm hyperalert, with one eye on the museum's big glass doors.

I begin walking through the airy rooms. The museum explains the work of the Swedish Academy, the Karolinska Institute, and how Nobel laureates are selected. I study the information given about famous scientists and their discoveries, described briefly on placards. I gaze at a model of the molecular structure of DNA, read quotes by Edison and Einstein on the nature of genius, touch a model of the structure of penicillin on a table.

On the ceiling, photographs of nine hundred laureates slide along a rail. Of these, only a small proportion are women. And very few of those have won in the sciences.

I know every one of these women by face and name. My favorite is Barbara McClintock, who studied chromosomes. Not only was she one of the few women to receive the prize unshared, but she endured ridicule from the scientific community for over thirty years about the very findings that eventually won her the prize.

In the museum's café, the undersides of the chairs are autographed by laureates. I sit on the one signed by Dan Shechtman, the 2011 prizewinner in chemistry. I buy some souvenirs from the gift shop: bookmarks of laureates, gold-foiled chocolate Nobel Medals showing Alfred Nobel in profile, and some chocolate in the shape of dynamite, which is the discovery that made Alfred so rich that he was able to fund the prize in the first place.

I'm a million miles away when I hear my name being called. I startle, thinking it's the guy with the red hair again. But when I look up, I see Rik standing above me in an overcoat, snow in his hair. I'm surprised to see him, but also embarrassed. For a moment I'd managed to push away thoughts of SFOF and the prize I didn't win. But now the shame of last night floods back. I'm aware, too, of my ponytail and jeans, my eyes red with crying and lack of sleep.

"You missed the announcement at breakfast," Rik says, dropping into the seat next to me. On its underside are the signatures of Christopher Sims and Thomas Sargent, the 2011 winners in economics. I know because I checked. "They're deciding what to do with you."

"What to *do* with me?" I say.

"You know, about the award."

He pushes his legs out and sits back in his chair. The snow in his hair melts, making his bangs wet. "I've been looking all over for you," he says. "Why did you walk out last night?"

I'm so embarrassed I wish I could walk out now, straight from the museum and onto a plane that would take me home. I can barely look at Rik, who seems genuinely puzzled.

"You were there," I say, my voice full of emotion. "You saw what happened. Everyone knows that I broke the rules. That I don't have a PhD."

"I saw William Drummond being a bully. I saw people being confused. Did you know there were press there last night?"

"Not Will's lovely Elsa," I say. It sounds like sulking even to me.

"No, but plenty of others. If you come back to the hotel you'll see they've returned, trying to get the story about the high school kid who somehow beat out postdocs for an SFOF award."

"But I didn't win the award. The rules—"

"Nonsense the rules!" he says, his eyes wide. "Who told you that?"

"Will—"

"Because he wants his brother to win!"

"Even so."

Rik sighs, then shakes his head. Among all the awful things I feel is a sense that I've somehow let him down.

"So, it's true?" he says, his voice thick with disbelief. "You don't have a doctorate? I mean—I can't believe I'm asking this—or *any* college behind you? Even a few credits?"

I shake my head.

He looks at me with a curious expression, as though not sure what to think.

"Please don't look at me like that." I feel small and stupid and impossibly naive. "I'm already embarrassed."

He shakes his head slowly back and forth, then says, "What's it like in high school for someone like you?"

I see myself suddenly back in the school cafeteria, sitting alone with a pile of books. Walking friendless in the hall. I used to think my aloneness was due to something about my appearance. I have glasses I try not to wear; I slouch so I don't seem so tall. I say nothing so that I don't draw attention. I've stood in front of the mirror for hours, trying to figure out what is the giveaway. My face, which has nothing striking about it? My hair, which is too curly to brush, too thick to braid? But it's none of that. I'm alone because of what's inside me, and I can't do anything about it.

"It's fine," I hear myself say.

Rik stares back at me, disbelieving.

"Okay, it's a little weird. So what?"

"Are you eighteen yet?"

I bite my lip, unable to bring myself to tell him I'm nowhere near it.

"I'll take that as a no," he says. I think I hear disappointment in his voice. It tells me many things: that he'd genuinely been interested in me, but also that he can no longer be so. It's as though he's offered me a gift I never even knew I longed for, and then, just as I realized it might be mine, he's taken it back.

"How old are *you*?" I venture.

"Twenty," he says.

"You must have skipped grades," I say.

"I went to college when I was sixteen. The question is, why didn't you? Have you ever had your IQ tested?"

"They used to give me tests. I never knew what the results were."

He looks at me and I know what he is about to say. I've heard it many times, and it isn't helpful. Maybe it isn't even true. "I'm not that smart," I say, before he can get the words out. "Loving science makes you seem smart, even when you're not. There is so much about life that I just can't figure out."

He doesn't say anything, not to agree nor to disagree. He keeps looking at me; I don't know why. I feel nervous, like I'm being evaluated. It seems as though I've spent my whole life being evaluated. "Anyway, what does it matter? I have to go home now and tell everyone I didn't get the prize after all. Do you think I'll have to pay back the hotel and plane fare?"

He leans forward. "That's not necessarily how it's going to pan out, Kira," he says. "They're deciding this morning how to handle it."

"But Will said the rules—"

He interrupts me. "*Will* doesn't decide. Anyone has a right to lodge a complaint and to argue his case. He's done that. But *you* also have an opportunity to state your own case."

It sounds good, but all I can think is, *What case?*

Rik smiles at me. "You think these rules are like the physical laws that govern the universe? Like Kepler's three laws of planetary motion?" he says softly. "That's not the way it works. The meaning behind the rules is what matters. And you satisfy the meaning behind the rules."

"I don't understand."

He looks at me as though trying to decide something. "Would you come with me somewhere?" he asks.

"Probably."

He laughs.

"What's so funny?"

"Most people would have said 'Where?'"

"Okay. Where?"

"I want to show you a place where there are no rules."

I shake my head. "Everywhere you go there are rules. Objects in motion stay in motion, laws of thermodynamics, general relativity. Not to mention gravity."

He laughs. I like that I can make him laugh, so I cheer up a half notch. But he's very handsome with his high cheekbones, his golden skin. It distracts me in a way I don't like. At least not any longer. I try not to remember dancing with him on the ship or our silence together in the chilled water of the stone pool. "Okay, where is this mythical place that has no rules?" I say.

His answer is surprising. "The Stockholm metro," he says.

We leave through the museum's frosted-glass doors. They are etched with the image of Alfred Nobel, and when they open, his head divides in half. I explain to Rik that I left my coat and suitcase in a coffeehouse, and he looks at me strangely because it's impossible to forget a coat in such cold weather. But he dutifully accompanies me to the coffeehouse, where, thank God, I discover that the man with the red hair is gone but my suitcase and coat are still by the table. We set off for the metro, Rik trailing the suitcase for me, its pink shell contrasting with his dark coat and shoes. I hold my bag of goodies from the museum's gift shop in one hand, a map in the other, but Rik knows the way.

He says, "True or false: Alfred Nobel not only invented dynamite, but at least two other explosives."

"That's true. I bought chocolate in the shape of dynamite," I say, holding up the bag. "It's got jalapeño as an ingredient."

"Too easy. True or false: Falcons in Australia fly burning twigs to places where they want to start fires in order to flush out their prey."

"That's ridiculous," I say.

"But true!" says Rik.

"Birds start fires?"

He smiles, pleased to have stumped me. "Your turn."

"Me? No."

"Come on. Take my mind off the freezing cold."

He's trying to cheer me up, and I appreciate it. But I really can't think of anything. Then I blurt out, "True or false: If p is a prime number, then for any integer a, the number a to the power of p minus a is an integer multiple of p."

I clap my hand over my mouth, realizing, of course, that it sounds like showing off.

Rik stops walking. "That's not how you play."

"I know. It was stupid."

"Not stupid, but—" He seems unable to complete his sentence. "Do you talk like that to your friends?"

"Yes."

"And what do they say to you?"

They just . . . uh . . ." I only really have one friend, Lauren. So I say, "They fix my hair and tell me not to wear stripes with plaid."

He starts to laugh, so I add quickly, "Just kidding!"

But I think he knows I wasn't.

The snow grows heavier. He thrusts his hands deep into his pockets and we walk into a breeze that pushes against us on the narrow cobbled street. "So was it true or false?" he says.

"You mean what I said? It's Fermat's little theorem."

"It stumped me," he says.

"Well, I didn't know that Australian birds could be arsonists. So we're even."

At the metro stop, T-Centralen, we stand beneath a huge arch, like the ceiling of a massive cave. It's painted with giant blue vines, its base a cool lapis like water against an uneven surface. The only way you'd know it was a metro station is by the trains that run on either side of the tiled platform.

"How does all this make you feel?" Rik asks, turning to take in the amazing structure.

"I wonder what they used in order to make the cement look like plaster."

"That's not feeling. That's thinking. Forget about how the artist made it. Tell me what it is like to stand here."

I look again at the blue vines and foliage, the shadowed darker colors, the cratered recesses. "It feels like I'm underwater. Or inside some colorful part of Earth not yet discovered. Calm. And it's all so, you know, intentional. Someone thought about me standing here."

This pleases him. "I couldn't have said it better," he says.

At Kungsträdgården, we gaze up at a ceiling mosaic. "This is a sculpture garden with all the pieces painted onto the ceiling," I say.

"It feels warmer here, as if the colors bring a kind of heat. Do you think the artist knew that?"

He nods. "Oh yes."

"That's real granite," I say, pointing at a wall.

"Yes, and that's real moss," Rik says. "There was no intention for it to grow here; it just happened. And they found some fungi in this section that had previously been unknown. And a spider that can't be found anywhere else in Scandinavia."

"Really?"

He winks. "Really," he says.

He tells me that the Stockholm metro is called the longest art museum in the world. It's 110 kilometers. I want to see it all, but we don't have time.

"We have work to do," he says. "You need to prepare your statement for the committee."

"My *statement*?" I say. I don't want to think about the committee, about the SFOF award, about rules and qualifications.

He nods.

"I can't write a statement. I can't write anything, really. I'm failing English. Or maybe not failing entirely, but close."

"*High school* English?" he says incredulously.

"Yes."

"Then we'll begin writing the essay in hell," he laughs, and we board another train.

By "hell" he means Solna station, where a jagged rock rises darkly against a black base and looks like a comfortable cavern from the underworld. In the craggy red, we could be standing in the middle of Earth's core. Rik gets out his phone and opens up a word processing app.

"We have an hour," he says.

"But the rules . . ." I begin.

"You're assuming that the committee chose their words precisely. But people aren't precise. Numbers are precise. Elements are precise. But people are like time; they bend. Wouldn't you say that what matters in science is the quality of the research? And not the educational background of the researcher?"

I nod. "The book of nature is written in the language of mathematics."

"That's rather beautiful. Why don't you start by saying that?"

"Because Galileo already said it," I tell him.

We ride the metro. I type a sentence into his phone. He types another.

"See, it's not so hard," he says.

"I feel like we are rejecting what is given in a mathematical proof. As in, 'Given that entrants to the prize have a PhD . . .'"

A look of worry flashes on his face. "Please don't mention that to the committee," he says.

Back at Gamla Stan, we make our way through the medieval alleyways as the snow gathers, crossing the bridge toward the hotel. I see a boat just like the one on which we'd had the party and danced. But the person who danced with Rik is not the girl crossing the bridge in jeans and sneakers now. Then, I'd been a scientist among scientists, a grown woman in an evening gown. Now things are different. I've already noticed the shift in Rik's attention. He walks with greater distance from me, nothing noticeable, just a few important inches. And he finds no excuse to touch me, not even when we sat together on the metro seats, poring over my statement for the committee. His leg had not touched my leg. His fingertips had not brushed my hand.

Rik had been interested in an invented person who doesn't exist. I'm back to being Kira Adams.

We cross the length of the bridge and approach the hotel. He says, "When we get back—"

"You'll have things to do," I say, finishing his sentence. I don't want to hear him say it.

"I was going to say, you might want to change your shoes."

"Oh!" I look down. My shoes were ridiculous, totally unsuitable. Red canvas sneakers with a hole in the toe.

"It's just that they're wet."

And freezing. But I already knew that.

Rik says, "I don't want anyone to see I've returned you to the hotel with wet feet."

"Anyone," I repeat. A thought suddenly occurs to me. "Rik, did someone *send* you to find me?"

His face darkens as though I've just discovered something he'd hoped would stay secret. "I wanted to find you," he says.

"But someone *did* send you, didn't they?" I say, more of a statement than a question. "Munn sent you."

This is so obvious to me now. It was only my vanity that made me imagine Rik had sought me out on his own. It's Munn who holds his allegiance. If Rik left the conference to come find me, it was because Munn sent him.

He keeps his eyes forward in the direction in which we are walking. As we climb the steps to the entrance of the hotel, he says, "Munn did send me, but—"

It sounds like the apology that it is.

"Of course," I say, interrupting him. I wish that it had been his idea. That he cared that much. I don't want him to see that it bothers me to know that he'd only been responding to his boss's orders. I concentrate on the hotel's icy steps, the doorman who draws open the wide door and welcomes us in. Suddenly, I can't bear to walk with Rik, who apparently fetched me out of obligation, not sentiment.

"Let me explain—" he begins.

But he doesn't get the chance. Standing in the lobby of the hotel as though he's been waiting all this time, is Dr. Munn.

"So you found her," he says to Rik. To me, he says, "This way, Kira."

9

A DOZEN COMMITTEE members sit in heavy leather chairs around a long table. Some of them served as judges, others as advisors. It's obvious they've been here for a while: empty coffee cups, balled napkins, crumbs from the many pastries laid out on a sideboard. Apparently, long discussions have taken place this morning over the question of whether I must be disqualified.

Some of the committee members glance sharply at me as I enter. Others regard me with weary compassion. I've brought them a troubling situation, that's for sure.

I'm given a seat next to Dr. Biruk, who chairs the meeting from one end of the table. I'd love a glass of water but I don't dare ask for one. My right leg shakes with nerves. My heart bangs loudly in my chest. Meanwhile, my cold feet ache in the warmth of the room. My head begins hurting so badly I can barely focus my eyes as I listen to what is being said around me. Dr. Biruk is explaining the rules of the award and how my paper somehow "slipped through the cracks."

The faces around the table look uneasy.

"We don't want to chastise you unduly," comes a woman's voice from the other end of the table, a committee member by the name of Professor Mavis Fogg. She wears her tortoiseshell glasses at the end of her nose and a gray suit jacket and a dress shirt with a ruffled collar that does little to soften her appearance. "But we do need to get to the bottom of this."

A small man with a freckled, bare scalp presses his thumb and forefinger into the space between his eyebrows as though all this pains him, then says, "We've checked again to see if your paper is original, and indeed it appears to be the case. We are relieved that you cannot be accused of plagiarism."

Someone sniffs as though she's not entirely convinced of this. I hear a remark being made and then the whispered response to it: "Yes, but we're not here to debate the merits of the paper—"

The room grows heavy with a verdict. I can't decide if they pity me or despise me or both.

A man's voice emerges. "We do acknowledge that we have some responsibility, as we ought to have been more careful," he says.

I look up and see the man, his lips drawn together tightly, his white beard floating above a brick-red bow tie. "We should have been meticulous in establishing the extent of your academic . . . er . . . career. Such as it is."

He is interrupted by someone delivering copies of my statement. Rik must have printed it out for them. I sit through an excruciating five minutes as the committee reads it.

"Well, thank you, Miss Adams," says Dr. Biruk, then puts my

statement aside. He is so polite, so respectful, that it makes me feel even worse.

I wish they'd just cut to the chase. I already know the answer. It's obvious all this is a buildup to telling me that I'm disqualified. I want to leave. I would leave, too, if only they'd give me back Lauren's suitcase, which is now parked at the other end of the room by the door. I glance over to it and see, beside the suitcase, Dr. Munn leaning against the wall, his long legs crossed at the ankles, looking straight at me. If I want to escape, I'll have to get past Munn, too.

"I want to make it clear that we do not consider you wholly to blame," says Dr. Biruk. He takes in a long breath as though readying himself for something unpleasant.

Here it comes.

"We do have one question, first," interjects Professor Fogg, patting my statement as she speaks. "Were you aware when you applied for the award that you did not qualify, strictly speaking?"

It is perhaps the worst thing they could ask me. Nothing that I concocted this morning on the metro with Rik provides a satisfactory answer. The statement we wrote only argued that the quality of the work should be the deciding factor, not whether I have a particular degree. But the committee is asking something else entirely, making it a matter of ethics. Was I aware that the award was for those with doctorates? Yes, I was. I recall only too well saying as much to Lauren when she arrived at my house with all her beautiful clothes.

"I knew," I say. "The rules state that a PhD cannot have been awarded more than a year ago."

"I see," says Professor Fogg, her words ringing with disappointment.

"Regrettably, this is what we speculated was the case," says the man with the freckled scalp.

"Well then," sighs Dr. Biruk, stroking his goatee.

Dr. Munn coughs, then steps forward and pours a glass of water from a jug on the table. Remarkably, he seems to know how thirsty I am and hands me the water.

"So, you *knew* that your PhD could not have been awarded more than a year ago?" he says.

Before this week, nothing could have made me happier than the thought of being in the same place as Dr. Munn, or any number of the other judges and committee members gathered. But now all I feel is shame.

"I didn't hear your answer," says Munn.

I think of the people outside the room: reporters, radio journalists, a small camera crew. I saw them all as I was hurried inside. Also, Carlos and Helmi, who stood helplessly as I was brought through the crowd. Will, too, who didn't look as smug as I thought he would. Rik had been with me at the start, of course. But he peeled off at some point, or was directed away. I try not to think of him now.

"Yes, sir," I say. "That's correct."

He pauses. I can feel him looking at me, feel the whole of the room staring. It seems so unnecessary. They should have let me leave. If I'd been able to say goodbye to Rik and get on a train, I'd be at the airport by now. I try to sip the water, but my hands shake too much.

Munn breaks the silence. "And was your PhD awarded more than a year ago?" he asks.

I wonder if he is being purposely cruel. I feel my tongue like a dry log in my mouth. Someone is going to notice my legs shaking.

"No," I say.

"When might it be awarded?"

My college applications sit unmarked in my bedroom at home. Even if I were able to pay the tuition, which I can't, even if I could leave my mother, which I can't, I'd need many years to work my way up to the PhD level. "I don't know," I say, staring down at the conference table.

"Well, why don't you guess?"

"If I only have to work part-time while studying, maybe seven years from now."

"But in any case, not more than a year *ago*, correct?"

Again, the room is silent, awaiting my answer. But this time, it's different. I'm not worried. I am stunned because now I see what Munn is doing. He's making a mathematical formula. My PhD is not in the set that includes those PhDs acquired more than a year ago. Very simple, easily proven, an elegant way to say I haven't cheated. I unfasten my gaze from the table and meet his eyes.

"You are correct, sir."

Munn addresses the others in the room now. "I'd like to remind the committee that unlike many other disciplines, science has an open and democratic character. Legend has it that a sign hung above the entrance to Plato's Academy. It read, 'Let no one who is ignorant of mathematics enter here.' It did not say, 'Let no one without an advanced degree enter here.' Mathematics is the barrier through which all great scientists must travel. Miss Adams has certainly crossed that barrier."

He pauses now, observing the committee members thoughtfully. "Even with the most pedantic reading of the rules, Miss Adams qualifies," he says. "That is, if what qualifies someone to enter this prize is that they haven't completed a PhD more than a year ago *as stated by the rules*. And Miss Adams has certainly not completed a PhD more than a year ago. We all agree on that, do we not?"

Again, he pauses, allowing those around the table to take in his argument.

He walks a few steps, then folds his arms across his chest and says, "So, as long as the committee still agrees that her paper is otherwise the winner, a conclusion is easily drawn. Dr. Biruk, do the judges still agree that Miss Adams's paper is the best among the applicants in that category?"

Dr. Biruk looks around the table, apparently reading the faces of the other committee members. "The judges do agree, yes," he says, then blinks several times. "Perhaps another vote is in order?"

Munn nods. "I, for one, am willing to extend an invitation to Miss Adams to work at the Mellin Institute. There's my vote, if you're asking for it. But I'll leave it to the committee to make their final judgment," he says. And with that, he slips out of the room.

I look at the faces of the committee members. They all appear a bit chastened.

"Miss Adams, you will be attending college, we hope," says Dr. Biruk.

"Yes, sir, as soon as I can, that is," I say. I don't say when. I don't know when. Anyway, I can barely think straight. Did Dr. Munn just announce he was willing to *hire* me?

Another of the committee members, a professor from the Karolinska Institute, addresses me. "Have a *kanelbulle*," he says, and passes the plate. "Would you like a cup of coffee?"

"This is cold; let me order some hot coffee," says Professor Fogg. She's transformed from the cross-looking, affronted committee member of only a few minutes ago into an almost motherly figure, asking if I need anything more. "Sugar? Cream?"

"Your parents," begins a German scientist, "they *do* know you're here, correct?"

I nod.

"Good," he says, and grunts. "Very good."

And in this manner, with no great fuss, it is decided. An announcement is made. At last, the doors to the conference room are opened and I see Helmi and Carlos standing outside. Someone whispers to them, and I watch as their faces light up. They come rushing toward me. There will be no more accusations, no worries about the prize. The committee members, too, seem relieved that the burden of a decision is over. They hadn't even found it necessary to disgrace anyone. They are out of their seats in seconds, exiting the room like horses running to pasture. Suddenly, it's only me and Carlos and Helmi at the long wooden table. I slip off my wet shoes, pull my feet up under me in the chair, and accept a kiss on the head from Carlos, a hug from Helmi.

I think, not for the first time, that there is something magical about Stockholm, about the Grand Hôtel, about the lore of Nobel.

All the inhospitable hours that scientists give the work they love, the vast brain power, the sheer effort of the laureates who have graced these same rooms, bring extra oxygen to the air. I tell Helmi it's okay now, not to worry. I hand Carlos a *kanelbulle*, then bite into one of my own. I feel for the first time the true elation of a prizewinner. I am with friends; these are my people, my tribe. The *kanelbulle* is as delicious as I remember from the first time I had one. As is the coffee, when it arrives.

PART TWO

LAB RAT

If we knew what we were doing
it would not be called research, would it?
—ALBERT EINSTEIN

10

THE PRIZE MONEY covers our debt to Biba. We even have enough left over to pay the notices that are coming in the mail with "Urgent" stamped in red ink.

But without a regular income, the prize money can only go so far. I know our debts will eventually mount up again. Biba knows this, too. He rides up on his motorcycle as I'm leaving, blocking my car so I can't pull out of the space.

"We're okay for money right now," I say through my open car window. I hate that I have to be civil to this jerk.

He pays no attention, sauntering over with a look of weary resentment on his face. "For your own good I'm telling you this," he begins. "Don't work for that Munn."

What man? I think. Then I realize he means Dr. Munn.

"People I know will not like it," he continues.

I want to ask him what people. Ever since the red-haired man I've felt uneasy. And how does he even know about Munn's job offer? It was made only once, in front of the committee members back in Stockholm, and I haven't heard anything since.

"But . . . why not?" I say.

"You won't understand."

I might tell him I understand all sorts of things, but the truth is, I don't want to prolong any conversation. The guy is dangerous. I wish he'd just go away and leave us alone. But I know that won't happen. He'll be around again, offering my mother another of his overpriced loans.

"Maybe you shouldn't lend my mother any more money," I say. He raises an eyebrow as though he finds my intrusion into his business with my mother both amusing and stupid. "I mean, I wish you wouldn't."

"Now I take orders from you?" he says, disgusted. "You are completely ignorant."

So are you, I think as he returns to his motorcycle. *You don't even wear a helmet.*

He climbs aboard, keeping his eyes hard upon me. He makes a little kiss shape with his lips as he starts the engine.

"No job with Munn," he says, revving up the engine so that it sends fumes into my face. Then he speeds away.

Lauren calls. She says there's a documentary about to start. An "absolute must-see!" she says. It's about a type of bird that cunningly deceives other birds into feeding and caring for its growing babies and that we have to watch it.

"Edge-of-seat stuff," she says, which I'm not entirely sure I believe. But I tell my mother, and she flicks to the channel.

"Got it," I tell Lauren, and promise I'll make popcorn.

Ten minutes later, my mother and I are glued to the screen where a fat baby cuckoo grows obscenely large inside a nest of reed warblers less than half its size. The reed warbler parents haven't figured out that the cuckoo isn't their own.

Out of nowhere my mother says, "Bring me a dollar."

I've got a bowl of popcorn in my lap, a handful by my chin. The cuckoo ruffles its feathers, nearly toppling the tiny reed warbler babies, who settle unsteadily around it.

"I think they're going to fall," I say.

"A dollar, please!"

"I know what you're doing, and I don't want it," I say, still staring at the reed warblers.

"Kira, I'm not going to argue."

"I know you're not. It's me. I'm arguing."

"There's no winning this one."

"Can't we just watch TV?"

She gives me a look. It's been a bad day for her. Tired. No appetite. I sigh and heave myself from the sofa. I go to the kitchen, dig a dollar from my school bag, and bring it back, slapping it on the coffee table.

"This is totally unnecessary," I say.

On TV, the cuckoo baby is now pushing the reed warbler chicks out of the nest. They drop, one, then the other, tumbling through reeds and into the water below. My mother clucks her tongue. "Until now, I didn't think it was possible to hate a baby bird," she says, tucking the dollar into her hand. "Now bring me that pad of paper, would you?"

The birds on the TV remind me of what Rik told me back in

Stockholm, that falcons create brush fires to flush out their prey. I know it's senseless to miss Rik, but I do. I miss all of them. I keep imagining that Helmi and Carlos and Rik are all still there at the Grand Hôtel, dining in the beautiful rooms or walking the magical cobblestone streets of Gamla Stan. Doing all the things we did during the SFOF conference, but without me. Of course, they've gone their separate ways.

My mother scribbles across a page of notepaper. "Here, sign this."

She has written out a bill of sale for the car, which is exactly what I knew she was going to do. The dollar makes it a legal contract. It's part of the preparation in case she suddenly dies.

"I don't want it," I say.

"I didn't ask if you wanted it."

She returns her attention to the show, her eyes fixed on the enormous cuckoo chick. "The little murderer," she says.

She wants to pretend that selling the car to me is of no great importance, that it means nothing. But arguing about it is like arguing about her disease itself, and she's not up for that.

"We may need another loan," she says, nodding at the corner of the room where a brown stain is growing on the ceiling. It's been there awhile, worsening with every rain.

"I don't care if the roof falls in; we're not taking money from that guy," I say.

My mother sniffs. "I can't see the bank giving us a dime."

"Try another credit card?" I suggest, but I know this won't work either. After a pause, I say, "I'll take some extra shifts at the store." It's a part-time job wrapping gifts at Stanford Mall. I've been working double shifts during the Christmas season, and I might be able to extend that into January.

"No, you won't." Her voice is stern. "Because that's how it starts."

"How what starts?"

"The Great Downhill. The Great Downhill starts because you don't have money, so you take a job and work it around school. You forget a few assignments, drop some grades, and now school isn't going so well. And guess what? You still have no money. So you take more hours. They up your wage fifty cents. You think you're doing okay. Maybe you finish school, maybe you don't. College? You can put it off, can't you? One year, then two, then you think you're a little old for college. You don't want to be in with all those young kids. Anyway, you've gotten a tiny promotion, just enough to scrape by. You might make assistant manager, even. Then you meet a man. The slope gets steeper. You're going down fast. But you don't know that. You're in love. First with him, then with the baby. Now you're working part-time and looking after a family. Another baby comes along—"

"Stop!" I say. "I'm not doing that!"

"Then go to college."

"It's not the same as it used to be," I say. "People who are good at sciences don't need school. . . ."

I realize all at once that I'm quoting the man with the red hair. I've thought of him a few times since getting home. His strange offer, the mention of a "facility," his boss in Moscow. I'm spooked by the thought of what might have happened if I hadn't gotten out of that coffeehouse.

"Everybody needs school," my mother says.

In her life, my mother has sold tickets for Greyhound, dispatched for Yellow Cab, fried for KFC, managed call centers, worked on cafeteria lines. She is weary and God knows she's sick. But she's got wisdom, and not just what you learn in books.

"You work all those hours, and you'll end up just where you are now," she says. "You need to go to college. I know you can't while we're in this . . . bind."

She means while she's sick. She means she is the "bind."

"But once I'm gone, sell the damned place. The house isn't worth anything, but it's the land, you see. It's residential. We've got a lot of loans against the place, but there might be a little left over."

I hate it when she talks like this.

"Mom—" I interrupt, but she shushes me.

"You're special smart. Always have been. Promise me you'll get yourself an education."

I'm late with my answer, so she says, "I *need* to know that will happen."

I know that life doesn't make an even distribution of anything: not money or luck or looks or talent. Long ago, my mother told me that there are things that are meant for me, and things that are not. I just wish that working at Mellin could be for me.

But I don't hear from them. Three days of rain and we're swapping buckets to keep the floor dry. I'm doing the double shifts my mother doesn't want me to do and we're still broke.

But then, just before New Year's, I'm driving home after finishing a shift at the store and see a shiny Mazda MX-5 outside the house. As I come up the porch steps, I hear voices, my mother's and another. Then laughter. My mother is *laughing?*

I hear a man's voice. Why would there be a man in the house?

My mother calls, "Kira, we're in here!"

I drop my school bag in the hall and step into the kitchen. There's a man seated at the kitchen table with his back toward me. By his left elbow is a cup of tea. Even before I clock the particulars—his tweed jacket, his brogues and blond hair, I know exactly who he is.

Will Drummond.

He rises from his chair now, turning toward me. He looks like he might actually try to greet me with a kiss on the cheek, but my expression makes him change his mind. He steps back, dropping his hands by his sides.

"Who'd have thought I'd open the door and find one of the prizewinners from your contest!" my mother says.

I direct my attention at Will. Everywhere else, I'm anxious, quiet. But at home I'm a different person. In my own home, I can stand my ground. "You didn't come all the way over here to persuade me to give your brother my prize, did you?" I say boldly.

He frowns. "I was in the neighborhood and thought I'd drop by, that's all. Your mother kindly offered me a cup of tea."

"In the neighborhood?" I say. "What happened, you get off at the wrong Tube stop?"

He raises his eyebrows in surprise. He's not used to me talking back, and I have to admit it gives me a little thrill to see his expression.

"Tube stop, very good," he says, nodding an acknowledgment. "Have you been to London?"

It's not a real question. He knows I haven't.

My mother says, "I couldn't let him leave before you got home! I mean, all the way from England! I was just telling Dr. Drummond—"

"Please, call me Will."

"—I was just saying to Will that I don't think I've ever met anyone from England before."

My mother gets up from the table and begins fussing with the microwave, putting something in and pressing a series of buttons until it starts. I realize she's unfreezing store-bought cookie dough so that she can make some cookies for Will. How can I tell her that a person like Will would never appreciate the effort, and that he will make fun of her later when he's with his real friends? I can just hear him: *Store-bought cookie dough! And then she microwaved it!*

And it isn't just the cookies he'll make fun of. He's probably never been in a house as shabby as this one. I look around at the kitchen. The pine table has watermarks and scratches. There are cracks in the linoleum on the floor. The chipped countertops are cluttered with mail and papers, half-filled medicine bottles, and some old scratch tickets from the lottery that my mother enters and never wins. It's a cramped, messy space, highly personal, and, to me, so very important. I don't want Will here, assessing everything about our home.

"We were just talking about college," my mother says. "I told Will you hadn't applied for next year's admission, and he thinks that's a mistake."

Will nods. "That's right, I do," he says, clearing his throat. "And I know a little about these things."

He's here with an agenda. I don't know what it is, but I'm certain he didn't stop by the house to talk about my education.

My mother says, "Will thinks he can help get waivers for the application fees and that you still have time to apply for a few colleges that have—what did you call them, Will?"

"Rolling admissions."

"That's right. Rolling admissions. You can apply any time of year. It's not too late."

I'm annoyed at my mother. She keeps pretending I have a choice about going to college when, clearly, I don't. Maybe she's just making a show of it to be polite to Will with his great "offer." To him, I say, "Since when do you care about my future?"

"Kira!" My mother's voice.

"Why don't you tell us why you're really here?" I say.

My mother interrupts. "Will, please excuse my daughter. She's very tired. She works too much."

I stare at Will and we size each other up like two animals in a cage.

Meanwhile, my mother puts the cookies in the oven to bake and boils water for tea. She tries to encourage me to show an interest in the courses Will is recommending as I sit stonily in a chair, saying nothing. The atmosphere doesn't improve despite the smell of freshly baked cookies. At last, my mother grows weary enough to excuse herself to go lie down.

"I really ought to be going as well," says Will, though I notice he makes zero effort in that direction.

"You stay," insists my mother. "I just need to rest a bit and I'll be fine."

As soon as my mother has left the room, Will unleashes his real personality. He leans toward me, speaking in a harsh whisper.

"I wanted to talk to you about Munn's enterprise," he says.

I try not to look surprised. "You mean the Mellin Institute?" I say. And then, hoping to hell I'm wrong, I add, "Let me guess, you work there."

"As a matter of fact, I do," he says, raising an eyebrow. "How did you know that?"

I had no idea. But I remember what Rik had said about how the winners at SFOF were often recruited shortly after the awards. As the grand prize winner, Will had undoubtedly received many offers, including one from Mellin. And he's here, after all.

"I'm not intending to have *you* there with me," he adds.

Now I am genuinely confused. "I haven't heard anything from them," I say.

"Well, you will. You're in," he says glumly. He leans toward me again. "But I wouldn't suggest you take the position. Mellin is a strange laboratory. They've got these *kids* running the place—"

"*You're* there," I say, interrupting.

"I'm young, but twenty-three is not a high school student." He gives me an I'm-being-reasonable expression, then continues. "Look, I know we didn't get on very well at the Science for Our Future conference. But really, that's not why I object to this . . . position you're being offered at Mellin. To be honest, it's just that I've come an awful long way to take this job, and I didn't expect to be having to teach a child—"

"I'm not a child."

"But you're not trained to work in a laboratory. You need an education first. I'll write you a recommendation for whatever college you like," he says. "I'll even ask some people I know, friends of my parents. These are very *respected* scientists, Kira. Your mother mentioned the difficulty of tuition, but there are scholarships—"

He keeps talking, but I'm not listening. I'm thinking about what it will be like to work in a laboratory. "I'm not going to college right now," I say when he's finished.

"Then you're a fool," he says, exasperated.

I'm hardly going to tell him the truth. I'd do *any*thing to go to college—work any hours, take any loan. I'd be the first to admit that someone like me has no business at Mellin, but I can't pay the bills and I can't abandon my mother. Plus, I want the job. Of course I do. Someone like Will has never worked in a kitchen or done double shifts on his feet. He doesn't know what it's like. I say, "I think working under Munn will be quite an education in itself."

"You'll barely *see* Munn," he hisses. "You want to know who you will be working under? Me. I'm supposed to teach you, and I don't think that's my job, frankly."

With that, he rises from his seat in a fury. But I'm a step ahead of him, running forward to swing open the front door. I want him to know just how ready I am for him to leave. He huffs out, stomping down the path that leads to the street. I slam the door, put my back against it, and try to regain my breath. I can be tough for a while, but he always gets to me. Gets to me in the end.

11

THE FIRST PERSON I meet at the Mellin Institute is April Chen, the animal tech and general organizer who keeps the place running smoothly. She greets me at Mellin's impressive glass entrance. She has straight black hair cut with geometric precision and is wearing a hoodie with Frida Kahlo's face on it billowing over her skinny black jeans. She looks more artsy than scientific, except for this one thing: a large white rat on her shoulder.

"Thanks for coming at this hour," she says, holding the door for me. The rat stretches forward, sniffing the night air with a pale nose framed by whiskers. I must be staring, because April says, "Sorry, I was just cleaning cages. This is Cornelius. Please don't be shocked. He's just a rat. His tail is just a tail."

I'd been nervous standing at the door, but when I see the rat, everything changes, my curiosity piqued. "Can I touch him?" I ask.

"Of course!" She scoops up the rat and plonks him on my shoulder, where he promptly hides beneath the dense curls of my hair. I laugh out loud.

April smiles. "Cornelius is my absolute favorite, and he never bites. To be honest, none of our rats do!"

I follow April into the foyer, feeling the rat sway a little, rebalancing itself by gripping my sweater with its tiny claws. We stop at an elevator and April stretches out her arm. The rat, as though by cue, climbs across to April's shoulder.

"Working here, you have to think *big*," she begins. "The bigger you think, the more you'll get wrong, but Munn doesn't mind that. You'll always have new ideas."

"How do you know I'll always have new ideas?" I say.

"Because that's the only type of person Munn hires for what he calls our 'innovation ecosystem.'"

"Innovation ecosystem?"

"It just means we learn from one another."

The elevator opens onto a brightly lit hallway. Directly across from where we stand, above a set of glass doors, is a gold plaque. It reads, *Science is about finding better ways of being wrong.*

Apparently, this is the "upstairs lab," and it is empty at this hour. I can hear the air purifiers with their HEPA filters humming away, various machines clicking on and off. It's pristine, nothing out of place or left unpolished. In fact, it looks brand-new, like it's never been used.

"We share space and equipment throughout the entire lab zone. That way, we share ideas. Oh, except Munn's office. That's off-limits."

Through an open door I can see the corner of Munn's desk, a big window behind it. His office backs onto the building's courtyards, filled with flowering trees and manicured beds.

"Will Drummond needs some help with a project involving our organ tanks, so you'll be working with him. As your mentor, he'll show you everything you need to know. And guess what? *His* mentor is none other than Dr. Munn. So you're in good shape!"

So she imagines. But I remember Will's words as he stood in the kitchen glaring at me. *I don't want you there,* he'd said.

April says, "What wrong? You *have* worked in a lab before, right?"

That's the other thing.

I guess the look on my face says it all, because April seems a bit shocked, then recovers, saying, "Well, just don't use other people's media, okay? And remember to aliquot into a separate container."

I have no idea what she's talking about, but I nod anyway, making a note to never, ever touch anyone else's solutions. We finally stop at the door to the stairwell.

"It's a beautiful laboratory," I say.

April shrugs. "The auditors think it is great. It's the only thing we let them see. But the rest of us don't like it much."

That seems incredible. "You don't *like* it?"

"To be honest, we don't do our real work here," April says.

She pushes through a set of double doors that leads into a brightly lit stairwell with recessed colored lighting. From the ceiling hang large icicle-shaped sculptures that wind down into fantastic shapes much like the crystal formations that hang from the ceilings of caves. It reminds me of the metro in Stockholm, the underground art gallery Rik showed me. I feel the heat in my cheeks, remembering Rik.

"Who did all this?" I ask.

"The same artist who did the sculpture out front," April says, pausing to admire the silvery formations. "I wasn't so keen at first. I was worried someone would be decapitated by one of these . . ."

"Stalactites?"

"Whatever. The artist donated his time, so it wasn't as though we were having to dig into the budget. Anyway, Rik likes them. He's the visual one."

My cheeks burn brighter at the mention of his name. I really wish he didn't have this effect on me.

I follow April down a hall until at last we arrive at a blank wall. "Are you ready to go back, Cornelius?" she asks the rat on her shoulder. She steps toward the wall, then places her head against it as though listening for something inside.

"What do you hear?" I ask.

April laughs. "Nothing. We use ear scans to open internal doors."

Just as she says this, a seam appears in the wall and the two sides peel back, making me jump. I'm so freaked out by the wall separating that it takes me a moment to appreciate the room now before us. Across an oak floor are dozens of vintage laboratory tables lit by pendant lamps made of conical laboratory glassware. In cabinets lit with pinprick lights is antique medical and apothecary glassware: flasks and beakers with ground-glass stoppers.

"It looks like an old-fashioned laboratory," says April, "but it's our dining room."

I walk forward, staring up at the walls. There are cast-iron mortars used centuries ago in apothecaries to crush ingredients, nineteenth-century English reagent bottles with the names of chemicals stenciled in white enamel beneath their short necks.

Also, an entire library of antique scientific books.

"It's . . . beautiful," I stammer.

April smiles, glancing up to the leather-bound editions. "I'll just put Cornelius back," she says, and disappears through a door at the end of the room, leaving me to walk among the vintage collections. Above a buffet table are pictures of historic laboratories: Edison's lab in Menlo Park, Louis Pasteur's cluttered tables, medieval laboratories with their great clay ovens.

I hear April's voice behind me. "Everything you see belongs to Munn. Some of the equipment was actually used by his father, who was also a scientist. When Munn moved to the US, he had to either donate it all to a museum or bring it with him."

"You said this was a dining room. Who eats here?" I ask.

"We do, of course!" she says.

I'm used to the school lunchroom, Formica tables that fold up, lunch on scratched trays, not soft lights and buttery wood and precious collections on shelves around me.

"I feel like I'm in another world," I say.

"We have all our meetings here. Wait until you've seen the rest of the facility! But first, you'll need to sign some papers." She opens a drawer and digs out a pen and a short stack of formal-looking documents. "These are just saying you won't tell anyone what you see here in the lab. There are a few details that are, like, low-key top secret," she says casually.

She checks the pen for ink, then hands it to me. I look at the papers and see immediately that they are from the US government. That much is obvious from the insignia.

April notices my hesitation and shrugs. "A lot of labs do government work. You'll have to get clearance and stuff, too, but that can come later."

I tell myself this is no big deal. Researchers at the Norwegian glacier laboratory have to trudge hours through a tunnel and work under seven hundred feet of ice. By contrast, signing some papers is easy. I sign everywhere there's an *X*.

"Great!" says April, once I've finished.

I follow her to the far side of the dining room, where a break in the bookshelves reveals another white wall with the same slightly metallic sheen as the one before. I watch with astonishment as, once again, April presses her ear to it, causing an undetectable seam to reveal itself.

This time, the seam in the wall doesn't lead to a room but to a whole new building, a giant dome-shaped structure dug deep into the ground. There are no windows, but round lanterns embedded into the walls glow as though the walls are studded with small, lit hearths. The stairs, spiraling gently down three flights, have spotlights along each riser. Clever use of mirrors makes it all bright enough, even welcoming, like an enormous cave of delights. I can see the tops of people's heads below, working in separate laboratories walled off by glass.

"We have a gym, a library, a file room, a computer room. For security reasons, you can't get any network other than our own internal one, however," says April, "so you can't use your phone. I'm sure you understand."

"It's amazing," I say, stepping forward. I suddenly have the strangest feeling, and when I look down, it appears that my feet are resting on nothing. There's no floor. Then I realize I'm standing on a shelf of glass that makes up a balcony overlooking the great dome. The glass is solid, but it feels like I'll drop into space. I lurch back, suddenly dizzy.

"You'll get used to it," April says. She walks across the glass floor, then hops up and down to show me how safe it is.

It's like she's walking on air. I follow her, staring at my feet as I cross the clear surface, feeling uneasy at the great drop below. Finally, I reach the balcony railing.

I peer down at all the different labs spread out like pieces of a puzzle. An area of marble tables at the dome's center looks like a coffee bar.

"Come on," April says. "Let me show you where you'll be working."

We begin down a long staircase, stopping finally on a floor full of what appear to be baby incubators. I look inside one, then lurch back. Instead of a baby, it holds an enormous lung. The lung is surrounded by a complicated circuitry of tubes and filters. Something is making it breathe. It is the most grotesque thing I've ever seen, and it produces a warm marine smell that hovers in the air.

Next to it is another incubator, this one holding a fist of tissue that pulses rhythmically with a familiar beat.

"Is that a human heart?" I say weakly.

April looks at me with amusement. "A *human* heart? God, no! A beating human heart is worth a million bucks. We don't keep them sitting around. That will be a sheep heart or something."

"And the lung?"

April squints at the enormous lung as it slowly heaves away, inflating and deflating. "It could be anything, but I'm guessing cow."

There are a number of kidneys, a few tracheas, and what looks to be a liver. All of them are housed in the same type of incubator.

"Walk around, learn everything you can, ask questions. Munn always says, 'Don't leave good ideas behind.' He'll be pissed off if he doesn't see you snooping."

I'm already snooping. I can't keep my eyes off the transparent tanks with their gory, live organs. "Why do you keep all these organs in what look like baby bassinets?" I ask.

"We call them the Innards. It's not the organs that are important here, but what you are calling the 'bassinets.' They not only keep the organs alive but repair them. Ideally, the repair would be a hundred percent, but we're not quite there yet."

"Why would work on organ repair need to be kept secret?" I say, remembering the nondisclosure agreements I signed.

"No reason, really. But our government work *is* secret. Munn put together a team that contributes to the work at DARPA, which is the Defense Advanced Research Projects Agency."

To me, DARPA means weapons, military, defense. I have to remind myself that they also developed Siri, Unix, and the Cloud, for example, so it's not all army stuff. "What do you guys actually *do*?" I ask cautiously.

"We just . . . you know . . . help them," April says with a light laugh. I follow her through a series of quick turns. "But you'll have nothing to do with DARPA. You'll be on the regenerative medicine side. You know, the organs you see here."

This is the work Mellin is famous for. I've never heard of this other stuff involving DARPA. "But . . . why did Mellin get involved with defense?" I ask.

This time it's not April who answers me. Instead, I hear a male voice with a heavy accent. At first, I'm spooked, because it's the same accent as the red-haired man. "Threats have been spurring on science for as long as there has been war," says the voice, and suddenly I'm back in that coffeehouse in Sweden, feeling cornered.

But it isn't the red-haired man. There, at a coffee bar with granite countertops and a gleaming espresso maker, a guy with dark hair perches on a barstool. He's young, maybe only a few years older than me, but nonetheless has an impressive five-o'clock shadow. His T-shirt, threadbare at the neck and with what look like chemical burns on one sleeve, reads *Never trust atoms. They make up everything.*

"The government bets that we will come up with remarkable ways to combat the enemy. It's a technology race, and America wants to be number one," he says.

Mellin is known for stem cell research, not military weapons. But I'm rapidly becoming aware of what they *really* do down here.

"Dmitry, I should have known you'd be here," April says, rolling her eyes.

"I'm always here," he says.

"I mean *here*, here. In the way. Stop talking, at least. You make us sound scary!"

He says, "We *are* scary. One of our researchers disappeared—*poof!* My theory? Kidnapped."

April frowns at him. "The *police* theory was that he had gambling debts and *wanted* to disappear. He's probably living on an island right now, drinking margaritas."

But Dmitry isn't persuaded. "Kidnapped," he insists, and sips from his tea. To me, he says, "You know James Bond? We are the people who invent his gadgets: false fingerprints, ring cameras, that sort of thing."

April rolls her eyes. "James Bond isn't *real*!"

"False fingerprints are real," he says with a certain glee. "But our guys developed a 3D fingerprinting device that takes in structures of the skin so fakes don't work anymore. It's in all the airports now."

April says, "Dmitry works on neutralizing attacks from foreign agents. You must forgive him. It's obviously affected his *brain*." She removes a couple of coffee mugs from a cupboard. "Milk or cream?"

"My brain is untouched," Dmitry says. "We have a contest against the Russians, my former people. We have Silicon Valley while they have Silicon Forest. I am sure you are aware."

No, not aware. About Silicon Forest, that is.

"Dmitry, please stop about *the Russians*. We're not some crazy espionage facility!"

He moves from the far stool to one closer to me. "But we *are* an espionage facility," he says, speaking only to me. "It is important you understand, but I hope you will stay despite this. Maybe you'll be assigned to me!"

"You don't get *everyone* for your own research, Dmitry!" April says. She turns to me and mouths the word *weapons*, then hands me a mug. "Don't let Dr. Gloom worry you," she says. To Dmitry she says, "If you don't shut up, Kira will never take this job. And Munn himself recruited her!"

"I'll take it," I say.

"What?"

"I'll take the job." I've never been so certain about anything in my life. I don't care about DARPA or Will or anything else. Just being here is thrilling. I never want to leave.

April looks confused. "Don't you want to hear the pay?"

"If you're paying me at all, that's fine."

Dmitry says, "Every year scientists get younger. Did you hear about the boy in Belgium who received his bachelor's degree at the age of nine? I used to think I was clever until I heard that," he says.

I smile. There is something appealing about his earnestness. April's cool clothes and precision hairstyle contrast with Dmitry, who wears mismatched flip-flops and baggy jeans. He looks like he hasn't had a proper haircut in years, but he has a charming manner and a lopsided grin.

He says, "Munn loves anomalies. I had the advantage because my father was a scientist. I grew up in laboratories. Did you know that Stalin was a botanist? He revered scientists so much he often had to murder them."

April rolls her eyes. "Are you *trying* to put Kira off? Nobody is getting *murdered*."

"April takes an optimistic view. But Russia will not tolerate any form of disloyalty. They killed my father and little sister, for example."

I glance at April for confirmation, but she's suddenly busy

refastening a set of papers on her clipboard. I look at Dmitry and read from his expression that he is telling the truth.

"Oh, I'm . . . I'm so sorry," I begin.

Suddenly, something that sounds like an egg timer rings in the laboratory. April calls over her shoulder, "Is nobody going to check those organs?"

"Will is over there," says Dmitry, peering across the laboratory. To me he says, "I'm sorry. I shouldn't have mentioned it. Such matters do not affect you."

I am stunned by what he has told me. His father, his sister? Meanwhile, I brace myself, readying to confront Will. I can see him now, ducking and bobbing along the rows of organs. He reaches the coffee bar, looking larger in his lab coat, his hair more golden under these lights. He stops abruptly when he sees me, his expression darkening.

"Hey, Will," says April brightly. "Look who you get to mentor!"

Will takes in a long breath. "I see you are incapable of taking good advice," he says to me. Then he splutters something else I can't hear before turning away and walking back to the organs, some of which are sounding alarms.

12

FOR THE FIRST time in my working life I wear no name tag. I don't fill in a time sheet or punch a clock. My official title is that I have no official title. I earn more than I ever did as a gift-wrapper, and my colleagues—if I dare call them that—hold advanced degrees, yet I address them by their first names. I'm surrounded by science, and I can access any piece of research within Mellin's system. It turns out *everything* is on their system. No more paywalls.

It has the strangest effect on me, as if I'm Cinderella enjoying the party, at least until midnight, when I'll be returned to mice and rags. The biggest problem, other than Will, is that I barely have time to eat or sleep.

There's a coffee place near work, and sometimes Lauren and I meet there for a latte. Last time she said, "What's with the dark circles under your eyes? Sleep deprivation is super bad for you. Acne!"

I told her that in 1894 the Russian scientist Marie de Manacéine kept puppies awake twenty-four hours a day, and by the fifth day, they had all died. She took a sip from her coffee then shook her head in disgust.

"I am *so* against animal testing," she said, wiping milk from her lips. I reminded her that this took place in the nineteenth century, but she stopped me. "I *know*," she said, rolling her eyes. "I was just pretending to be clueless." Then she offered to hang out with my mother some evenings. "Just to keep her company. But only if you promise to speak to that cute boy," she added.

She meant Rik. And no, I don't dare speak to him. I'm still too embarrassed about what happened in Stockholm.

When I'm not in school or looking after my mother, I study everything I can about tissue engineering, renal disease, transplants, dialysis outcomes, drug therapy. I try to be thoughtful toward everyone at the lab. They are incredibly nice to me, except Will.

He's determined to get me fired or convince me to quit. Day one, he relegated me to the position of scrub maid, imagining that no one can stand being elbows-deep in organ fluids. This means that for hours every day I wear long gloves and a plastic apron and sometimes even a garment that looks like a shower cap so that I don't get any of the gore from the Innards on my hair. Meanwhile, he sits in a chair, using his heels to roll across the floor, swiveling left and right. Evenings, he slips off his unstained lab coat and goes off in his pristine car while my lab coat makes me look like I've been butchering livestock. I scrub my skin raw getting off the smell.

Once in a while he attempts to teach me something, but even then he makes it as unpleasant as he can.

"Think about it," Will says this morning in a rare moment of instruction. "What happens to raspberries when you unfreeze them?"

"They turn to mush?" I say. I'm squatting under a table, cleaning up a small spill. In my hands are a scraper and a pan. In my pockets are leakproof bags for the guts.

"And why is that?"

"Ice crystals form between cells and squash them," I say, edging myself farther under the table.

"*Squash* them?" Will snorts. "Exogenous ice crystals exert pressure on cell membranes as well as cell structures within the cytoplasm," he says, in a tone that is meant to sound *instructive*. "*Please* work on precision. I heard you describing how one of the dangers of dehydrating rabbit embryos was that they 'dry up like raisins.'"

I don't understand his criticism and answer straight. "But they *do* dry up like raisins," I say, looking up at him from beneath the table.

"Damn you! I am trying to teach you something!"

It takes me a moment to figure out where I went wrong.

"Sorry. It's 'raisins' that upset you?"

He throws his head back and rolls his eyes. "Oh, forget it," he says. "Just go—*please*. Finish what you're doing and find someone else to pester."

"Pester? I'm sitting on a *floor*!"

"Yes, but that's exactly it. You need to learn to clean up more discreetly."

* * *

One of the researchers, Chandni Bhatt, told me to drop by any time. So with Will annoyed at me, I take the opportunity to look for her lab, known as the "Bhatt Lab." I find her there, feeding nutrients to an array of pig kidneys. They've been stripped of cells and washed clean, then repopulated with human stem cells.

"You're bleeding," she says as I come in. She's noticed where I've chewed off just a little too much fingernail. I push my hands behind me.

"Sorry."

"Sorry you're bleeding?" she says. Then she turns and looks at me. "So what crime got you banished from the kingdom this time?"

"Using the word *raisin*."

"There is nothing offensive about the word *raisin*. It's a very cute word."

"Too cute for Will."

"Ah yes, always use big words around Will. Big *masculine* words." She laughs. She has a huge smile and beautiful brown eyes, and she never looks exhausted like I do. "Put on some gloves and check my stem cells, would you? Stamp anything that is differentiating."

It's like Chandni to include me in whatever task is at hand. I pull up a seat and peer into the microscope. Then I begin marking cells in which the borders are no longer clean because the cells are spreading apart and transforming into heart or lung or blood cells.

She's brave to trust me with this. I appreciate her confidence and work carefully, silently.

Eventually, Chandni says, "So, we are considering transplanting an organ into a human that originally came from a pig. Give me a well-documented objection to doing so."

When I don't answer right away, she adds, "You have no concerns about putting something from a pig into a person?"

I wince. "I'm probably wrong—"

"Then be wrong," she says. "Wrong is okay."

"Maybe worry about a pig retrovirus being transmitted to humans?" I say, then watch with relief as Chandni's face lights up.

"Bingo!" she says. "So why don't we just treat the pigs for the virus before using any part of the animal's organs?"

"Because it wouldn't work. The retrovirus is built into the pig's genes."

"*Correct*!" Chandni yelps. She seems so pleased with me that I blush. "Anything we can do to remove them?"

"We can use gene editing and remove the gene from the DNA of the pigs. But the big problem is getting people to agree to the procedure. And it's expensive."

Chandni nods. "So you understand what prevents us isn't what is in *here*," she says, pointing to her temple, "but what is in our wallets. Science is business. We can be as clever as we like, but the truth is simple: *money makes the world go round*."

"Is that why this laboratory works on biological weapons?" I say. "Because of money?"

"That's why this laboratory works on *countering* biological weapons," she says. "And yes."

Dmitry finds me at the sinks, scrubbing yet another bassinet, and pulls me away.

"Where are we going?" I ask as we pass by his lab without stopping.

"To a jungle," he says, leading me to another part of the building.

We arrive eventually at something called the Greenhouse.

"This is Betty," he says, pointing to a spray of leaves that rises up from a yellow ceramic base. "She withers in the presence of high levels of radiation."

I look at Betty, who appears to be an ordinary fern.

"Smart plant," I say, "being a natural-born biosensor 'n' all."

"Well, not exactly *natural*," Dmitry says. "We edited her genes first."

"How do you dream this stuff up?"

He looks at me shyly, as though wanting to impress me but not wanting to have it show too obviously. "One of my researchers is a botanist, and we were having a chat one day and somehow we just came up with it!" he says.

One of his researchers. He's only a few years older than I am and already has people working for him.

He brings me to another area, where he is trying to turn chemical weapons into harmless organic substances. It looks a little like an abandoned garden shed, with pots and tubs of soil instead of vegetables, and a distinct humus smell.

"I'm trying to neutralize chemical weapons using bacteria," he says.

I think about that for a moment. "You make chemical weapons into *dirt*?" I say.

"Yes, and it's brilliant idea! But my finicky bacteria don't work outside of optimal temperatures."

"What do they do instead?"

"Die."

"Oh. Well, what else are you doing?"

"Little of this, little of that." I love the way he speaks, his accent making the word *little* into *lee-tel*. "I will show you. You will become my student and I will become your student. That is how we play at science."

That sums it up. Science is a game for Dmitry. With his threadbare clothes and disheveled hair, he looks like a large child, moving around his laboratory as though it's a playground. But the "playground" is also a serious place.

"Do you ever sleep?" I ask.

"Do you?" he says, and we both laugh.

One night, when I get home, there's Biba with his greasy hair and his stupid motorcycle, watching me as I get out of the car.

"What?" I say, passing him.

"Your mother says no more money."

"That's right," I say.

"But your house needs improvement. Look, I took photos."

He gets out his phone and flicks through images on the screen, all of them shots of my house, the roof collapsing.

"What did you do, climb a tree?"

"You need money for the roof? I'll give it to you."

"I like the roof as it is," I say.

"Whaddya do in that lab?" he says.

I say, "We imagine answers to problems not yet posed. We

think big and loudly and fearlessly."

He makes a face. "What exactly?" he insists.

I might tell him that one team is developing programmable microbes that can produce flu medication on demand, while another is growing a human heart. Or maybe that Dmitry neutralizes weapons. Instead, I say, "We grow plants."

"This is ridiculous. Perhaps you can give me information," he says. "Information worth a roof."

"Worth two roofs," I say.

"Don't get greedy. I will arrange a meeting."

"Like I said, we grow plants. And then we name them. I met Betty today."

"Crazy. You're all crazy," he mutters.

In school I eat alone, but here I have lunch with physicists, biologists, chemists, cytologists. And, of course, Dmitry and Chandni—that is, if I can get here quick enough from class. I'm stuck with Will, sure, but he's just one among a crowd.

Rik arrives. As always when I see him, I find the urge to tidy my hair or sit more elegantly or smile more broadly, hoping he'll notice. I see he has a pile of paperwork with him, a clipboard, a laptop.

Everyone scoots around so he can sit down. He chats with Chandni about some logistics on lab equipment. Then, out of nowhere, he turns to me and says, "Munn mentioned you."

Me? I'm embarrassed.

To Will he says, "It must be very exciting working with Kira."

Rik knows exactly what Will thinks of me and is just trying to irritate him. Meanwhile, I turn red.

"Why would that be exciting?" Will says.

"Because Munn thinks so highly of her!" Rik smiles.

I'm sweating with embarrassment, but there's nothing I can do. Rik loves to tease Will. And he knows the greatest counter to Will's low opinion is Munn's high opinion, and it is something about which Will cannot argue. But this kind of talk will only strengthen Will's resolve to get rid of me. If he could have me scrubbing the floor with a toothbrush, he would.

"Do you want to hear how many times your paper has been downloaded?" Rik asks me. "More than *any other* at SFOF."

"Because of the *scandal*!" adds Will quickly.

"What scandal?" says Rik.

I feel my cheeks growing hotter. The last thing I want is to draw attention to the debacle in Sweden.

"We keep acting like it's fine to have a high school student hanging around," Will says, "but we're keeping her like a pet. It's no good for us and no good for her."

"Oh stop," says Chandni, waving him away.

"You act as though it's a good thing to have a child in the building," he says, "as though what we do here has no consequences."

"Now you're pretending to worry about children?" says Chandni.

"I think it's imprudent. That's all."

"Ha!" laughs Chandni, unconvinced. "It's your ego. You don't like being shown up by a teenager—"

"I'm hardly being shown up!"

Dmitry looks uncomfortable as the arguing continues. Finally, he says, "I think you have an overinflated notion of how dire these consequences might be."

"Really, Gloom?" shoots back Will. "Anything dangerous in your lab? Maybe a few microbes or pathogens that could potentially cause severe epidemics?"

"I am not exposing Kira to any danger," says Dmitry.

"Yes, you are," says Will. "We all are. She should be at a school. Here she's just in the way."

With that, Will gets up and moves swiftly through the dining room and then upstairs. If he's going to complain to Munn about me, I need to be there to defend myself. I race after him, his words echoing in my head: *Here she's just in the way.*

"Why are you always so mean to me?" I call up the stairs. He turns and walks down a few steps.

"Well, it's scarcely astonishing." He makes a gesture with his hand as though to punctuate his point. "If I'd been told I'd be babysitting, I'd never have taken the position."

"Why don't you ask Munn to move me?"

"I already have."

For some reason this hurts me more than all the other awful things he's done and said before.

"You shouldn't be in a laboratory like this. It's not appropriate. It might even be dangerous," he says.

"Dangerous *why*?"

"Other than the *toxic* chemicals you haven't been trained to handle?" he says, Then, lowering his voice, he adds, "And I'm sure you've heard the rumors."

At first I'm stumped. Rumors about what? Then I remember Dmitry talking about the researcher with the gambling debts who'd gone missing. *Poof*, Dmitry had said, and reasoned he'd been kidnapped. "Are you talking about the *kidnapping*?" I say.

Will comes closer now, whispering, "Do you know how old he was? Fifteen."

"That guy is probably living on an island." I'm trying to sound like April, trying to sound confident and breezy and all the things I'm not feeling right now. Because I'm thinking that fifteen-year-olds don't generally rack up gambling debt. And I'm wondering if the guy really was kidnapped.

"Munn found him living on the streets selling card tricks for a dollar. He walked in here and within months was running two different labs. He had a once-in-a-century kind of intelligence. Even more interesting because he hadn't had access to computers."

"What do computers have to do with anything?"

"Just that his brain was unaffected by technology. Our generation was raised on computers. All that information spilling in at once as we surf the net gives someone like you a bloated working memory."

"People like me but not like *you*?" I say pointedly.

He sighs. "I don't pretend to be your equal in raw ability," he says. It's the only time he's ever said anything remotely complimentary, and for a moment I'm stunned. "But I'm trained and you're not. Nor are you an adult. And this boy . . . I don't know . . . I just find it weird that Munn hires so many baby geniuses."

I think about what the red-haired man told me about his boss. Something about hiring people with unusual talents and training them up himself. Maybe this is a new idea taking shape across the globe.

"Plenty of places do that," I say.

"Oh really? Well, I find it odd. *Very* odd. I don't think any of us should be too comfortable here. I heard Munn say something once. He said, 'A certain type of mind is as valuable as plutonium and just as dangerous.' *That* is your friend Dmitry, a thousand times over."

"Dmitry isn't *dangerous*," I say. "He's sweet."

"Fine, don't listen to me. Do whatever you like," Will says. He walks off, calling over his shoulder, "Go keep Dr. Gloom company. You know how certain birds create elaborate nests to attract their mates? Well, I'm sure he's using his death agents to call you."

Dmitry's lab is the largest and messiest in the place, cluttered with beakers, tongs, strikers, ring stands, everything clumped together as though on a flea market table. It looks like the inside of a tent that bears have ravaged, and right now it carries a trace of something that smells like paint thinner.

"You're not dangerous, are you?" I say.

He stops what he's doing. "Sorry about the smell," he says. "I was testing a strain of *D. radiodurans*, a chemical found in radioactive waste sites."

"Is *it* dangerous?"

He shrugs. "Well, yes. But I'm hoping that *D. radiodurans* can break down radiation in the case of nuclear attack," he says matter-of-factly. I notice his T-shirt reads, *Bacteria: It's the only culture some people have.*

"Doesn't radiation kill bacteria?" I say.

"Not this one. *D. radiodurans* is strong. It eats sewage. We call it Conan the Bacterium."

"So does it work?"

"Hmm, not sure. I'm hoping for a fortunate accident. You know, like when the Germans came up with sarin gas. They were looking for a good insecticide, but then it killed an ape."

"Oh!" I've still got Will's words in my head, so I say, "You want the bacteria to kill something?"

"No!" he says, lurching back at the idea. "I mention the unfortunate ape only because its death is an example of unintended consequences."

He disappears out of the lab, leaving me standing in the mad disorder of his workspace, then returns carrying two giant mugs of hot chocolate. "Come with me. I will give you a primer in toxicology," he says. "Also, predictive toxicology, that is with computers. It would be a waste if you didn't study computer science along with everything else. You'd be very good at it."

"But you definitely don't develop nerve agents, right?" I ask cautiously. I'm sure he doesn't, but I have to ask.

"The opposite," he says, sipping from his mug.

I breathe a sigh of relief.

"I develop antidotes, detection systems, diagnostic tools. I told you that my father and my sister were killed? It was nerve gas that did it. I vowed to dedicate my life to solutions that neutralize biological weapons so that, perhaps, I can contribute to saving a future Alina."

"Alina was your sister?"

He nods. "I used to have a dream where I injected them with an antidote, set up fluids, rushed them to a hospital, and saved the day. Like, you know, a hero." He smiles, embarrassed. His round face is flushed. "But of course, that didn't happen. I did not save them. But I do have ideas about how to recover people who have died in such a way. To bring them back from the brink of death or even after they've died."

"That's impossible." It slips out faster than I intend.

"But as you've heard, I'm crazy," he laughs. He looks a little nutty, his hair wild around his head, sweat glistening above his upper lip. But his dark eyes are intelligent, defiant. "I usually keep my ideas to myself."

I smile. "I like your ideas," I say. "And I don't think you're crazy."

We sit together at the coffee bar. He tells me there's little that can't be fixed in the human body if treated fast enough. Then he writes out a few examples. It's the kind of lesson I've never had. Another person might find our conversation difficult to follow because of the leaps and references and the way we constantly interrupt one another. But I'm used to the way Dmitry talks. And he understands me intuitively. Our minds sync up. It feels a little like magic.

Then he says, "People make you nervous," as though it's just another fact.

I look down at my bitten fingernails. "Not you," I say.

"Then can I tell you my craziest idea?" He leans forward.

"Is it . . . dangerous?"

"No . . . ! Well, I don't think so," he says. He begins scribbling on the paper in front of us again, drawing out his idea as he describes it.

It really is a crazy idea. Brilliant, in fact. But I can see where he's erred already. Not in the science, but in how he evaluates it. Because the idea that he's describing, that he's showing as perfectly viable, would change the way we understand death. And I imagine that when you start redefining what it means to die, you can find yourself in some dangerous territory.

"You want to cure death," I say. A statement, not a judgment, because I don't know if what he's dreaming up is good or bad.

"Of course," he says. "Don't you?"

13

WILL HAS A new strategy to get rid of me. Instead of keeping me on the sidelines, he puts me right in the middle of everything, expecting me to perform functions in the lab that I've never been taught to do.

Inevitably, I make mistakes: unbalancing the centrifuge or using media so hot that it kills all my bacteria. Every mistake is carefully documented by Will, presumably to show Munn at a later date.

"I think you'll agree it just isn't working out," Will says.

I'm falling even further behind in school and have to cut hard into my sleep just to hand in assignments on time. I ran into Greevy in the hall and he said, *Mind you graduate.* Meanwhile, Will is making sure I fail at the lab, too.

"Why don't you show me how to do stuff, and then I can be more useful?" I say.

He shrugs. "I suppose that is the reason why students get an education," he says.

The words sting. Not because he's being mean again, but because he has a point.

A few days later I'm bending over a burner that isn't lighting. I stretch down, listening for the sound of forced gas. All at once the stream of gas lights up against my ear. I spring away from the flame, screaming. A burning sensation blazes on one side of my head and I can't see for the blurring of tears or stop the pain or even find a sink; I'm yelling for help when Will charges over. "What is that awful smell?" he demands.

Then he realizes it's my hair.

He tugs me by the arm, pushes my head into a sink, and holds the faucet over my painful ear as I cry out in agony, gripping the edge of the countertop, trying to keep my balance.

I hear footsteps and voices and Will saying, "No reason to gawk!"

Finally, he straightens me up. I'm dripping wet and my face feels like it's on fire.

"*Now* can you see why you need a proper education?" he says, holding me by the shoulders.

He just doesn't get it. I can't go off to college and get a "proper" education like he can. I don't have the money, and even if I did, I couldn't leave my mother.

But what's the point in explaining? "Let go of me," I say through gritted teeth.

As soon as I can, I stumble to the bathroom, lock the door, and soak the side of my head in water. It hurts like hell, but at least with the water running nobody can hear me crying. Eventually, I turn off the tap and sit on the closed lid of a toilet seat, dripping onto my clothes. I don't move for a long while. How can I have been so stupid? I really am as much of a liability as Will describes.

I can't decide what's worse: being fired or quitting. I guess quitting would look better on my résumé. I don't want to, but I need to resign before they fire me. I stay in the bathroom, enduring the pain, which is nothing compared to the pain of leaving Mellin.

At last, I emerge into the hallway, squeezing my stinking, burnt hair between paper towels. There's April, standing in the corridor, waiting for me.

"Are you okay?" she says. Her own veil of dark hair cuts across her forehead in a perfect line, then down to her shoulders as straight as a pencil. Her clothes are so cool: a stripy skirt, a jean jacket. Meanwhile, I look like a fire has been put out on my face. Because it has. The flesh has a powdery yellow coating on it and is puffy around my ear.

"I'm fine," I lie. "It's nothing."

"Oh good. For a minute there I thought you'd cooked yourself. Listen, you know when I told you that Munn wants you to make mistakes? I meant make mistakes while asking great questions, not burning your ear by trying to listen for gas coming out of your Bunsen."

She laughs now. I try to laugh along with her but find it difficult.

At my station, I collect my bag, my car keys, my sweatshirt. I want to go home. Go home and hide. I feel as though my accident proves that Will was right all along. I don't belong in a laboratory. I don't have any useful skills except standing at a sink, scrubbing. Who am I to play at being a scientist? I'm not a scientist.

Will strides over and says, "Good to see you're all right. Regulations stipulate I log an accident report."

I say nothing. He knows that I've provided another reason for my dismissal. He's practically gloating.

"I hope you're proud of yourself," I say.

"I hope that's the last of your injuries," he fires back. Then, more softly, he says, "It's not like I wanted you to hurt yourself. Really, Kira. I'm sorry this happened."

I walk past him, searching for the exit on the lower floor, which is the fastest way to the parking lot. I'm on my way out the door, a hand cupped over my ear, fighting back tears, when I see Dmitry. He's holding a latex glove filled with water and ice cubes, tied at the wrist like a water balloon.

"Come with me," he says gently.

He brings me to something like a school dormitory, or what I imagine a school dormitory to be. Sets of bunk beds, chests of drawers above which hang small mirrors. I realize all at once that this is where Dmitry sleeps. He must never even leave the lab. I can tell which is his bed, too, because it's made up with a Snoopy quilt with his favorite T-shirt scrunched at one end. On the floor beside the bed, stacked several feet high, are his books.

He sits me down, assessing the damage. He doesn't touch my ear but he uses a penlight to get a good look. "It's not as bad as I thought," he says finally. "But you should see a doctor."

"It costs hundreds of dollars just to walk into an emergency room," I say. "Thousands at some hospitals."

He places the glove filled with chilled water over my ear again. It's a clever thing to have come up with. The glove shapes itself over my jaw and provides huge relief. "It's important not to burst the blisters," he says gently.

"I have *blisters*?"

He moves the burned hair carefully out of the way. "A bit worse than blisters. You will need some pain relief. Also, to rest. I'll get pillows."

He drags pillows from every bed in the place, including his own, and stacks them so that I can stretch out on a mattress while keeping my head up and the ice pack in place.

"I'm so stupid!" I say. I feel tears gathering at my eyes and pray that Dmitry doesn't notice.

"You make mistakes because you are exhausted and because that *zhopa* won't teach you anything," he says.

"He wants me to leave. I guess he'll get his way."

"No," he says. "I will talk to Munn. Munn will listen to me."

"That's very kind of you, but whatever you say, Munn will still feel obliged to let me go."

"Kira," he says, drawing my name out as though I am being stubborn. "You don't know what it's like to have an ordinary mind, one that doesn't process research papers like a computer."

"Will says I have a bloated working memory," I say.

"What he ought to say is that you can do things he can't. The programmers in the upstairs lab can't. Frankly, none of us can."

"He hates me."

Dmitry looks at me carefully. "Why does that matter?" he says.

I don't know why it matters. It just does.

"Anyway," he says, "Will better get over it, because in the next few years you are going to leave him in the dust."

"I can't even set up a Bunsen burner."

He pats my shoulder. "Those things are easy. I am going to teach you."

"Why should you be stuck with me?"

"We will start tomorrow when you are feeling better."

"Tomorrow is Saturday."

"Saturday is good. Saturday is perfect."

I look at the bed at the end of the long room. Dmitry's bed. "You live here," I say, a statement, not a question.

He nods. "Where else would I go?"

"What if I burn the place down?" I ask.

He points up to the ceiling and smiles. "Sprinkler system," he says.

My mother already doesn't like Mellin, says it cuts too much into my schoolwork. Now this.

"Do they not have health and safety over in that lab of yours?" she hollers. "And now you're working *all* weekend?"

"I'm *learning*, not working," I say.

"Don't you already go to school?"

Part of my mother's frustration is that she doesn't understand what goes on in my life. When I'm not at school, I'm at Mellin. It's hard to get everything done, not just homework but laundry and shopping. She sees me hustling and still we're always short of cash. Biba came around the other day. He said my mother borrowed money from him for groceries.

You mean lottery tickets, I'd said to him. Because I'd already bought all the groceries. *Stop giving her money.*

I don't give her anything, he said. He flashed an ugly smile. *I lend it.*

"I'll make dinner," I tell my mother now. "*Don't* let Biba anywhere near you. We'll have a picnic in front of the television and watch a movie. Lauren might even come over. She always cheers you up."

She tells me Lauren isn't going to like my blistering skin and crispy hair. "She already thinks you should moisturize."

"I know," I say. I hold up a tub of medicine that Dmitry gave me. "I am moisturizing."

Saturday morning, Dmitry is waiting for me by the espresso maker in a T-shirt that says *Do not approach space debris*, a giant mug of tea beside him.

"Does it hurt very much?" he says, pointing to his own ear.

The pain woke me up. And my hair still smells. Not that Dmitry will be able to tell. He must have been evaporating toluene again, because the whole laboratory stinks of it.

"Do I need a mask?" I say.

He shakes his head. "Safe levels," he says, meaning the toluene. "This morning we will concentrate on lab skills. All very easy. Then, we will look at a glove box, a rotary evaporator, and how to handle Schlenk lines. We will also find out what happens if you heat a closed system—spoiler alert: it acts like a bomb. So expect our session to end with an explosion. Sound okay?"

"A real bomb?" I ask.

He raises his eyebrows, grinning. He has the most expressive face, and I can see he's excited about teaching me, though I can't imagine why. "We'll be busy," he says in a singsong tone.

Some may call him Dr. Gloom, but nobody can doubt Dmitry's work. Nor his importance at Mellin. Even though he's the youngest scientist here (apart from me, who can't call herself a scientist), people line up to ask him questions. But I have him mostly to myself today. He shows me a piece of brain tissue, explaining that the brain makes an effort, however feeble, to repair itself even when clinically dead.

"The tissue wants to tell us all about the dying process," he says enthusiastically. "We should listen."

I describe to him the game Carlos played with the audience at SFOF, figuring out the time of death of all those scientists. "He uses genetic activity in brains to tell the time of death in people. He's worked with the police and everything."

Dmitry nods with recognition. "Munn brought Carlos here to meet me when he was just starting out on this mission."

"Carlos was *here*?"

"Of course! From Texas! We had dinner together. He loves barbecued meat. He was fascinated to learn that we are the same in Russia with our *shashlik*. Munn offered him a position, but he has moved to Europe. Apparently, he's met a Finnish woman—"

A Finnish woman?

"You must mean Helmi!" I say. "I was there when they met!" I'm so excited. I tell Dmitry all about the Science for Our Future awards, about how Helmi and Carlos presented their papers the same day and how they had seemed to like each other very much, though I had no idea an entire romance had followed.

"Ah," says Dmitry wistfully. "It is good to find love."

We work all day. As promised, we end up in blast shields and goggles, watching the first law of thermodynamics in action by replicating, in miniature, several common laboratory mistakes that cause explosions. Afterward, I suggest we get a sandwich, but Dmitry suddenly looks uncomfortable.

"Perhaps you can bring one back?" he says.

I get out my car keys. "I'll be right back."

When I arrive back from the deli I find Dmitry in the dining room. He's set out plates and a flask of water with two glasses. Also on the table is an impressive wooden chessboard.

I put down the paper bag of sandwiches and potato chips and look at the pieces, arranged across brown and white squares. "Did this belong to you in Russia?"

"Oh, no," he says. "At home in Moscow, we had an old Soviet tournament set. Much less ornate."

I pick up a knight. The weight of the piece in my hand is substantial, as though the knight is a wooden artifact, not a simple game piece.

"Do you play?" says Dmitry. "If not, I will teach you!"

I shake my head. "You should play with people who understand the game."

He works his right eyebrow into an *S* formation, then says, "If I want to challenge myself, I can play on the computer. Do you know the pieces and how they move?"

"I think so."

"Then we skip lesson one!" he says, sounding delighted.

In all the years I've studied and learned and tried to understand, I've never come across anyone like Dmitry, a natural teacher who wants to share everything. He eats his sandwich and teaches me a few openings, all very casual. After a while, I ask, "Do you never leave the lab? I mean, at all?"

He stops chewing and looks at me.

"Sorry," I say. "None of my business."

He holds up a finger. "I leave only on special occasions. The people who killed my father did not want him to grace the United States with his skills and knowledge. They may feel the same about me."

"That's why they killed him? Because he was working for the United States?"

"You shouldn't look so surprised." He takes a long sip of water.

We play a few more moves, and then Dmitry says, "My father was a scientist, but he also taught himself Turkish, Polish, and English. That made him very interesting to the KGB, who wanted him to work for them. He said no. He thought that settled the matter. Years later, after the Soviet Union broke up, the KGB was dismantled. The organization that replaced it approached him afresh. He refused again and managed to evade them for years. But intelligence agencies are clever. And they approached him a third time when they discovered there was something my father wanted very much. That would persuade him."

"What did he want?" I ask. But what I'm thinking is how the red-haired man had approached me at a conference.

He puts down his sandwich, then wipes his fingers on the balled napkin on the table. "He wanted me to go to MIT," he says. "And he agreed to the work as long as I was permitted to attend. But this time it wasn't Russian intelligence that wanted him. It was the CIA."

I stop chewing. "Your father worked for the *CIA*?" I say.

"The Department of Defense, but it took the CIA to get him out of Russia. By then, he wanted out. I was fifteen. Don't ask me why MIT; he had his heart set on it. The deal was done at a science conference in St. Petersburg. He was on a plane within a few hours."

"With you?"

"No. I was looking after my sister at our apartment in Moscow. Some men came to our door in the middle of the night and told me to wake my sister and get into a car. I wouldn't do it. They said that I had to and that our lives were in danger. But my father had left me in charge of my sister, and I was not going to get into a strange car because a couple of men in suits told me that I should. They got angry and shouted. When that did no good, they rang my father and gave the phone to me. He told me to do what they said. He said, *Please, Dima, this is not so much to ask you? To get into a car, no?*

"My father told me I must bring all his papers, so I got a suitcase and stuffed it full. I took my books and some clothes for my sister. I didn't have another suitcase, only plastic bags. We were driven out of Moscow. We had to get to a landing strip in the middle of a forest. The landing strip was one of those—I don't know what you call them—areas that are cleared in case of fire."

"A firebreak?"

"Yes, a firebreak. We had to walk through the forest to get there. In Russia, we have bears. Alina was terrified. The men told her to shut up; there were no bears in this part of the country. But one of them went to the trunk of the car and got out an ax just in case. My sister started to cry. She didn't want to walk through the forest in darkness and she was scared of the ax. I held her hand. I could not tell if she was shaking from fear or from cold. The men told me to make her stop crying. I whispered a story to her as we walked, the wooden suitcase banging against my leg. At that moment, I cursed my father."

Again, another silence. Then Dmitry says, "We began life in America. My father worked for the US government. I went to MIT. My sister forgot about Russia. She was watching *The Simpsons* and playing computer games. She spoke English fluently and sounded like an American, not like me with a terrible accent."

"I like your accent."

"Okay, maybe it is good then."

I wait a beat, then say, "I'm so sorry about what happened."

He sighs. "It was graduation day," he begins. "We had breakfast together on campus, as people do. I bought my father a pair of binoculars so he could see the ceremony clearly from the audience. He thought they were a wonderful gift. It was very warm with the cherry blossoms and flowers everywhere. Then they were killed."

I don't know how to respond to this. So simple and so final: *Then they were killed.*

"I'm sorry," I say. With hesitation, I add, "How come you got away?"

"That depends on who you ask. My theory is that they made a mistake. My father asked another graduate, a Polish boy, to join us for breakfast so he could practice his Polish. He was always doing that, pulling people in to talk with him so he could practice his languages. Meanwhile, I was standing in line to collect my graduation gown. The line was long. The next thing I knew I was walking across the green and there was an ambulance and the . . . you know . . ." He stumbles for the word.

"Paramedics?" I say.

"Yes, paramedics. My family was roped off and someone in a protective suit was yelling to the public to clear the area. For some reason, I had my father's new binoculars in my hand. I put them to my eyes and I could tell immediately what had happened. All the typical responses—spasms, convulsions. I knew they'd been poisoned. I could see them all dying right there on the grass. The Polish boy—the one that they had mistaken for me—was on the ground beneath the table. I cannot tell you how much I wished I hadn't bought those binoculars."

"Oh, Dmitry," I say.

"Now I am Dr. Gloom. Everybody talks about me. They say my father was a spy or my father was *bratva*. You know, a criminal. People make things up."

"But why your sister?" I say. It's too appalling to think about.

"Killing a family is a good deterrent for others still in Russia who might wish to do the same as my father. But Munn believes they never meant to kill me. He doesn't believe it was the Russian government who assassinated my family."

"Who does he think, then?"

Dmitry shrugs. "A private enterprise. A rival, perhaps. Science has become very big business," he says.

"Would it be the same people who took that researcher, the one everyone says had gambling debts?"

"His name was Arturo. *Is* Arturo," he says. "He would have been an easy target. No family. His father rejected him for being gay. Such idiocy. He snuck across the border to America, nearly dying on the journey. He showed up with nothing but the clothes on his back and a deck of playing cards he always carried. I mean *always*. He was a heck of a poker player and he rarely lost. I never believed that story about gambling debts."

"You think he was kidnapped?"

"Of course," Dmitry says, as though this is obvious.

I thought of how, at various times, I've imagined myself to be living under difficult circumstances. How my mother has always had to work so hard and for so little. But it's been far worse for Dmitry. And for Arturo.

"And this is why you live in the laboratory?"

He nods. "My work helps American soldiers. That makes me a traitor in Russia."

"And they definitely know you're here?" I say, pointing to the ground.

I hear him laugh a single, bitter "ha."

"They know everything," he says.

14

THE LABORATORY LESSONS give me new confidence. I come into Mellin feeling as though I am, at last, up to the job.

Unfortunately, Will doesn't agree. He wants me sterilizing bassinets, scrubbing everyone's glassware, and sweeping up the floors. Nothing more.

"You're very good at it," he says brightly.

Lauren and I have long talks about Will. She thinks he's secretly in love with me. I think he's openly at war with me.

"Wouldn't it be cool if it turns out he always had a crush on you?" she says.

"No."

"Not now, but like in the future. And one day you tell your kids about how when you guys first met he hated you and—"

"Don't be gross," I say.

I try not to think about Will. Anyway, right now he's the least of my tormentors. The high school prom is nearing and there've been all these promposals. One day, a boy arrived outside class with a huge, painted sign that read, *Nobody but you, Kira!*

I hadn't wanted to go to the prom with him, but it felt mean to say no especially because of that painted sign. So I'd agreed.

Within a few seconds, I realized my mistake. At first, it was just the look on his face. Then he started laughing. Then his friends appeared. They'd been watching the whole thing. And they started laughing, too. I moved away from them, backing up, but they crept nearer. Finally, I turned and raced down the hall, walking as quickly as possible through the crowds while they charged alongside me like a pack of dogs. It wasn't until I turned the corner and into a classroom that they stopped. I spent the entire period worrying they'd be waiting for me outside when class finished.

I blame myself. The kid is very popular and has a girlfriend who is likely to be prom queen. If I were halfway aware of what goes on in my school I'd have known as much. But now, every few days, I get another of these "invitations," fake promposals that arrive without warning. School has become nearly intolerable.

By comparison, Will is just an annoyance.

I take a dirty bassinet to the sink. *Dirty* isn't the right word. It's like someone murdered their pet in it. If I don't look too closely I'm okay. I've worked plenty of hours in the cafeteria where my mother once worked, so standing at an industrial sink with a lot of hot water steaming around me is almost second nature. If Will thinks he can scare me off with blood and gore, he's wrong. He can ignore me and he can give me gruesome tasks. But he can't run me out of here.

I'm scrubbing away at the sink with my stack of bassinets when April shows up, a pair of rats on her shoulder. "Would you be really annoyed if I asked you to help me with something when you're finished?" she says. The rats tip their noses to sniff the steamy air. "It would be a big favor," she adds.

I nod, then put out my finger to stroke one of the rats. "How come these ones are so smooth?"

"Because they're female. The does have sleeker, shorter coats. This is Daisy and Not Daisy."

"Not Daisy?" I laugh. "That's the rat's *name*?"

April rolls her eyes. "I've run out of names for them over the years. Come by animal tech when you can, okay?"

There's a running tension between April and anyone at Mellin who dares to ask for the rats for experiments. She's an expert on testing models that don't use animals and will give long lectures on the alternatives: in vitro, in silico, cell cultures, computer models. As far as she's concerned, animals are the last thing anyone should use for testing. But it still happens.

I arrive to find April bent over a shallow cage filled with a dozen rats, all with the same peculiar bald patches across their middles. Judging from the sites of the patches, I imagine some kidney experiments have taken place.

"This is my hospital cage," she says. "They sleep in that corner where the soft bedding is, but it has to be changed daily or else they risk infection. You can leave the rest of the bedding, but just do that part—"

"You want me to clean the rat cages?" I say.

April stops herself at once, and looks up at me. "Oh, sorry!" she says, her hand flying to her mouth. "I haven't even asked you!"

She suddenly stands at attention, heels together, hands clasped in front of her, looking at me with great urgency. "I'm going on a training course, and then taking a few days' vacation. Can you *please, please* look after the rats for me? I'll show you how to do everything. It's the ones that have been recently operated on that I worry about most. They look like they are going to be fine, but there's always the possibility the wounds may abscess or they'll pull out the stitches. See?"

She picks up one of the rats and holds it out to show me what she's talking about. The two sides of the incisions, undoubtedly once neatly knotted together, are gaping slightly where the stiches were gnawed away.

"I don't suppose you can stick a cone on their heads like dogs?"

"Ha! Don't think I haven't tried!" she says, squinting at the rat's incision. "The surgical glue should keep that together, but we still have to watch it."

Despite the stitches, the young rats are racing around, looking for food among the bedding, as though they've already forgotten the trauma of surgery.

"Rats must have amazing pain thresholds," I say, though I spy a bottle of painkillers nearby.

"I have a feeling they're going to do a whole new bunch early next week, which means you'll have fresh casualties," says April. "But don't worry. I'll make sure the hospital cages are all set up for you."

It seems April and I are now Team Rat. I follow her around as she shows me the little creatures, so eager to come out and play.

They crawl across the bars of their cages, splayed out like starfish. She shows me how to dose the water bottles with antibiotics, which food packets go into what hospital cages, and gives me a list of people to call if I see any sign of a wound opening or a rat getting sick. "If they seem a little depressed," she says in a conspiratorial tone, "just slip them cake."

"I love how you give them nice homes," I say. The cages are full of colorful ladders and bridges and fleecy hammocks the rats can sleep in.

"They're sweethearts. You remember Cornelius, don't you?" she says. She puts her arm into the cage and Cornelius uses it like a bridge to climb out. "You met him the first day you were here. He's my favorite. Don't tell the others."

Cornelius is one of the bigger rats, his ivory fur laced with streaks of blue. His size and whiskers and long, naked tail may frighten some people, but not me. And it's clear that he adores April. He curls around her hand and begins licking her fingers. "When I get back, I'm taking him and his brothers home. He's getting older now and deserves his retirement," she says. She gives him a kiss on the top of his head.

"He's adorable," I say truthfully. "Do you take a lot of the rats home?"

She puts a finger to her lips. "Shh, it's secret. Munn wouldn't approve. People don't think these animals have value outside being available as tools for experiments. You're the only person I trust to look after them with *care*," she says.

I promise that I will and she gives me the paper with all the phone numbers on it, underlining her cell number three times.

"Night or day," she says. "And feel free to, you know—" She hesitates now. In the world of science, it is best not to fall too hard for the lab animals, but clearly April already has. "Feel free to play with them, okay?"

15

I TOLD DMITRY not to tell the others, but he unleashes his newest "crazy" idea right in the middle of an otherwise ordinary lunch. Everyone pounces on him.

"You want to bring back *dead* people?" Chandni says, stabbing at her salad. "You mean like in those awful newspaper headlines, 'Pregnant Dead Woman Kept Alive,' when anyone with an education knows it's the unborn baby that is being kept alive and that she was brain-dead weeks ago?"

"Yes!" pipes up Dmitry. "I want to bring back that poor lady!" he says, as though he knows her.

"What rubbish," says Will. He pushes his fork around his plate. The lunch today is vegan, and it infuriates him that he is being asked to eat something he describes as "New Age." "We're scientists. We shouldn't even be having a conversation like this."

"But we should be!" insists Dmitry. "I believe it is possible to repair neurons. That does not mean we ought to be doing so in all cases—if a person has a painful, terminal condition before their brain begins to die, they will still have it when recovered—"

Will interrupts him. "You've made a classic mistake. Did you hear yourself? You said, 'before their brain begins to die.' I'm telling you the brain is already dead. You won't 'recover' anyone. But if you want to try to raise the dead, then be my guest."

I'm waiting for Dmitry to argue that the brain doesn't die all at once. After all, he was the one who taught me this.

Instead he says, "I will need to borrow Kira for this investigation."

I am stunned by this announcement. "What?" I say.

"You want *Kira*?" Will says.

"She is my first choice."

"Fine, have her," Will says, as though trading a horse. "Did Munn agree to this work?"

Dmitry hesitates. "Not exactly."

"I thought not," Will says. "I take it you're not exactly close to proof of concept?" he adds sarcastically.

"More the theoretical side of things," Dmitry admits.

"The *theoretical side*," Will snorts. "You're paid to analyze chemical weapons for the Department of Defense, if I'm not mistaken. Aren't you *boy wonder* of antidotes and countermeasures? This 'crazy idea' as you call it is an unauthorized lark!"

Dmitry sits very still, his lips in a thin, tense line. A lot of money and responsibility rests on his shoulders. And it's true this new thing is, indeed, a distraction.

I say, "If you ask me what I think—"

"Not asking," says Will.

I continue anyway. I may not always stand up for myself, but I can sometimes stand up for people I care about. "Raising the dead, as you put it, is a great antidote to chemical agents, possibly the *best* antidote," I say.

Will turns to me. "So that acetylcholine can flood the parasympathetic nervous system all over again and the victim can die the same excruciating death a few extra times?" he says, then realizes what he's said and stops himself.

Everybody freezes. Death from a nerve agent really is excruciating. The victim dies in convulsions. It's terrifying and it's painful. Dmitry looks as though he's struggling with that now. His father, his sister. He pushes his hand through his hair. "There would be some challenges," he says flatly.

The table is silent.

"There would be some difficulty with timing," he admits.

"And that's not all, mate," Will says, his voice kinder now. He knows he's crossed a line. "It's a nice idea but maybe a stretch too far."

But it's not a stretch too far. At least, I no longer think so. In my "free" time, I've been studying the concept, and I think it's possible. I wait for Dmitry in his lab and tell him that if he meant it about me helping, I would love to do so.

"You don't mind appearing to be mad?" Dmitry says.

My face is still marked with burns around my ear and my hair looks like it's been melted on one side, so I'm not particularly worried, no.

We begin, seated at one of the waxed tables in Mellin's dining room, surrounded by the smell of old books. I bring Dmitry everything I can dig up about agents that send blood flow back to areas of the brain where it has been starved of oxygen, about neurogenesis and DNA damage response. I discover experiments in which drugs are injected into the spinal cord and electrical currents are used to stimulate the brain with some success. Paper after paper. Dozens, hundreds.

I bring home printouts every night, reading in the armchair in my mother's room while she dozes. Or sitting around with her, half watching TV.

"Do they pay you for this?" she asks.

Beside me, hunched over a cardboard box, Lauren laughs. "They don't need to," she says. "She's obsessed."

Lauren is one to talk. That box houses a nest of baby birds. The birds' parents were killed and the babies went to the rehab center where Lauren volunteers. Now she has to feed the chicks every thirty minutes from dawn to dusk. Needless to say, the nest is not supposed to be out of the center, but I'm not telling.

I want to do a good job for Dmitry. I read, analyze, summarize, draw elaborate pictures of various processes in the body. But I'm tired. I fall asleep at dusk just like the baby birds. One evening Rik finds me in the dining room fast asleep with my cheek on the table and gently shakes me awake.

"Hey," he says. "Are you okay?"

Normally, there is a little bit of electricity any time he's within ten feet of me, but I'm so tired I barely register it's him. "Sorry," I say, and fall back to sleep.

I don't wake again until it's so late that only Dmitry is left on site. I slump into his laboratory and drop into a chair.

"You want a bed in the dorm?" he says. "It's surprisingly comfortable."

I tell him no. School in the morning.

One afternoon my mother finds me parked outside the house, dozing with my head on the steering wheel. She says, "Kira, that's enough! You could have fallen asleep driving. You need a day off."

"Okay," I agree. It seems a waste, but Saturday I sleep until noon, then spend the rest of the day with my mother. We sort laundry into neat stacks, squeeze lemons into a big glass pitcher for lemonade, bake homemade bread so the house fills with a lovely yeasty smell. We do all the gardening chores, and it feels good to be outside, the sun on my back. I look up and see my mother with her iced lemonade, watching me thoughtfully.

"You have such a young, strong body," she says.

"The house," I say, pointing at a section of the low gray roof with new asphalt tiles. "You had it repaired."

"You wanted it to cave in on our heads?"

"I want—" *Oh, what's the point?* "Fine," I huff.

Lauren stays over for supper. We eat burritos at the picnic table, searching for hummingbirds among the flowers. We watch a movie together, all three of us, until my mother dozes off. I get out my papers again.

"I think you're a workaholic," Lauren says.

"More like desperate," I say earnestly.

"Are you going to graduate?"

"I hope so."

"Meet me at the café on your way in to work tomorrow," she says. "I have a surprise for you."

* * *

It's the café near work. Lots of people from Mellin use it, including Rik. It's not wise for me to develop a crush—Rik is a hundred levels out of my league—and I've been kind of avoiding him for this reason. But I don't see him here, thank God, and the coffee smells good, so I get in line, hoping that Lauren will join me shortly. I'm peering up at the menu deciding between a latte and a cold brew when I hear someone call my name. I look up and there's a guy wearing a pair of shorts, a T-shirt, and matching socks in my high school's colors. He's walking toward me with his arms open, as though he intends to hug me.

"Kira," he says, his voice full of mock longing, "why do you forsake me?" He reaches the decorative iron railing that separates those standing in line from those in the seating area. There he pauses, tilting his head to one side, and fixing his pale eyes upon me. "Why won't you go to the prom with me?" he says, his voice steeped in sarcasm.

I know him. Mike. One of my prom tormentors. There are more and more of these phony invitations as prom nears. I don't know if they do it to other girls. I hope not, because it's really mean, but I also hate the thought that I'm the only one.

"Stop it!" I whisper.

"Just say yes," he urges. It would be easy for a bystander to imagine that he really means it. "I love you!"

"Please go *away*!" I say in a low voice.

Over his shoulder he calls, "She wants me to go away!" He clutches the bottom of his T-shirt and brings its hem to his face as though wiping away tears. I turn my back to him, staring up at the menu on the wall above the espresso machines, hoping that if I ignore him long enough he'll give up. But then I hear laughter from somewhere deeper within the coffeehouse. I turn to see another guy from my school, dressed in the same sports uniform.

"She's going with *me*!" he tells Mike. "Are you trying to steal her?" He shoots me a nasty grin, then says, "You said yes, don't you remember?"

Unfortunately, I remember all too well, him with his sign, *Nobody but you, Kira!* The bold way he asked if I'd go to the prom with him. My stupid reply.

"You have to decide between us," Mike says, punctuating his words with a sniff. "We need to know."

Each pushes the other out of the way and pokes his face toward me as though urging me to choose him. Meanwhile, I'm pinned in line, blocked by the counter and dozens of people. I don't think it can get any worse when suddenly a third one appears from the back. He, too, is wearing a sports uniform. I guess they stopped to get breakfast before a game. I've never had any classes with this particular boy, but I know who he is. He's come to school drunk a few times and has been in trouble for fighting. He looks pretty sober right now, marching toward me as though at a ball he's going to kick.

"You're so hot," he says, eyeing me up and down.

I am many things, but not hot. His statement only makes this fact more obvious.

I try to ignore them. I turn away, peering through the glass front door, watching for Lauren. But Lauren is nowhere to be seen.

I consider rushing for the front door. I'm wondering if I can make it to my car without them following.

I hear, "What's the matter? You don't like me?"

I spin around and say, "Stop it!" as menacingly as I can. This sends them into peals of laughter.

Then, "Ah, don't be mad. Let me buy your coffee!"

"No, let me! I'll buy your coffee!" says another.

"She don't want coffee. She wants me!"

I turn my back toward them again, pushing my vision up to the menu behind the countertop, trying to settle the rising panic within me. Something hits my shoulder, then falls to the floor with a ping. I look down and see a coin rolling across the tiles. I feel another thump on my back, and a second coin drops at my feet. The coins come faster now, first one, then another. It's my turn at the cashier, and I try to order coffee and ignore them, but it's impossible. A quarter hits me on the side of the head and then bounces against the display.

The cashier shows no sign of noticing. "I think you've dropped some money," he says innocently.

Meanwhile, the crowd is thinning by the exit. I can see through the door to the wide sunny street beyond. I'm itching to run.

The cashier asks for my order. Another coin hits me, this time in the back of the head. Anger roars inside me and I turn, not quite believing I'm doing so.

But then I freeze. It isn't the sight of the three leering guys in sports uniforms that horrifies me; it's the sudden appearance of Rik behind them. He's walking quickly from the back of the shop, his eyes on mine. He must have seen all this—the fake tears, the sarcastic pleading. I pray he hasn't seen the coins being lobbed, but just as I have that thought, I feel a jab on my chest and realize I've just been hit by a nickel directly on my right breast. And there is no way Rik hasn't seen it.

"Bull's-eye!" one of the boys cries.

It's too much—the humiliation and Rik seeing it all. I look at the door again. I wish more than anything that I'd chosen to run. But it's too late now.

"Kira! There you are!" Rik says brightly, pushing past the boys. He puts his arm around my shoulders as though I'm his girlfriend and he's been expecting me. Then he wheels me around toward the cashier again. I look at his face, hoping to get a sense of what he's really thinking behind the mask of good cheer. But he appears to be concentrating on the menu, leaning his cheek against the top of my head with ease, as though he does this all the time.

"What are you having?" he asks.

I feel the adrenaline coursing through me. A bead of sweat glides down my back. On top of everything else, I'm going to smell. "Latte," I croak. "Medium."

I hold my breath, waiting for the next nickel to fly. Are they going to lob coins at Rik, too? And what would he do if they did? I find him elegant and handsome, but he isn't the tallest or broadest guy in the world. Meanwhile, Mike and his pals are big slabs of milk-colored meat and muscle.

"Well, well," I hear from behind me. "I guess we have our answer."

Another line of attack is imminent. I look desperately at Rik. He seems unbothered and gives my shoulders a squeeze.

And then I see a flash of blond hair and Lauren coming

through the open door. She pauses briefly, stretching her vision down the length of the café, then at the line at the front where I stand with Rik. She smiles when she spots me, then her eyes go wide as she realizes Rik is there, his arm still looped around me as he pays for the coffee.

I turn to Lauren now, the heat roaring through my body, my cheeks so red I can feel them burning. Being bullied is bad; being bullied in front of Rik is beyond the worst humiliation. But here's Lauren—who goes to a totally different school and who may never have seen this kind of stuff before. What if they start on her?

"Lauren, we have to *go*—!" I say urgently.

"What are you talking about? I just *got* here." She smiles her dazzling smile at Rik. "I think I might have heard about you."

"Really?" says Rik, amused.

"Really," she says, again flashing her beautiful white teeth.

All I can think is that at any moment the guys from school are going to launch an attack on Lauren.

But I see a change come over them. Mike's eyes become rounder. The tension in his forehead might even be fear. The one who'd started all the teasing over the prom in the first place looks down at his shoes, then over his shoulder as though searching for a safe place to hide. Even the last one, the enormous guy who'd started the coin tossing, looks sheepish, his height and size giving him a different appearance that is no longer menacing but instead awkward and ungainly.

I'm confused. Why is it that Lauren could never be a target? But of course, I know exactly why the guys from school slink back now, preparing to leave the café altogether. In her skinny jeans, platform sandals, and floaty off-the-shoulder top, Lauren embodies a particular kind of California gorgeous. It isn't just her natural beauty that scares the boys, but the fact that it is combined with signs of wealth, of status, not to mention the confidence all that brings. Lauren's hair is highlighted and lowlighted, falling down her back in lush, layered waves. Her bronzed skin, her big Italian sunglasses, her Louis Vuitton shoulder bag all tell a story, just as my messy curls, eyeglasses, and clothes from Target tell a very different story.

As for Lauren herself, she hasn't even noticed them.

"Here you go," Rik says, handing me my coffee. "What can I get you?" he asks Lauren.

"Oh, don't worry. I'll grab something in a minute," she says, then goes in search of an empty table. "I'll find us a spot," she calls over her shoulder.

I look at Rik, feeling my face flushed with embarrassment. "Join us?" I say unsteadily.

"I wish I could." I can't tell if he means this.

I nod. I wonder if there is some chance, however slim, that he hasn't seen what happened.

Then he says, "You shouldn't let them stop you, you know. If you want to go, that is. It's *your* prom."

So, he heard it all. Everything. And this makes it even more real and unbearable.

"I don't want to go," I say. This is true. In fact, it never even occurred to me to go. The ticket price alone prevents it, and then there is all the crazy fanfare of prom: girls spending days shopping, getting their hair and makeup professionally done. Even in my school, where the families of most of the kids don't have any money, limousines are rented, elaborate parties planned. The last thing I want is to get involved in all that. "I only said yes the first time because I thought I had to, but it turned out to be a prank—" I slam my palm over my mouth, realizing I've confessed more than I'd needed to.

Rik waits a beat, then says, "You're too remarkable a person to put up with guys like that."

I shake my head back and forth, unable to hear anything nice about myself right now.

"And not just because you can do math like Hypatia," he adds.

Hypatia lived during the fourth century and edited Euclid's *The Elements*, the most important Greek mathematical text. As a result she was declared a vessel of Satan and murdered by Christian monks. I'm not sure if Rik knows this last part.

He waits for me to look up at him, then says, "I'll see you soon, okay?"

I nod. He fishes his car keys out of his pocket and walks out the door and into the sunshine. I watch him for a few minutes, then head to the back of the café to find Lauren. She's waiting at an empty table, elbows propped up, chin resting in her hands, a giant grin stretched across her face.

"So that was kind of amazing!" she says, her eyes wide with anticipation.

She's talking about Rik, not the high school assholes.

"He looked *very* interested," she continues.

There's nothing between us, but I'm not sure Lauren will believe me if I say so. "He's not going to date a high school girl," I say.

"You won't be a high school girl forever, and listen to me—" Lauren eyes me carefully, then says, very slowly, "He had his *arm* around you."

While this is true, it's not what Lauren thinks. "He was just pretending," I say.

"He was just pretending he had his arm around you?"

I shake my head. "Never mind."

She reaches over and takes my latte. "Sip?" she says. As though suddenly remembering something, she digs into her bag and pulls out a small robin's-egg-blue box. She slides it across the coffee table as though it's a hockey puck.

"Surprise!" she says.

I've never been to Tiffany. I can't even recall a time when I've seen a Tiffany gift box. But somehow I know that particular shade of blue, that logo, and I know that anything inside such a box is precious and unaffordable.

"What is this?" I say.

Lauren looks at the box as though it is a tiresome pest, then sighs. "Tiffany does something like sixty-five women's watches, right? But my ridiculous parents—two people who never even *speak* to each other—gave me the same damned watch for graduation."

"They gave you a watch? I think that's nice."

"Not *a* watch," she says, "but two copies of the same watch. Graduation was, like, really tense. My parents sat on different sides of the theater. But then they gave me these watches. I didn't realize until later that they were the damned same!"

I point at the box. "And this is one of them?"

"Open it."

I take the box in my hands and carefully remove the lid. Inside is a beautiful watch with a powder-pink face and diamonds to pick out the hours. "It looks like a sculpture you'd keep in a glass cabinet," I say.

"And here it is again!" she announces. She pushes back the sleeve of her top and shows me her wrist, around which is an identical watch. "I would return one of them, but I can't. If I return my father's watch, he'll think I prefer my mother. If I return my mother's watch, she'll say he always gets his way. It will become a living nightmare. So, I'm keeping both watches. That way, my parents are both happy."

"And you have two very nice watches," I say, laughing.

"One," says Lauren, holding up a finger. "*One* very nice watch. I think you should have the other."

"*Me*? Why me?"

"Why *not* you?"

It never occurred to me that the gift box had been meant for me. I don't know what to say.

"I just can't," I begin. "I mean, it's beautiful and I am very grateful, but—" I pause, staring at the watch. It's so exquisite, glittering in the spotlights of the restaurant. "But it's just not mine."

"It wasn't *mine* before my mom and dad—I don't know which one—gave it to me. I'm giving it to you. What's the difference?"

I look at Lauren—lovely, gorgeous, smart Lauren. "But it *is* different," I say. "Your parents. Your watch."

Lauren rolls her eyes. "What if it were a puppy that needed a home?"

"But it's not a puppy. It's money strapped to your wrist."

"It will sit in a drawer for years doing nothing. Anyway, I like the idea of us having the same watch."

"I can't—"

"Also, I'm leaving soon and I don't have any other parting gift for you, so you're stuck."

She's got an internship that starts any day now. And then there's college. She's going to Cornell, about as far away as she can get from her parents.

"You're my best friend," Lauren says with a pained expression. She isn't the sort of girl who cries, but I can see the emotion on her face. "Why don't you let me give you something nice?"

"You give me nice things all the time. For most of my life you've been my only friend," I say. It's a startling revelation. "And that's a gift."

"Yeah, well, that's because high school kids are infantile," she says. "I'm glad you're at Mellin. At least there are some people there who see what they've got in you. And that Rik is charming. Seriously. But be smart and take the watch. You can always sell it if you get into a tough corner."

But that's just it. I'm always in a tough corner. I'm thinking about the recent repair to the roof. My mother got the money from Biba, and he'll be back for it soon enough, along with a hefty rate of interest.

I smile, but I push the box in her direction. "I can't," I say, and we look at each other for a long moment.

At last, she picks up the Tiffany box and drops it into her bag like it's a tin of throat lozenges. Then she stands, pushing away the chair with the backs of her knees. She loops her bag over her shoulder and says, "Okay, you win round one. But this is *not* over. Now let's get out of here. I'm bored of this place."

I'm looking forward to another day with Dmitry. But when I get to the lab there's no chess game set up, no mugs on the marble coffee bar or any of the usual signs that Dmitry is expecting me. In fact, there's no sign of Dmitry at all. I look around for him, first at his usual place behind the glass walls of his lab and then in the dining room, just in case he's rummaging through the kitchen looking for food.

But the dining room is tidy and polished with no signs of crumbs from toast. I do find some leftover vanilla cake, however. Perfect for the ratties. Then I wind my way back downstairs to the dormitory and knock gingerly on the door.

I hear Dmitry's voice, hoarse and strained. Pushing open the door, I find him lying in bed, his pajamas buttoned high on his chest, a wad of tissues balanced on his belly. "Stay back," he says. "I'm contagious."

The air in the room is stale and unmoving and I can practically feel the heat coming off him from six feet away. "How long have you been like this?" I ask.

"Since last night. Can I have water?"

I see it's a struggle for him to talk. "Water coming up," I say. "I'll get you tea, too. It'll help your throat."

At the coffee bar I make him a cup of his favorite Red Rose, bringing it back to him along with a big tumbler of cold water and a piece of fruit from my bag. But he's already asleep, lying on his back, the perspiration slick on his brow. A box of tissues on his chest rises and falls gently with his breathing. I remove a book about chess from his night table to make room for the water, marking his place with a wooden swab stick he uses as a bookmark. Then I leave him to sleep.

I make myself a cup of coffee, then spend the afternoon reading up on neural regeneration, or "raising the dead," as Will sarcastically calls it. I read paper after paper, researching neural recovery patterns, neural progenitor cells, bone marrow stromal cells, anything that might help heal dying cells in the brain. When I check the time again I see it's evening.

Back at the dormitory, I find Dmitry still asleep in bed. The air around him is dense and heavy. A smell of menthol and fever permeates the air.

"Dmitry?" I whisper. When he doesn't move, I reach out and put a hand on his shoulder. He's warm to the touch, his fever raging. "Dmitry, wake up."

He turns slowly, his eyes closed. His forehead glistens with sweat. "What time is it?" he asks.

"Time for you to drink something."

Even in the shadowy light I can see his eyes are sunken, his skin ashy. He takes a sip of water.

"Thank you," he says, then, "I think I need aspirin. Tylenol. Pretty much anything would do—"

"I'm going right now," I promise, fishing out my car keys from my back pocket. Then I remember where I am. This is a science laboratory, where people work long hours in windowless rooms with the constant hum of forced air around them. I don't need to drive anywhere. There is probably aspirin in every drawer here. "I'll be right back," I say.

Ten minutes later I return with a huge beaker of opened drug packages: Advil, Excedrin, Aleve, Bayer. It looks like I've gone trick-or-treating for medicine in a neighborhood full of doctors.

"Thank you," Dmitry says. "Alternating doses of ibuprofen with acetaminophen acts as a stronger antipyretic than using only one of the drugs. Let me explain why—"

I interrupt him. "Dmitry, please. You don't need to teach me when you're sick."

He nods weakly, then plucks a couple of pills from a foil pack and swallows them with water. "Wake me in four hours," he says, then he's out.

I clear the night table of Kleenex, tidy his collection of pens as well as some scraps of notepaper on which he'd been writing. I'm about to leave the papers on the small desk by his bed when I notice a flowchart he's made. It's full of arrows and boxes and a whole range of symbols used in biological sciences, including the most famous one, the cross that means death. I take the paper into the light and study it more carefully. It would look like gibberish to anyone else, but I've worked with Dmitry long enough to understand the thinking behind the symbols he's drawn.

I get out my own notebook.

I've been jotting down some ideas today while studying. It seems they aren't so far-fetched. In fact, if I take out some of Dmitry's mistakes—or what I believe are mistakes—and substitute my own work, I can answer some of the questions he's posed with double question marks along the margins.

I put his notepaper into my jeans pocket, feeling thrilled, almost jittery about what Dmitry and I are working on. But it's suppertime for the rats, and I promised April I wouldn't be late with their food. So I head over to animal tech.

Quiet and sleepy during the day, the rats are alert, active, and desperate to come out and play this time of evening. They leap from shelves in their cages and crawl along the bars, hoping that I'll come over to give them some attention or feed them treats. I scoop their mix from a big plastic tub, luring them to one end as I clean out the litter trays from the other. Some are so friendly they prefer crawling up my arm to eating, and I can see why April is so fond of them.

I check the ones with surgical scars, looking for signs of infection. I hand out bits of cake, letting them eat from my palm. I've grown very fond of the rats since April has been away. I check Cornelius and his brothers, the ones April is planning to take home when she returns from vacation.

I find the brothers all right, but not Cornelius. He's usually the one clamoring at the cage door. It's unlike him to stay sleeping when there is freedom to be had, and very strange for him to sleep through dinner. I see his tail poking out from under a cardboard box that April has set up as a hiding space. Lifting the box, I find him hunched up, his fur standing on end, his sides heaving with each breath. I'm about to scoop him up to have a closer look when he suddenly shakes, then loses his balance and topples to his side. He lurches forward, all his muscles stiffening, then lies still.

I gasp, grab up Cornelius, and cradle him in my arms. Then I run out of the room to the glass balcony, charging down the staircase to the floor below. I don't know what I'm doing exactly, but I grab a stethoscope off someone's desk, wrap the headset around my neck, and insert the eartips. I can't hear breathing, or the rapid tap of a rat heartbeat. I can't hear anything at all, really. I adjust the bell and try again, then pinch a forepaw, the classic way that researchers determine death in lab rodents. No response.

In all likelihood, it's a heart attack. There's no rodent-size defibrillator around here, but Dmitry has oxygen in his lab. I run to his lab, throw myself into a chair, push oxygen in the rat's direction, and begin chest compressions.

After six minutes, I give up.

I want to call out for help, but there's nobody around. The giant building with its lights and beeps, its breathing lungs and pumping hearts feels empty except for me and Cornelius. Anyway, there's nothing anyone can do.

Suddenly, I remember the piece of notepaper in my pocket: Dmitry's chart that maps out, in theory, a way to bring back dead neurons. It won't work if I follow the procedure as Dmitry has written it, but I have some ideas of my own. My modifications might help the brain create glial walls around hopeless cells and stimulate the hypothalamus to create an excess of new neurons. A few additional modifications and maybe—I know it sounds insane—but *maybe* I can help Cornelius.

I grab ice from the kitchen and bury Cornelius in it to bring his temperature down and slow the rate of neural death. Meanwhile, I assemble everything else I need inside Dmitry's lab. If my experiment fails, at least I'll be able to tell April that I tried my hardest.

And if it doesn't fail?

People have done crazy things in this place—persuaded human skin to grow on pieces of apples denuded of their cells, grown kidneys to the size needed for humans, tested tiny vascular implants that wrap around blood vessels and clean the blood. In such a place, it doesn't seem so odd to be working late at night on a dead rat.

I place Cornelius on a bed of paper towels. I have to get a cannula into the vein of his tail. A cannula is like a tiny intravenous tube. With it in place I can give him injections. I've never done anything like this before, but I've seen it on videos. I bite back my nerves and begin. It's a terrible feeling to pierce his skin like this, but I do it. Then I study Dmitry's notes, adding in my own ideas, the ones I've dreamed up over the past many weeks. Solutions come to me freshly as I work. It's as though I'm connected to something greater than myself, the answers arriving as I move toward them. I just have to keep going.

Cornelius's reentry into the world begins very subtly. The tone of his skin changes. His toes unfurl, one by one. He takes irregular, shallow breaths. I'm not even sure he's breathing at first. He gains color in his nose, his ears, his feet. He's still a very sick rat as I take him from the table and hold him against my belly, warming his body against me. Then the trembling starts. He's shaking, which terrifies me, and his feet twitch. He gasps and gasps as I maneuver the oxygen nearer. It seems to help, but he's barely hanging on. For a moment I regret bringing him back. The suffering is obvious.

Unless I do something quickly, his heart will stop again. But if the blood is restored too quickly to his brain, he could suffer a brain injury. I remember a Danish study about MEK 1/2 inhibitors—that's an idea! Then I add some ordinary nitroglycerin to Cornelius's IV.

He's still alive fifteen minutes later, then half an hour later. No longer struggling as much. He's even attempted walking. An hour later, I'm still sitting with him and he's breathing almost normally. I wrap him in my lab coat, then bundle him into a plastic tray and cover the tray with wire mesh. It's been four hours and is time to wake Dmitry for his medicine.

I'm at the door to the dormitory when the weight of what just transpired finally hits. I stop suddenly, putting my hand against the wall to steady myself.

I just brought something that was dead back to life.

16

I WAKE UP feeling rat whiskers against my cheek. I open my eyes and see Cornelius chewing one of the many electrical cords that weave across Dmitry's work station. I sit up quickly, startling him so that he runs, and then I have to fish him out from behind a ring stand. The clever rat has even managed to chew off his IV.

He's in fine shape for an animal that was dead hours ago. He still has signs of a heart condition, his sides working hard as he breathes. But he's alive, bending his head up to sniff me as I hold him against my chest.

I can't wait to tell Dmitry. Between the two of us we've come up with a kind of protocol for bringing back recently dead organisms. Cornelius is proof. The strangest part is that it doesn't feel strange. Just another of science's discoveries that will one day be taken for granted.

I don't know exactly what to do with Cornelius. Do I put him back with the other rats? Do I keep him separate and show him to Munn when he arrives this morning? What will Munn think, anyway?

I take Cornelius off to the coffee bar and let him lick sugar water from my palm as I prepare some tea for Dmitry. I find some cookies and offer one to Cornelius. It gives me a special thrill to see him take it in his paws and chew off a piece.

"You're going to be a famous rat," I tell him.

I hear footsteps, then a loud moan of disgust. I don't need to look around to know that it's Will.

"Oh *Gaaawd*!" he says, stomping toward me. "Do we now have *two* mad women who carry rats around like handbags?"

"Good morning, Will," I say. "Did you have a nice weekend?"

"Not particularly. Do you realize how many violations of good laboratory practice you are committing? First, we shouldn't even *have* a coffee bar right here in the middle of the building like this. Second, that disgusting little creature you treat like a teddy bear ought to have been pronged ages ago—" Despite his protests about the coffee bar being in breach of laboratory practice, he begins setting up his own double espresso. "Why are you here, anyway? It's the morning. Aren't you usually in class in the mornings?"

"I—" I'm bursting to reveal everything that happened last night, but Will doesn't deserve to be the first to hear of the experiment's success. By all rights, that should be Dmitry.

"Get rid of that," Will says, pointing at Cornelius.

"He's very important. Leave him alone."

He reaches for Cornelius, clasping him by the tail.

"Don't touch him!" I say. But it's too late. Will has Cornelius upside down by the base of his tail. Cornelius lets out a screech.

"Stop it! He'll have another heart attack!"

Will finds this amusing. He starts to laugh while I wrestle Cornelius out of his hands. Then I rush to the staircase.

"Where are you going now?" Will says. "We've got work to do."

We're supposed to be gathering the final data on the experiment he's in charge of, determining the efficiency of the bassinets. But that is going to have to wait.

"Munn's office!" I say, racing up the stairs.

"Are you going to go crying to him now? Telling him how awful I am to you?"

I ignore him and keep climbing.

"If you are going to complain to Munn, it will only reflect badly on you," he calls up to me. I hear him curse, then his footsteps charging up after me.

He says, "You'll look as though you are whining, which you are. Has nobody told you that Munn loathes whiners?"

I won't be whining. I'll be telling him what happened to Cornelius, who Will nearly scared to death a minute ago.

Will says, "You'll say I'm unkind to you, and I'll say you're unprofessional—which you are. I've kept careful lab notes on all the things you've tainted, ruined, or miscalculated in the laboratory, including the time you set your head on fire."

"I don't care!" I say, though I do.

"You realize you are going to address the top man while hugging a lab rat?"

"Yes!"

"So you intend to make yourself look even more ridiculous? Well, balls out, I have to admire it. But it's your word against mine.

Who do you think he will believe?"

I pause and glance down at him. "I'm recording this conversation on my phone, so I imagine it will be me," I say, holding up my phone.

I think I hear a little gasp. Then, "Kira, really, I was only kidding! I think you're a wonderful mentee, a real gem. Come have a coffee with me. Bring the creature if you must."

I'm not really recording him—the thought only occurred to me as I said it. I shoot forward up the last stairs to the upper lab, and finally to Munn's office. By the time I reach the door, I'm breathless.

I haven't had a conversation with Dr. Munn since joining Mellin. He's rarely down in the labs, and he'd have no reason to talk to me anyway. I've certainly never been in his office. But I barge through the door without knocking, closing it quickly behind me to shut out Will.

"Sorry," I say, by way of greeting.

Munn is sitting at his desk, the window behind him filled with a view of flowers and fan palms. If he's startled to see me, arriving at speed and panting in front of him, he doesn't show it. He looks up from his papers, pushes his reading glasses down on his nose, and says, "Good morning. Can I help you with something?"

"This rat," I say, swallowing hard.

He nods as though rats are often brought to his attention. "The rat climbing onto your shoulder, you mean?"

"Yes, he was . . . uh." I don't know how to say this. "He was . . . um . . . dead. He died. Last night. And I spent some time reviving him."

Munn sits back in his chair and looks from my face to Cornelius, then back again. "Well, that's good."

Munn doesn't seem at all convinced, so I say, "I'm not making
this up."

He studies me for a moment, then says, "I have to admit the rat
looks very much alive, and as far as I am aware, that isn't normally
the case in previously dead animals."

I hear a single "Ha!" from behind the door. That would be
Will, of course, with his ear to the keyhole like a schoolboy. At any
moment Munn will invite him in. "Did you know that Dmitry has
been working on a way of regenerating dead neurons?" I say.

Munn raises an eyebrow.

"It's an effort to revive those that would be declared brain-
dead."

"Not much would surprise me about Dmitry's abilities, but I've
not heard that he's downstairs undoing death."

I hear another burst of laughter from the other side of the door.

"Well, he *is*," I say boldly. "Or trying to."

"So, this has happened *before*?" says Munn. "Why wouldn't
Dmitry have told me himself?"

"Because it hasn't happened before. And to be perfectly honest,
Dmitry wasn't there when Cornelius came back to life. He missed
the whole darn thing. He's sick."

Munn clears his throat. He gives the impression that while
he is somewhat amused by the conversation, his attention is now
wavering. At any moment I think I'm going to be asked to leave.

"Dr. Munn, please," I say urgently. "I made some changes to a
protocol Dmitry developed, and when I tried it, the rat came back

to life. I don't know how else to describe it. What are you supposed to do, anyway, when something important happens in an experiment?"

"Well, you could write it up, for a start," Munn says, and gives a little cough. "As a report."

The realization hits me like a stone. Of course, a report! That's what I should have done. A paper like the one I wrote for the Science for Our Future award.

"Just out of curiosity," says Munn, "how did you kill the rat to begin with?"

"*Kill* him?" I'm shocked he'd think I'd do such a thing. "Why would I kill him?"

Munn cocks his head in surprise. "For the purpose of experimentation," he says slowly. He looks at me carefully, appearing in turns charmed and mildly exasperated. "All right, forget the report. I will hear about it now. Do have a seat."

"Are you sure?"

"Please," he says, gesturing toward a chair.

I lower myself into one of the armchairs, clutching Cornelius in my lap so that he doesn't wander off over the chair's soft leather.

"Put the rat on the desk," Munn instructs. I do as I am told. Then I watch as Munn takes a mesh wastepaper basket from next to his foot, dumps its contents onto the carpet, and turns it upside down onto Cornelius so that it acts as a type of cage. "Now, please explain exactly what happened."

I tell him how I've been doing research for Dmitry. And how when Cornelius died in front of me, I ran downstairs to Dmitry's area and somehow, by a miracle, used the set of instructions that

Dmitry had written as a base and brought the rat back to life.

"Where are these instructions?" he says.

"They're downstairs. In Dmitry's area. But I added to them. And subtracted, too. Basically, I changed them."

"And it was definitely dead? The rat, I mean."

"Yes, sir."

"What would you say, five minutes?" he says. "Six? Seven?"

"Oh, longer than that."

Munn smiles knowingly. "Did you know that the longest record for a person going without oxygen and surviving with no apparent brain injury is twenty-two minutes? Remarkable, isn't it? I think we may have had a similar occurrence happen to your little fellow here." He nods at Cornelius.

"Sir, the rat was dead. He had no heartbeat."

"Decades ago, that would have meant dead, but—"

"He was dead for almost thirty minutes." I suddenly realize I've interrupted him. "Sorry," I say.

"Thirty minutes?" Munn considers this. His face is dark, his brow furrowed. All at once he says, "Very well, if you say so. Follow me!"

Suddenly, he springs to his feet, reaching the door to his office in giant steps. He grabs his lab coat off a hook, swings the door open, and says, "Good morning, Will," as Will moves aside to allow him to pass.

Will and I follow Munn down the corridor and into the animal tech room, where he opens a cage and pulls out two rats, young does I recognize immediately. I've never before seen Munn in the animal tech room, let alone with rats in his hands. He handles them expertly, if coldly, and strides back out of the room, through the dining room, then down the spiral stairway until he reaches the bottom floor, with Will and me struggling to keep up with him.

"Do you still have your gear set up from the experiment?" he asks.

"Yes, sir. In Dmitry's area."

Munn moves quickly toward Dmitry's lab. At the door he stops and turns toward me, holding up the rats, one in each hand. To my horror, I see that they are now both dead.

"Asphyxiation," he says, by way of explanation. "This is completely unorthodox and not considered humane killing, but I am making an exception here because you have promised me you are genuine in your claims."

"I am," I say, my voice shaking.

"I certainly hope so. Check your watch. We'll want to time this."

He opens the door for me, then turns to Will. "I'm sure you have something to do?" he says, and with that he turns his back on Will, who remains outside the glass walls, silently peering in.

At Dmitry's desk, I immediately start switching on electricity, charging up the scanner, rushing to get the correct-size needles and syringes. Munn hands me one of the rats, then fishes a cotton swab out of his pocket and checks for a corneal reflex on the other. The rat doesn't respond. He then listens for a heartbeat and looks closely for any sign of respiration before declaring the rat dead.

"The standard for determining death is one minute with no sign of respiration," he says. "Check vital signs. Did you do that last night with the other rat?"

"I didn't check for a corneal response," I admit.

"Well, do it now."

I set to work, my heart beating wildly, praying I'm able to remember the same procedure as before. I work quietly for five minutes, ten minutes. If I make a mistake now, I'll never be believed. The hardest part is an injection into the lumbar region, but here I go, trying to be as precise as possible and keep my hands from shaking. I watch the ultrasound screen, moving the needle with its guidance until at last it is positioned correctly. Only then do I release the contents of the tiny syringe.

"I need a zap," I say, reaching for a laser that will stimulate the heart. A few more adjustments, and then, just as with Cornelius, the rat begins to transform. First, the erratic beat of the heart, the occasional breath. She starts to quiver as Cornelius had done. After what feels like an eternity, the shaking resolves and I see the little feet unfurling toe by toe as a wash of pink floods the translucent white of her skin, signaling that the heart is beating. The rat is alive.

"I think it's going to be okay," I whisper to Munn.

"Too right it is!" says Munn, grinning. He tries to contain his emotions, but I can see he is amazed, as though he's just witnessed a miracle, which I guess he has. He pulls at a whisker and watches as the animal shrinks back, a sign of life. The rat isn't upright, isn't able to walk or orient itself, but it certainly isn't dead.

Munn bursts into laughter. Clapping me around the shoulders, he says, "You've done it! Good God, you've done it!"

I allow myself a small gasping laugh, more in relief than anything. Then I reach for the other doe, desperate to help her. I feel confident now, moving through the steps as Munn sits with the first rat, who is slowly recovering on a towel in front of him as he scratches hurried notes onto a pad.

I'm not sure when the procedure takes a wrong turn, but it does. Maybe I damaged the tiny rodent spinal column or syringed too quickly the substance between the vertebrae. The second doe comes to life, as the other rats had, but her response is far weaker. She only moves the legs on one side of her body; her color never resurfaces. I work desperately to save her, but she dies again, going limp in my hand.

I've made a mistake—I don't know where. The blood hasn't circulated correctly back through the brain. Or perhaps it has, but returned too quickly, causing further damage. In any case, the little doe cannot make it back from where she has been sent. And while Munn tells me that this is a great day, a great day indeed, I feel I've failed because this second little rat is gone. Perhaps it bothers me especially because of the grotesque manner in which she died, strangled between the thumb and forefinger of a man who, for all his tenderness toward humanity, does not value the life of a creature like her. Or maybe it is because the recovery process itself required me to manhandle her body as she fought to recover. It makes it all the worse that I knew the rat's name, and because the name seems strangely prescient. As Daisy, the rat that survived, begins to take her first slow, awkward steps into a second life, Not Daisy, the rat that died, lies unmoving on a folded cloth.

Munn, Will, and I go to the dormitory, me with Daisy in my hands.

"Dmitry?" Munn says, knocking.

Will whispers, "I think I hear something."

I say, "I'll go in."

"Are you quite sure?" asks Munn.

I press the door gently open with my shoulder. The only light is from Dmitry's laptop, glowing from its place on the bedclothes. Dmitry is sitting up, his earphones in. I'm willing to bet he's listening to Tchaikovsky.

"Kira?" he whispers, removing the headphones. His throat sounds sore. Though he is able to sit up, he looks terrible.

I wish I didn't have to barge in like this, especially with Munn and Will in tow. Also, I feel guilty that I haven't brought him anything to eat or drink. He should have a big glass of freshly squeezed orange juice and a plate of hot food, not that he'd necessarily want either.

"Don't talk if it hurts," I say. "I'll get you tea in a minute."

I hear Munn behind me say, "Will, get him tea."

"Of course," Will says. Then, in his most polite and ingratiating tone, he adds, "Milk and sugar?"

It's amazing how agreeable he can be in front of Munn. Or my mother, for that matter. She still refers to him as "that very nice young man."

Munn addresses Dmitry. "It's Gregory here," he says.

"Dr. Munn!" says Dmitry, his voice full of surprise. He pushes his laptop away and runs his fingers through his hair, but it's all cowlicks and it sticks straight up no matter what he does. "I didn't realize it was you!"

"Don't feel you have to move, my boy," Munn says.

"I have a virus," Dmitry says. The word *virus* conjures up all kinds of concerns, but Munn isn't fazed. He drags a chair over to Dmitry's bed and sits down with a sigh. Tissues overflow in the wastepaper basket, littering the floor around it. Several near-empty glasses crowd the small night table, along with the beaker of medicines I had collected earlier.

"As sorry as we are to see you so unwell, that's not why we're here," Munn says. He nods at the beaker of medications and adds, "Anyway, it appears you are well supplied."

Dmitry tries to smile. He looks terrible, dehydrated and sallow, with dark circles under his eyes.

"You wrote out a kind of chart that showed what one might do to encourage the brain, after death, to partition away damaged neurons and restock with fresh ones. Do you recall this chart?" Munn asks.

Dmitry says nothing, so I remind him, saying, "You used a black pen and then wrote questions out in red ink."

"Oh!" says Dmitry. He looks a bit embarrassed. "Those were just ramblings."

Will returns with a tray on which he's placed a pot of tea, cups, and saucers.

Munn says, "You might be interested to know that your young colleague here had a bit of a lark with those ramblings and tried the process. You see that rat she is holding?"

Dmitry squints at Daisy.

"I can confirm that the rat was dead for at least eight minutes before Kira began the process. We haven't done a thorough analysis to determine the extent of brain damage, but there is no question it was recovered from a state that is considered legally dead."

Even in the dim light, I can see Dmitry's bewildered expression. I can imagine the dozens, if not hundreds, of questions flashing through his mind. Munn watches his face as intently as I do, then pours from the teapot, offering a cup to Dmitry before taking a slow sip of his own. Then he leans back in his chair. "You don't seem that surprised," he says.

Dmitry sits up straighter. "Is this true? About the rat?" he asks me.

"Of course. And another upstairs."

"My notes," says Dmitry. "Where are they?"

"On the table in your lab," I say.

"You did this?" he says. More of a statement than a question.

It doesn't feel fair that after all his years working doggedly on a problem, I came along and beat him to the final discovery. "It wasn't really me. It was *you*, Dmitry. You did it." I look from Dmitry to Munn.

"I would say the pair of you make a very fine team," Munn says.

I hope Will heard that. I glance over to where he's been standing in the doorway, but he's gone.

"May I have the rat?" Dmitry says.

I carefully hand him Daisy. He tries to hold on to her, but she is gaining strength now. She walks across the bedclothes, moving in a circle.

"That's either a nerve issue or a stroke," Munn says, observing Daisy's odd movement. "It will be interesting to see how it does after a few hours."

"And another rat upstairs?" says Dmitry. "The same?"

I stumble through the whole story, feeling a little apologetic for the presumption I've shown in working out of Dmitry's lab, from his very notes, without permission. I feel I've taken advantage of him, of his wealth of study and years of steady progress to bring about what happened. "I got very lucky," I say finally.

He shakes his head. "No. If you had followed my notes, both rats would be dead." He takes a sip of his own tea now, then clears his throat painfully. "Thank you, Kira. You brought me medicine and then redesigned my experiment so that it would actually succeed."

Munn says, "We have to talk about what happens next. There are many serious issues surrounding this particular discovery." He pauses, listening to footsteps that come from outside. "Will?" he says.

I see Will's head pop back through the door. "I was just checking on the other rat. Still alive!" he says, sounding as though he is pleased for Cornelius, which I know is impossible. I wonder what he was really doing.

"Please, come in. Close the door."

With the three of us assembled, Munn explains that while it is clear that a very significant breakthrough has been made, it's been done without the benefit of the scientific method, and this is a problem. "As much as we allow for creativity and flair here at Mellin, we cannot publish vague and what some would call outrageous claims. We need to conduct a proper investigation. Meanwhile, it is imperative that we keep this secret. The discovery is newsworthy and sensational. Any leak to the press—even rumors that post-death recovery is possible—may cause chaos."

Why would a scientific advancement cause chaos? My confusion must show, because Munn looks directly at me and says, "Kira, the truth is, we don't really understand what happened here. Imagine families refusing to bury their dead for years while we work on this."

"It's okay, I can keep a secret," I say.

"It would affect organ donors," adds Will, undoubtedly to please Munn, who keeps close watch on what affects donor numbers. "I mean, who would sign up as an organ donor if it was even remotely possible they could be brought back from the current definition of dead? People needing transplants would die in droves before we even got our research off the ground."

Even Dmitry agrees. "I'm afraid we've invented a bit of a monster," he says, almost apologetically. He smiles slyly at me. "You and I are like Dr. Frankenstein," he says.

I think he means it as a compliment.

17

EVERYTHING CHANGES. MUNN, rarely in the lab before, spends all morning with us. Will seems to have forgotten his list of grievances against me. He treats me like a real colleague and even makes coffee for me before I return home for some much-needed sleep.

It's as though my life has turned 180 degrees. And yet, as I'm coming up the path to my house, the day looks like any other. I hear birdsong, a radio playing in the open window of my neighbor's kitchen, the drone of a jackhammer in the distance. I want to shout to the world that we can now bring back a previously "dead" brain. But secrecy is everything.

My body is sore from sleeping in a chair. My head aches as though my skull isn't quite big enough. I know I need sleep, but I'm too keyed up.

But then I look up and see my mother in the doorway. "What's the matter, your phone broke?" she says sternly.

I suddenly realize I've been out all night with no explanation.

"I'm sorry. You know what it's like at Mellin. You can't make a phone call. It's a closed system."

"You should have gone outside the building and called. What were you doing anyway?"

I was bringing back animals from the dead.

"Dmitry has the flu. He was really sick, and then one of the rats had a heart attack. It's okay now."

I step inside, kick off my shoes.

"You're very fond of this Dmitry, aren't you?" she says.

It's true. I like him. I'm sad that he has no family. The loss is more glaringly apparent when he's sick, as he is now. I'll go back to the lab later with soup. I wish I could bring my mother. She's the best at looking after you when you're ill.

"Lauren was here," she says now. "She wanted to say goodbye. I really wish you would answer your phone."

How can I explain the events? I can't. Not without violating Mellin's confidentiality agreement. And not without going directly against Munn.

"What do you mean, goodbye?" I say.

"She went off this morning to that *thing*," my mother says.

I feel a pang. That "thing" is a three-month residential skills training program that prepares people for working with conservation groups. She'll be gone all summer.

"She left something for you. It's on the kitchen table."

I feel even more guilty now. I follow my mother into the kitchen and see a small box gift-wrapped in SpongeBob paper. On a card it says, *I'm going to miss you, Science Girl. Lauren x.*

I feel a weight in my throat. Lauren is always doing nice things for me: taking me with her on birding expeditions, lending me clothes, giving me presents. And what have I done for her? Not even been here to say goodbye.

"Aren't you going to open it?" my mother asks. Perhaps she sees the emotion in my face, because it's gentler than before.

"I know what it is," I say. I can tell by the weight and shape of the package that it's the elegant pink-faced watch with tiny diamonds marking out the hours.

I'm a person who adds up the grocery bill in my head as I shop, checks gas prices at several stations before choosing which one to fill up at, repairs my own eyeglasses because they cost too much to replace. I've avoided phone calls and front doors for as many years as I can remember, ducking debt collectors. But it's not the cost of Lauren's gift that overwhelms me. It's the fact that this is the same watch that Lauren wears. Her good watch. Her best. She'd wanted the same for me.

I drop into a chair, studying the little box. SpongeBob has been Lauren's favorite since she was eight years old.

My mother takes an onion out of a basket on the countertop and sets it on a chopping board. "I'm making you an omelet," she says. "You need feeding."

She pours oil in a pan, adds onions, then mushrooms. Like anyone who has worked in a restaurant, she does three things at once: whisking, pouring, flipping. She garnishes the omelet with herbs from the garden and hands me a glass of orange juice, serving up breakfast on a warmed plate. It isn't until I've taken the first mouthwatering bite that I understand the significance of what I've just seen. My mother is operating at full capacity—at least this morning she is.

I've almost forgotten what she was like before she became sick.

"You're feeling better?" I ask cautiously.

"I've been having some good days," she says.

Midway through our meal my phone rings. I think it will be Lauren, but there's no caller ID, and when I put the phone to my ear I hear Rik's voice.

"Is it true?" he says, his words rushed. "Were they really dead?"

He's talking about Cornelius and Daisy, of course.

"When did you hear about it?" I say.

"Munn has me setting up meetings. He's going to Washington to talk to some people there, get some funding. It's all very hush-hush. This is serious, Kira."

"Are you going, too?"

"Yes, of course. I take the notes," he laughs. "I want you to know that I'm really happy for you."

Rik has never called me before. Lauren insists he's just waiting until I'm eighteen to ask me out, but that's not the vibe I get. Whole weeks go by without him even looking my way.

He says, "Are you free at all? I think there has to be a celebration. Something to mark the occasion. I mean, after Washington, that is. Would you like that?"

I feel my heart speed up, my mouth go dry.

"Sure," I say. The words arrive as a whisper. "That would be great."

I hope my voice is the right mixture of confident and pleased, like guys ask me out all the time.

"Great, I'll organize everything," he says, with excitement.

And as quickly as that, the phone call is over.

I look up to see my mother is staring at me, a dishcloth over her shoulder. "You look as though someone just gave you some very good or some very bad news," she says.

"It's possible I just got asked out on a date." I can't help but marvel at this fact. I'm happy, but also astonished, more because it seems so unlikely than anything else. I don't even know how to *be* on a date.

My mother smiles. "Well, I'm not surprised," she says. "Senior year and all."

Munn and Rik leave for Washington. Dmitry slowly combats the flu. Meanwhile, Will and I wind up phase one of the experiments involving the Innards. The study reveals the normal rate of deterioration of organs over time given different media. It also shows how we can improve the condition of organs if we use Mellin's new "organ restoration units," what I call the bassinets.

It's good stuff. Not *bring-back-from-the-dead* stuff, but good.

Will does the writing part. I draw up the notes and organize the data. We're busy, but Will finds time to angle for more information on post-death recovery. He wants to know everything about what I studied and what I did.

"Right now?" I say. I'm in the lab, bent over a laptop and working through the data.

"Yes, now. Why not?"

"We're not supposed to talk about it," I say. It's the one thing we can't share with our colleagues in Munn's *innovation ecosystem.* "Someone might hear."

"Oh *please,*" he says, scoffing.

But I won't talk about it. I wish I *could,* especially to April, who has no idea why she can't bring home Cornelius as she'd been promised. And why suddenly Daisy can't walk right and her sister is dead.

I've been avoiding April for days. I realize now that I'd better face the music. "Excuse me," I say to Will, and then, because I feel I really should at least acknowledge what happened to her rats, I climb up the stairs to the animal tech room.

"Hey," I say to April. She's cleaning cages, her back to me. "I'm really sorry about Not Daisy."

"You might *at least* give me an explanation," she says without turning around.

I wish I could. She deserves to know. "I can't tell you much."

"Can't or won't?"

"I'm not allowed."

She swings around, and the look on her face about kills me. "I'll have you know I've been at Mellin since you were in junior high. I know everything about this place. And for goodness' sakes, I think I know how to keep a secret!"

I stare at the floor. "I'm sure you do. It's only that Munn specifically said—"

"Oh *stop!*" interrupts April. She takes a long breath, steadying her temper. "I leave you in charge and suddenly one rat can't walk correctly and another is dead, its brain extracted and the body left for me to deal with. I don't care what Munn says, I think I'm owed an explanation!"

I realize all at once that Will left the rat dead for April to find. "That was Will's fault," I say desperately. "He was supposed to dispose of the—"

"I left *you* in charge!"

I have no way of telling her the truth. No way to make her feel better. "Would it help if you knew the experiment was very important?" I ask.

April makes a clucking sound with her tongue, then turns away again. "Everything we do is 'very important,'" she scoffs. "Or imagined to be so before it is revealed later, as usual, that the experiment was unnecessary. Or that it hasn't worked."

"I don't know what to say. I'm really sorry—"

"Nothing! Say nothing," April says. "Just leave."

I turn to go, catching a glimpse of Cornelius. He can't go home with April now as he's way too important to the lab. Daisy, still clumsy in her movements, has to live in a cage with only a single level.

"Maybe I'll see you later," I say.

April doesn't respond. She's cleaning again, ignoring me as though I've already left the room.

I know April can be prickly, but it's only because she takes seriously her husbandry of the animals. I wish I could at least tell her why Daisy limps, why Not Daisy is dead. Not only dead, but missing her brain. Will was told by Munn to dispose of the rat's body properly, and I assumed he would do so. I should have known better.

I find him at the coffee bar, the one he disapproves of so much, typing on a laptop.

"April blames me for the rats," I say. "You could have at least *cleaned up.*"

He stops typing. I'm waiting for him to tell me he didn't get a PhD from Cambridge to be a lab maid, that it's my job to clean, not his, and that I should stop whining. But instead, he says, "I agree, I should have been more tidy."

"You *agree?*" I've never heard him say such a thing.

"Of course. Especially because it's you who is being blamed. I'll speak to April and try to put it right."

It's like he's changed personalities. "That would be very nice of you," I say. I look at him, studying his face to see if he's only pretending and will shortly return to his usual self. But he remains as before, understanding, compassionate. It's like he's been replaced by his brother, Aiden, who had struck me as a nice guy.

"It was a very strange morning," he says. "And I was distracted. Not that this excuses my oversight regarding April's rat."

April's rat? He actually acknowledges April's care for the rats and the need to respect that?

"I still can't remember all the details of post-death recovery," he continues. "Maybe you could help me with that. This paper is sucking up all my available brain cells, it seems. I can't remember *exactly* what you did to bring the rats back to life."

When I don't say anything he adds, "It's a project we are both going to be involved in. I'm curious, that's all. *Exactly* what did you do in there? Talk me through it step-by-step. I have time."

Of course, he's correct that we'll be working together and that he needs to know everything he can about post-death recovery. But something isn't right. I've never seen him behave like this, and it's making me nervous.

I tell him I'll fill him in later. Right now, I'm due over at Dmitry's area.

Then I get the heck out of there.

I walk off as though I'm heading toward Dmitry's lab, but instead I track toward an exit. Outside, in the bright sun, I text Lauren:

Will acting more oily and devious than normal. I think he's the cuckoo and I'm the baby reed warbler.

She sends me back this:

Push him out of the nest. Anyway, why are you worried about him? What is happening with RIK?

18

I'M SITTING ACROSS from Dmitry at the coffee bar playing chess. He's pinned my bishop and I'm in deep concentration, trying to figure out how to hang on in this game, when Rik's voice pulls me suddenly to attention.

"What about Saturday night?" he says. I wheel around on the stool, and there he is, fresh from Washington. His jacket is draped over his arm and his hair is wet with rain so that it's glossier than ever. "It's awful out there," he says, wiping a sleeve across his brow. "I thought eight o'clock. That okay with you?"

He's going to have the entire lab talking about this date.

"Saturday is, uh, good!" I say. I sound weird, even to myself.

"Will there be food?" says Dmitry.

I glare at him. "Dmitry!"

But Rik only laughs. He pulls up a barstool and says, "You'll love the restaurant. Fabulous views, beautiful décor. It even has floor-to-ceiling aquariums."

"With *fish*?" I say.

He laughs. "Yes, fish."

I'm flattered by the effort he's put in. I'm also very nervous. I look at Rik and smile. I notice his eyes with their sweep of soft lashes, his open, inviting face. I think (not for the first time) that it would be easier for me if he weren't so handsome. Maybe I could relax more.

Dmitry points at the chessboard. "Why are you protecting your bishop at the expense of your queen?"

"Where is it? The restaurant, I mean," I ask Rik.

"It's up on a cliff overlooking the water."

"Your *queen*," says Dmitry.

Rik has clearly found the perfect place for our date. I'm overwhelmed, speechless. But then he says, "And you can eat indoors with security."

Security?

"That'll be for me," Dmitry says, still with his eyes on the board.

"*You?*" I say.

Dmitry glances up from the game. "Munn prefers me in an armored car. It's not necessary, but—"

I don't hear the rest of what he says. My cheeks burn as I start putting the pieces together. This isn't a date. Not at all. This is a dinner for all of us. Munn, Dmitry, Will, Rik. And me. The "celebration" is for our secret little group that knows about post-death recovery.

"Oh," I say. "Oh, of course."

Dmitry points at a spot on the board. "This is the move. There."

But I'm not thinking about the game. I'm thinking that for

almost a week I've been daydreaming about a date that isn't even a date. It has nothing to do with Rik and me. There *is* no Rik and me. How could I have been so foolish, so stupid as to think Rik had asked me out? I want to run out of the room, change my identity, and return as the girl who never imagined Rik would ever ask her out.

"You're leaving your queen?" says Dmitry.

I move a piece, trying desperately to appear nonchalant. As long as Rik doesn't figure out that I'd thought we had a date, it will be all be okay. *Don't let him figure it out*, I think. *No no no no no.*

"What is no?" Dmitry says. And I realize with horror that I've spoken aloud.

"Um . . . nothing," I say. I move another piece on the board, somewhat randomly, my mind a jumble of thoughts all coming at once. I don't even know what I've done until Dmitry makes a face.

"If you insist," he says, then shrugs as though to say if I'm going to let a queen go that easily he's certainly going to take it.

Rik says, "I'll arrange for a car to pick you up." He writes out the name of the restaurant on his business card and hands it to me. "You might want to check it out."

Dmitry says, "Kira, are you paying any attention to this game? You could still win this, you know."

But I can't win this. I can't even think straight.

"You're an excellent player! Don't give up. Remember that it was you who revived the rats. I am two rats behind you, as a matter of fact."

Rik laughs. "We're *all* two rats behind Kira," he says.

* * *

For the rest of week I think about this date that isn't a date. To Rik, I'm just that awkward girl he met at SFOF who gives Will a headache. Nothing more. And there I was imagining being alone with him in the restaurant with the views and the fish. How naive I've been.

Even so, Saturday arrives and I freak out about what to wear. The website for the restaurant shows a glamorous glass structure set into cliffs overlooking the Marin headlands. It is just as beautiful as Rik described. I can't exactly show up in jeans.

The only good dress in my closet is the dragonfly dress, which isn't even mine. I tried to give it back to Lauren, but she refused, claiming it doesn't fit her. "Too long!" she'd said, when I tried to return it.

I tell myself it doesn't matter what I wear because this is not a date. It may as well be the blue skirt and blouse, the outfit I wore for my giftwrapping job. Nobody will care.

But I can't resist the dragonfly dress. I take it to the window, turning the fabric in the light, admiring the beads that shimmer and flash. I remember the last time I wore it: that cold December night on a ship alight with bulbs, dancing with Rik.

"Stop it," I say, this time out loud. "He's not interested in you."

Meanwhile, my hair has gone all Medusa. And tonight I can't just pull it into a ponytail and forget it, which is what I normally do.

I'm miserable and I don't know why. I should be happy.

I go to the kitchen and drop into a chair. "What do I do with my hair?" I ask my mother.

She's wearing a headscarf because her own hair has never fully grown back after all the rounds of chemo. She gives me a stern look, crosses her arms in front of her, and says, "Be grateful for it."

"I know, Mom, sorry. But—"

She comes closer, peering down on my head. "Nothing wrong with your hair."

I try pinning it up, then get out a straightener and experiment with that. No luck, so I wash it freshly, filling my palm with conditioner and working it in. I rinse it again, but only lightly, hoping that the conditioner weighs down the curls. By some miracle, this works. When finally I put together the whole thing—dress, shoes, hair, makeup—I check the mirror. With the dark frames of my eyeglasses I look like a fashionable bookworm. That's not so bad, is it?

My mother comes into the room, walking slowly toward me, touching me as one might touch a work of art.

"Then you *are* going, after all," she says quietly.

I have no idea what she's talking about. "Of course I'm going. It'll be good—I think. I don't have a . . . you know . . . a bag."

She holds up a finger, signaling for me to wait as she disappears into her bedroom. She returns with something wrapped in tissue paper. I'm a little worried it's some kind of hideous necklace. My mother is given to "statement" jewelry involving big glass beads. But when I unwrap it I find a beautiful sequined clutch bag.

"I wasn't much older than you when I last wore it," she says, nodding at the bag. It's a lovely rectangle of sparkles with a kiss-lock closure. "It's yours now."

I touch the sequins, feel the texture of the beads. There's something old-fashioned and elegant yet strangely contemporary and boho about it. I couldn't have asked for a more perfect bag. "Thank you," I say, and kiss my mother's cheek. "It's stunning."

I'm watching out the window for the car that Rik has arranged. At last, I see something fancy, but it's definitely not what I expect. For a moment I think it's Lauren and my heart leaps at the thought that for some crazy reason she has left her post for the weekend. I miss her so much. I want to show her the dress again and the bag from my mother, and of course the beautiful watch now strapped to my wrist. It hadn't been easy for me to take it from its box, but if I'm not going to wear it tonight, then when? And I know that Lauren would want me to wear it.

But it isn't Lauren. It's Will's little MX5, a different shade of red from Lauren's car and lower to the ground. I'm suddenly on my feet, my heart pumping. I watch him get out of the car and walk the short path to the house. I don't want him in our house again. I don't want him to see me waiting here, all dressed up. It embarrasses me. I don't know why. But the doorbell rings and suddenly he's here.

My mother remembers Will, of course. "So good to see you! Do come in!" she says.

I want to run away. It would be possible to slip through the window and get into my own car, but we've got three locks on these windows and, anyway, I can hear my mother talking to him now. I peek out of my room and there she is, smiling broadly and holding his arm. He's being super polite, attentive, and is somewhat dashing in his dark blazer. Of course, I hate him for all that.

"Kira, there's someone here for you!" my mother sings, escorting him into the living room.

It's a room I grew up in and love, a place I feel at home, however battered the furniture, however old the carpets. I can imagine Will having some hateful remark to make about it later.

An ache erupts at my temples as I enter the living room. This is so awkward. Will stands with his feet slightly apart, his hands clasped in front of him. He takes in the sight of my dress and bag and efforts with hair and makeup. His face is controlled: a fixed smile, nothing you can read.

"Let's go," I say, heading for the front door.

My mother catches my hand. "Wait! Would you both mind if I got one quick picture?" she asks sweetly.

I feel a greater humiliation, every part of me wanting to scream *No!*

"I don't see why not," Will says. His smile is pinched and he rubs his fingers together impatiently, but he stands like a soldier, dutifully waiting as my mother retrieves the camera.

It isn't until we are outside, taking the path to Will's car, that I figure out why my mother is so happy, why the evening means so much to her. She thinks the sudden appearance of a beautiful dress and all this effort is because I'm going to the senior prom.

Even worse, she imagines that Will is my date. Can't she see he's too old and too much of a jerk to be anyone's prom date?

Will politely opens the car door for me, and I drop into the bucket seat as gracefully as is possible given the dress and long legs and the fact that the car is so small it's like getting into a roller-coaster car. I look back at my mother, framed in the doorway in her housedress, her floral scarf, a Kleenex clenched in one fist as she waves with the other hand. She blows me a kiss.

"You didn't have to come inside to get me," I say to Will.

"Shall I park at the curb and shout out the window next time?"

"*What* next time?"

He shakes his head. "You really are a most difficult creature," he says. "I was being polite. What was all that picture-taking about, anyway? I thought for a moment she was going to insist on videoing us."

"I have no idea," I say. But, of course, I do know. So would Will if he understood the excitement (bordering on hysteria) that a senior prom brings, with all its promposals and pageantry.

"Are you all dressed up because your boyfriend is going to be there?" he says.

"I'm dressed up because it's a nice place," I growl. I notice that Will wears a tie and a pair of cuff links, simple silver knots that grace his sleeves. "And he's not my boyfriend. He's like that with everyone."

We pull up to a stoplight and Will gives me a look. "I can assure you that he is *not* like that with everyone," he says.

"It's his job to be nice."

"If you imagine he takes every new recruit under his wing, tells them his secrets, and teaches them how to play chess, you are very much mistaken, my girl."

And that's when I realize he's talking about Dmitry. "*Dmitry?*" I say, before I can stop myself.

"Who did you think I was talking about? Oh, I *see*," Will says knowingly. He pulls forward onto the entrance to the highway. "You thought I was talking about young Rik."

"No, I didn't!"

"That's exactly what you thought," he teases.

I wish he'd shut up. Also that I could get out of the car. And why am I *in* his car, anyway? Rik said he'd send an Uber, not send Will.

"I think Dmitry is the better man," says Will. "Not that you're asking my opinion."

A few miles pass in silence, and then he says, "I'm sorry." He's putting on the nice act again. "And I'm sorry about how I've treated you in the past. I've been trying to put things right. Or haven't you noticed?"

Yes, I've noticed, but I say, "Just tell me what you want." Because I'm sure it's something. "And explain to me why *you* arrived instead of the car that Rik had arranged."

He sighs. "Because I thought it would be more pleasant to ride together. Far more personable and, as the venue is thirty miles away, a lot less costly to Mellin."

"Since when do you think about the cost of anything?" I say.

Will makes a little *tsk*-ing sound. "I don't think about cost. I think about value," he says pompously. And then, as though he's tired of having to defend himself, he adds, "There isn't any value in your being ferried by a stranger up a highway. There is value in our talking about the post-death recovery project before our dinner. Don't you agree?"

"Not to me," I say. "I already know all about it."

"I'm talking about the *project*. We can't think about ourselves. You insist on seeing everything as a personal attack, Kira, have you noticed that? I think you might be depressed."

He's like a politician, angling one way, then another, saying anything that might further his campaign.

"You don't always notice the things people do for you, do you?" he continues. "Just tonight, for example. I might have spoiled what appeared to be a very special event to your mother. It seems she was quite moved to see her daughter all dressed up, being escorted to dinner. I might have refused the photographs or been much less friendly. Think about it, Kira, and you'll know I'm right."

My mother had been happy tonight. Even joyful. Seeing her in the doorway as we left in the car, so proud and loving and somehow, too, a bit nostalgic. Yes, Will had given her that. He'd stood for the photographs, grinning as though he was actually looking forward to spending the evening with me.

"Thank you," I say genuinely. Then, because it doesn't sound like quite enough, I add, "Will."

I look away from him, up at the sky where the sunset fills the horizon with orange light, the fog forming a bluish cast beneath it.

He reaches over and opens the glove compartment. "Do you see a pen and pad in there?" he says. "I wonder if you could write down the procedures you went through, step-by-step, in recovering those rats. I couldn't see exactly what was happening that morning, and I'm a bit fuzzy on the details."

"You want me to write it out for you?"

"If you don't mind—"

"What, *now*?"

He clears his throat. "I'd rather not look as though I'm totally clueless in front of Munn and Dmitry tonight."

So that's the reason he volunteered to drive me this evening. He wants me to tell him what I've done. He's correct that we're working together and that he's part of the little circle Munn has drawn of people who know about post-death recovery. I really ought to tell him. But as I take the pen from the glove compartment, I find myself hesitating.

"It was mostly Dmitry who figured it out. You should ask him," I say, putting down the pen. Dmitry and I have talked extensively about post-death recovery. I still insist it's his baby, not mine.

"Dmitry's protocol as it stands doesn't seem to work," Will says, fishing out a page of notepaper from his coat pocket, which he then drops onto my lap. It's Dmitry's original instructions, the ones I'd seen on his night table and modified in order to save Cornelius. I can't imagine why Will has them. "I tested it today and nothing happened," he says.

I'm holding Dmitry's original sheet of instructions in my hand. "You tested *this*?" I say, appalled. "On live creatures?"

"Just some rats."

"*April's* rats?" I feel an ache inside. "Does she know?"

"She was in the dining room showing off her holiday photos. She didn't even miss them."

She didn't even miss them? I don't dare ask which rats, and it wouldn't matter if I did. Will wouldn't remember what color they were or what cage he'd taken them from. "Why did you do that?" I say. "I mean—"

"I wanted to see for myself."

I feel a rush of anger. It's all I can do to stay still in my seat. If he weren't driving, I might even have hit him. "But you *had* seen!" I yell.

"I repeated the experiment," Will says. "A perfectly normal thing to do in a laboratory."

"But you used the wrong information!"

"So I gather. Please stop shouting and give me the *right* information." When I don't move, he adds, "What's the matter? Don't tell me you've forgotten the protocol. That *would* make for an awkward dinner!" He tosses out a little laugh.

"How many rats?"

"Oh, only three or four. I don't know. Maybe a half dozen. Why? What's the difference?"

I want to call April right away, both to tell her how sorry I am and to explain that Will had acted on his own accord. But she'll be at Mellin now, and Mellin blocks all calls outside their secure system.

God, I hope Will didn't leave the bodies for her to dispose of.

We pass San Mateo in the fast lane, following signs for San Francisco. I write on the notepad furiously, filling line after line with information about what I did to save the rats. But instead of the real protocol, I just make stuff up. *Three drops of India ink, half a mil of jelly beans . . .*

"You know, this ability to bring back an organism after it has been declared dead may be the most important discovery you make in your lifetime," Will says. His voice is deep and clear, devoid of any regret. He's already forgotten about the rats. "It can be difficult to navigate a career in which the most significant contribution you make happens in your twenties."

I continue the fake instructions, adding a whole set of symbols drawn from my imagination that mean nothing.

"I'm not in my twenties," I say, then write, *Add two molecules . . .*

"It's easy to be taken advantage of when you're so young."

We pass through the city, heading north, gaining elevation as the MX5 rumbles forward. He keeps chatting. I keep writing nonsense.

"I haven't told you yet what a lovely dress you're wearing," he says.

Equipment required: cauldron, pickle juice, ginseng, paper pulp, three hairs from your left forearm . . .

"I know you're only humoring Dmitry when you say it was he who developed the protocol. It was you who figured it all out, wasn't it?"

. . . three microns of beetle dung, a milligram of wasp venom . . .

"This being able to read papers very quickly and synthesize the information. It's a useful gift you have, isn't it?"

I roll my eyes. "I can read, yes. Shall I write that down, too?"

He ignores the sarcasm. "Not even Dmitry can deal with such large data sets in his head. It's most extraordinary."

I write down, *Find Dmitry and ask him how he understands this stuff because you certainly never will. . . .*

"And he's neglectful in some ways," Will says. "Sloppy. Or do you think he cultivates that look and the whole sleep-at-the-lab thing to lend him more intrigue?"

I look at Will with his beautifully cut jacket, his silk tie, his recently styled hair. A handsome man, his profile is classic, his skin tanned. By contrast, Dmitry's clothes never fit well. His jeans are too long, his shirts too boxy. He's short and has enormous shoulders that seem too wide for his body. Plus he needs to shave twice a day if he doesn't want a blue cast of stubble over his face. But I like him, everything about him, how his hair stands away from his head at the sides, how his shirts always come untucked. I can't allow Will to insult him.

"I think Dmitry is a genius," I say.

"Oh yes," Will sneers. "We're *all* geniuses, aren't we?"

How is it that he makes anything I say sound absurd and juvenile?

"Geniuses bring into focus what the rest of us fail to see," I tell him. "And that's Dmitry through and through."

Will shrugs. "Even so, it wouldn't kill him to iron a shirt."

I swear the man is like Teflon. I hand him the page of "instructions" for post-death recovery and watch him fold it into the pocket of his jacket without reading it.

At last we reach the restaurant's pebble driveway. A valet steps forward and opens the door for me. I climb out of the car, which isn't easy in a long dress. Then I look up at the building, set high up on the cliffs. It is more beautiful even than the pictures on the website. I feel the chill from the sea air, smell the salt in the wind. Will motions for me to lead the way.

"You're awfully tall, aren't you?" he says. In my heels, I am as tall as he is.

"Not really," I say, because I can't stand to agree with him.

We pass through the giant doors of the restaurant and into its bright interior. As Rik promised, it's spectacular, with walls of glass overlooking the water and an enormous aquarium worthy of a public space of its own. I can smell grilled salmon, lemon, warm butter. Huge pots of fresh herbs sprout from corners: mint, parsley, rosemary.

We are shown to a table in the corner by one of the glass walls. I see Dmitry first, then Rik catches sight of us and gestures to Munn. All three rise as we reach the table. Munn says, "Kira," as though my name itself is good news. Dmitry tells me I look like a princess, which embarrasses me so much I begin to stammer, barely able to say hello properly to Rik, who beams a smile at me.

They've saved me the seat with the best view. I'm between Rik and Will, looking out over the water. Low tide. I can see Seal Rocks and the colors of sunset as daylight dwindles. Munn tells us about a friend who got it in her head to swim out to the small islands but stopped when she saw shark fins.

"She liked swimming in the sea. That was nothing to her; she'd swum the English Channel. But sharks are sharks," he says.

A bucket of champagne arrives. I can't drink it—they've forgotten I'm under twenty-one—and I cringe as they realize this. Rik says it doesn't matter. He's not twenty-one either, of course. In fact, I'm not sure that Dmitry is, but that doesn't stop him from drinking.

"I'm Russian," he says, by way of explanation.

Meanwhile, Rik disappears for a moment and then reappears with a small bottle of ginger ale and pours it for me like a good waiter. I hold up the flute and toast along with the others. "To more discovery," Munn says as we raise our glasses.

"Why were you late?" Dmitry asks me gently. Then to Will, "I was worried."

"She wasn't late," Will says.

"She was. I was waiting!"

"Holding your breath, Dmitry?"

"*Will*," I say, shooting him a look. He shrugs.

His next remark is about the view and how, whatever else, you can't fault the physical beauty of America.

"You've not seen Idaho," says Rik. "I drove across it once. One straight line, like a zipper that separates potato fields."

"I've never been to the Rockies," says Dmitry. To me he says, "I miss snow. We should go to Idaho for a vacation."

Munn clears his throat. "There are cities in which underground laboratories span whole city blocks," he tells us.

"Disneyland for scientists," Dmitry says. To me he says, "We really should go."

Munn explains more about these laboratories, unknown to most of the residents who live above them. Meanwhile, I try to figure out the menu. What's a *crostata*? Is *cappelletti* another word for pasta?

I'm not the only one. Dmitry reads the menu with his brow furrowed as though it's a difficult mathematical equation. He rarely leaves the laboratory, which means he doesn't really go to restaurants.

Meanwhile, Will glances at the menu as though it's a stage prop and not anything he actually has to read, then puts it aside.

"I find the notion of all these secret laboratories fascinating," he says quietly to Munn, as though it is only he and Munn at the table.

When it comes to ordering, I stumble through my choices. By contrast, without referring to the menu at all, Will says casually, "I'll have the lobster salad and then the lamb."

Munn orders raw oysters for the table and they arrive in a wreath of shells and lemon, looking dangerous and alluring. I have no idea how to eat one. Rik shows me how to loosen the oyster in its shell.

"Don't use too much garnish. The garnish will kill it," says Munn.

"You mean they're still *alive*?" I say.

Will laughs. "We don't ask that question."

"He meant kill the flavor," Rik explains.

"But it *is* alive?"

"Oysters have no brain, just two masses of ganglia around their body," says Dmitry. "Does that help?"

Rik holds up a glistening oyster. "Try it just for the experience. I'll have one at the same time."

He makes it sound so inviting.

"I think you have to watch out for that guy," Dmitry says, pointing his fork at Rik.

I bring the oyster to my lips as Rik does the same with his own. "Are you ready?" he says.

"I think so."

"Close your eyes."

"Why does she have to close her eyes?" Will scoffs, as though everyone is making too big a show of a simple appetizer. But he can't ruin it. We're having too much fun. I'm in the most glamorous restaurant in the world, and Rik has prepared me the perfect oyster.

"Ready?" he says quietly.

I close my eyes and slurp the oyster off its shell. It tastes like the sea, like salt and lemon, like fresh air and wet sand. When I open my eyes again Rik is looking at me, his face full of anticipation.

"That was good," I say.

Another bottle arrives. I cover my glass with my hand.

In the end, I have a few sips anyway. Munn tells of his meetings in Washington. The conversation flows, everyone sharing ideas, coming up with protocols. I listen as though to a symphony. I don't hate Will quite as much, or maybe I'm just too busy admiring Munn. Even with his white hair he's youthful, forward-thinking, progressive, and as smart as a whip. I can't believe I'm in his company.

"You know, I didn't believe you at first," he says to me now. "I thought, what is this girl telling me, that she's brought a rat back to life? Is she experiencing some kind of psychotic break? Do I call a doctor?"

Dmitry lifts his glass to me. "I have the best research partner."

"She *is* clever," says Will. "More importantly, she can't drink, so she's very convenient as a designated driver." He raises his wineglass. To me he says, "I'm thinking of letting you drive my car later."

"I always get a driver," says Dmitry, nodding toward one end of the room. "Being an enemy of Russia has its rewards."

I look over in the direction Dmitry indicated and see a man quietly seated at the bar, watching. Dmitry's security guard.

Munn explains that not only will we receive funding for our work on post-death recovery, but a sizable grant for more work on renal disease and regenerative medicine. "I stressed that post-death recovery puts into jeopardy hundreds of thousands of people on the transplant lists here and abroad. Somehow I talked them into giving us enough money to work on the two projects in tandem. Naturally, they wanted to hand the neuro work over to a larger organization, but for now, we'll be spearheading the research at Mellin."

"Marvelous," says Will. "Do we need another toast?"

More champagne, then the waiter comes along with dessert menus and everyone talks about how they can't possibly eat another bite.

"But you'll have something, won't you, Kira?" says Munn.

The dinner menu may have confused me, but the dessert menu does not. "I'm having the chocolate cake. *Obviously*," I say.

"Excellent," says Munn. The waiter disappears with our order.

"Rik, trade seats with me. I'm sitting next to Kira so I can sneak forkfuls," says Dmitry.

"I doubt there's any shortage of cake," says Will. "Get your own."

"I'm on a diet," says Dmitry. "I am only allowed to *steal* cake."

Munn says, "Rik, would you ask the waiter to bring an extra chocolate cake to the table?" He looks at Will, then at Dmitry, and adds, "For whoever might want it."

I think Munn is only joking, but Rik excuses himself and gets up from the table, then walks toward the back of the restaurant.

"I'm taking his seat," says Dmitry, coming around to my side of the table.

"Of course you are," says Will, rolling his eyes.

"Well, I'm going to the ladies' room," I say. "If the waiter comes, can someone order me a coffee, too?"

I step across the restaurant floor, again stunned by the beauty of the wide restaurant. Through the windows and the skylights in the ceiling I see the sky is now dark, pinpricked with stars. I move past the pots of herbs with their delicious scent and down a hall to the ladies' room. Leaning against the heavy door, I enter a space full of soft music and fragrances of sweet orange and lavender.

In the mirror I see that my hair is still surviving. It flows in a soft veil of spirals without frizz. My skin is clear, unmarked by the dark circles that are so often present. It feels as though somehow I've grown into the dress and the lovely, heartbreaking gift of Lauren's watch. And I feel like a true part of Mellin now, no longer the awkward intern who Will resented in his space. For the first time I belong somewhere. I'm not an object of ridicule at school. Or a gift wrapper who can't even tape down the ends of the paper correctly. I'm a valued researcher, and I owe it all to Dmitry. He believed in me from the start. Scared me a little, too. *Threats have been spurring on science for as long as there has been war*, he'd said that first night.

Well, he is right. When Munn says he's been to Washington for meetings, he means to the Department of Defense. Work on post-death recovery will be classified. If I'd wanted to be taken seriously as a scientist, I've certainly been granted my wish.

On my way back to the table I feel someone touch my arm. I turn and it's Rik, his tie looser than it had started out tonight, his shirt less crisp.

"Are you stalking the ladies' room?" I tease. He's standing only inches from me, looking right into my eyes.

"I was hoping I'd find you," he says.

"Has Will done something awful to Dmitry?"

"No," he laughs. "Believe me, Will can't do anything to upset Dmitry. Dmitry may seem comic, but he's tough as nails. Nothing bothers him."

"Like you," I say.

"Me?"

"You always look so in control."

My remark surprises him. "I'm not so sure," he says. Then, "I know we're here for a work-related event, but my whole life is work, and . . . well, I've enjoyed this."

Suddenly, I can barely look at him. "Me too," I say.

He looks from my face down the length of me and I feel my cheeks flush.

"I remember the first time I saw you in that dress," he says. "We danced on the ship."

It's almost too much to be reminded. I nod.

"Things are changing so fast," he says, and I sense a hint of longing in his voice. "You're a star. You don't know it yet, but you'll see. Forget high school and whatever happened there. You're on to great things."

I look at him. I realize that he isn't just saying I'm nice or helpful. He means I am going somewhere. I think of what my mother said about the Great Downhill. The Great Downhill isn't going to happen to me.

"I don't know what to say," I tell him. "I don't feel like a star."

He shakes his head slowly, as though he cannot understand why this should be the case.

"Do you like the restaurant? Maybe you'd let me take you again on your birthday," he says. He sounds most unlike the Rik I am used to, who is always confident, organized, unflappable. He almost sounds shy. "You can try another oyster," he adds.

It's such a simple request on the face of it, just dinner. But it's not just dinner. He's asking me on a date for real this time. And not just any date. My birthday is months away. I'll be eighteen.

"You plan ahead," I say.

He nods. Then he leans toward me, his face inches from mine. There's time for me to move away if I don't want the kiss. But I don't move. And now I feel his hands on my shoulders, his lips on my cheek. His kiss is chaste in every way and loaded in every way. The moment is innocent, yet not.

And then it is over.

"This never happened," he whispers.

I realize how long I've been waiting for that kiss. Since the time we locked eyes in the stone pool at the bottom of the Grand Hôtel. Since sharing coffee in the warm café on a chilly winter's morning in Stockholm. Since he took me under his wing as the boys from school harassed me. All that time.

I watch as he retreats. One step, another. Part of me wants to tell him that of course I'll have dinner with him. That we don't have to wait until my birthday. But I have another feeling, too. One that surprises me.

I don't want Dmitry to know that Rik has asked me out. Even less that he kissed me, however innocently. When I think about an event like my birthday, I want to share it with Dmitry. I realize that there could be no real celebration without him. I want to buy a giant ice-cream cake and watch him freak out over how delicious it is. I want him to make jokes and help me blow out the candles. I want to introduce him to my mother, to Lauren. There's a bond between us, one I can't describe. And it can't be rivaled, not even by Rik.

I know this is ridiculous. Dmitry and I are just friends. But these are my feelings. And they're real even if I don't admit them to anyone but myself.

"I'll see you at the table," Rik says. And then he dissolves back into his role as Munn's assistant, signaling the attention of a passing waiter and asking for the extra chocolate cake, just as Munn had instructed.

19

THE REST OF the evening passes as in a dream. I can only think about that kiss, about Rik, who glances at me every so often as Dmitry jokes about the wonders of chocolate cake. And about Dmitry, who makes me laugh and feeds me crumbs and speaks to me in Russian even though I don't understand a word, because it cracks me up when he does this.

I don't notice when Munn takes the check, or when Will sinks deeper into the wine. Coffee comes and goes, then suddenly we're out in the night air.

Will puts his hand on my arm and gives me his keys. "How about you drive?" he says, his words slurring ever so slightly.

Munn nods his approval. "I think that's a good idea," he says, before disappearing into the car that has been hired for Dmitry.

Stuck with Will, who is too drunk to drive or even help navigate, I can no longer let my thoughts linger on that kiss with Rik or how to work out my feelings about Dmitry. Instead, I pay close attention to the GPS on my phone, navigating my way to the highway. Luckily, the night is clear, the traffic thin.

"That was a very good evening," Will says. "Amusing company although . . ." He sighs heavily. "There really aren't enough women in science."

He smells of sour wine and aftershave and is sprawled out, taking up as much room as possible in the small front of the car. He removes his tie and stuffs it into his jacket pocket, then undoes the first three buttons of his shirt. I can see his pale chest, his flushed cheeks. He'll have a hell of a headache in the morning.

"I don't know your address," I say.

"Oh yeah, we'll need that. You know what else we need? Coffee." He sits straighter in his seat, pointing ahead at a big sign ahead advertising doughnuts. "Pull in over there. Do you see the sign with the . . . what is that painted on the sign anyway?"

"A chocolate doughnut," I say. "No, I don't see it."

"Oh, come on, be a sport. It's a drive-through. Anyway, I need the loo."

He gets his way. Of course. When he comes back with his coffee, I notice he's swaying.

"Why didn't you want one?" he asks. He takes a sip through the plastic lid on the cup, then makes a face and blows across the rim. "Afraid to spill it on your dress?"

"Yes," I answer truthfully.

"Pretty dress," he says. "Nice watch, too. Does it belong to you?"

"Please shut up."

"I was only joking."

"No, you weren't."

He sighs. "You looked lovely tonight. No, I mean it. You are a lovely young woman. And you're going to be very successful. There's no stopping that," he says, almost as though he wishes otherwise.

He takes a few more sips of coffee, looking out into the night, then adds, "Munn is being very foolish with post-death recovery. He's letting the government be in charge of it all. But if he were serious about it he'd do it through a private company. The discovery process would be halved, maybe quartered. Instead, he wants *us* to do it all. But we're not big enough. You need giant organizations for this sort of thing. And you need them managed properly. Not by these . . . strange gifted children he hires. Don't you agree?"

I check the GPS to see how much longer I have to endure him.

"Well?" he says.

"I don't know how it all works," I say, "but I do know we have a contract with the government. Even if Munn wanted to work with a private company, he couldn't."

"That's where you're wrong. There are *no* contracts for work on post-death recovery. We hadn't set up a study on it yet!" He gets excited now, turning in his seat to face me. "There was never even a discussion about post-death recovery—no paperwork, no plan. You were in a laboratory late one night and got adventurous. It wasn't like you were operating under anyone's instructions. Post-death recovery is *your* intellectual property, not that of the Mellin Institute."

"Well, then, I bequeath it to Mellin," I say.

He chucks himself against the back of the seat. "Throwing away money!" he declares.

"What am I going to do, set up a lab in my bedroom?"

"Sell it," he says, his voice suddenly gruff.

I realize that Will is serious. Yes, he might have had too much to drink, but he's clearly given this a lot of thought. I concentrate on the road, hoping the conversation will drift to another subject or peter out entirely. But he continues.

"Munn wants to protect the world from post-death recovery because he fears some sort of social chaos, people demanding their long-dead relatives to be brought back to life or some such. That's all nonsense. Do you know how many people have heart attacks in America? One every forty-four seconds. And don't forget stroke victims, babies born with umbilical cords around their necks, the list is endless. We could help all these people, but Munn is in our way."

"We *work* for Munn," I remind him.

"That problem," he says, "is easily solved."

I wish he'd shut up. Just sitting in the car listening to him makes me feel like I'm betraying Dmitry and Munn.

"Kira, you're a clever girl. But you're young. You think it's thrilling to be at Mellin. I agree it *is* far more innovative than anywhere else. But Mellin isn't a moneymaker. You may not be worried about money now, but you will be eventually. And eventually may be too late for you. You've hit upon this opportunity early in your life. You either make something of it now or live with the regret."

I try not to listen. I've got other things on my mind anyway. I have to sort out my feelings about Rik. He's so nice and so good-looking. Why wouldn't I want to have dinner with him on my birthday? I mean, I do want that, right?

"Perhaps you aren't aware of how much money we are talking about," Will says. When that doesn't provoke me, he adds, "Don't you want things? If not for you, then for your mother? You could live somewhere nice instead of that—"

"*Stop!*" I say. A guy like Will can't even imagine what it means to "want things." I'm only too aware of the debts my mother has. And how much medical care costs.

"What I mean is that you could make your mother's life easier. Don't tell me you're not interested."

For years, all I've thought about is how to provide for my mother. I've dreamed of what it might be like not to live in debt. But Will is wrong to imagine that post-death recovery is my intellectual property. Everything I learned at Mellin made it possible to recover those rats. If he thinks I'm going behind Munn's and Dmitry's backs when I owe them everything, he's crazy.

"I think Dr. Munn will make sure we have enough," I say finally.

Will grunts as though it causes him actual pain to hear this. "Munn doesn't give a toss about you," he says. "Look at him, taking us out to a fancy restaurant like he's the king. Buying you off with chocolate cake. You don't seem to understand, *you* were the one who did all the work."

I can't bear for him to sully the evening. I loved the restaurant, loved the views and food and company. I can picture Dmitry, sitting beside me with his cake fork. The unexpected kiss from Rik. But mostly I remember feeling as though I belonged. I've never felt like that before. The only thing that could have made it better would have been if Lauren had been there. I glance at her beautiful watch on my wrist.

Will shifts in his seat. "I don't think you understand just how lucrative this discovery of yours is. I've been talking to some people. Very quietly, of course. These are very important people, Kira, and they'd like to meet with you," he says.

"*What* people?" I say, appalled.

"You should be thanking me."

"Will, *what* people?" I say fiercely. For the first time in ages I think about the red-haired man, about how he seemed to know everything about me, the pressure to meet his boss. "We're not supposed to talk to *anyone*—"

"We're not supposed to do a lot of things," he says. "Anyway, since when do you follow rules? I seem to remember you being very happy to pretend you were qualified for the SFOF award."

I'm furious now. "Who did you talk to, Will? Because I swear, if he's the guy who stalked me at SFOF—"

"Pipe down," he says. "God, you're so dramatic."

"Did the guy have red hair?"

"I don't know," Will says, then belches. "Why does it matter?"

I'm fuming, and actually quite scared about who he's let know about post-death recovery. We reach his road and the small complex of condominiums where he rents.

"You're an idiot," I tell him.

"That's my space," he says, pointing.

I pull into a bay and take the car out of gear. My phone sounds with a text, but Will grabs it before I can.

"Oh *look*," he says. "Rik is wishing you a good night. Isn't that nice? I think that's very nice."

"Give me my phone," I say, my jaw clenched, my hand reaching.

"I'm surprised there isn't a text from Dmitry. He's moony over you. I speak too soon!" he says. "There's one from him as well!"

"I remind him of his *sister*."

Will guffaws. "Oh, don't be so stupid. He's a man, if you hadn't noticed. And I think you almost prefer him to Rik."

"Give me back my *phone*!"

He holds the phone next to his shoulder, away from me, then gives up and tosses it on the dashboard. "You do prefer him, don't you?" he says.

"Please, Will. I'd like to go *home*."

"Fine, go home. I'd let you take my car, but I need it in the morning. We'll get you an Uber." He reaches across and pulls the keys out of the ignition, then gets out of the car. Stumbling forward, he says, "Come on! Let's not wake the neighbors."

I watch through the windshield as Will finds his house key on the key ring. He glances toward me impatiently, looking young and cocky and very drunk. Then a noise or movement catches his attention and he scans the cluster of flowering trees along a low wall. A worried expression crosses his brow. Something is wrong. I'm about to get out of the car when I see two men appear from the shadows, one on either side of Will. He doesn't even have time to call out before his body hits the ground. Suddenly, there he is, sprawled out, the soles of his shoes catching the moonlight as he lies on the sidewalk. And now I'm losing all control, trying to lock the doors with hands that no longer seem to work, trying to call out with a voice that no longer makes a sound. I look for the keys, but they're not in the ignition. Of course not. Will took them. The two men vanish as quickly as they appeared, and all I can think is that I need to call an ambulance, call an ambulance *now*!

My phone is in my hands, my fingers skidding across the numbers when the door flies open and I'm yanked from the car. A weight bears down on me. I can't stand properly. Someone pushes my head. A jolt of pain hits high in the muscle of my right arm. I can't remember falling to the pavement or how I land or what happens after that. I know I can't move. Can't breathe. Things are happening around me, the men crowding in. I have one thought: that I won't be home tonight and that my mother will worry. And then it's as though I've fallen through a rabbit hole into another world.

PART THREE

DRAGONFLY

Whoever leads in artificial intelligence
will rule the world.
—VLADIMIR PUTIN

20

I'M LYING ON a shallow mattress, a pine ceiling inches from my face, a noise roaring through my head. I shift slowly onto my side, feeling a hammering in my temple. I can make out a patch of carpet and a tiny closet without a door. A square of light comes into focus. It's a window that is for some reason below me. Through it I see a plain of grass passing under an evening sun. Even this much light is too much. I wince and look away.

I've never been in a sleeping compartment of a train before, but I recognize it, maybe from the movies.

And then, bizarrely, I hear Will's voice below. "I thought you were dead," he says. I realize now we're in bunks, him on the bottom. The springs of the mattress squeak as he stands to look at me. His hair is uncombed. His normally clean-shaven cheeks show a day's growth of golden stubble.

"What happened?" I croak. The sound of the train is like a drill in my temple.

"I'm not sure. I keep trying to get the door open. They've locked us in here."

"Who is 'they'?" But he doesn't answer. It's hard to talk. My lips are stuck together and my throat feels like sandpaper. "Do you have any water?" I say.

"I wish I could take it off its hinges. The door, I mean. Do you know there's not so much as a penny in this room I could use to turn a screw? And no water, either. Just cans. Here," he says, and hands me a lukewarm can of 7Up.

I try sitting, but I feel nauseated. "I might throw up," I say.

Suddenly, he launches into action, hooking one arm under my knees and another around my shoulders, dragging me off the mattress, the blanket flying. It's all too fast. I'm dizzy. But he gets me to the bathroom just in time. It's humiliating to retch like this in front of him, but I have no choice.

"Sorry to pull you about like that," he says when I'm finished. "But if you'd been sick on the carpet we'd have to live with it for God knows how long."

I reach above me and close the lid of the toilet, then flush. I feel better, though moving is a terrible effort. I realize I'm in bare feet and the dress from last night.

"What's going on?" I ask.

Will sighs. "I don't want to say."

But I think I know what's going on.

Kidnapping doesn't even sound like a real thing. It sounds like what happens somewhere else, to other people. But every thought in my head points to it.

"That Mellin researcher with the gambling debts. He's not on an island drinking margaritas, is he?" I say somberly.

Will shakes his head.

"But why on earth would anyone *want* us?"

He shrugs. "You think *I* know? I'm going crazy in here. We've got cheese sandwiches—that's it for food. Cans of fizzy drinks but no water. And you can't even open a window."

I rise slowly from the floor, leaning over the small sink and rinsing my mouth with the water from the tap. "Can we drink this?" I ask, pointing.

"I wouldn't."

I wash my hands, my face, letting the water run over my dry lips. It's hard to resist the urge to drink it. Above the sink, where there may have been a mirror at one time, is a bare spot on the wall. No personal items, not a comb or a toothbrush.

Will sits on the lower bunk, leaning forward, his head in his hands. I see the band of paler skin where his watch once was. My own hand flies to my wrist and I feel a spear of loss as I realize that the watch Lauren gave me is also gone.

I move slowly along the walls, touching them with outstretched fingers, feeling for a weakness. The door is fastened by two bolts, locked from the outside. I can see where the screws had almost come through from the other side, two sharp lumps. Whoever put us in here meant business.

"I keep looking outside trying to figure out where the hell we are," Will says. He stares out the window as we pass a field of wildflowers picked out by a low sun. "I can't even tell if that's sunrise or sunset. It's like an endless blue cast."

There's a socket by the bunks, a plastic surround with two

small holes made for round prongs, not the flat pins of American electrical plugs. I look for more clues and find a sticker with a pictograph that shows cigarette smoking is not allowed. At the bottom of the sticker is tiny writing. I've seen the same alphabet across Dmitry's chess books. The Cyrillic alphabet.

I turn to Will. "It's Russia," I say. "We're on a Russian train."

"I don't believe it," he says, though I notice him regarding the window curtains with fresh interest. With their tassels and unusual design, they have a distinctly Eastern feel.

"How long have you been watching that sunset?" I say.

If you go far enough north the sun never entirely disappears at the end of the day. I wait as Will figures out what I'm suggesting. "It could be Scandinavia," he says finally. "They get white nights, too."

"Maybe. But look at the lettering here." I point at the sticker.

He squints down to where I'm pointing.

"Can't you be wrong?" he says, his voice rising. "Just once in your life, can't you *please* be wrong?" He swipes his hair out of his eyes, balls his hands into fists, and springs for the door, pounding it.

Nobody comes. It's as though we're traveling on a ghost train, running along tracks without anyone else aboard. If I think about it too much, I could convince myself we'll eventually jump the tracks and crash.

After some time, we pass a body of water so large it might be an ocean.

"Russia is landlocked," Will says. "So you're wrong after all."

"Not to the north, it isn't."

"Oh," he laughs dryly. "So you think that's the Arctic Ocean, do you?"

"I think it's Lake Baikal." Lake Baikal is the largest single source of fresh water on earth. They must have flown us west from San Francisco. "I bet we're heading farther west across land, toward Moscow or St. Petersburg."

"And you know this *how*?"

It was Lauren who told me of Lake Baikal. Imagine what she'd think if she knew I was staring out the window at it now. "I have a friend who loves birds. If you go to Lake Baikal at the right time of year, you can see up to two hundred species in a week."

"Oh, jolly good. I'll book a holiday," he says, and flops onto the bunk, his arm over his eyes. Every once in a while he says "dammit," then goes silent again.

The night carries on, the sky dimming. Blue light appears in the room, not from lamps but from spindly fluorescent tubes that glow at the edges of the ceiling. They give our skin a ghostly hue like we're already dead. I'm terrified and curious in turns. Sometimes I stare out the window, unseeing. Other times, I notice the landscape. When I spot a mass of legs and fur moving like a cloud through the blue-gray darkness, I say, "Will, look! A whole herd of deer!"

But he remains in the bunk, unmoving.

"I believe you," he says.

There's nothing to do. Not just now, but for hours to come, and hours after that. We don't know what time it is. We don't know what day it is. We sit on bench seats by the window, our heads propped up on our elbows. I knead the spot on my arm where they injected me in the parking lot outside Will's apartment, a hard lump that throbs beneath my fingers.

Will says, "I used to like Russian history. We did it in school. Do you want to hear about Napoleon's failed invasion?"

"When did it happen?"

"1812."

"Then no."

"What about Ivan the Terrible?"

"I think the name sums it up."

"Then what *do* you want to do?"

"Go dancing," I say, and he bursts out laughing.

But then we get a little hope. We see lights in the distance, way out behind a hillside. The lights grow brighter, larger. And now, like a miracle, buildings come into view, so tiny they might be from a doll's house. But they are buildings nonetheless.

Will grabs me with excitement, saying, "We need a way of drawing attention!"

The window is locked shut and its thick glass would not be easy to break, even if we had something heavy to bash it with, which we don't. Will tries kicking it out, but that doesn't work for a number of reasons, one of which is that they've taken our shoes. There's nothing to write on and nothing to write with. If we had a bar of soap we could scrawl on the window with that. But the bathroom dispenser's thin foam won't form letters.

But then we remember the cheese sandwiches. Will tears through the packaging and comes up with a wedge of yellow cheese.

We smear the word *SOS* across the glass. If we pound the window hard enough at the station we might attract the attention of travelers on the platform outside, and maybe, by some miracle, someone will tell the police that there are people trapped in here.

A few minutes later, the train rumbles toward the brightly lit station with big, Russian lettering above a wooden facade. It slows and slows as we pound the glass. But instead of stopping it continues, passing gently through the station along an outer track until, at last, the station is left behind.

We are left standing at the window, our palms against the glass, as the buildings grow smaller and the city light fades. Once again, we are returned to the darkness of the rural countryside and the enormous, starry sky. I feel even worse for having hoped, emptied out, like someone has carved into me and taken out all the stuffing. My eyes fill with tears of anger and frustration. I want to lash out, but there's nothing to hit.

"There'll be another one," Will says.

The train climbs, then dips, clacking along the tracks. I step up to what is now my bunk, more weary than tired, and pull the blanket over the thin fabric of my dress. I wish I had a phone, a Tylenol, an escape plan.

"What city was that, do you think?" Will asks.

"I don't know. Maybe the Siberian capital."

"I doubt it. Maybe it's Novosibirsk," he says. "I only know that because it was a major supply source for the Red Army during the war. My father and all my uncles were in the British Army. My family has an apparently endless interest in military trivia."

"I thought your father was a scientist."

"He is. But my grandfather acted as though the Second World War ended last Tuesday. He's dead now, of course."

I shift in the bunk. I think of my mother back in our little house in California. I remember how she'd looked as Will and I set off for the restaurant, her face soft and sad and full of longing. I wish I could run back home now, hug her close, and tell her everything will be okay. All my life, my mother has done that for me. Told me it would be okay. And now it appears that for the first time this will not be the case.

I feel myself starting to cry, and I don't care about anything so trivial as whether Will hears me.

"Don't panic," Will says, his voice gentle.

But I can't help it. "That guy you talked to about post-death recovery, let me guess, he was Russian, wasn't he? With thinning red hair?"

"Sounds a bit like that," he says. "I haven't revealed a single detail of the procedure, if that is what you're asking."

But that's not what I'm asking.

The train is noisy and slow, clattering endlessly through the night. Occasionally I drift to sleep, but it never lasts long. Sometime in the early hours Will gets up and goes to the sink. He takes his shirt off and I can see his naked back, the long hollow between his back muscles. He washes his shirt in the sink, his head bent in concentration. He looks like a young man away on a vacation, traveling the trains from one side of Europe to another. When he turns, I see his broad shoulders, the hair that thickens across his chest. He returns to his bunk and I hear the sheets as he stretches out. The noises are reassuring. I try to imagine we are going on a trip together, just a trip.

In the morning, there's a brown paper bag inside the compartment, placed there as though by magic.

"Look," I say, waking Will.

The bag holds four packaged sandwiches, wedges of cheese, two apples, two packets of small cookies, and some unripe pears. It isn't much for a day's food, but the miracle is the water. Three liters of a brand called Berjomi, with a picture of snowcapped mountains on the bottles.

"How did they know when we were asleep?" I say.

"Or that we wanted water," Will says. He's still missing his shirt, and it feels a bit too intimate in this tiny compartment.

"There has to be a camera. Or at least a listening device," I say.

We search the cabin, every corner and ceiling tile and light, but come up with nothing. Through the window, I see the sun peeking through low clouds. It would be a nice day, if you could get outside.

Into the air Will calls, "Hey, can we have some vodka as well?"

"They might not know English."

"They know the word *vodka*."

The hours pass slowly. We gaze out the window at the countryside: green hills, woodlands, long stretches of grasslands studded with wildflowers. Whenever the train slows we think it is finally coming to a station, but then it rounds a bend, or climbs a hill, or slides noisily through a tunnel. We stop once about a half mile outside a station, and for a moment I think the journey is over. We hear some noise outside but can't tell what's happening.

"Perhaps they're picking up other prisoners," jokes Will.

"For someone who is grumpy in normal life, you've evolved into a remarkably cheerful captive," I say.

"Cheerfulness is a military value. My father taught me that. He's always best when there is a foot of snow on the ground, blocked roads, and a power outage. Meanwhile, someone has suffered a minor fracture. In such circumstances, he's a gem. Otherwise, he stalks the house like an angry spirit looking for something to rattle."

"That was you back at Mellin," I say. "I was almost afraid of you."

"Are you afraid of me now?"

I realize all of a sudden that I'm not. It seems there are two Wills. The bully back at Mellin and this one, in his bare feet and messed-up hair, his beard growing daily.

"Do you hate me?" he says.

I shake my head. I don't hate him, but I want to hate something right now and he's here in front of me.

"Well, I do," he says. "I hate me."

You'd think I'd stay terrified the whole time but, strangely, I don't. For minutes, then hours, I forget to worry. The train rumbles at a snail's pace as we play tic-tac-toe on the glass window.

"I'd do a lot for a steak right now," Will says.

The bag which we discover by the door every morning, is always full of the worst food imaginable. I take it now, empty the sandwiches (some kind of meat on a bed of cabbage), then tear the paper into something approximating squares.

"Look," I say. "Place mats."

"Let me know when you get to the finger bowls," Will says.

"Oh, come on," I say. "We have to do *something*."

We drink water from plastic bottles, eat with our hands. We arrange some cookies in a circle and play games with them. First dominoes, then checkers. That gets us through many hours until, at last, the sun begins to wane once more and the sky glows yellow and orange.

"It's beautiful," I say. "I've never appreciated sky so much."

"It looks like a Turner painting," Will says.

I have no idea who Turner is. A famous painter, I guess.

Will says, "I look outside and I just want to walk around, you know? I want to run up a hill. When I was a boy, I used to take long walks with school. Do you know what the Munros are? Mountains in Scotland. We were a bunch of schoolboys terribly underdressed for the weather. We slept in mildewed canvas tents. But we loved it."

I can imagine him on a long walk up a rainy Scottish mountain. He's vain and spoiled, but he's also practical and determined. He probably led the way.

"I wish I had my glasses so I could see properly," I say. No glasses, dirty hair, skin breaking out, and teeth I'd do anything to brush. I'm jealous that Will is now in a clean shirt while I'm in a dress that needs laundering. "I wonder if you could do me a favor. I wonder if you could—" I can barely bring myself to say it. "I need to wash my dress," I blurt out finally. "I've been wearing it for days. I smell."

"You'll find it difficult to change clothes in there," he says, gesturing toward the bathroom. "Not enough room. Why don't I step into the WC and you slip out of your dress and wrap yourself in a sheet like a toga?"

He smiles. I hadn't known he could be so nice. He really is like his father, needing a dire emergency to bring out his better side. "Then I'll swap with you," he continues. "And you can wash the dress in the sink."

It's a good plan. While he waits in the tiny bathroom I change into a makeshift toga. Then we trade places. Of course, the dress is supposed to be dry-cleaned, but I really have no choice. I rinse out the soap and hope it will be okay.

Later that night—it's impossible to know the time—I wake suddenly as though from a nightmare. I'm covered in sweat, every muscle tense, feeling as though at any moment I will be pulled from bed and pushed out into the cold night. I tell myself not to be silly, but stranger things have happened. I can still feel the place on my arm where they injected the drug. And I'm still captive on a train.

"Are you awake?" I say.

"Hmmm?" Will murmurs. I can imagine him on his bunk, his arm over his eyes. "Do you need something?" he says sleepily.

"Sorry. Go back to sleep."

"No, tell me. What's wrong?"

"I'm scared."

"Me too. But it will be okay," he whispers. "You'll see."

"Why do you think that?"

"Because you're special. You were born to do something big with your life, not to die in Russia on a clanking train."

"What should I do when I panic?"

"Are you panicking now?"

"Yes." I'm thinking of my mother, alone in the house. Not even Lauren around to help her. I'm thinking of the type of people who would kidnap a high school girl. All the things that are happening and that might happen.

Suddenly, I feel the whole of the bed frame almost lift from the floor with Will's shifting weight. And then he's here, his face near mine.

Very slowly he says, "We aren't important enough to kill."

"Are you sure?" I say.

He gives me the briefest of smiles, then touches my shoulder. I'm glad he's close and am grateful that he doesn't move, not for a long time, but stands in the dark with his hand on my shoulder, saying nothing.

It helps; I don't know why. Lately, I've begun thinking of him like a big brother, someone who teases me and scolds me but who also cares for me.

"You don't resent me anymore," I say.

"Shh," he says. "Forget all that."

Minutes pass. The night seems dark and endless and forever.

"Who is Turner?" I whisper.

"A famous English painter," he says, but he doesn't scoff the way he usually does, as though I'm an idiot for asking.

"Of course," I sigh.

"My father made us memorize British paintings, at least the most well known of them. When I looked out the window of the train today I thought immediately of Turner's painting *Rain, Steam, and Speed*. It's in the National Gallery in London. I'll show you one day."

"London," I repeat. It sounds as impossible as it is.

"We'll go to Knightsbridge and have lunch, then a walk through St. James's Park. There are pelicans there, you know."

"Pelicans?"

"They were a gift to King Charles the Second."

"Who gave him pelicans?"

He blurts out a laugh. "The Russians," he says.

"Is that really true? Or are you just saying it to distract me?"

"Both. Now sleep. Things will be better in the morning."

"Stay here for a little while longer," I say.

"Okay."

"Until I fall asleep."

"Yes."

We develop a routine of washing, eating, playing tic-tac-toe. We have races to see who can answer fastest when multiplying four-digit numbers in our heads, we do crosswords the same way.

"Six-letter word for *brought up*," I say.

"Is the first letter an *R*? Is it *raised*?"

We talk while lying in our bunks, while sitting on the floor, while splashing water on our faces at the tiny sink.

"You mean his blackboard is just sitting there with his *actual* writing still on it?" I say when Will tells me about Einstein's blackboard, one he used during a lecture on cosmology, hanging on the wall in the History of Science Museum in Oxford.

"People came to set up individual *chicken* farms?" he says when I tell him how my great-grandparents came to California to be chicken farmers.

"So, what do you do? Buy two different-size shoes?" I say when he discloses that none of the men in his family have feet that match.

Then, late one night, Will asks gently, "What happened to your father?"

"He was hit by a stray bullet." It sounds better than *he was shot.*

"That's . . ." Will has no words. "Where I come from you might get the occasional stolen bicycle. Or maybe someone breaks a potted plant."

"My neighborhood was different back then."

"So it seems. Do you remember him?"

I think for a moment. "Barely. And my mother doesn't really talk about him." I haven't thought of this before, and now I realize it's true. It's like my father never existed. "My poor mom," I say, thinking of how she must be feeling right now with me so far away, lost, stolen.

"I'm hoping my parents don't know," says Will. "Though I must say, if my father can blame me, he will. If being kidnapped and transported across Siberia can be my fault, he'll be sure to say so."

"But it *is* your fault," I say.

"Can we change the subject?"

There's a silence, and then I say, "Did I tell you that Rik kissed me?"

"He *did*? I don't believe it!"

I'm about to describe that moment in the restaurant, but a thought strikes me. "Why *don't* you believe it?" I say, mildly affronted.

"Well, I just can't imagine him putting down Munn's briefcase long enough to do such a thing. When did this happen?"

"At the restaurant. Just a really short . . . well, it was barely a kiss. Not what *you'd* call a kiss."

"What would *I* call a kiss?"

"I don't know. Something more."

"Oh please," he says, rubbing his hand across his eyes. "You think you know everything about me. Did his lips touch you? If so, it's a kiss."

"I don't know if I'll ever see him again," I sigh.

"Are you in love with him?"

"What do you mean, am I in love with him?"

"A simple question."

"The truth is . . ." What is the truth? The truth is that Rik is kind of perfect. He's the guy whose shirt is always ironed, whose hair is just the right amount of messed-up without it looking deliberate. Hell, he even impressed Lauren, and that's hard to do.

But when I think about love I think of Dmitry. Dmitry with two mugs of hot chocolate and a smile on his face because he has a surprise for me. I think of him appearing out of nowhere with a latex glove full of ice. Or joking that he's two rats behind me when, in fact, he's always so far out in front of me. I wish I could tell him this. I wonder what he'd say.

"Love isn't a simple question," I sigh.

Will says nothing, then, "Perhaps not. I had a girlfriend in England. I broke up with her to come to the States."

He shakes his head slowly back and forth as though unable to recall what had persuaded him to leave a woman and go to America.

* * *

"I miss music," he says, sometime around midnight. "This bloody train, rumble, rumble, clack, clack. It's like a flat line of sound that never ends."

"Can you sing?"

"I sang in choirs as a boy."

"What's your favorite song?"

He moans. "I can't tell you. You'll only say I'm being a snob."

"I won't say that. I mean, it's true that you *are* a snob, but I won't say it."

He laughs. I realize that I like it when he laughs. "Allegri's 'Miserere,'" he admits.

"Allegri *what*? Sing it."

"I can't. It's a choral song."

"So?"

"So, it's got a soaring high C that only children and sopranos can sing. It was considered so sacred that for over a hundred years the pope forbade it to be transcribed."

"When did the pope change his holy mind?"

"He didn't. Mozart heard it as a boy and memorized it in a single sitting. There *are* geniuses in fields outside of science."

"I *know* that," I say. I feel a little sad that I may never hear the "Miserere," this sacred song with all its mystery. I tell Will this, how I wish I'd heard it and that now I may never.

"Don't be silly," he says. "You know that day in London we're planning? I'll take you to a choral concert in the evening. I'll make sure the 'Miserere' is being sung."

"You mean after lunch and the walk and seeing Turner paintings? That will be a long day."

"It will be a lovely day. Now, don't fret."

"I'm not fretting."

"Yes, you are," he says.

And it's true. I've been crying. Again. "Promise me that if you get away without me you won't forget. You'll find a way of rescuing me, okay?" I say.

After a beat, he says, "Of course I will."

"And I'll do the same for you. I swear." I mean it, too. I won't leave him behind.

"Oh, Kira," he says, his voice so sweet it doesn't even sound like him.

I drop my hand down along the side of the bunk and he reaches up and squeezes my fingers. I hold his hand and we lie like that for a long time.

Then I sleep.

When I wake, he's still there. He's not holding my hand anymore, but shaking me gently.

"Wake up," he says. "We've stopped." There's urgency in his voice. Fear, too.

"What? Where?" I say.

He pulls me gently down from the bunk and we stand, huddled in the dark. Through the window I can see a lamp. Also, a train platform and what appears to be the corner of a tiny station behind it. The thought of leaving the train is suddenly worse than the thought of remaining.

"They're coming," Will says. "Listen."

An involuntary sound comes from deep within me, something between a cry and a gasp. I clutch Will's arm. He throws a blanket over my shoulders and hugs me toward him. "It's going to be cold outside," he says.

21

THE MEN ENTER the train compartment as I stand helplessly beside Will, holding on to him. In such a small space they seem enormous. Pale and ragged and threatening. I don't know how Will keeps his head, but he does, stepping forward and demanding to know why we've been taken. He looks urgently from one man to the other. One of them takes a gun from beneath his sweatshirt.

"What is going on?" Will says.

The man with the gun speaks to us in English. One word: *"Go!"*

We're herded through the train, my bare feet struggling with the uneven floor between cars. I see now that the train isn't set up for passengers. It's a postal train. There is no other compartment like ours, or at least none that I see.

At last we reach an open door. The night air has a wet, mechanical smell. I pull the blanket closer around me, surprised by how chilly it is. The wildflowers we passed had been blooming in a cold sun, far colder than back home. It's difficult to walk without shoes, and I nearly fall down the step onto the platform, stubbing my toe in the process. I limp on, shivering, as we're urged forward, faster and faster in the weak light, the rough pavement scraping the soles of my feet. It's the middle of the night and the small station is empty. If you could even call it a station. It's more like a bus stop built of gray bricks. Calling for help would be useless.

"Can we at least have our shoes?" Will says. But it's easier to control people who cannot run.

We're shunted into the back of a small van. No seat, no windows. We sit together, feeling the vibration of the road. I catch a glimpse of the shaven head of the driver, his scalp darkened with a tattoo. The one with the gun is in the back with us. He puts his finger to his lips to tell us no talking, then gets out a cigarette.

We travel for what feels like hours. Will sits with his back against the side of the van, his face stony and unreadable. The man with the gun smokes cigarette after cigarette.

I can tell when we finally enter a city by the number of traffic lights and turns in the road. At last, the driver pulls up next to a building and opens the window, then punches some kind of code into a security system. The van moves again, but only a few feet, as though positioning itself into a parking space. I hear the engine go off, the humming of a motor outside. Then we're being lowered into the ground.

For some reason, being taken underground freaks me out. Maybe it's all that cigarette smoke. I begin to gasp. The man beside us, the one with the gun, gives me an angry look. I put my hand over my mouth, but I'm losing control of everything. My breathing is uneven, my vision blurry with tears.

Will looks at me, his eyes full of emotion. *Watch me,* he seems to be saying. *Breathe in, out, in, out, like this.*

I hold his gaze, linking my breathing with his as the elevator comes to a series of faltering halts. The van jiggles, then is still. The driver opens his door, then gets out and comes around to unlock the back. I slide across the floor of the van, then step out into a parking lot, the cement grimy beneath my bare feet. As quickly as we were dispatched off the train and into the van, we are now ushered up a series of metal steps to a door lit by a single bulb. Will asks for the dozenth time why we've been taken but is silenced by the man with the gun, who pushes him hard against the back of the neck, saying "Shut up!" in English.

We climb a set of steps, go through another door and into a wide hallway, drafty and dark, with ceiling lights that either blink on and off or fail to light altogether. Puddles on the floor, unused equipment, a humming sound from an aging ventilation system. We're marched down one last dark hall, brought to a room, and forced inside. The door locks behind us and now, once again, we're alone.

The room is windowless and gray, about a dozen feet long and perhaps eight feet wide. It looks like it was used as a closet, with unpainted cinder block walls and light coming from a fluorescent tube on the ceiling. At the far end is a thin mattress without sheets. Beside it, a bottle of water. In the corner is a bucket, which I assume is our toilet.

"Are they mad?" says Will.

I shiver in my dress. The building's damp walls bring a chill.

I go to the door, pressing my ear against it. Will paces and shouts through the keyhole.

After a while we give up. He says, "Sit with me."

We drop onto the awful mattress, our backs resting on the wall, knees bent, ready to jump to our feet if we have to, ready to wait for hours if that is what is necessary. Will spreads the blanket over us and puts his arm around me, rubbing my shoulders for warmth. Instinctively, I clutch his fingers and we wait, watching the door and listening for sounds outside.

Mostly what we hear is the strip light above us. If we turn it off the room goes black. Leave it on and it hums like a pylon.

"What do we do?" I say.

"Whatever they want."

Hours pass. There is no more joking or remembering or imagining a day in London. I curl up in a ball, my head beside Will's knee. The mattress smells like burnt dust.

"I am so sorry about all this," he says. "So very sorry."

"Talk to me," I say. "Tell me something good. Anything."

He touches my hair. At first he says nothing, and I think how we've reached a place where even Will has finally given up. But then he says, "I'll tell you about lambing, how about that?"

"What's 'lambing'?"

"When mother sheep have babies," he says, as though explaining to a child. He gives a short laugh and I'm surprised. Not just by the fact he can still laugh but the power of it. The laugh ignites hope.

"Do you think anyone in America has sent help?"

"Munn is hardly going to sit there and do nothing," he says.

"But it's happened before—" I say. Arturo, the fifteen-year-old, still gone.

"Shh," he whispers. "We're talking about lambing."

He describes how they went for Easter to his family's house in Devon. A man who worked for his father rounded up all the pregnant ewes into pens inside the barn. He and his brother spent freezing nights among the straw bales waiting for the ewes to give birth, then bottle-feeding the weaker lambs. Orphans were brought into the kitchen, warmed by the Aga.

"What's an Aga?" I say.

"Like a giant oven that stays on through winter. Keeps the place warm."

I doze off, imagining warm kitchens, green hills, deep straw beds. I'm half awake when I hear footsteps. They grow heavier as I come to full attention. Then, all at once, the door flies open. The brightness of the hallway fills the room.

It's the men from the train. One motions for Will to come. Will looks annoyed, pulling himself up from the floor in no particular hurry. I get my legs under me, ready to join him, but the one with the scalp tattoo holds out his hand to stop me. I step back, then fall uncomfortably upon the mattress.

"You can't just take him away!" I say. Of all the things I imagined might happen, it never occurred to me that we would be separated. I suddenly realize that this is the most frightening thing they could do to me. Will is my one comfort in this grim nightmare.

But there's nothing either of us can do. The guy in the sweatshirt prods Will forward. "Move!" he says. Will won't be rushed. He tucks in his shirt and smooths back his hair in his usual self-possessed manner, moving with quiet dignity as the men shout at him in Russian.

He's incredible. Meanwhile, I rock on my heels, crying and shaking. The one with the gun takes it from his belt, and I lose it completely. I reach forward, grabbing at Will's ankle. "You can't go!" I cry. "I can't do this on my own—"

"Shh," he whispers. He loosens himself gently from my grip, then kneels down so our faces are close. The men pull at him, but he won't be budged. He says, "From the moment I met you I found you infuriatingly clever. And all these months I raged because you could do *anything*. Now, listen to me, because I know you. I know how tough you are and how resourceful. I saw it every day at Mellin." He touches my cheek, almost smiling. "You're going to be fine," he says.

"But Will—!"

"Outsmart them. You can, you know."

I want to tell him that in a fight between brains and guns the guns always win. That's something my mother always said. I want to tell him that all my hope walks out the door with him. All my courage.

But he's gone too fast, his hair shining golden in the light. He moves with a grace his military family would be proud of, his head up, his back straight. As the door locks behind them, I listen for his footsteps in the hall. I listen for his voice.

But there is nothing.

I shout myself hoarse, kick the crap out of the door. It doesn't matter what I do.

Hours pass before I see another human being. And then, it's the guy with the shaved head and tattoos. A giant, he takes up the whole doorway, staring down at me as though I'm a terrible inconvenience. I back up, tripping on the hem of my dress. Why's he in the room with me? Not speaking, not moving, just staring?

"Where's my friend?" I say.

He gestures for me to follow him out of the room and down the hall. Maybe he's taking me to Will. We pass through a set of doors to a large stairwell walled with big plates of glass. A filmy gray light tells me it's morning. Then I'm ushered into a kind of industrial elevator from which I can see nothing.

"Are we going to see Will? The man you took?"

No answer.

"The Englishman, where has he been taken?"

Again, nothing.

The doors open into a poorly lit laboratory with banks of worktops, some with fume hoods and sinks. The furniture is old and tattered, but you can see that it was once well-used. I see the other man from the train, standing by a wheeled cart on which there are stacks of chipped cups and saucers.

With them is another man who I recognize at once, the man with the red hair. His beard is longer since I saw him in Stockholm and he wears a lab coat instead of the navy blazer he wore at SFOF. But it's him, all right, with the same pale skin and weary expression. He stands with his arms folded across his chest, staring at me with watery eyes.

"Finally, we are properly introduced, Kira," he says. "I am Yegor Vasiliev."

22

I'M TOLD TO sit in a chair, so I sit. I'm asked if I would like some tea and I say no.

Vasiliev tells one of the men to pour the tea anyway. I know this because he barks orders and almost instantly a cup is on the table before me.

"Drink," he says.

It is very strong, black, and only lukewarm.

"There have been developments since I saw you in Sweden," he begins, his English heavily accented just as I remember. "This 'post-death recovery.'"

I say nothing.

"You know about this process?"

"I want to see Will," I say. I'm desperate to see him. I keep looking around, hoping to catch a glimpse of him. But it's only Vasiliev and his men.

"Your colleague told us it is only you who can do this procedure. Much to our surprise, he cannot."

If we'd been working on hypersonic missiles or laser weapons—both of which are being developed on the military side of Mellin's research—I might understand why we've been kidnapped by a foreign power to show them a "procedure," as Vasiliev describes it. But bringing a couple of rats back to life? That hardly sounds like something that can be weaponized.

Vasiliev pushes his glasses up on his nose. "The damaged brain has only limited ability to regenerate itself. But it is said that you can bring back a dead brain. Is that correct?"

"Who *are* you?"

"Correct?" he repeats.

"What have you done with Will?"

Vasiliev drops into the chair in front of me, looking suddenly exhausted, as though my presence is a terrible imposition. Then he looks up at me from beneath heavy eyelids and says, "Don't be difficult."

"I want to see my friend," I say.

"Why?" he says, as though this makes no sense to him. "He's just another person. You have three persons before you. Why add another?"

What? "I want Will," I say clearly, slowly.

He bangs the table hard, startling me and sending the tea flying.

My dress is wet, the tea staining one side. At my feet is a broken cup.

"You've spilled your tea," says Vasiliev.

I'm given another cup of tea. This I leave untouched.

"I won't tell you anything until I've seen him," I say.

The men who kidnapped us look at Vasiliev, then at each other.

Vasiliev crosses his arms in front of him, staring at me from across the table. He looks even more exhausted as he says, "Perhaps he's already dead."

The words hit me like a blow. I begin to hyperventilate. My hands are shaking. All I can think, all I can hear in my head is *perhaps he's already dead.*

"We'll check later and tell you," says Vasiliev. "But first." He takes a pad of paper from his clipboard and pushes it to my side of the table. "Write down this procedure that you will show us later."

He nods at the paper.

I gesture around the empty laboratory. "I couldn't even do it here. Everything I use is at Mellin. A Rho antagonist, rat stem cells from a tissue bank, actual rats—" I begin.

Vasiliev says, "Write down these things you need."

"Not until I've seen Will—" I say, suddenly standing.

He shakes his head, his eyes half closed, as though everything about me is giving him a terrific migraine. Suddenly, his men are shouting at me in Russian. One of them forces me back into the chair. I've never been touched by strangers, let alone manhandled like this. I scream as I'm pushed down onto the seat. They press my head down so that I have no choice but to stare at the paper on the table in front of me.

Weirdly, Vasiliev acts as though none of this violence is taking place. "Are you hungry?" he asks. "Would you like some toast?"

I can't think but I start to write just to keep Vasiliev at bay. What gauge needle had I used for the lumbar injection? Twenty-five gauge? One-centimeter length? I don't want to tell them anything, but I have to tell them everything. And I'm trembling from my toes up.

"Have you experimented yet with human subjects?" Vasiliev asks.

Is he *kidding*? I shake my head.

"The method will work for people," he says, as though this is a well-known fact.

His words chill me. Of course, post-death recovery will eventually work for people. But as Munn said, the ethical questions involved are huge. If we bring people back, it can't be into a state of profound brain injury, paralysis, or vegetation. I think of Daisy, the rat whose motor skills will never fully recover. And Not Daisy, whose brief moments of consciousness were soon lost again.

"You mean in the future, right?" I say.

"Now," he says.

Would they bring me rats, then . . . *people*? Are they insane? But look at them, surrounding me like a pack of wolves. They seem capable of anything.

I cover my face with my hands. "Rats and human beings metabolize drugs differently," I say through my fingers. "I wouldn't even know what to do!"

"We will begin with rats."

"But for all I know, the rats I worked on in the US are dead now," I say.

Vasiliev shrugs. "Does not matter."

I have an idea. I'll write down Dmitry's original protocol. That way, I can make a big show of trying to save them but fail. Maybe this will persuade Vasiliev not to try the procedure with human beings anytime soon.

But maybe not.

What if they really are crazy enough to bring me people to work on? I have no choice but to hedge my bets, considering what I need to work on both rats *and* humans. I begin listing all the drugs, equipment, and papers I need to look at, including as much detail as I can recall. I think hard, blocking out the men before me, moving into the realm of my brain in which I become machinelike, unwavering, processing data from studies I've read, working out possibilities. I once described to Dmitry the way I feel when I'm "in the zone" like this, and he told me he was addicted to that feeling. It's why he plays chess.

Finally, I review what I've written the way I might a set of answers for an exam. "I'll need additional equipment and drugs once I've read the papers listed," I warn.

Vasiliev regards the list, squinting from beneath pale, nearly invisible eyebrows. "You won't have time to read all this information," he says, taking a bite of toast.

"I read fast," I say.

He grunts. "Very well," he says stiffly, flicking buttery crumbs from his fingers. He hands the list on to one of the other men, speaking to him in Russian. "We go now."

I'm escorted to the bathroom. The door shuts behind me and I hear the men outside guarding it. The bathroom is flooded in places and the sink tap is rusted. No window from which to escape. But at least there is a toilet.

Then they take me to the cinder block room, which is empty save the mattress and bottled water. I fling myself down onto the mattress, feeling drained.

There is still no Will.

I sit for hours listening to the ugly sound of the light humming above me. I must have fallen asleep, because at some point I open my eyes to the man with the scalp tattoos in front of me carrying a tray of borscht, brown bread, and a soft drink that is something like orange soda.

I'm scared out of my mind at the sight of him.

He hands me the tray.

My voice trembles as I say, "I'm not hungry."

But he insists I take it.

Until the research papers arrive, there is nothing to do but eat when food is brought and sleep when they leave me alone. Wait and wait. I lie on the mattress under the thin blanket in my ridiculous dress. This must be what prison is like. Or solitary confinement. I miss my mother so much it feels like a great chunk of me has been carved out. She depends on me for shopping, cleaning, driving. Who will help her now that I'm gone? Lauren is at an internship. She won't be dropping by as she used to do.

All that feels so far away. My old life is evaporating, has evaporated. I fight against the sense that it is forever gone, recalling how it felt to be in the woods with Lauren, the concentration on her face as she peers through her binoculars, her joy as she identifies birdcalls. And Dmitry, setting up a chessboard, grinning when I make a clever move. I think of Rik and Chandni, wondering what they will make of my sudden disappearance. Dmitry will be frantic. I know that.

But more than anything, my thoughts are with Will. If he's alive he's as alone as I am. I long to hear his voice; I miss his displays of indifference. They gave me courage while facing all the threats of violence. He got me through the train journey. I need him even more now.

Hours later, what might be the middle of the night, I wake to a bar of light from the hallway extending as the door opens again. There's the same man, the one with the scalp tattoos, his body taking up the whole of the doorframe. Leather jacket, jeans, boots. I lurch into a sitting position, my back against the cold cinder blocks. He's terrifying, but in his hands is another blanket. Also, a pillow, which he holds out now, an offering.

"Thank you," I whisper.

In answer, he puts a finger to his lips. Then he leaves.

The pillow makes it possible to get into a comfortable position. And the blanket is a godsend. At least I'm no longer cold. I lie on the mattress, staring up at the blackness, trying to figure out how to save a person using post-death recovery. It's a barbaric notion that they'd ask such a thing from me, but I should be ready if they do.

I wake up at some hourless moment in the day or night, not knowing at first where I am in the darkness. The door opens and I see that the guy with the sweatshirt has changed it for a gray one, almost identical. Behind him is the guy with the scalp tattoos, his face showing none of the kindness it had when he brought me the blanket.

I'm handed a towel, on top of which is a folded set of surgical scrubs, a small bar of soap, toothpaste, and a toothbrush.

I'm taken to a changing room with a big drain in the middle of the floor. There's a row of lockers on one side, a few toilets, and showers with old-fashioned metal showerheads fixed onto the tiles. I feel a rush of joy at the thought of a shower.

Then I think that this is how they grind you down. Little "luxuries" meted out for good behavior. The last thing I should feel is joy. Or gratitude.

I peel off my dress, hanging it on a hook on the wall. It looks silly there, a ball gown in a locker room. I step under one of the showerheads. The water is lukewarm. I shiver in the weak spray, but the tiny bar of soap is a luxury so precious to me, I hold it under my nose to sniff before beginning to wash. Gliding it over my shoulders, I can feel days of sweat and dirt dissolve beneath my fingers. I scrub my skin with my fingernails, use up all the soap. I stay in the shower until the water runs cold. Then I turn off the tap, listening to the pipes bang around me.

The surgical scrubs are big, but at least they are clean. I've just tied the waistband when I hear a knock on the door. Time's up.

We wander back through the halls. The building is huge and dilapidated: damp patches in the ceiling tiles, brown water stains, cracked glass. Clearly, it was once a well-used laboratory but has been long since abandoned.

Finally, we reach a room, smaller than a classroom but with a classroom feel to it. At the center is a desk on which breakfast has been laid out: two slabs of dark bread, juice, coffee, and three fat sausages.

I eat quickly and voraciously, pleading for more, and get another slice of bread. Vasiliev arrives, and with him a cart of research articles and books, pens, and a calculator.

"We are still sourcing some of the items you have requested. Once we have located everything, you will perform post-death recovery on our rodents," he says. "Please check that we've brought you all the necessary reading material."

"I'd like to see the friend I came with. Will."

"He is unable to help us with the procedure," says Vasiliev. "We were misinformed."

"Where is he now?"

Vasiliev checks his watch, heads for the door.

"Why won't you let me see him?" I call.

But Vasiliev just disappears, leaving me with the articles.

23

I FEED MYSELF page after page, swimming in a haze of thoughts and emotions, thinking about the information on the printouts before me, then drifting into worries about what's going to happen. To me. To Will. I scribble notes, boxing some, drawing arrows to link others. I look around for ways to escape. The sun streams into the room, heating the air so that its antiseptic smell grows heavier. It's the same sun that shines back home, where I long to be.

I'm allowed to pace but not to stray too close to a door or a window. I'm allowed water and tepid tea but not coffee. Eventually, a second meal arrives on a tray. Stew and vegetables, slabs of bread and margarine. At some hour, deep into the night, I am told I must return to the bedroom now.

The bedroom? Is that what they think it is?

The second day passes much like the first. No shower this time, but the research papers wait for me as before on a cart beside a table. I read, leafing through one article or study, then another, always under armed guard.

It couldn't be more crazy, I think. And then it is.

The man in the sweatshirt arrives through the double doors, balancing a plastic tub. He crosses the room and drops it in front of me, then tips the tub so I can see inside, rattling its contents as though it were a pot of pennies. There, on a layer of shredded paper, are a half dozen albino rats, their pink eyes like jewels against their ultrawhite fur, their delicate toes as pink as carnations.

"Okay?" he asks.

I look at the rats' faces, fearful but curious. I don't like the thought of putting them through this ordeal.

"Vasiliev wants you," he says. "Go."

He and the guy with the scalp tattoos bring me down a long hallway to the stairwell. I can hear noise in parts of the building and I wonder if it's very windy outside. I peer through the industrial windows along the cold cement steps and see fat clouds moving across an azure sky.

"I want you to know that I hate you all very, very much," I say in a tone that might be used to comment on the weather.

They have no response. Either because they don't understand or because they don't care. I may as well be one of the white rats in the tub.

Eventually we end up at a laboratory, but it has been transformed, no longer disused and filthy but brightly lit with a shining floor. Across the counters are drugs, solutions, syringes, imaging machines, monitors, ice, a padded incubator rich in oxygen. The stethoscope and all the syringes and needles I had requested are laid out carefully on a table.

But there is also a tripod and camera. These I did not ask for.

Vasiliev greets me with a nod, his red beard catching the sunlight, his clipboard angled to take notes. "I would like you to speak very clearly, so that we can record what you are doing as you proceed," he instructs me.

I say nothing.

"You do understand?" he says.

I shrug.

"Please check that we have made all necessary items available to you," he says, gesturing toward the table.

I have no choice. I study the equipment they've brought. Vasiliev tells me to prepare the syringes. Meanwhile, he makes sure the electricity is working.

He says, "We will induce cardiac arrest in rat, then bring to you after eight minutes dead. Agreed?"

I do nothing to signal that I agree, but after a short interval the first rat arrives anyway, brought in on a white lab towel. Its eyes no longer sparkle. They are half closed now, lifeless. The blood has drained from its muzzle and feet. I'd estimated the rats' weight at 250 grams each and have already loaded the syringes for a correct dosage. I place the one before me on the scales now before taking it onto my lap.

"No!" Vasiliev says. "You will work here! On the table!"

So. That is a requirement. It is also a requirement that I not allow my hair to fall down, obstructing the view of the camera.

One of the men steps forward, gathering up my hair roughly, then balling it into a rubber band.

"Ow!" I say, as the rubber band pulls at my hair.

"Proceed," says Vasiliev.

"I prefer to work on my lap," I say. "It's easier that way."

It's not easier, but I have a plan, and part of that plan requires fooling the camera.

Vasiliev shakes his head. "Here!" he orders, slapping two fingers on the tabletop.

Again, I have no choice. I follow his instructions, working quietly. I try not to think of the passing minutes and the men surrounding me. The limited space in the rat's spinal column makes the procedure challenging. I concentrate, becoming immersed in what I'm doing, my thoughts flowing easily one to the other.

But Vasiliev interrupts me. "Aloud!" he commands.

Apparently, I'm supposed to talk the whole time, explaining what I'm doing and why I'm doing it as though to a group of students.

So it continues. If I work in silence, he blasts, "Speak!" disrupting my concentration. If I narrate as I work, my precision wavers. I have no intention of showing them what to do to bring the rat back. I just have to make it look like I'm trying. But everything about what is happening now is exhausting and infuriating. At last, I lay the rat down in the incubator, then fold a towel to provide a padded wall along the edges of the tank.

"Why did you do that?" Vasiliev wants to know.

"Convulsions," I say.

"I see no convulsions." He leans toward the rat, then pokes it with his pen. "It's still dead."

The room is silent, the men standing around the plastic incubator, watching the rat, unmoving and pale. Vasiliev's irritation grows as the seconds wear on, the tension in the room mounting. Finally, he exhales angrily, his eyes hard on the rat.

"It isn't alive," he hisses.

I shrug. "You killed it."

"Make it live!"

When I do nothing, he steps forward, then back again, as though stopping himself from rushing at me in anger.

"Do it!" he screams.

He signals to his men, and one of them swats me hard on the back of the head so that I fall forward onto the table. Then they are screaming at me in Russian, slapping me, pushing me.

It's humiliating, and it hurts, but they aren't damaging me. Not much anyway. I suppose they can't knock me senseless and still expect me to think straight. But then Vasiliev holds up a hypodermic needle filled with some kind of fluid, and now I really am scared.

"Do you know what is in here?" he says.

I shake my head.

"You've heard of an epidural?"

I nod. "To block pain," I say.

"Yes, exactly. Normally, it is a simple injection into the spine providing pain relief so that mothers can have babies without so much screaming. Correctly placed, the patient has no feeling below the waist. But if you place the needle higher in the spine, it numbs the nerves to the lungs and the patient stops breathing. I'm very good with placement and will ensure the needle is precisely positioned so that you can still breathe, just not very well. During the hours you are gasping for air, you can consider all your options. By the time you can breathe normally, I am certain you will agree to show us the procedure *properly*, as we've asked."

"No!" I say, and begin backing up, but his men grab me, holding me so I can't move.

It takes both his men to force me down, rolling me into a ball so that my knees are touching my chin. I'm told to shut up as the needle goes in. And not to move unless I want to die.

For the next four hours, the sensation is as though I am being strangled, because I am. I have to think about every breath I take, willing my lungs to expand, then contract. I can't get enough oxygen no matter what I do. The only way to cope is to stay as calm as possible, as still as possible, so that my body requires less oxygen. I lie on the lab floor, feeling for all the earth as though I'm asphyxiating. The first hour is the worst. After that, I seem to gain a little more breath, and the knowledge of this gives me a measure of hope. I stare up at the bright lights, trying not to panic, seeing water marks on the ceiling just like the one back home. The roof is caving in, slowly but surely.

They bring me another dead rat. This time, I perform as they wish, exactly as they wish, because I don't want to get that needle again.

The rat comes back to life in a series of spasms. The feet twitch, then the legs and tail, then the whole spine as it convulses and shakes, moving sideways. I find this uncomfortable to watch. But there are good signs: the ears bloom pink, the muzzle twitches and moistens, the eyes flutter open. I set up the oxygen and wait as the rat slowly gains strength. At last it rights itself and sits, leaning against the plastic wall of the tank. Hunched over, its fur standing up, the rat sways its head from side to side in an effort to see, but one thing is certain. It's alive.

"Bozhe moy," says Vasiliev.

It's as though a spirit has wandered into the cold body of the rat and, there, lit a fire. We are all transfixed as I put the rat on the table and watch it shuffle across the surface. Within a few minutes I can see improvements in its balance. In fact, the little white rat does better than the ones back at Mellin had.

"He's off and away," I say.

Nobody thinks about prisoners or threats. Nobody thinks about guns. We're all amazed at what we've seen. Even Vasiliev appears pleased for a moment.

Then he turns to me. "Repeat," he says. "Rat number three."

My new plan is to vary the procedure slightly, undetectably, saving some rats and not others. I want to show that post-death recovery isn't reliable and therefore cannot be tested yet on humans. But I sure don't want another needle in my spine.

I try not to look too nervous as they bring in the next rat. It will be hard to fake the injections under the close watch of the camera lens. The men hover as I fill the syringes. Vasiliev leans so close I can smell the coffee on his breath.

My idea is to place the tiny syringe under the skin and then out again, plunging the solution onto my hands instead of the rat. It's only 0.1 milliliter and shouldn't be noticed. If I do it well it should appear as though I'm giving the rat an injection when I'm not. Then, of course, the rat will never recover.

Sorry, Rat Three, I think.

But Vasiliev is making this difficult. He's figured out I'm left-handed and so he stands to the side and slightly behind my left shoulder. Positioned this way, I can't tell what he's looking at exactly. Meanwhile, the camera's eye records everything. I continue with the rat, going through the procedure as before, waiting for the moment I can fudge an injection.

But the moment doesn't come. If I want a distraction, I'm going to have to create one. I turn over one of the vials, push a needle through its stopper, then draw out several more milliliters of the solution than I need. I pretend to be checking the measurement, tapping it to remove air bubbles, all the while aiming the needle just behind my left shoulder. Then, all at once, I squirt the solution.

It hits Vasiliev square in the face.

"Idiot!" he shouts, and with his exclamation comes my window of opportunity.

While he's dabbing his eye with his sleeve, I turn quickly to the rat. I bend over the rat so that hopefully my head obscures the camera's view, then push the needle through one side of the skin and out the other, making sure to miss the muscle.

Then I place the empty syringe on the table. Proof that I am following the protocol.

Everyone is watching but seems none the wiser. I continue with the procedure, eventually nestling the rat into the incubator. It stays motionless, just as the first had done. No signs of life, no twitching of legs, no color returning to its pale ears or lifeless paws.

We wait and wait, but the rat remains dead.

"What is wrong with this one?" Vasiliev says.

I shrug, holding my breath, hoping he'll declare it a failure and move to the next rat. If my trick worked, I could "fail" with every third rat. Given such a performance, working on humans would be out of the question.

But Vasiliev isn't convinced. He walks around the incubator, his hands clasped behind his back.

"You did something wrong," he says.

"It doesn't always work," I say. I try my hardest to seem disappointed in the result. "I told you that."

He stops at the camera, rewinds it back to the beginning of the procedure on the third rat, and watches silently. I focus my gaze on a spot of sunlight that makes a rainbow across the floor. The video continues minute to minute until the point at which I staged the accident with the solution. I feel a sinking in my chest as Vasiliev calls over the other men and they all crowd around the monitor.

The video is rewound, played again, then again. A feeling of weakness floods over me. My head is pounding. My arms feel light and useless. I'm terrified and trying not to show it. Then the guy with the sweatshirt points at something. Vasiliev squints into the viewer. I feel the sweat gathering at my neck, rolling down my back. A minute passes, another.

Vasiliev comes toward me. He stands directly in front of me, hands on his hips, looks me in the eye, then spits straight into my face.

I scream. Somebody slaps me hard across the ear, sending me flying. I'm on the floor as Vasiliev signals to one of the men to take away the dead rat. Then he turns to me again, hovering above me as I shield my head.

"You think we are *stupid*?" he shouts.

They pull me up by the elbows and I stand unsteadily, my head ringing, as another rat is presented. For a moment the room seems to throb in and out of focus. I struggle to stay standing.

Then I see it again, the hypodermic needle.

"*Please!*" I beg.

"Stop playing games," says Vasiliev, the needle poised beside him. "Because we are not."

The sight of the needle brings tears to my eyes. I start to cry and Vasiliev yells at me, telling me to stop making noise, stop complaining, stop acting stupid.

I'm falling apart. I know that. And I realize all over again how much it had mattered to have Will near. He'd always known when to distract me, to humor me, to reassure me. Where is he now?

"Fix this!" yells Vasiliev, handing me the dead rat.

Eight rats, one after another, hour by hour without pause.

When the final one has been restored I think I'm finished. I look at the rat, newly undead, bracing itself against the towel that pads the inside of the incubator's wall, and pray that there will be no more of this.

The stress of the day has stopped me from feeling hungry, but it doesn't stop me from feeling light-headed. I'm about to ask for a cup of coffee when Vasiliev speaks.

"Again," he says.

Again? At first I think he wants me to stun the rats' hearts so that they die all over again and he can watch as I revive them a second time, an unnecessary and cruel thing to do. But it turns out he wants me to revive the rat that I'd let die hours ago.

"You're kidding," I say. There's no point. Too much time has passed. The damaged neurons have already shed their mitochondria. There are no longer organelles inside those cells. One of the things I do in post-death recovery is to support the brain's astrocytes, another type of cell, so that they replace damaged neurons. But it's too late for that now.

"We kept it on ice," he says. I begin to protest, but his expression tells me I have no choice.

I take in a heavy breath, then tear open a package of syringes. They bring me the rat. It looks terrible, with stiff limbs, a mouth gaping to reveal yellow incisors, staring lifeless eyes. I work quickly and not very carefully (I'm certain this won't work), eventually placing the rat into the oxygenated incubator.

Then I unclip my lab glasses and drop into the chair, exhausted. I turn my attention to one of the windows, wishing I could at least go look out over the trees. But the rule is no windows, no doors. Perhaps they fear I might jump.

"I read about you in America," Vasiliev says.

I shake my head. "No, not me."

"About a girl with a brain like a calculator. She went to university at age twelve."

"You've got me mixed up with someone else."

"You read documents then process the information like a machine."

This is kind of true. "Perhaps you can replace me with a machine and I can go home," I say.

Vasiliev makes a sound, "Puh!" Then he comes closer, bringing his face down to mine. "If it were possible, I would do just that!"

I don't look at him, or answer as he launches into question after question.

Where did you study?

How did you come up with the procedure?

Who taught you?

He wheels me around so that I face him. "Does America have secret academies where they keep their best and brightest?"

Secret academies?

"Of course not," I say. "I'm a high school student."

"They give you drugs to make you smarter?"

"*What?* No!" I say.

"Alter your DNA?" he says. "Your parents had this done, yes?"

And then, all at once, Vasiliev's attention goes elsewhere. He cranes his head around to the incubator, then claps his hand over his forehead.

"*Smotri!*" he shouts. "The rat! He lives!"

And sure enough, there it is—the little rat I'd had no hope for is trying to get upright. Damaged, yes. Weak, yes. But alive.

"I'll lower the oxygen a bit," I say. "It won't do him any good to have too much."

The little rat fights his way back into life. Meanwhile, I come to the uncertain realization that I am of no further use to Vasiliev. Now that everything is recorded on camera, they can dispose of me without consequence. And I have no doubt they'll do just that. I feel my heart beat loudly in my chest. I have to get away somehow.

I wonder if I ran toward a window as hard as possible whether I could break through it and fall with the shattering glass below. I'd rather die like that than however they're going to kill me. And maybe I wouldn't die. We're not that high up in the building. Maybe a miracle would occur and I'd live after all. I think of myself running through Moscow, escaping these men. It's only a daydream, but it's a nice one.

A sound brings me to attention. A gurney is being wheeled unsteadily through the doorway. I rise to my feet, my eyes fixed. When I see what is happening, I gasp, then rush toward the gurney, screaming.

"Will!"

Will is asleep on a white sheet, another covering him up to the chest. At first, I'm overjoyed to see him, but then I realize that he isn't asleep. In the stark laboratory light, he no longer even looks like Will. His shoulders are pale and bare and cold to my touch. I see, too, that he is naked beneath the thin cover and that the whole of his body, once so tall and powerful and young, is lifeless and unmoving. He will never again be the menacing presence I'd feared back in Stockholm, nor the confident chum who'd used cheerfulness as a military tactic to get us through our days locked together on the train. I think of how we played checkers to pass the hours, how he held my hand. In death, he is younger, not much more than a boy. His golden hair still gleaming, his face unlined.

I scream, a single shrill sound that echoes across the laboratory and carries on in waves. I look desperately around at the men—the guy in the sweatshirt, the guy with the scalp tattoos—as if they could help. Their faces are unreadable, remote, as though a dead man is simply one of nature's casual losses, no more important than a fledgling found dead outside its nest.

"It didn't need to be *him*!" I say. But of course, I know it did. They want me to be super motivated. They figured out exactly how to make it so. I say, "You can't just . . . just . . ." I have no words.

Vasiliev says, "I have every confidence in you."

I've never seen a dead person before, let alone touched one. The only way I can approach him is to tell myself that he is not dead, not really. I recall what Dmitry once said, that death happens not at once but in stages. *You must think of it as a process,* he'd explained. *Not like a closed door but like a revolving door. Only then can you imagine a way to interfere with it.*

I shoot into action. "Get ice around his head!" I yell. "And the larger syringes! Those! In the back!"

"I will assist you," Vasiliev offers. I glare at him as he expertly fills syringes, placing them one by one on a sterile cloth as I grab a large arterial cannula and look for the pump.

It's hellishly difficult to work on such a large body. Turning Will, sticking him, keeping him in place, is all physically unmanageable, requiring assistance not only from Vasiliev but from the other men as well.

Unlike with the rats, everything becomes impossibly slow, as though I'm trying to ski through a jungle. The injections are much larger. I have to work periodically with the pump; the laser I used with the rats is inadequate. They bring out a larger one, but it works differently and I have to waste precious minutes figuring it out. Meanwhile, the clock ticks away, not only on the wall above me, but in my mind. Seventeen minutes, eighteen minutes. I know one day this procedure will be routine, but I'm failing now. Beneath my hands, Will's skin grows colder, his lips darken. I want to reach up and hold his head in my hands. I want to cry out and attack Vasiliev with my fists. Instead, I stare hard at the monitor that shows me where my needle is moving inside Will's spine. Twenty-four minutes, twenty-five . . .

Vasiliev sets up a machine that registers brain activity. There is some activity in the brain even after death, but the signals are very weak. I try not to be discouraged. I work on. It seems as though the whole enterprise is hopeless when, at last, Vasiliev leaps forward. The look on his face tells me that something has happened. And then I see it: a line of red peaks on the monitor, then peaks again, which shows activity has improved, not just by a small amount but by a significant margin. Will's brain is working again, at least to some degree.

I begin CPR immediately, pumping his chest. If the heart begins to beat again, however irregularly, there is hope. "Defibrillator!" I call at Vasiliev, but he's already on it, positioning the electrode pads.

Vasiliev calls loudly in Russian, then one of the men pulls me from Will before the charge from the defibrillator hits him. I watch as Will's body jumps, then is still. I begin CPR again, placing the heel of my hand on Will's chest, the other one above it, and pressing down rhythmically, *one, two, three* . . . Once more, I stand back as the machine sends a current through him. At last, his heart begins weakly. Vasiliev sets up an EKG machine and they roll Will into recovery position. I can see his heartbeat on the monitor and a brightening on his face as the skin pinks up as it had with the rats, indicating he has a functioning circulatory system. I work on him with new hope, a thrill rushing through me as though I've just outrun fire.

He comes to eventually in a series of unsettling spasms, his legs jerking out from the gurney, his arms flailing. It takes several minutes for him to stop convulsing violently, the involuntary jerks and spasms carrying on but with less intensity as the minutes pass.

"Will, can you hear me?" I say, my face inches from his. He's too disoriented to answer. His eyes stare without focus into the distance. A strange sound emits from his throat and then he is silent.

"Blink if you can hear me," I say.

Blink.

"Are you in pain?"

Blink.

"Is the pain between here and here?" I touch his hip bone, then his toes. No blink.

"Is the pain between here and here?" I touch the area between his hip bone and his shoulder. No blink.

"The pain is in your *head*?" I say.

Blink, blink, blink.

His head hurts. Also, he can hear. But when I swipe my hand in front of his eyes his pupils don't contract. His optic nerve may not yet be back "online." Then it occurs to me I've damaged his retinas with too much oxygen. Rats have bad eyesight. Albino rats can be nearly blind from birth. I'd never have known if the rats' vision was worse after post-death recovery. I never had the opportunity to test anything.

"Will," I say, my voice heavy. "Can you see?"

No blink.

24

THEY TAKE HIM away with me shouting down the hall after them, screaming and crying until at last the guy in the sweatshirt pins me against a wall and reminds me he has a gun. I go silent as the gurney turns a corner out of view. I tell myself that they can't do this, *they can't*, but of course they can do anything they like. Where will they take him? Not to a hospital, that's for sure. What if they have no intention of helping him, but are planning only to study him?

I understand part of Vasiliev's strategy is to keep me disoriented and alone. He's succeeding there. I'm woozy with it all. But worse than the way I feel, worse even than being so far away from home and worried about my mother, is knowing that Will is somewhere else, apparently blind and in pain. He's far more alone than I am. Every bone in my body wants to chase after him, but the guy who is holding me now pushes me aside, then fixes me with a look that says, *Don't move.*

I stand for a moment, stunned. Then, incredibly, he gets out a pack of cigarettes and offers me one before lighting up right there in the laboratory.

"Geez, is there *nowhere* you won't smoke?" I say. He looks at me with a blank expression. "Oxygen," I tell him, pointing at the oxygen cylinders all around us.

He purses his lips and shrugs.

"You don't mind if you explode?" I say.

He takes a long drag off the cigarette, then spits on the floor.

"Fine," I say. "I hope you explode."

I'm brought back to the cinder block room, pushed inside, and told to change my clothes. I wonder what I am expected to change into, but the answer comes in the form of the dragonfly dress. It's been cleaned and is carefully folded on the mattress with a tube of red lipstick and some blush arranged on top of it.

Amazing. They kidnap me, cage me, asphyxiate me, kill my friend, but bring me lipstick so I can look my best.

I dial the base of the lipstick until a chunk of red emerges. Then I write across the wall's gray blocks the words *I hate you*, though I suspect they already know that much.

There is another surprise. When I hold up the dress something falls out: my eyeglasses.

"Thank *God*," I say aloud. And I've got shoes again, too. They're under the dress.

I pull off my scrubs and step into the dress. Then I sit on the mattress, my stomach growling, wondering if I'll get any dinner tonight. I remember sourly what Will said on the train, that cheerfulness is a military tactic.

And then I think of Will.

I wish for the thousandth time that he were here. And that someone would help us. I think of Munn, who has all those contacts at the Department of Defense—surely, he'd know how to get us out of here.

And my mother. I wonder if I will ever hear her voice again.

And then I think—I hope—that the fact of this dress means that I can go home now. I'd happily travel the long train journey back, eat the cheese sandwiches, wash my clothes in the tiny sink, endure all the hours with nothing to do. I'm so tired of being scared, so altogether tired.

I hear footsteps and I jump. The door opens. Vasiliev has sent one of his lackeys to get me. It's the one with the scalp tattoos.

"Where's my friend?" I say.

"No English."

"I see you gave me back my shoes. Where's my watch?"

"No English."

"My *watch*," I insist, circling my wrist with my fingers, then pretending to check the time.

He shrugs.

"It was a gift from my friend. Another friend, not the one you killed. Or tried to kill, anyway. Can he even *see*?"

"No English."

"You probably gave my watch to your girlfriend. Maybe you sold it."

I wait for him to get angry, but he shows no response. Either he really doesn't understand English or he doesn't care what I say. I notice he pays no attention to my big red lipstick sign either. Nothing I do, other than bring back the dead, matters to these people.

We go out to the cold staircase once again. It feels weird to be wearing shoes again. I clomp along the dark halls, then down the stairs, out the door, and into the van where days ago Will and I crouched together.

I keep thinking he'll be around the next corner. But he's not.

We ride the car elevator up to the street level, then head out. The guy with the sweatshirt drives, the one with the scalp tattoos beside him. My visibility through the front windows is limited. We could be anywhere in Russia, anywhere in the world really, and I wouldn't know.

"Where are we?" I ask. But there's no response.

We ride in silence. When eventually the van stops and they let me out, I'm in front of a pale building with fat pillars and grand windows. The house, if it is a house, is giant. As I'm taken through an iron gate and up a set of steps to a wide wooden door, I think it must belong to the man Vasiliev works for. The one he described back in Stockholm as a man of great power.

"You want me to go in *there*?" I say to the guy with the scalp tattoos.

He rings the bell, then returns to the van, leaving me on the doorstep. I'm nervous as hell, but what can I do? The guy with the sweatshirt leans out the open window, smoking and glaring at me with an expression that says running will be futile. The front door opens and he begins waving the gun, signaling me to go through. I'm terrified to move, but I do it, wondering how on earth the door opened with nobody there.

Once inside, I see that there is someone there. A small, stout woman in a black dress and a long, white apron. She looks like an actor from a living history museum. I'm half expecting a man in a frock coat and top hat to arrive behind her, announcing the prince's ball.

"Where am I?" I say. "Whose house is this?"

The woman says nothing, but ducks her head in greeting.

I step onto a gleaming wooden floor in a hall, vast and elaborate, with giant chandeliers and gold-leaf ornamentation along the walls. My mind flashes back to the Grand Hôtel and all the gold and crystal of the Hall of Mirrors.

That was a lifetime ago.

I hold my hand to the side of my head as though on the phone. "Can I use your phone?" I say. "Phone?" I point to the imaginary phone in my hand. If only I could call someone, call Munn. If not him, then Lauren. She'd tell her dad or the police or someone. She'd figure it out.

But the woman only gestures for me to follow. We climb one side of a double staircase that arches upward toward the floors above. I stare at walls of oil paintings in overwrought frames, intricate molding, a huge decorated ceiling. Through a set of wide doors is a room with a giant ugly chandelier. It hangs from the center of a ceiling rose with a pattern of leaves that snake toward the walls. A set of tall windows frame the branches of the flowering trees outside. The sparkling lights of the city ignite in the slow dusk of evening. I wouldn't have thought I'd recognize the skyline, but I do. I'm in Moscow.

A man stands at the window, his hands behind his back. He turns as I enter the room and comes toward me, smiling.

"I am Mikhail Petrovich Volkov," he says. His English is good, less accented than Vasiliev's, and he guesses correctly that a Russian name is difficult for me and that he needs to speak slowly. "You may know me as Volkov," he says. He pauses as though his name ought to mean something to me, but of course it doesn't.

I nod and smile and shy away, not wanting him too close.

"What? You are afraid of me? I'm not going to hurt you," he says. He seems to find this amusing. When I say nothing he adds, "I understand you had a rather thrilling day, Kira."

He knows my name. He also knows what we were doing in the laboratory.

"Is Will still blind?" I say.

He ignores my question. "Vasiliev told me of this person who can make the dead live again. I thought, who could do such a thing? A magician? Then into my house walks a young woman little more than a child. My dear Kira, you are magnificent."

It pains me to hear him speak like this, as though I've done something great. I've done nothing great. And when I cannot join him in his blithe description of the day's events, his mood changes as though a curtain has been drawn. He frowns. "Come here," he says after a moment. "Let me look at your hands."

I try not to shake as Volkov takes my hands and turns them over gently in his own as though getting ready to tell my fortune. He looks hard at the rough skin, the bitten nails. "Your hands reveal that you are full of worries," he says, noticing the chew marks. "But also, that you work hard. There is a Russian saying, 'The man who does not work, does not eat.'"

A warning.

He points to a patch of skin above my knuckles. "But I suspect you have been doing too much of the wrong kind of work," he says. "See this? The red, rough skin? I understand you have been used in that American laboratory only to wash chemicals from laboratory glass?"

So he knows about Mellin, too.

He points to a shiny patch of skin in the shape of a crescent moon. A burn I received, like so many others, from working in kitchens. My hands and forearms are full of such tiny scars.

"You should protect your hands," he says. "They are going to be very important. *You* are going to be very important."

Volkov loosens his grip and takes a crystal decanter from a tray set on a table beside us. He fills two small ornate glasses and then offers me one.

"To your health," he says. He downs his shot, then holds up the empty glass as though saluting me with it before placing it once again onto the tray.

"Drink!" he instructs.

I look at the little glass of clear liquid in my fingers. Then I hold my breath and force myself to throw back the shot, trying not to wince.

"And now," he says, holding a plate in front of me with pieces of toast and pickle.

I can feel the warmth of the vodka radiating outward inside me as though I've lit a small furnace in my belly. I'm so nervous, I'm afraid I'm going to bring it all back up. But I'm hungry, too, so I take one of the miniature toasts from the plate.

"Another," says Volkov, offering a second shot. I don't want it. But this is not a man who will be told no. So I steady myself for the jolt that is coming, then feel the liquid burn a trail down my throat.

Suddenly, I'm light-headed, as though I could float across the room. But I'm still scared; the alcohol has done nothing for that. One time, when I was a child, I sat down on the forest floor and discovered too late a rattlesnake near my foot. My mother, a few feet away, had calmly but sternly instructed me not to move, not a leg, not even a finger. We waited like that for what had felt like an eternity, silently observing the rattlesnake until, eventually, it unwound itself from its fist of coils and slithered off into the brush.

I feel the same now with Volkov, as though I better be still.

"May I show you something?" he asks. "It's only a flower, but it is a very special flower." He goes to one of the enormous windows and takes a small plant in an ornate pot, placing it on the coffee table. We sit down, and he says, "Let me tell you the story of this flower. One day, a team of scientists were digging below the permafrost in Siberia. They found all sorts of things—woolly rhinoceros bones, hooves of mammoths. And then they found, entirely encased by ice, something like what you see before you."

"They found a potted plant?" The words slip out, a result no doubt of too much vodka. I slap my hand over my mouth.

Volkov looks at me stonily, then laughs. But it is a strange, unnatural laugh, as though he's trained himself to make the noise, as this is what Americans do, they laugh like fools. "No, my lovely, the scientists found a treasure of seeds stored some thirty-two thousand years ago by one of Earth's prehistoric squirrels. This very plant was born of those seeds."

I study the flowers, delicate white blossoms with robust stamens.

"Imagine!" says Volkov. "They came back to life after such an age. It's a miracle, don't you think? But your miracle is even greater." He leans toward me now, whispering. "You can bring human beings back to life. You can cure death. I cannot imagine what it is to feel that power."

"Will can't see." I know I shouldn't speak like this, but I can't stop myself. "Is anyone going to help him?"

Volkov's expression changes at once. He's grown tired of me spoiling this important moment, a moment he's paid dearly for and wishes to enjoy.

"You have an unfortunate habit of dwelling on details," he says coldly.

It's clear that the effort he makes to appear congratulatory thinly veils a great well of anger. Also, that he's a man who makes people afraid. I saw as much in the behavior of the housekeeper, or whoever she is, when she escorted me up to the grand living room to see him. She stood at the entryway, unwilling to enter, her hands folded across the front of her apron, her head bowed, eyes cast down, as though she did not wish to provoke him with so much as an unwelcome glance.

I do the same now, staring down at the silk carpet beneath our feet.

"It has been a long day. You are tired," he says finally.

An enormous growl from my belly sounds, and I automatically press my hand against my stomach. "Excuse me," I mutter. "I worked through lunch."

An understatement if ever there was one.

He lets out a long breath. "My dear girl!" he exclaims, his role as host in full sail once again. "How can you be expected to enjoy the evening if you are hungry? Did Vasiliev not feed you? What is the matter with that man, anyway?" He laughs again, making us into a friendly duo with a common foe in Vasiliev, whose great crime had not been to kill a man but to forget to order in sandwiches. "Let me get you something right away."

He moves to the staircase, calling down. Ten minutes later, the housekeeper appears with a tray of caviar and deviled eggs, slivers of bread and smoked salmon, and tiny warm pastries filled with pureed olives and cheese. I try not to be too greedy, but I eat like I've been starved, which I suppose I have been.

"In a little while we'll have a proper dinner," Volkov says. "I hope that is acceptable to you."

It's clear he is used to people being charmed by his invitations. While I am anything but charmed by him, I could use some food.

Volkov shows me more of the grand house, telling stories about the artifacts he's collected: fossils, dinosaur bones, pieces of meteorites, a medieval medicine chest, a microscope with sapphire and diamond lenses.

"Of course, you have heard of Fabergé eggs," he says, stopping at a sculpture of gold and emeralds in its own glass display case. "Did you know that the nephew of Alfred Nobel had one commissioned? The family was very wealthy, you see. Science is expensive business. And it is becoming more so."

"Did you have this one commissioned?" I ask, peering through the case at the egg, covered in jewels and with a whimsical beauty.

"Oh no," he laughs. "This egg is far older than I am. It was tracked down for me by a fellow who knows that I like such things.

I have a few people who look after my interests in this way."

"Are you a collector, then?" I say.

He considers this. "Yes, I suppose I am. But I am far more excited about the future than the past. And you are the future."

I don't understand what he means. I'm exhausted, and the vodka is still swimming in my head. At last we enter the dining room. At the end of a banquet table are two place settings, elaborate and detailed like every aspect of the giant house. There are several wineglasses and a complete set of silverware, including a tiny fork and a knife with a weird edge. Enormous red-and-gold plates are whisked away and replaced with warm ones when the food arrives.

If you have been fed only sausages and sandwiches for days on end, there is nothing more appealing than crisp green beans, roasted carrots, and grilled peppers. I want it all. I want the tomato, the bright lemon, the pieces of garlic, the herbs. The food is beautifully presented, abundant, and delicious. Perhaps it is the vodka, but everything tastes richer and deeper than I'm used to; even the lemon seems more fragrant.

After a little while, Volkov clears his throat and says, "Vasiliev forgets how much young people need to eat." He pauses, his face registering mock disgust, as though Vasiliev really needs a good telling-off for having fed me so infrequently. "However, he has been useful in finding you, so we can thank him for that. Only occasionally, a person of great potential is brought to my attention, someone worthy of investment."

I freeze, mid-bite. "What do you mean?" I say.

"I would like to see you enriched. Many people are interested, *very* interested, in developing our work. Since the pandemics that have swept our globe, we search for the best people, not just from Russia but from the ends of the earth. And we need them young so that the investment is worthwhile."

I recall something Dmitry said the first time I met him, that the Americans had Silicon Valley and the Russians had Silicon Forest. "Is it true you have whole cities devoted to science?" I say. "Tucked away in forests?"

He leans back in his chair, lacing his fingers together. "The first was Akademgorodok, a science park in Siberia. At its peak, it housed sixty-five thousand scientists. But Brezhnev was not so keen. After the breakup of the Soviet Union, we lost many of our great scientists." He makes a gesture with his hand as though the scientists had vaporized like ghosts. "Now it is coming back, the science. At last, politicians understand its value. We have many hubs. Skolkovo is only twenty kilometers away, for example."

I nod. I have a feeling it is only a matter of time before he tells me I am to work in one of these "hubs."

"You are remarkable—and very young," he says. "Given the right guidance and opportunities you can accomplish great things. Why not pursue post-death recovery here in Russia? I could make this very easy for you."

When I say nothing, he adds, "The type of education you require is expensive. Of course, you already know this. I am aware that you don't have many resources. I mean, of course, money."

I wonder how he knows so much about my circumstances. But, of course, Dmitry warned me about the Russians. *They know everything,* he'd said.

Volkov takes my wineglass and places it in my hand. "Think

of me as Uncle Misha. I can provide all you need to become a great scientist. I run an academy of my own, you see," he says, clinking his glass with mine.

I watch him carefully. "Why would you do that for me?" I say.

Volkov gives a mock jolt of surprise, then says, "You can bring people back from the dead and yet you are asking *why*? Work for me and you will have opportunities you never imagined. No strings!" he says, pulling his hands back, palms up, to show he has no expectations.

I don't believe him for a minute. I'm willing to bet that a man like Volkov has nothing but strings.

"Can you think of me as your benefactor?" he says. "It would be such a pleasure for me."

A benefactor. A patron. It sounds like something from centuries past. But then, the entire house and all the beautiful things around me—the Fabergé egg, the works by great artists, the meteorites and asteroids and ancient bones—are all part of a collection of antiquities. He collects scientific things, and he wants to own the girl who brings the dead back to life.

"That plant you showed me, the one grown from prehistoric seeds?" I wait for Volkov to nod. "Well, who told you that the seeds existed?"

Volkov shrugs. "There are people who know I am curious about such things."

"What people?" I say.

"Friends," he says.

I remember what Vasiliev told me, that he has science scouts. And that one of those scouts is related to Biba.

The pieces all fall into place now: Vasiliev brought me to Volkov to consider for his collection. If I pass this "interview" I will be kept. To what end, I am uncertain. And if I fail the interview?

Volkov looks at me fondly. "You love science, don't you, Kira?"

I nod.

"This is all I ask," he says.

As though I'd be stupid enough to believe that.

We have coffee and chocolate in a room that overlooks a large courtyard, beautifully spotlit to show off the trees and flowerbeds. A fountain, illuminated from below, sparkles with silvery water. Nothing inside Volkov's palatial house can rival the trees through the windows, the flutelike song of the thrushes, the comforting coos of wood pigeons. I wish I could go into the garden. I want to take off my shoes and feel the grass between my toes.

Volkov pours the coffee. "I hope you will accept our arrangement," he says, offering me chocolate from an ornate box. "I will finance everything you need, make sure you are working with the best people, and you will have a comfortable life. How does that sound?"

"You want me to work for the Russian government?"

He lets out a single bark of laughter, then says, "The *government*? Of course not! This is nothing to do with the government. I have my own laboratories. A private enterprise, I can assure you."

I'm scared to death of him, of Vasiliev, of everything around me right now. The house is supposed to be beautiful and interesting, but it reminds me of a mausoleum, a great tribute to dead science. Volkov himself possesses a kind of darkness that he masks, playing the cheery host. I want to run out of here, but where would

I go? Outside are Vasiliev's men. I have no choice but to play along.

"What would you want me to do?" I say.

He smiles, conveying a warm, avuncular air. "I wouldn't presume to tell you what to do," he says, as though it is me who controls him and not the other way around.

I imagine that Volkov is a criminal like everyone involved in kidnapping Will and me, but there's a chance he doesn't know what happened. Perhaps all Volkov has been told is that a girl with a special process for recovering the dead is in Moscow.

"That's a very kind offer. I am more than grateful," I say as politely as I can, "but I'd like to go home."

Volkov nods as though he understands. "Of course you do. But little girls grow up. Eventually, they leave their homes and make their way in new places."

"Sir, I can't," I say, my voice almost a whisper.

He leans toward me. "Oh, but you can. You only need to say yes."

I say nothing. Volkov adjusts himself in his seat, then says, "Tell me why not." He leans back, his brow furrowed, taking a long look at me as though sizing me up. "After all, we are negotiating, you and me." He makes a gesture with his finger, pointing it back and forth between us to emphasize the idea that we are in this together, brokering a deal. "I have made you a generous offer and you have declined. That is perfectly acceptable, but now it is only right that you tell me *why* you have declined so that I have the opportunity to meet your demands."

I have no demands, other than my plea for them to help Will, but I don't dare mention that again. "I just want to go back to America," I say, stumbling through the words.

"America," he repeats, as though confused over why anyone would want to live there. "Has it been so great a life for you? I've been led to believe it has been very hard. For your mother, in particular. Until her illness she worked two jobs at the same time, if I am not mistaken."

He's not mistaken. Two jobs and still things were very tight. But I'd do anything to be back on US soil.

I shrug. "It's my country."

He draws in a breath. "Patriotism is a fine trait," he says, regarding me with a serious expression. "Is there a second reason other than this admirable patriotism?"

A second reason? How about that I've been dragged here against my will, tortured, and forced to live as a prisoner? Or the fact that they put Will's dead body in front of me so I could demonstrate on it? Or that he's made me afraid over the tiniest of infractions, including not wanting to do vodka shots with him in his ghastly living room?

But I won't say any of that. Not if I know what's good for me. Anyway, he'd refute anything I said, explaining it as a "misunderstanding" or "miscommunication" or some gaffe on Vasiliev's part. But he can't change my allegiance to my birthplace. I've given him the one reason for which he has no solution. "Only that," I say.

Volkov nods. "Thank you for being honest with me. It is important for me to know what stops you from pursuing a life in science here in Moscow. Still, you cannot blame me for wishing that a person with a mind such as yours could be persuaded to use it for the benefit of the people of Russia. If you wish to reverse your decision, you know where to find Uncle Misha, no?"

I force a smile. "Yes, I do," I say. "Thank you."

We finish our coffee with no more talk of deals. He tells me the garden is visited nightly by an owl. I half expect one to fly out as though at Volkov's command. But the owl stays hidden. The sky darkens with almost imperceptible slowness. At last, the housekeeper arrives, asking if we would like more coffee.

"I believe a car is waiting for me," I say. *A car.* It's laughable. What I mean is a dirty van.

"Of course," Volkov says.

We say our goodbyes. I wonder if he really will allow me to leave Moscow, to go home. A man like Volkov can summon up any number of scientists. Perhaps he'll move swiftly on to the next. It's only a question of money, of which he has lots, and power, of which he has even more.

On my way out, I ask the housekeeper if I can use the bathroom and am directed to a door at one end of the hall.

The bathroom must be three times the size of my bedroom at home, with a large mirror and another gleaming floor. The ceiling is so high the room echoes, and when I wash my hands it's at a sink so ornate it's like a fountain. Beside it, mounted on the wall, is a lovely glass cabinet. I see it is filled with curious trinkets and am drawn to a set of crystal jars with delicate stoppers. I imagine there are stories attached to each one, just as there had been a story about the pot of white flowers in Volkov's living room. And then my gaze focuses on a single jar with a thick base filled with tiny air bubbles that have been trapped during its making. It has a ground-glass stopper and stenciled lettering across its front, written in English.

This is an old apothecary glass, just like those in the dining room back at Mellin. I gently open the cabinet door, remove the jar, and hold it up to the light. The jar isn't only similar to Munn's laboratory glass, it *is* Munn's laboratory glass. A tiny sticker underneath reveals the name "G.P. Munn."

A chill passes through me. Why would Munn's glassware be in Volkov's house? It doesn't seem possible. A Russian man so enthralled by science that he is willing to pay for me to stay here and work on post-death recovery just *happens* to have one of Munn's laboratory glasses in his cabinet? It's too great a coincidence. I feel my stomach lurch; everything I think I understand is coming apart. Munn knows Volkov. It's a startling fact. And if this is the case, Munn may even know that I'm here or at least suspect it. And then I remember Biba's words: *Don't work for that Munn.*

What does Biba know about the relationship between Volkov and Munn? Volkov said he had friends throughout the world's scientific community. But he may just as easily have enemies. Perhaps one of those enemies is Dr. Gregory Munn?

The contrast between Volkov's palatial house and the dirty van could not be greater. The van smells of burgers and beer, and I can tell by the way it weaves that the driver is drunk. We speed down the road, miss a light, run an intersection, then careen to the left as I tumble in the back, looking for something to hold on to.

We're up and down huge boulevards, zipping in and out of buses and other cars moving as crazily as we are, everybody sounding their horns. Meanwhile, my brain is full of questions about Munn. Of all the people I've ever known, I admire him the most.

But that laboratory glass is as stark a sign as any. They know each other. Had the two of them drunk vodka together in Volkov's upstairs veranda, looking out over the rooftops, and made decisions about my life?

I'm also plagued by thoughts of Will. Nobody speaks of him. It's like he doesn't exist. I keep remembering him dead on the gurney. I imagine him, lost and blind.

"Would you stop driving like a maniac?" I yell to the guy with the sweatshirt. He pulls out his pistol and waves it around, shouting drunkenly in Russian. The guy with the tattoos takes the gun from him, replacing it with a can of beer. They drink and speed and laugh, playing a game now in which they take corners at a pace. I brace myself as they jerk to a stop, then roll like a ball in the back of the van as they swerve through traffic, yelling their heads off. Finally, they take a corner too fast and—*bang*—the van clips the curb, hits a trash can, and does a one-eighty before landing on the sidewalk. It's not the worst crash in the world, but the guy in the sweatshirt wasn't wearing his seat belt and he nearly knocks himself out against the windshield. The guy with the tattoo seems to have done something to his foot. Meanwhile, my hip feels like a boulder dropped on it, but I can move while they can't.

I have a chance here.

Sliding across the van, I step over the back of the guy in the sweatshirt, hearing him scream as I push open the door. I fall onto the sidewalk, banging my knee, then pull myself up onto my feet, limping, but moving. I make it to the end of the avenue and search desperately for a way to cross. But there are cars everywhere and no crosswalk. I run up and down, searching for a route across the traffic before finally seeing the underpass that tunnels beneath the ground.

I'm charging down the steps when I feel a grip on my shoulder. Somebody grabs my hair. I push forward but it's no use. My head lurches back; my feet come off the ground. I feel the same pressure on my neck and head as that night in Palo Alto when I was attacked. That time, they'd used some kind of drug to knock me out. I don't know what they used because there's really no such thing as a knockout drug. Even a rag soaked in chloroform and held over a victim's nose and mouth isn't instant. It takes about five minutes to work.

But this isn't chloroform. The guy with the sweatshirt, his face bloody from the crash, holds me in a locked position as the other one gets a needle high into my arm. I feel the scratch of the needle, then my arm filling with cold. Suddenly, it's as though my muscles have dropped from my frame. My eyes stare forward like headlights; my heart beats loudly in my chest. I have no control of my body at all, certainly not to stand, but not even to gasp for air. As hard as I try, I can't get oxygen into my starving lungs.

It dawns on me now that they've used a paralyzing drug, which stops all voluntary muscle contractions, including breathing. I'll be dead soon; I see no way around this fact. I suppose that if I won't work for Volkov, I'm a liability, a witness to an international crime. Will, too.

Every cell in my body aches for oxygen. My vision begins to close. My chest is bursting with the pain of asphyxiation. I'd do anything to breathe, such a simple thing. And then someone pushes a finger into my mouth, and I feel a current of rubber-scented air. Perhaps I'm imagining it, but what looks to be a portable ventilation unit, no bigger than a laptop, suddenly comes into my vision. A tube slides painfully down my throat. The machine works away, one breath, two. I feel my body gaining strength, my vision clearing. Volkov must not have ordered me dead after all, which means, among other things, that there is a possibility that Will is alive.

25

I WAKE WITH the same throbbing headache I had on the train. Nausea, too. My stomach lurches, but when I try to get up I'm stopped by a heavy restraint on my wrist. I can only get so far. I bend over the edge of the bed and retch onto the floor.

I pull myself back onto the mattress, covered in a sheen of sweat. Where I banged myself during the crash is sore. And the pain in my temples throbs like a wound. The feeling is familiar, but this time there's no Will. No cool hand to brush the hair off my forehead and tell me not to worry. Nobody at all, as far as I can tell. The bed is in the same building where I've been prisoner for days. I recognize the smell and the sagging, stained ceiling. But the room has been fitted out like a hospital room. I make out a sink and a set of drawers on wheels. An IV sends fluids into my left arm.

I'm not going to be a prisoner any longer. I just can't take it. I consider how the IV needle might be used as a weapon. I only need to get it out of my arm.

But just as I have that thought, Vasiliev huffs into the room, trailed by a dark-haired assistant, a boy about my age, with a long face and a clipboard in his hands.

Vasiliev says something to him and the boy disappears, returning with a plastic tub and paper towels. He begins cleaning the floor while Vasiliev checks the monitors.

"Water," I croak. There's a sink I can't reach and a stack of paper towels on a countertop. "Something to clean my face with?" I ask. "Those paper towels."

My voice doesn't sound like me. It arrives slow and thick, as though I haven't spoken in days. "How long have I been out?" I ask.

Vasiliev says nothing. He presses a floor pedal and a motor starts, tilting the bed so that I am more upright. My head swims.

"Sick?" Vasiliev says, and thrusts a bedpan onto my lap.

"Thirsty."

Vasiliev shrugs, then instructs the boy, who drops what he's doing to fetch the tiniest of paper cups, barely a swallow of water and it's not even cold.

I wish they'd go away, both of them. I can't stand the sight of them.

"Let me go home," I say.

"Sleep," says Vasiliev. He signals the boy to leave, then follows him out, shutting the door behind him.

But I don't want to sleep. I want to go home, to sit in our little kitchen with its oiled table where I set up Legos as a child, where I'd done my homework, read papers, celebrated birthdays. I want to see my mother, who will be scared and alone. To talk to Lauren, my good and wonderful friend. And Dmitry. He'd be so angry if he saw what they are doing to me.

But I suddenly can't stay awake, no matter how I try.

The next thing I'm aware of are footsteps. I wake again, my head feeling like there's a weight upon it, my limbs like dumbbells. They probably guessed my weight wrong when they medicated me, a simple miscalculation that can kill a person.

When I open my eyes I see Vasiliev. He's wheeling in a metal cart with a television on it. Behind him is the boy who cleaned up the vomit earlier, balancing a tray with a pot of tea and a bowl of broth.

"Why are you keeping me here?" I say. "I've already shown you everything I know."

Vasiliev doesn't even acknowledge the question. He unwinds the cord for the television. The boy places the tray on a table so I can eat. I get the feeling it wouldn't matter if I screamed and yelled. They'd still ignore me. And I can't do either right now. I'm too weak.

"Can I have my other hand, please?" I'm left-handed, and right now very shaky.

But instead of unfastening the restraint, Vasiliev gives the electrical cord to the boy to plug into an outlet on the wall.

"I want to go home," I say.

"Shortly, you will not want to go home," he says.

This would make me laugh, if I could laugh at anything right now. But all I can think about is whether somewhere, even somewhere close by, Will is being held captive in a similar bed. Are they telling him he won't want to go home, too?

"I want to see Will," I say.

"Will?" He pronounces the name as though the *W* is a *V*.

"Is he okay?"

Vasiliev grunts.

"Is he dead?"

But Vasiliev is too busy monkeying around with the television, then conferring with his assistant, who pushes the cart cable farther into the back of the monitor. I can't understand all this fuss with the television.

"How long have I been out?" I ask.

"You've been ill some few days now. Car crash."

Ill? Drugged up to my eyeballs, he means.

I should probably try to eat. The broth suggests they have no faith that my stomach will hold solid food. I unwrap the spoon from the napkin and take a few messy mouthfuls.

"Watch," says Vasiliev, pointing to the TV. The boy gives me my glasses.

Across the screen are familiar images. Cars, streets, sidewalks. It's America—I'm not sure where yet. A headline scrolls across the bottom: *Resurrection Drugs on the Horizon.*

The TV fills with stock footage of laboratories—a gloved hand taking up liquid with a pipette, test tubes being carefully lifted from centrifuges. Vasiliev ups the volume and I hear a broadcaster's voice:

"Post-death recovery could mean people live not one, but many lives, as researchers investigate ways to bring people back to life even hours after they are declared legally dead."

The voice goes on to explain that post-death recovery was developed at the Mellin Institute as part of a classified, government-funded research project.

"But early last week, an employee at Mellin broke ranks with the institute, uncovering this research and bringing US secrets to Russia . . ."

The report cuts to a man standing on a street outside a government building. The heavy frames of his eyeglasses balance awkwardly on his handsome face as though he isn't used to wearing them. "We don't know why she did it," he says. "We only know that what ought to have been an American technology is now available in Russia, where this researcher is currently residing. And, of course, we don't know to what end this technology will be used."

He raises his hand, offering a brief wave before turning away from the reporters, then pushing his hair out of his eyes in a gesture I've seen a hundred times before.

It's Will. The glasses are to help correct his vision, which was damaged during his post-death recovery. But everything else about him is exactly as it was.

I look desperately at Vasiliev, but he directs my attention back to the screen. The clips are recent, but they aren't in any order. They seem to have been taken over the course of many days, mapping out the world's response to post-death recovery. I watch various versions of Will giving that same sanctimonious remark to different audiences. He keeps talking about a "researcher," by which he means me, of course. Like I intended to come to Russia and tell everyone about post-death recovery. Like I'm some kind of rogue informant.

Then I see Munn being accosted by reporters outside the doors of the Mellin Institute. Munn explains there has been no threat posed by the leak of information.

"Is it true Kira Adams is currently residing in Moscow?" asks a reporter.

My name. My name on television. I'd never imagined I'd hear such a thing. Why would I?

I watch as Munn states that he is unaware of my whereabouts. For the hundredth time, I wonder how this could be the case. I keep remembering Munn's glassware in Volkov's bathroom. It's hard to believe he has no idea what's going on.

More footage. There's April, a knapsack over one shoulder and the animal carrier she uses for rats in her hands. She's trying to get through a group of reporters, ignoring the questions that fire at her from all sides. But then somebody asks what it was like to work with a person who can bring back the dead, and she pauses for a moment.

"Are you *kidding*?" she says, flicking back her hair. "Kira was just learning how to work in a lab, you know?"

"How long has she been working on post-death recovery?" asks the reporter.

April shrugs. "I'm going to get in my car now, okay?"

"What's in the carrier?" another reporter calls. "Are those rats that were brought back from the dead?"

The camera zooms in on the carrier. I bet that's Cornelius and his brothers in there. Perhaps in the chaos of Will's announcement about my "defection," April made sure to "lose" the laboratory notes about Cornelius.

Now comes footage from school. I see Greevy, sitting at his office desk, saying he is surprised and sorrowed by the news. But he doesn't look sorrowed. He looks harassed. I see kids who barely know me saying I am a loner, a geek, a loser, a "total brain." There's Mike, acting like he's freaked out because he's been in school with a traitor to the country. Someone else says it's gross that I touch dead people. One girl a few grades down from me says she's glad I can bring back the dead. "Doesn't this help people?" she asks reasonably.

She's sharp. You can tell. I bet she's good at science.

The interviews continue. They find signs of treason and conspiracy in everything about me. Someone tracks down Lauren, way out in the hills of California at her internship. She's very clear on the subject (me). She stands with her hip angled toward the camera, staring over her sunglasses at the reporter with contempt. "Do I have a *comment*?" she says. "Yeah, like, have you heard of *trial by media*?"

You have to hand it to her.

Most painful is watching my mother barricading herself behind the closed door of our house, trying to shoo away the reporters. I tense up, rising out of the bed until the restraint at my wrist pulls me back, watching her as she asks them politely to leave her be. My mother looks exhausted. She looks ill. Then she's gone.

I want to stick my head under the pillow, blocking out any more of this, but on comes a new clip and I can't turn away. It's Rik.

He seems nervous and self-aware; I've never seen him like that. He's always so confident. When we walked through Stockholm, or danced on the ship, or held each other's gaze across the chilly water in the stone pool, I'd been the nervous one. Not him. But right now, he looks as though he hasn't slept in days.

"What are your thoughts on Kira Adams?" they ask him.

He shakes his head, his eyes down, as though they are talking about a dead person. "No comment," he says.

"Were you personal friends with Miss Adams?"

"Not really," he states.

Not really?

I want to reach through the television and tell him that none of this is my fault. How can he possibly believe what Will is saying about me? He knows I'd never betray Mellin.

But maybe he doesn't know that. And I remember, too, how he helped me prepare my statement for the SFOF committee. That was kind of him, but he was under instructions from Munn. Maybe he's still under instructions from Munn. Say nothing. Deny knowledge. Pretend you hardly know her.

I shouldn't be surprised. His allegiance to Munn is steadfast.

But nothing explains Will. He looked after me on the train. He soothed me when I had nightmares, made me laugh as we waited out the long hours. He promised we'd stick together. I can't imagine what would have made him turn against me.

It hurts more than it ought to.

"What did you tell Will to convince him to go out there and lie?" I say fiercely.

Vasiliev is nonplussed. "What lie?" he says.

"Did you threaten to kill him? Because he certainly knows I didn't come here by choice to hand you information belonging to the US government."

He shrugs. "Are you not here in Moscow now, surrounded by Russian scientists?"

"You forced me!" I say.

He makes a face, then snorts. "You don't know force," he says slowly.

Oh, but I do.

Another clip, this one of the chairman of the Science for Our Future committee, Dr. Biruk. His bald head shines darkly under the television lights as he describes how I misled the SFOF judges about having a PhD. He comes across as being very sorry to have to say this, very sorry indeed. His statement is made worse by how likable he is.

"Turn it off," I say. But Vasiliev doesn't move.

"I'd have thought a clever girl like you would have more friends," he says.

I look away. I can't let Vasiliev see how much all this affects me, how it destroys me. I stare at the grubby wall beside me and try my damnedest not to cry.

But then I hear a voice. I turn back to the television and see Mellin's grand glass front once again on the screen. There's someone standing at the entrance, positioned exactly where Munn had been in the other clip. But this time it's not Munn. It's Dmitry.

His khakis are cinched up properly with a belt so they don't sag around his hips. His hair is more tidy than usual, his face clean-shaven. He's not only wearing a dress shirt, he's even wearing a tie. He takes a few steps, then stands still, a page of notes in his hand as he faces reporters.

"I'd like to make a statement," he says.

He pushes his glasses up on his nose, then squares his shoulders. He looks poised, but I can see the almost imperceptible shaking of his hand as he begins to read. "I had the pleasure of working with Kira Adams for many months. She is an honest and compassionate individual. She wished always to serve those around her, to work hard and learn as much as she can for the good of science, and the good of this country—"

I feel the emotion swell in my throat.

Vasiliev snorts. "Only one colleague defends you, and he is Russian," he says sourly.

Meanwhile, Dmitry continues on screen. "If she is now in Russia, then she was taken against her will. The criminal you seek is not Kira Adams, but whatever brutish group the Russian government is allowing to act. The Russian government tolerates almost any form of criminal activity in order to bait the United States and has been punishing scientists or killing them outright since before the time of Stalin—"

Vasiliev swears, then reaches down and yanks the cord of the television from the wall. The room falls silent. If I didn't have the restraint on me I swear I'd wrestle Vasiliev for that cord, because I desperately want to hear the rest of what Dmitry says.

Or maybe just his voice. I wish I could tell him what it means to me to know that he believes in me.

The boy with the dark hair knocks at the door, then enters the room carrying a shopping bag.

"Your clothes," says Vasiliev. "Get dressed and we will talk."

"I can't put them on if you don't unshackle me," I say.

"Shackles," he says, making a *tut-tut* sound as he unfastens my wrist. "Such babies, you Americans."

He pats the pocket on his lab coat and comes up with an envelope, which he drops onto the bed. "From Volkov," he says, and disappears out of the room so I can dress.

I look at the envelope. It has already been opened, undoubtedly by Vasiliev, who doesn't concern himself with matters of privacy or decency. Inside is a card with a picture of the Moscow skyline in a rainbow of watercolors. The message is in Volkov's own hand. It reads:

DEAREST KIRA,
WHEN THE WORLD TURNS AGAINST YOU PLEASE REMEMBER UNCLE MISHA. MY HOUSE YOU VISITED IS ON KRIVOARBATSKY LANE. ALL THE TAXI DRIVERS KNOW IT. COME DIRECTLY FROM VASILIEV. IT WILL BE FAR BETTER FOR YOU THAT WAY.

MIKHAIL

And there it is, not a clue, but an answer.

I see that I've walked straight into his trap. And the realization of what has happened stops my breath.

Volkov had asked me what prevented me from staying in Moscow. *It is only right that you tell me . . .* he'd said.

My answer was that I wanted to return to my country because I love my country. He couldn't argue with such sentiment. So he did what he could do: turn the country against me. I can love America all I want, but from what I see on the news, it doesn't love me. If I show up at the embassy now, I'll be placed under arrest for divulging government secrets. Even if I'm not ultimately convicted of a crime, nobody will ever trust me again in America. There will be no job at Mellin. No job at any laboratory. This is why Vasiliev said that soon I would not want to go home. Home means jail or blacklisting.

No doubt this is what Vasiliev's "talk" will be about.

Well, to hell with that.

I grab the shopping bag, pull out the dress, and hold it up. The dragonflies have seen better days, that's for sure. But the dress is still beautiful. I take the shoes from the bag and am shocked to discover at the bottom, wrapped in tissue, the pink watch that Lauren gave me. I handle it carefully, as though it's a live thing, admiring all over again the beautiful watch face that catches the light. I hadn't wanted to accept it because it was too expensive. Now I see the price tag is irrelevant. Its value comes from something else entirely.

By the time Vasiliev returns I'm dressed. A formal gown is the silliest thing to wear under such circumstances, but Vasiliev can see me in a werewolf costume for all I care. I hold my wrist up to show him the watch and say, "Volkov made you give this back to me, didn't he? I'm surprised one of your henchmen hadn't already sold it."

His pale face registers no emotion. He takes a chair from the corner, scraping it across the floor, then drops heavily onto the seat.

"Volkov's laboratories are the best in the world," he says. He leans back in his chair, his lashless eyelids drooping as though the effort of keeping me prisoner has exhausted him. "There are other young people."

"Why on *earth* would I work for you?"

"We work for Volkov. Perhaps you have learned it is better not to cross him."

"You mean, if I'd agreed to stay in the first place he wouldn't have turned my country against me?"

"Your country," he sneers. "You know Twitter?" he says, pronouncing it *tweeter*. He gets out his phone, showing me the little blue bird along with a list of trending hash tags, including #KiraAdams, #Traitorscientist, and #securitythreat.

There is talk of criminal charges, long sentences in federal prison, the importance of making me an example. Apparently, I'm not too young to be executed for treason.

How can the #military **do its job with** #nationaltraitors **like** #KiraAdams **running free?** #lockherup #executespies

As for post-death recovery itself, some think it sounds great. You see #Liveforever and #CheatDeath in their tweets. But many find it creepy. I'm called an offense to God, a sick child, a quack, and a criminal. Always, it comes back to that.

"How much of this nonsense did you generate with your own troll factories?" I say, pulling on my shoes. My head is still hammering and my balance feels wrong.

"You work for Volkov or you are arrested. Not by the Russians, but by the Americans. Your CIA. Already, they are looking for you.

We can help them find you faster, of course."

"Nobody ever got in trouble for telling the truth," I say, sounding braver than I feel.

He looks at me like I'm really very stupid, then says, "You will go to Volkov. He will give you the protection you need. United States will not be able to harm you."

I'm wondering how much more he knows that he isn't telling me. He's impossible to read, appearing either angry or depressed. Perhaps he's failed with me in some way I don't understand. Or perhaps he just doesn't care. He works for a tyrant who uses scientists like slaves. He's a tyrant himself.

He plucks Volkov's note from my hand, puts it in the pocket of his lab coat, and says, "Volkov is expecting you. You will go directly from this location to his house—"

"No!" I interrupt.

But he carries on, indifferently. "I suggest you show gratitude. Not to me. I don't care. But to Volkov. He is very powerful, very . . ." He taps his temple with a forefinger. "But you probably think you are clever enough to fool everyone. I assure you this is not the case."

He heaves himself from the chair, as though he's been working too many hours. "We will leave shortly."

"Absolutely not."

He looks at me for a long minute, then says, "What is the message you wish to communicate to Volkov?"

I have plenty of messages I'd like to relay to Volkov, none of them flattering. But I recall something Volkov himself said to me, as we sat in the palace of his house. He said, *Little girls grow up. They leave their homes and make their way in new places.*

"Tell him the little girl has grown up," I say.

Vasiliev takes that in. "You wish to sound brave," he scoffs, as though this amuses him and disgusts him in equal measure.

He shakes his head, then leaves the room.

I watch him leave, expecting the door to lock behind him. But the door remains open. I stare into the empty threshold, waiting for the men to arrive, Vasiliev's little posse of armed guards. But none come. No guns or threats or that awful constant feeling of being watched. I look around and realize there isn't even a camera on me. At least, none that I can see.

It seems that without any great announcement, I've just been released. I remove my shoes again and step soundlessly into the hall. It feels so odd to be able to do this, to walk out of a room on my own, to move freely once again.

But now I see the dark-haired boy who had been in the room earlier. He's coming toward me, holding a box of supplies. He freezes when he sees me. I begin to run, but I hear him call out, "Don't go yet! They can still find you!"

It isn't just that he speaks great English, but that his accent is exactly like that of so many people who live near me, literally in my neighborhood. It stops me in my tracks.

I turn to face him. He's smaller than I am. He may even be younger. "Where are you from?" I ask.

He looks down, saying nothing.

"You're American?"

After a moment he says, "Mexican. But I lived in America."

"Why are you here?" I say.

No answer. He stares at the floor, unmoving. I walk toward him. He's wearing a white lab coat, just like the one Vasiliev wears, and his hands are pushed deep in his pockets. When I get nearer I see that in one of them he is clasping a deck of playing cards, thumbing through them like they are worry beads.

Munn found him living on the streets selling card tricks for a dollar.

"Arturo?" I whisper. "Is that *you*?"

He raises his head and meets my gaze. He has huge brown eyes, a young boyish face. "Tracker," he says, and points at my leg.

"Where?" I say.

He licks his lips, glancing over his shoulder. "Here," he says, and points around my hip to the back of my thigh.

We return to the room and rifle through the set of drawers near my bed, finding bandages, syringes, antiseptic wipes, latex gloves, then finally the thing we need: a small scalpel blade. I douse it in alcohol, then hand it to Arturo.

"Be careful," I say, pulling my dress up.

Arturo nods, blushing crimson.

The tracker is tiny, but getting it out is bloody and painful. I have to lie on the floor with my leg in the air like a tumbled ballerina while a boy I don't know stares right into my underwear.

Arturo keeps apologizing and I keep telling him "Just get it out," until, at last, he leans back on his heels, and presents a tiny black cylinder to me, balancing it on the end of a forefinger.

I say, "I'll remove yours now. Then you can come with me."

"No," he says.

"But I can't leave you," I say.

He starts shaking, then saying, "No! No!" louder and louder. "Go!" he says finally, then backs up away from me and, to my astonishment, turns and runs.

26

I DON'T CHASE after Arturo. Instead, I race from the building into a glorious day, the wet air of late spring all around. Slipping off my shoes, I step barefoot across the grass. The moment of freedom is so exquisite I forget all about the pain in my thigh. I have no idea where I'm going or how I'll navigate the city, but for a single hard-won moment I think only of the sun on my face and the cool grass between my toes.

I follow the sidewalk, heading God knows where. Heading out. The sky is cloudless and blue. I see a gathering of sparrows at a bus stop and watch them for a full minute, amazed at how much I've missed the small details of living. A dog passes on a leash and I want to drop to my knees and hug it. I have no money, not a cent, but at least I'm no longer locked in a room.

The tracking device is in my hand, still bloody from where Arturo fished it out. I wish Arturo were here with me instead of back in that monstrous disused laboratory with its rotting structure, but I can't think about him just yet. I have to think of where to put the tracker so that Volkov's people don't realize I've ditched it. The answer comes by way of a city bike, wedged among a bank of others. I stick the tracker under the seat. It'll ride for miles, I imagine.

I hop buses, evading the drivers because I don't have fare. Amazingly, I only get kicked off once. Did the driver swear at me? Who knows? I can't understand a word he says anyway.

I should go straight to the embassy, if I knew where that was. But I'm not ready to answer questions or to be locked up again, if that is what is going to happen. I may only have a few hours of freedom.

I travel by bus to Red Square, vast and full of tourists standing in line to get into the museums, talking among each other in all languages, taking pictures. I stare up at the grand clock on Spasskaya Tower, above which sails a single red star. I marvel at the colors of St. Basil's Cathedral. All around are restaurants and bars and kiosks. The smell of food is overwhelming, and suddenly the only thing on my mind is that I'm starving. But a sandwich costs money that I just don't have.

I don't want to turn myself in, but I've got no money and nowhere to stay tonight. There's no other choice.

But then I think, *What would Lauren do if she were here?* Would she waltz up to the embassy and say, *Hi, I'm the agent working for a foreign power who you've been looking for?* Would she turn herself in?

I can almost hear her now, that brassy confidence, that fantastic sense of fun. She'd say, *If they want me they can come and get me!*

So I channel up some Lauren, and before I know it, I'm feeling like I did back in Stockholm, back when I was sipping champagne. In the dragonfly dress I was able to fool people. And while, to my mind, the dress has evolved into my prison clothes, it still says money to everyone else, as does Lauren's watch.

A realization hits me all at once: The dress is my entrance ticket, my letter of recommendation. Wearing this, I can walk into any restaurant in the city and be treated with respect. And into any hotel. If I'm going to be arrested, I may as well have some fun first. So I stand up, put on my high heels, and set off across the street to the Ritz-Carlton.

The Ritz-Carlton, Moscow, parks expensive cars out front to show how wealthy their guests are. It's huge and glitzy and kind of terrifying. I stand at the entrance, about to go in, then change my mind. But it's not because the hotel intimidates me. It's because I see the Hotel National next door, an Art Nouveau building with more of an old-world feel, and there's a family arriving at its doors. Two children and their parents, dressed as though they've been to the theater and laden with shopping bags. I head toward the Hotel National, arriving just in time to slip into line behind them. The parents don't notice. The children regard me curiously, then glance away. I try to appear casual, as though I'm part of the family and I belong in a place like this.

Nothing could be further from the truth, though I look the part.

I pass through the lobby, which is enormous, with expensive furnishings, marble floors, and shrub-size flower arrangements.

The family I'm following calls for an elevator, and I wait with them, then remain in the elevator when the family gets out on the third floor. I have a plan . . . sort of.

I go searching for a cleaning cart outside an open hotel room door. This takes all of ten minutes to find. Standing in the lobby, I gather the courage to enter. Then, like a diver embarking on a complicated series of flips, I set my concentration and burst into the room, arriving in what I hope looks like a flurry of frustration. I see the cleaner right away. She's my mother's age. She even looks like her, but is wearing a stiff uniform and sturdy pumps.

"My glasses?" I say, making circles with my thumbs and forefingers, holding them against my eyes.

At first, the cleaner regards me suspiciously. I feel the dread of discovery. What if she knows that the person who occupies this room has already checked out? But she begins poking around, searching for the glasses I've pretended to lose, her low heels clicking against the parquet floor. Meanwhile, I stash my actual glasses behind the television and then make out that I'm hunting for them, too.

In fact, I'm looking for the internet access code, which I find on a sheet of instructions on the desk. Then, a stroke of luck: a card key sleeve is sitting right there by the phone. Waving the card sleeve will likely get me past the doormen.

But when I tuck the card sleeve into my palm, I discover it isn't empty. I feel the stiff plastic of a card inside. This is like treasure. It must be that the occupants had been given an extra key or simply left it behind. I stuff it into my shopping bag just as the cleaner finds the "lost" glasses. She holds them up to me carefully and I make a show of looking genuinely relieved. "*Spasibo!*" I say. It's what Dmitry always says by way of thanks.

I retreat to the lobby and head down the hall, turning into a stairwell, where I have to pause, leaning against the wall, waiting for my heart to stop racing. I think of Stockholm and how, in those days, I'd been almost too afraid to enter a hotel in which I'd had an actual reservation. Now look at me.

First things first. I need a shower. The hotel has a fitness center and a pool. All I have to do is wave my new card key at the attendant and I'm straight into the changing room. This room couldn't be further from the cold shower in the abandoned laboratory. For one thing, the floor is heated. Also, the tiling is beautiful and might, in fact, be marble. Banks of mirrors and sinks occupy one side of the room, big shower stalls the other. I peek through the doors and see the pool area. A wall of glass shows the city in sparkling light. If I had a little more courage and a bathing suit, I'd swim in the glow of the sun that streams through.

But for now it's enough to take a shower, not lukewarm like in the abandoned laboratory, but a hot shower full of steam, with shampoo and scented shower gel, even hair conditioner. I stay in the shower so long my skin wrinkles. Then I wash my underwear, drying it under a hand dryer. I dress again in the steamy warmth, feeling clean and smelling good for the first time in a long while.

My plan for dinner is whatever is left on trays outside room doors. Eating room service leftovers isn't exactly stealing, and anyway, my stomach is roaring with hunger. The first tray offers cold coffee and an after-dinner mint. The next is nothing but an empty wine bottle and two stemmy glasses. But then I discover a true gift:

half a deli sandwich, totally untouched, that a guest has left behind. I eat it in a laundry closet that will be my bedroom for the night. Of course, the door was locked, but I waited for someone from house-keeping to leave with a load of towels in her arms, then caught the door just before it closed. I've never been so grateful for a meal.

The business center is just a few computers and a printer in a small yellow room, but it's all I need this morning. I wish I could email Dmitry, but as far as I know the only time he hacks out of the closed system at Mellin is to play online chess. I'm desperate to contact Lauren but am almost certain that all Lauren's social media will now be under surveillance, and I don't want the FBI knocking on her door. However, there is one person I must communicate with whatever the consequences. I open up a fresh message and type in her email address. *Dear Mom*, I begin.

But then I have to stop and pull myself together. This is so hard.

I try again, typing, *You're going to hear a lot of misinformation about me, but this is the truth, as hard as it is to believe* . . .

She may not get the email—she hardly ever checks her inbox. But it may be my last opportunity to contact her for a while, and I have to try. I want to reassure her, but also warn her that what is said about me on the news will probably get much worse before the media grow tired of the story. I tell her the truth, at least what is safe for her to know, which isn't much. Specifically, I don't tell her anyone's name. I don't mention Munn. If I did, she'd be at Mellin, threatening his life if he doesn't get me out of Russia. But he can't get me out of Russia.

Moscow has over a hundred sixty thousand CCTV cameras. Its facial recognition software is among the most sophisticated in the world. I know this from Dmitry. And I also know from Dmitry that the Russian government keeps a bank of images so vast that if you are on the Russian social media site, VKontakte, you are in the system. If you have a passport or any photo ID, you are in the system. Certainly if you have a criminal record or are understood to be a fugitive from justice, as I am now, you are in the system.

So, once I leave the hotel and am out on the street again, I know I'm being clocked. I better do something about that. I see an old lady at a kiosk selling straw hats. While she's sorting out change for a customer, I do something awful, grabbing a navy-and-white bonnet with a flouncy pink ribbon. It will help me fool the cameras. I move quickly away, hiding in the crowds, the hat pulled low across my brow. Then I duck into one of the nicer cafés to perform another act I'd never do in regular life: steal a tip off a table. Stealing a tip takes stealth and true thievery. It's also just mean. When my mother waitressed, her tips made up most of her pay.

The waitress shows me a table and offers me a menu. I hold the menu, pretending to read the complicated script. I consider leaving, trying another restaurant with a waitress who is rude or lazy, and not the lovely girl who brings me ice water and this basket of black bread that I'm scarfing down fast.

But I really don't have a choice.

Deeper in the restaurant, I see a group get up noisily, readying to leave. It appears a guy is looking for the waitress, a few bills in his hand, but she's in the kitchen, so he drops them on the table. If I'm quick I can get there in time. I make my way toward the table as though looking for a bathroom, pocketing the money as the guys reach the door. I wait until they are out of sight entirely, then turn on my heel and walk swiftly out of there.

The money is for the metro. There's a shop I saw from the bus on the way in yesterday that looked like it sold secondhand clothes. I've been in enough secondhand places to have a nose for such things. If I'm lucky, I can sell the dragonfly dress and buy some jeans and a pair of shoes I can walk in.

I enter the metro, still thrilled to be traveling on my own. No locked rooms. No men with guns. The metro turns out to be incredibly fancy: wide, tiled floors, marbled walls, all beautifully lit by brass wall lamps. It's a surprise, just as in Stockholm when Rik showed me the world's longest art museum, underground.

Above me is a surveillance camera. Along the platform are more. It seems the whole of Moscow is one big observation tower. I pull my hat deeper onto my head and angle my gaze down, waiting for a train to Novokuznetskaya. It's not long before I emerge back into daylight, searching now for the shop front I was sure I saw. I get lost, of course, and Lauren's shoes are unforgiving. By the time I find the secondhand clothing shop my feet are sore with blisters. But the windows are stocked with nice clothes, and a cheerful set of jingle bells announce my arrival.

Inside, a woman in a handcrafted dress is marking price tags on earrings spread across a glass counter. She looks up when I come in and I feel her eyes sweep the dress, then rest on Lauren's watch.

"Do you speak English?" I say.

"Little," she says, pinching her thumb and forefinger together.

She has dark eyes, heavy features. She moves slowly as though she's just woken from a nap.

"Do you think you can sell this dress?" I wonder what Lauren would say at the idea of selling the dress to a shop like this. But then, Lauren is a practical girl. She'd sell it and not look back.

The woman eyes the dragonfly dress freshly. Coming around the counter to where I stand, she touches the fabric, then pulls back the neck to check the label. "I can sell," she says finally. She offers a price, but of course I can't understand. I ask her to write it down, which she does.

"How about this?" I say, countering with a larger number, "but I take it mostly in clothes?" The negotiation goes on for a few minutes, with me desperate to get the best deal I can and the woman looking spectacularly bored with it all.

At last, we settle. I begin searching through the store. I want jeans, at least two shirts, and a pair of comfortable shoes. Also, another dress. I may need to keep freeloading off the hotel and have to look respectable.

"Do you have raincoats?" I say.

She doesn't understand. "*Plashch?*" she says, pointing to a rack of jackets.

For shoes I take a thin pair of pink sneakers because they are the only shoe in the place without heels. I try to get the rest in cash, but the woman balks.

"No money," she says, pushing a large velvet box of rings and necklaces my way. "Jewelry."

"I really need money," I say apologetically. Walking around

penniless isn't going to work for much longer. And I'm hungry again.

"The watch," the woman says, eyeing my wrist again. "I give cash."

I need cash. But Lauren's watch is the only thing I've got left from my old life, and I won't give it up.

She purses her lips in disapproval, but she tallies up the totals on a pad and hands me a copy along with some old bills that are perhaps too dirty to give to paying customers. She also throws in a tote bag for free.

"I want to sell my hair," I say.

The woman looks only mildly surprised. "Not Moscow," she says. "Kyiv."

Kiev, Ukraine. "Nowhere in Moscow?"

I can see the woman thinks it's a bad idea. "You keep long hair. Men like," she says. But she gives me an address.

The address takes me farther out of the city to an apartment in a building that looks like the half dozen buildings next to it on a nondescript residential street. A heavy woman wearing black answers the door, glaring at me crossly as though I'm intruding. I don't have the language to describe why I'm here, so I grab my hair, holding it up like a rope. "Sell?"

At first, the woman says nothing. But then she steps forward, inspecting my hair as though for lice. I can hear her breathing, smell her perfume. Finally, she nods and ushers me inside.

I sit in a chair in the middle of a living room lined in fake wooden paneling with windows that look as though they would fall apart if anyone tried to open them. The woman brushes out my hair and speaks slowly in Russian as though I will understand if she takes the time to sound out each word. The steam from a stew is thick in the air, along with the smell of onions.

It turns out the woman makes sheitels, wigs worn for religious reasons. The place is set up with sewing machines and Styrofoam heads, stained by dye. Two beautiful finished wigs, one blond, one brunette, perch gracefully on a tabletop like floral displays. Nearer are boxes of hair marked by color, blond in one box, brown in another, black in a third. Freshly washed clothes drape the radiators, above which the white paint peels due to years of rising moisture.

I sit quietly as over a foot of my hair is lopped off, feeling the scissors flutter around my head like birds. The woman is careful with the hair, not losing a strand to the floor. She then divides it into three bunches and wraps each with a band before putting them into plastic bags like specimens.

The dress shop owner was right—you don't get much for hair in Russia. You also don't get much of a haircut from it. I can feel the woman working away, the whisper of scissors close to my scalp. She's giving me the pixie haircut that I drew onto a page of notebook paper before we began. She frowns with disapproval, as though being forced to make me ugly. *Girls should have long hair,* she seems to say.

Eventually, she holds up a mirror for me to see, and I understand why she hates it. My hair is so short now it doesn't really curl, but neither will it lie down flat, sticking out in little ledges and peaks. A long section in the front obscures one eye and a bit of my cheek and there's a flat bang straight across the eyebrows. I nod my approval.

"Okay?" she says.

"Okay," I mutter.

"Vsio budet horosho," she says in an encouraging tone.

I have no idea what this means. Perhaps that it will grow.

Back on the street, I hold my palms against my choppy hair, thinking how strange it feels. It looks terrible—and creates a silhouette that I don't recognize as my own. But that is the point. It's exactly the right hair to trick the facial recognition cameras.

Anyway, my hair isn't important right now. I've got to stay focused. I try to imagine what Dmitry would say. He was the one who cheered me up when I burned myself, the one who always saw the good in any situation. He'd say, *This is great! The cameras won't pick you up now.* He'd say, *Hair is just protein that sprouts from your head.*

I concentrate on the positives. It feels great to be in jeans, to have pockets and shoes I can walk in, to have a little cash. I find the hat lady and carefully place the hat I stole earlier back onto a hook in her kiosk. I return to the restaurant on Arbat Street and give the waitress I stiffed her tip. Her eyes grow large; she doesn't understand and it's frustrating not to be able to explain.

"Just take it," I say, closing her fingers gently over the bills.

At a big department store I find a makeup counter and try on dark lip liner, tracing a slightly different design to my natural lip line, then I walk outside to the market and purchase a pair of cheap sunglasses.

You'd never recognize me, sitting at a bar wearing Russian clothes, drinking ginger ale and eating salted nuts, and watching a television that plays soundlessly in the corner. There's more coverage about post-death recovery, but this is Russian television, not American, so I can't understand what's being said.

I think of Munn's glassware arranged so delicately in Volkov's cabinet. And Volkov's enormous house replete with scientific antiquities. I'm missing a piece here, but I don't know what it is.

I have no choice but to return to the hotel. Dinner is an uneaten roll left outside a room on the second floor. A large bowl of green apples in a picture window on the landing is also a welcome find. I search out the laundry closet that will again be my bedroom for the night. I spend a few hours asleep in an enormous hamper, hiding beneath a stack of freshly washed towels.

Morning comes too fast, but at least nobody finds me. I'm able to sneak out of the closet, heading to the fitness room for another luxurious shower. An unexpected perk of choosing the laundry closet is the abundance of linen and towels stored here. With my own clothes rolled into a clean towel, I walk the corridors in a hotel bathrobe and slippers taken from a cart, appearing like any other guest. One of the staff even opens the door as I pass.

If there is a weirder way to live, I don't know of it.

In the business center I read the news from America. The story is being rehashed in different ways, but at least I'm no longer trending on Twitter. Will certainly is. He's being touted as some kind of boy genius. I can imagine what Dmitry thinks of that.

I can't stop myself remembering the days and nights we spent comforting each other through that awful train journey, playing checkers with cookies, telling stories. I'm so alone without him now. But he'd wanted to be a big shot. He'd wanted to be rich. I guess he got both in the end. His new thick-framed glasses lend him a distinguished air that suits his new position as the scientific director of a laboratory in Maryland. I try not to remember how he said he wouldn't leave me behind. How he promised.

I miss him and hate him in equal measure.

Everyone else I just miss. I will never have a better friend than Lauren. I will never know anyone as smart and kind as Dmitry. I try not to think about my mother. It just brings tears.

I type in search after search on Munn. Like Will, he was born in Cambridge, England, where his father was a professor. He's a member of the Athenaeum Club and the Royal Society. There's a list of his prizes and papers. I see he is affiliated with the Swiss Federal Institute of Technology, same as Einstein. I look for every possible association with Russia or Volkov but I find nothing.

And then I notice something, a single reference, a citation to a paper published decades ago cowritten by Volkov and Munn and published in a journal I've never heard of. Eventually, I dig up the paper. In it, I learn many things, including the little-known fact that up to the age of eleven a child with a severed fingertip can grow a new one. There are many additional papers by Munn, of course. But Volkov's scientific career stops there, with this one paper he published with Munn, the original of which is in French. Nothing on him again until the breakup of the Soviet Union, at which time Mikhail Petrovich Volkov somehow becomes one of the richest men in the world.

Their connections are few but deep: a paper they wrote together, a gift of the family's collection of glassware.

I need to find out more.

Mellin's cybersecurity is too hard for me to get through. My only hope is Rik's phone number, which I am pathetic enough to have memorized.

The biggest threat to a phone's security is its data connection. If Rik has recently used a network outside of Mellin's VPN, I can download everything I need with an app.

And so I get busy, hacking Rik's phone, working away. It doesn't take long to find what I'm looking for, a message to Munn sent through an unprotected network. It's about a flight leaving at 13:50 and tickets, which are attached.

I'm about to open the attachment when I'm startled by a noise. I look up and there's a man standing in the doorway. He's got his arms folded in front of him and a look of accusation on his face, but it's his uniform that panics me most. My heart pounds wildly. I look for somewhere to run. I tell myself to calm down. *Calm down now!*

But it's not a police uniform. It's from the hotel. The guy is a front desk clerk. I'm guessing he clocked me coming into the business center and is thinking that a teenage girl online so early in the morning is probably searching for stuff she shouldn't be. Plus, my weird haircut and old clothes no longer make me look like a rich American but a scruffy street urchin.

The man asks what room I'm in and I tell him, then hold up my card key. My stomach flip-flops but I smile bravely, praying that he'll move on. He looks at me for a long time, as though trying to decide whether I'm lying, then apologizes somewhat insincerely and disappears again.

As soon as he is out of sight, I close all my windows, erase the history, empty the cache, delete all cookies, and shut off the computer. I move as fast as possible, but not so fast that I forget about Rik's email to Munn. Holding my breath, I click on the attachment.

It's tickets for a flight that left yesterday. Munn is in Moscow.

I haven't been approached by police and I haven't seen Vasiliev and his men. I doubt they'd recognize me anyway. I barely do. Every time I pass a mirror, I flinch.

But at least I have some facts I can work with: Volkov and Munn know each other. Munn has flown to Moscow.

I think about Arturo and I pray that Vasiliev doesn't discover that he helped me remove the tracker. But I can't help Arturo right now. I'm in too much trouble myself. I can't stay in the hotel any longer either. The guy will have checked out the room number I gave him and discovered I'm lying. I'm willing to bet there's someone placed at the front door right now, instructed to stop me as I leave. But I know what to do. I enter the restaurant and head for the kitchen. If you've worked in enough kitchens you know exactly where to go. I grab a cloth off a door handle, pinning it around my waist like an apron as I walk, behaving as though I work here. I'm a busgirl or a pot cleaner or one of the millions of people who prep vegetables for salad. My attitude says, *Hey, I do this every day!*

My mother always said that working in the food industry teaches you more than you know, and she was right.

The high turnover in a kitchen means that a new face goes unnoticed. And there's always a door next to a kitchen that will be open no matter what the weather to combat the heat and steam of the cooking. I look for that door now, skirting the backs of the staff. If anyone notices me they see an aproned teenager, one of many who work in the kitchens here, nothing unusual. Soon, I'm outside. I step past two guys, sitting on the steps in their chef jackets and checked kitchen trousers, smoking. And then I'm gone.

27

MY GOAL IS to find Munn. He's in this city somewhere. I stay out of the way of police and cameras as I search every bar and restaurant, squinting through my sunglasses. I miss my normal prescription glasses, safely stored in my tote bag. And this new short cut feels like someone else's head. I get a lucky break, though, finding a tube of lipstick left behind in a bathroom. I use it to alter my lip shape again, so that I look even less like myself. The lipstick is bright red, expensive stuff that lasts all day. Lauren was right, makeup is magic.

Munn always stays in fancy places, the best bars and restaurants and hotels. He should be right here in the tourist part of the city. But I can't find him. After several days, I begin to wonder if he's got an apartment somewhere and that's why. Or maybe he never got on the plane in the first place.

Then one evening, I see someone walking out of the glass doors of the Four Seasons hotel and across its vast plaza. He's got Munn's same lanky body and sweep of white hair. I step forward, following him a short distance. It's Munn all right. I'd know him anywhere.

I follow him as he passes the fountains and flowers, then under Mokhovaya along the pedestrian underpass. I can't imagine where he is going until, at last, I catch sight of him heading back onto Tverskaya and entering the Ritz-Carlton, where I've taken up residence since abandoning the Hotel National.

In the laundry room, of course.

Munn crosses the lobby with its marbled floor and gilded everything. He fits in so perfectly here, as he does in all grand places. Striding confidently to the concierge's desk, he stops to ask a question, then walks off, turning the corner to the elevators. I wait for him to get into the elevator and for the doors to silently close. The progress of lighted numbers tells me he's reached the top floor. Floor twelve, the O2 Lounge.

The O2 Lounge serves Kamchatka crab, caviar, sea bass, and ribs. But nobody comes here for the food. It's the views they're after. The open-air bar looks out over Red Square, the studded towers of the Kremlin wall, and the fairy-tale rooftops of St. Basil's Cathedral.

It's still early, the patio dotted with people sipping cocktails. Light jazz floats on the breeze.

I search the tables and see the back of Munn's head as he sits beneath the shade of an umbrella. I can't quite shake off the idea that he's my idol, my boss, the man who plucked me from a terrible situation at the Science for Our Future awards. I revere him. I know I shouldn't. Look where he's landed me, alienated from my own country. And so very alone.

I realize that I need him. And he must need me, too, because he's come an awfully long way to find me. I have to think about what I want from him. I have to guess at what he wants from me. One thing's for sure, I can't afford to be shy. Or tongue-tied. I can't allow his age or fame or all his credentials to cloud my judgment.

I walk across the bar, sit at his table, and stare into his face with what I hope is a venomous look. Closer up, I see he is elegantly dressed, as always. His hair is raked back from his head, his gaze fixed upon me. I need to speak to him as a peer, not as a student. I need to be unafraid.

I take the glass from in front of him and drink. The dry vermouth isn't nearly as refreshing as I'd hoped.

A small smile creeps across his face. I think he's only now recognized me. After all, with my short hair and sunglasses, I'm practically disguised. He takes in a breath, then says, "The martini is said to be the only invention as perfect as the sonnet."

Another sip. This time the taste is different, not quite as bitter.

"Perhaps you'd like your own drink?"

I look at the glass and get a little happy thinking how my lipstick has marked it. I hope this annoys him.

"I'm living in a laundry hamper," I say. "Is that what you wanted? Or did you want me to work for Volkov?"

It's a genuine question.

"One moment," says Munn. He goes to the bar, returning with a menu. "Order something," he says. "You look gaunt."

"I looked worse when I was locked up," I say, surprised by the way I'm able to speak to him. Months ago, I'd have barely managed a few words, and here I am being brash. "Did they send you pictures?"

"I'll order for you," he says, summoning the attention of a waiter.

"What would happen if right now I walked into the US embassy?"

This gets his attention. "I wouldn't do that if I were you," he says. "Slow down on that martini. I don't think you realize how strong it is."

"I've been drugged up to my eyeballs for *days*. Imprisoned, scared out of my mind, in fear for my life, and now I'm a national scandal. I'm so nervous I can barely function. Don't talk to me about *strong*!" I finish the glass. "The news keeps reporting that everyone wants me brought to justice. As though I've done something *wrong*."

"Yes," says Munn. "I understand that."

My head swims, probably from the drink. "Maybe you can explain what's going on," I say.

He launches into a summary of what is happening back in America. Post-death recovery is on every news channel. People want to know how the dead can be brought back to life. Some have even stopped burying their relatives.

"I know all this," I say. "Internet."

The waiter arrives with a glass of orange juice and plate of asparagus, or what I think is asparagus. It's not green, but white.

"Can I have a burger?" I say. The waiter begins to remove the plate, and I say, "No, leave it. I want this, too."

Munn orders a burger, another martini, and more juice because I've already downed the first glass.

The asparagus is delicious, whatever the color. The alcohol has dialed me back, helping me to relax. I chew slowly, savoring every buttery bite. Munn allows me to eat undisturbed. I finish the plate, then say, "Are you part of the CIA? Or the FSB? Or MI6?"

I sound like I know more than I do about intelligence agencies. In fact, I only know what Dmitry has told me in his stories about his father. And while I don't know exactly who Munn is working for, he has to have something to do with intelligence.

"I can assure you that I was not responsible for putting you in your current situation," he says. "However, I have relationships with certain people who are in a position to *help* you."

"Help me not get arrested for something I didn't do, you mean?"

Munn takes a long breath, leaning forward as though he's going to touch my forearm in some kind of comforting manner, but I stop him with a glare.

"Volkov has taken a shine to you," he says, withdrawing his hand. "This has some disadvantages but also some advantages."

Hearing him speak Volkov's name sends little shock waves through me.

"Do you work for Volkov?" I ask. After all, it's a possibility.

My question surprises him. "Certainly not," he says. "We've been trying to gain intelligence on Volkov's scientific undertakings. If you were to work for him, you'll be privy to what is really going on in his laboratories. That's very valuable information to America. And to its allies. Great Britain, for example."

"You want me to work for Volkov? Because that *is* an interesting coincidence. He offered me a job."

"Which you declined," Munn says gently.

"And you knew that."

"Only because you're here now."

It's like we're playing a game of chess. His move. My move. I remind myself that Munn is always utterly in control of himself, and good at presenting an image. I can picture him in the conference room at the SFOF meeting during that awful moment when they were deciding whether to award me the prize. He'd leaned casually against the wall as though he was merely interested in the facts of the case, nothing more. Nobody would have guessed that he'd sent Rik not only to find me but to coach me through writing a statement.

I say, "Every Russian troll on Twitter and Facebook has convinced ordinary US citizens I'm anti-American. I'll never get a decent job no matter what I do. But that doesn't mean I want to work for someone who looks an awful lot like a criminal."

"*Is* a criminal," Munn corrects. "This is why it is so important to us to know what he is doing. The public will change its mind about you once we reveal how helpful you've been to us. And we will. That's part of the deal."

The deal. So there's a deal in play. And what strikes me, too, is the use of the word *us*. Munn must be desperate. Any normal person would be trying to get me away from Volkov, not push me toward him. But it appears this is what Munn wants. He's flown all the way to Moscow to persuade me to work for a criminal.

"Why does Volkov matter so much?" I say.

Munn looks uncomfortable. "There are some prickly rumors circulating about Volkov," he says. "I'm happy to share them, but tell me, Kira, what else do you know? I'll fill you in, don't worry, but I'm interested in what you've surmised thus far."

But I haven't surmised anything. A minute ago, I thought Munn worked for Volkov.

I glance out at the evening sky, thinking aloud. "First, Will leaked information, and that's how I ended up here," I say.

Munn considers this. "Possibly," he says, "but I suspect Volkov pegged you earlier. Will may not have been much of a factor."

I remember Vasiliev at the Science for Our Future conference and I realize that, of course, Munn is right. Volkov had tried a legitimate means of "acquiring" me, sending his man, Vasiliev, to the conference. But of course, I'd said no.

"And now the US sees an opportunity for me to leak information back about what they're doing in Volkov's labs," I say. "Volkov must be up to something bad."

He nods.

"It's a unique situation. Volkov imagines I now hate America simply because America hates me. But you know I'm used to being hated, and it won't change how I feel. So you're certain of my allegiance."

"All true," he says.

My burger arrives and I eat like a starved dog. Munn nurses his martini. After a minute he says, "This is all very dangerous. In truth, I rather hope you don't agree to it."

"I saw your laboratory glassware in Volkov's cabinet," I say. "Why should I trust you? You and Volkov are friends. You've even published together."

Munn clears his throat. "That was a lifetime ago. I can assure you we are no longer friends."

"Did you have a falling-out over whose name came first in the research article?" I say snarkily.

"Over a woman," Munn says, taking a sip from his drink.

From below come church bells, drawing our attention. We sit until the last note has rung.

"There is a legend about St. Basil's Cathedral. Do you know it? Ivan the Terrible blinded its creator so that he could never create anything to rival it. An awful waste." Then, quietly, he adds, "Don't let post-death recovery be your last beautiful invention, Kira."

I take a long breath. "It didn't look so beautiful when I saw Will dead under a sheet," I say. "And I don't want to be a spy."

Munn looks at me carefully. "You won't be. At least, not for long."

"Will and I promised each other that if one got away, the other wouldn't forget. But he turned his back—" I have to stop now. My throat feels cottony. My eyes fill. The sad truth is I'd never have done that to him. I'd never have left Will behind.

Munn leans toward me and whispers, "You're angry about Will," he says, "but there are a few facts you don't know."

"What facts?"

"For example," he begins, "Will was dumped on a gurney in a corridor because they thought he was too incapacitated to go any-where. He escaped that place—wherever it was they kept you—and arrived at Volkov's house, half blind and shoeless."

I think about Will, whose lab coat is always pristine, whose shoes always look fresh out of the box. For him to arrive in such a state into the palace that is Volkov's house is unimaginable.

Munn continues, saying, "He offered Volkov a plan that would keep you in the country and, yes, it meant whipping up the media and defaming you. That's a pity, but it was a smart move. Volkov hates America and has a pathological rivalry with me. You're the girl who can bring back the dead. Volkov would never have let someone that valuable return to the United States. If it weren't for Will, Volkov might have eliminated you altogether. Will saved your life."

I let his words sink in. *Will saved your life.*

I don't know what to say.

Munn continues, "Will did the only thing he could think of to make you safe. You're too well-known now to simply disappear."

Disappear. Like Arturo, I think.

"Volkov is probably hoping you'll come to your senses, so to speak, and go work for him," adds Munn.

"How did Will know where Volkov lived?"

Munn smiles bitterly. "He didn't," he says. He closes his eyes as though pushing away a memory, then says, "He got somebody on the street to lend him a phone. He rang me and I told him what to do. If you want to hate someone, hate me. Not Will. The boy was scared to death. He was scared for *you.*"

I nod, taking this in. I have to use every ounce of strength to stop myself from crying.

"There are some facts *you* don't know," I say finally.

Munn tips his head with interest.

"Arturo is still alive. I saw him."

He looks at me for a long moment, then he says, "And you'd like to help him. That will be difficult."

I think about how Arturo had refused to come with me from

the laboratory. It was like he was too scared to save himself. "I have to try," I say.

Munn raises his eyebrows at this.

"Volkov is expecting you to go knock around the city, then return to him desperate for shelter and food. But Volkov is clever. He will know that with every passing day there is more of a chance that someone like me will tap you on the shoulder. He won't trust you. Oh, he'll say he will. He'll put an arm around you and announce to a roomful of people, *This is Kira, I trust her with everything important to my heart!*"

His impression is actually quite good.

"But don't believe it," Munn says.

"I don't know what to believe. You still haven't told me why your laboratory glassware is in Volkov's display cabinet," I say.

"Oh, that." He acts as though it's an afterthought. "Mikhail and I studied together decades before you were born. Things were different then. We were just two young men interested in the truth, which is what we thought science was. The glassware was a parting gift when we went our separate ways."

"You published together in 1982. You must have been good friends."

"All that was a long time ago," he says. He looks sad for a moment. "But know this: when Volkov found out about post-death recovery, it wasn't post-death recovery he was after."

"Then what?"

He takes a sip from his drink, folds his arms across the table, and says, "It was you."

The sky is darkening; the tables glow with candlelight. Before us is a bottle of sauvignon blanc. Anyone looking would think we are father and daughter out celebrating. A birthday, maybe. Or graduation.

"Why me?" I say.

"Because you came up with a revolutionary procedure. And because you work for me. He couldn't stand that."

"That's crazy," I say.

"Not if you understand the history. He married young to a very beautiful woman. That woman left him to live in America. With me, for a time."

"I see."

"And there's something else. Dmitry believes he was meant to be killed along with the rest of his family that day at MIT. That is not the case. The death of his father and sister was deliberate, but almost certainly Volkov was there to kidnap Dmitry and bring him here to Russia to work for him. Instead, I stepped in. I saw what happened and I understood immediately—"

"You were *there*?"

"Of course. Dmitry was doing work for us even while he was at MIT. I was at the graduation. When the incident took place—" He pauses for a moment and blows a sigh through his lips. "I knew exactly what was happening. Because I know Volkov, you see."

"But the Polish student who was killed? The one that was mistaken for Dmitry?"

"Volkov's people made no mistake. The young man was just in the wrong place at the wrong time. They didn't get ahold of Dmitry because I got to him first. I shoved him into a car so fast he didn't have time to resist," Munn says.

I take this in. Dmitry's life was destroyed because of two men with a bone to pick.

"And Arturo?"

Munn shrugs. "That was payback for me having scooped Dmitry out from under him."

I am stunned. I don't know what to say. We sit in silence for a moment while I take in this new information. I feel a pang from somewhere deep inside me. It may be my heart.

"Dmitry will be the only person inside Mellin who will know of your new role," Munn says finally.

Dmitry. Oh, how I miss him. "Tell Dmitry to think of me whenever he eats chocolate cake," I say.

Munn smiles. "He thinks of you more often than that, I can assure you. Nothing cheers him." He sits back, crosses his arms over his chest, and says, "Are you with us?"

So simply put, but not a simple question.

"Perhaps," I say.

"You must be certain."

"Can we help Arturo?"

Munn shrugs. "I don't know."

"Who will look after my mother?"

He considers this. "If money starts transferring to your mother's bank account it will be obvious you're working for us. However, we could hire her at Mellin. Say she was a cleaner. But she won't have to clean, of course. She won't have to do anything at all but she'll get full medical benefits and a salary."

All my life I've wanted to make things easier for my mother. Munn knows this.

"I don't want to develop weapons to use against my own country," I say. "I don't want to become the person that the media thinks I already am."

Munn leans toward me. "But that's exactly what we need you to do. And then you will share the information with us so we can neutralize the threat. Just like the Cold War, but colder."

He tells me I have to return to Volkov, the sooner the better. "Tell him you thought about it and have changed your mind. That America is no longer your home."

I take a long breath. I'll do as Munn says. I've already decided that much. But I won't do it in order to please him or to avoid facing the media or awkward questions from the Justice Department. I'm not going along with this simply to help my mother and our dire financial situation either. I'm doing it in order to satisfy my own conscience. I haven't forgotten the boy my age who stood shaking in the corridor and pointed to the tracker in my thigh. I've known what it is like to be under the control of Volkov. Of Vasiliev. And I've felt that big needle in my back.

"I think there are more kids like Arturo in Volkov's . . . custody," I say.

Munn nods. "This is what we fear," he says. "Would you like to help find them?"

The question sounds so casual, as though he's asking if I'd like a cup of tea. Unpack it and it sounds more like this: Would I like to help find kids who've been kidnapped? Would I like to take my chances on being caught, tortured, killed?

Perhaps he knows me well enough to guess my answer. I nod once, then am still.

"So you'll do it," he says, a flat statement.

We sit for some time as the night grows around us. The lights brighten against the Kremlin. It's all very beautiful, and it bothers me that this is the case. I'm so desperately unhappy, but in some ways I shouldn't be. For the first time, the things I want are within my grasp. My mother will have no money problems, no medical bills that go unpaid or treatment that goes undone. I can put to use the gifts I've been told that I possess. And who knows? I might even do something great in the end.

"Do I get a code name?" I say.

"They are usually designated. What would you like to be called?"

I think about that. Everything started because I wrote a paper about the dragonfly, a creature with skills that exceed expectation, a creature science doesn't really understand.

"Dragonfly," I say.

Munn nods. Then he says, "I would tell you to be careful, but you don't know how to be careful yet. Dear girl . . ." But he doesn't finish the sentence. It's almost as though he regrets that I've agreed to his offer. He takes my hand, then lets it go as I stand, glancing one last time over the city.

"Volkov says he'll provide an excellent education," I say. "Tell that to Will. He was always so worried about me going to college."

"Oh, you'll be educated all right," says Munn. "You'll have every piece of equipment you need and every opportunity to shine. But no matter how valuable you are to Volkov, never forget that he'll dispense with you at once if he finds out about our . . . arrangement. Oh, another thing. Until this moment we've been hidden beneath this umbrella." He glances at the table umbrella above him. "But now you're standing. I don't know for sure, but consider the possibility that you are exposed. We don't want anyone seeing us together."

I look around and see, indeed, on the other side of the bar, a black box that could be a camera.

I say, "They're everywhere."

"This is a very difficult undertaking, Kira. Think hard, be thorough. You're one of the few people in the world who has the brains to succeed."

For some reason, this makes me laugh. It's funny, this idea that I could succeed under such unlikely circumstances. I may as well play poker to see if I'll live to tomorrow, toss dice and bet on my own life. I pick up my tote bag. In it is everything I possess: a few articles of clothing, a lipstick, some cash. I lean over and kiss Munn goodbye. One kiss on the right cheek, then on the left, then back to the right. Because if someone is watching us, I'd like them to imagine I'm not American.

"Where are you going now?" he asks.

"Volkov's," I say.

He nods. "You're so young," he says, as though noticing for the first time.

I smile. "Fortunately, science works no matter what your age."

And then I leave, back down the elevator and onto the street. I'm on my way to Volkov's, but I have one other place I want to visit first. Somewhere just outside of Red Square is what is called Kilometer Zero, the center of Russia and the place from which all its roads are measured. I will go to Kilometer Zero and make a wish, then toss a coin over my shoulder in accordance with the tradition. Some say that if the coin lands on the bronze, the wish will come true. Some say the wish isn't important but that the coin landing on the bronze means good luck.

Either way, it seems like a good starting point.

ACKNOWLEDGMENTS

Dragonfly Girl is a work of fiction but is informed by the very real work of doctors and scientists who have lent me their expertise, either through papers they've published or their own personal accounts.

I am indebted to Mr. Andrew Ready, Consultant Renal Transplant Surgeon at University Hospitals Birmingham NHS Foundation Trust and Medical Director of TLC, a charitable organisation dedicated to supporting renal transplantation in the developing world. Andrew generously read an early draft of the novel and helped me understand a little more about organ transplants and the potential of technology to improve the condition of donor organs before transplantation. Anything that is true regarding Kira's observations about organ transplant research is down to Andrew's guidance, while I am entirely responsible for all fanciful notions.

Also, many thanks to John Gregg, CEO of Balinbac Therapeutics, for his primer on drug development and helpful remarks on an early draft of the novel.

Many science writers have written about the dragonfly's phenomenal hunting abilities though none have connected it to uni-hemispheric sleep with supporting mathematical models as Kira does. This is for the very good reason that there is no established connection—I made that up. But I never would have known the first thing about dragonflies had I not come across Matteo Mischiati, Herel H. Lin et al.'s article published in *Nature* in 2014, Internal Models Direct Dragonfly Interception Steering. I'm so glad that the authors took the time to explain the dragonfly in terms that even a layman like myself could understand.

Helmi's talk was inspired by the real-life TED talk, "You can grow new brain cells. Here's how," by neural stem researcher, Dr. Sandrine Thuret. Any incorrect exaggerated information would be my own invention.

Carlos's talk about how changes in gene expression can help specify exactly the time of death isn't just make-believe. I read an article in *The Scientist* (www.the-scientist.com) about the work of Roderic Guígo and his colleagues at the Centre for Genomic Regulation in Barcelona, and extrapolated from there. As for Carlos's game, there are a number of internet articles about scientists who died as a result of their own experiments, including Alistair Field's article "Scientists Who Died In Pursuit of Great Discoveries," on www.knowscience.org. However, no such game exists (yet!).

Experiments with zebrafish really have led to the discovery that our genes stay active after death, at least for a time. I learned this from reading *Discovery Magazine*'s article on Peter Noble and his colleagues at the University of Washington.

The basis for the research described in Will Drummond's talk about genes following a predictable time schedule is the work of Seth Grant, Professor of Molecular Neuroscience at the University of Edinburgh in Scotland, about what he calls a "genetic lifespan calendar." For the real-life, true version of this phenomenon, I recommend Dr. Grant's own explanation on *Brain Science*'s September 2017 podcast in which Dr. Ginger Cambell talks to Dr. Grant about his work. Ginger's podcast is accessible to anyone with an interest in neurobiology. I write her fan mail.

Conan the Bacterium is a real thing. Dmitry wouldn't be the first to try to find uses for Deinococcus radiodurans. I read about it first in an article by Sarah DeWeerdt in *Genome News Network*.

Chandri's work on growing kidneys from stems cells from pigs is the sort of thing being done by DNA researchers around the globe in response to the shortage of donor organs available for people who need them.

Peter Dockrill was the first to alert me to the unsettling truth that Australian fires have been started by at least three different birds, including the black kite, the whistling kite, and the brown falcon.

Kungsträdgården station on the blue line in Stockholm is, indeed, the only place you can find the *Lessertia dentichelis* spider in northern Europe. I read this fact on the website www.visitstockholm .com and found it so interesting I had to include it!

And finally, it was writer and scholar H. L. Mencken who called the martini "the only American invention as perfect as the sonnet."

—Marti Leimbach